OUTSIDE the LINES

mary perrine

DEDICATION

To Aileen Demenge. Thank you for sparking the idea for this book.
I hope you find peace and hope in Bella and Tilly's story.
Valerie loved you more than you will ever know.
Together you filled the world with love.

Valerie Netland: October 10, 1942 – September 6, 2021

To all the families who have lost loved ones to cancer.
Their journey was cut short, but their impact will not be forgotten.
To my friends who passed from this disease.
Thank you for teaching us how to live even in the darkest moments.

Kay Brekke Hartzell: May 5, 1960 – September 12, 2014
"If you want something magical to happen, first you have to believe in magic."
Melissa Zahn: March 19, 1984 – March 7, 2018
"Faith over Fear!"
Jessica Zaback: October 13, 1974 – November 17, 2020
"Today I choose joy!"
Heather Miller: August 13, 1974 – June 12, 2021
"Be the light!"
You live on in our memories.

And finally, to my mom, Bee.
She is my Tilly—the woman who encouraged me to follow my dreams.
I'm finally listening, Mom.
I love you.

OUTSIDE the LINES

mary perrine

Water's Edge Publishing, LLC

PROLOGUE

One Year

Bella hadn't planned to run, but she also hadn't expected to be handed a death sentence that morning. The words echoed through her like clogs in an empty marble hallway, making it impossible to hear anything else. *One year—if you're lucky.*

At twenty-three, Bella had just begun to live. College had barely faded from her rearview mirror, and dreams of her future were still polished and shiny, waiting to be lived out. She was still a virgin for crying out loud. *That* was something she'd saved for the man of her dreams; he just hadn't surfaced yet. Her biological clock was still on the dance floor, shrouded beneath the driving beat of the drums.

Three minutes ago, every dream she'd ever had was terminated by those five words. Her brain trumpeted her failure as a human. Neither husband nor children would ever be hers.

Bella raced down the back stairs of the clinic. Doctor Sloan's voice trailed her until the metal door slammed shut with a bang that rattled her soul. Rounding the corner, she sideswiped some young intern, disheveling his precariously balanced tower of folders. Attempting to safeguard the stack, his hand snagged her silk scarf, tugging it from her head. She made a half-hearted attempt to grab it but lost the battle, continuing without it. As she ran, the breeze fluttered the peach fuzz that had sprouted since her last chemo session.

"Wait!" the man called as she descended the next set of

stairs. "Your scarf!" His words rebounded off the brick walls of the stairwell, but they were nothing more than noise.

The weight of the parking ramp door battled her near skeletal frame. Worming through the meager opening, she burst into the drafty ramp. A black sedan narrowly skirted her as she rounded the corner and dashed through the garage in the general direction of Sunny, her Volkswagen Bug.

Unable to locate her compact car in the congested parking ramp, Bella pressed the panic button on her key fob. If life had a panic button, she had no doubt she'd be squeezing the hell out of it.

Veering left, she headed in the direction of the flashing lights and annoying blare. She flung the VW door open and climbed inside. Catching a glimpse of herself in the mirror, Bella collapsed in a fit of laughter. In an alternate universe, where she hadn't received news of her impending demise, that wannabe doctor in the short white lab coat, the new owner of her scarf, could have been her Prince Charming. And Bella could have been his Cinderella—the elusive owner—the one he would spend his entire life searching to find.

But she wasn't Cinderella. He wasn't Prince Charming. And this wasn't a fairy tale with a happy ending. It had just become a miserable existence of waiting.

For a brief moment, her world fell silent before gut-wrenching sobs swallowed everything she'd envisioned. Before her fairy tale morphed into reality. Before her dreams turned into a vivid nightmare.

CHAPTER 1

Where she'd come to die

The neon lights of the city merged into one long streak as the coach bus sped south along the highway heading away from Bella's past. Her ticket read *Miami*, the furthest this bus would take her. It didn't matter. She would bail when the mood struck—when it felt right. Five years ago, at the age of eighteen, Bella had become a free spirit. Before then, she'd been a rule follower. First with her parents and nannies, then later in the perpetual revolving door of foster homes.

At each stop, she followed a parade of passengers out the door and onto the sidewalk. The moment her foot touched the pavement, she began counting. It was always the same number of steps, always the same direction. Once there, she drew a deep breath and held it. She closed her eyes and let the vibe of the town wash over her. The more distance she put between herself and the bright lights of New York City, the more she could breathe, and the closer she came to outrunning her past. So far, all previous stops had sent her and her overstuffed backpack retreating to the seat she had warmed for nearly fourteen hours. When it was the right place, she would know.

The sign above the driver's head flashed *Lawson Beach*. Her heart raced as she watched the murky green ocean with the enormous waves pass by on her left and the quaint town on her right. According to Google, the population was ten thousand, four hundred twenty-two. If her intuition was correct, Lawson Beach was about to gain a new resident—for the short-term anyway.

Bella followed a teenage girl who had boarded with her in New York. Her knees began to tremble as she neared the front of the bus. The backpack weighed heavily in her clammy hands as she descended the narrow stairs. Ten steps from the bus door, she set her pack between her feet, closed her eyes, and drew a deep breath. *Home.* She hadn't known it when she started her trip, but Lawson Beach was where she'd come to die.

Bella awkwardly hoisted her bag onto one shoulder and across her back before hooking her other arm through the strap. She steered her way across the street with those who had disembarked. Her heart skipped a beat as she watched fellow passengers embrace family and friends. Loneliness squeezed her chest, chipping away the confidence she'd felt only minutes earlier. Had she made a mistake? Was there a better place farther down the line? But if she got back on the bus, how would it be any different at the next stop…or the one after that? No, this was to be home. She could smell it in the salty ocean air and the aroma of flowers in the planters on every corner.

Bella released a long breath and contemplated her next step. She had no plan. The entire trip had been spent reflecting only on dying. Living hadn't even crossed her mind.

The sun settled on the tops of the buildings opposite the ocean. Sweat rolled down her back beneath the cumbersome pack. October 2nd's early morning temperature of fifty-three degrees in NYC was poles apart from the seventy-nine and high humidity of Lawson Beach, South Carolina. Dropping her bag onto the sidewalk, she slipped off her Notre Dame sweatshirt and tied it around her waist before continuing aimlessly.

Help wanted signs hung in nearly every window she passed.

She didn't need a job. Money wasn't an issue; it never had been. What she needed was a place to live—and food. Besides a few peanuts and raisins, Bella hadn't eaten since before her appointment with Dr. Sloan the previous day. For the past fourteen hours, she'd pecked at a bag of trail mix. Her water bottle and stomach were both begging for a refill.

The bell above her head tinkled quietly as she pushed the Table for Two Bistro door open. Heads turned and eyes peered in her direction as she quickly dove into at a chair at a small table near the door. A lump grew in her throat and her eyes stung as she hid behind the oversized menu. Never again would she need a table for two. From this point forward, she would be alone. Getting close to anyone wasn't an option; she wouldn't put them through the pain of losing her the way she'd lost her parents.

"What can I get for you, hon?" The slender middle-aged waitress wore a white t-shirt, black jeans, striped apron, and unsightly black tennies that were one step from old lady orthopedic shoes. Her name tag read *Maggie*.

The diner's aroma made Bella's stomach stir. Nausea or hunger? She wasn't sure. Nerves? Definitely. She stared at the menu. *Calamari, shrimp and grits, mussels, pork belly and scallops, and lobster bisque.* Her eyes misted over, and she blinked several times.

The waitress cleared her throat. "Not from around here, are you?"

Bella shrugged. "How'd you know?"

Maggie laughed. "Because the menu scares you." With the end of her pen, she pointed toward Bella's pack lying on the second chair. "And that thing's a dead giveaway."

A lone tear escaped. Bella hastily wiped it away with the back of her hand as the waitress flipped the menu and tapped her pen on the kids' section.

Her shoulders drooped. "Mac and cheese," she whispered. "And lots of water." The woman scribbled something on her notepad and turned to walk away. "Wait!" Bella called. "Thank you."

"Sure thing, hon."

Bella fished her phone from her back pocket. Twenty-nine text messages and fourteen calls. She'd felt each arrive, but she'd ignored them all. From the moment one of her roommates walked through their apartment door and read her note about leaving, the messages kept coming. While she waited for her food, she blocked each number. They would only try to talk her into another round of chemo—that would do what? Extend her life for another six months? Leaving her sick and weak and exhausted in the meantime. No, she wasn't doing that. Not ever again.

Before she left, she'd placed four months' rent in an envelope with the signed title for her car and a note. Bella hadn't told them she was dying; instead, she said she'd gone on an adventure. Everything in her room was up for grabs. Her roommates could keep it, sell it, or donate it. At the end of the letter, she asked them to remember her as she had been in college, the party girl—the first one on the dance floor and the last one to leave. Then, she sealed the envelope, packed her bag with only what she needed, closed her bedroom door, and walked away from the life she once saw as a beginning—but now recognized as the end.

"Here you go, sweetie." Maggie set a blue plate in front of her.

Bella shoved her phone back into her pocket and shoveled in the double-size portion of cheesy pasta. Suddenly aware of her eating frenzy, she embarrassingly scanned the room to see if anyone had noticed.

A middle-aged man dropped a twenty-dollar bill on her

table as he walked past. "Sir, I don't..." But he had already passed through the door.

"Takin' a break, Lou," Maggie yelled into the open kitchen window as she headed toward Bella. She lifted the backpack from the chair and set it on the floor before joining her. "So, what's your story?"

Bella put her hands in her lap and played with the paper napkin beneath the table. "Story?"

"Who are you? What brought you to Lawson Beach? Are you passing through, or are you planning to stay a while?" Maggie sipped the soda she'd brought with her. "You seem kind of...*lost*." She tipped her head. "We all have a story."

Except for her roommates and the Atwood Hills Oncology staff, no one knew her story. Just thinking about it felt like dredging up sludge.

"I, ah, um." Unsure how much to share or where to begin, Bella stumbled several times before settling on a lie. "My name's Bella. I live in New York City, and I just needed to get away for a while."

Maggie slowly nodded. "Abusive boyfriend? Meddling parents?" She paused. "Cancer?"

"What? No!" Bella insisted. "None of those."

The waitress reached over and grabbed her hand. "Honey, the stocking cap in this weather is pretty much a giveaway."

Bella touched the forgotten pale blue cap. "Oh," she murmured.

"Tell me what you need. Money? A bed? A job? I know most everybody around here. I can get you whatever it is."

A watered-down smile spread across Bella's face. "Just a place to stay."

Maggie rapped on the table before she jumped up. "I know the perfect spot. Wait here," she called over her shoulder before disappearing into the kitchen.

Minutes later, she handed Bella a piece of paper torn from her server notepad. *354 Sweetwater Lane* had been scrawled across the page. "Tilly's expecting you. She's good folk. You'll like her once you get to know her." She smiled at Bella. "Just give her a chance. She's a little rough 'round the edges at times." Maggie stepped back. "Promise me you'll get to know her before you make up your mind about her."

A ragged sob tore through Bella as she stood up and threw her arms around Maggie. "I can't thank you enough."

"Sweetie, if you need anything, you come find me. There's nobody in this town that wouldn't give you the shirt off their back." She held up the twenty-dollar bill as evidence.

"Maggie!" The deep voice boomed across the emptying restaurant. "Order up."

Maggie winked as she poked a thumb over her shoulder toward the kitchen. "Even Lou."

CHAPTER 2

Tilly

354 Sweetwater Lane was no more than a few blocks from the bistro. Bella traveled the sidewalk on the ocean side, catching glimpses of the water between houses. The thumbnail moon illuminated the water, casting a narrow path of golden light through the center of the ocean. Never had she been this close. Its size scared her, but its beauty mesmerized her.

After landing in the system at twelve, she rarely glimpsed anything of beauty. There were kindhearted families, but most were poor people who had decided to foster for the income. They hadn't chosen to house broken kids out of want. No, doing so guaranteed a consistent monthly income. But that commitment came with an extra mouth to feed and another pair of shoes to buy. Most of her foster parents had been close-fisted, providing her with nothing more than a warm meal, a bed to rest her head, and an occasional pair of underwear.

And vacations? As far as the families were concerned, that was squandered money. No one took a foster child on a trip. So, besides traveling to and from school, Bella spent her time close to home. Books had been her window to the world. They also kept her from focusing on her turbulent past before she became an orphan.

In New York, Bella had always lived in condos or

penthouse apartments. Compared to the country, city living felt like being crammed into a crowded elevator with doors that never opened. On the sidewalks, people shouldered past you, always in a hurry. No one knew your name. No one ever asked. Day and night, the traffic was so deafening, Bella could barely think. Buses and taxis raced up and down the streets, honking out messages that kept the stream of vehicles flowing in a synchronized promenade. In the city, Bella always felt like she was holding her breath.

Lawson Beach was everything NYC was not. The endless sky provided a breathtaking backdrop for the stars that lived above, an infinite cache of tiny sparks that flickered against the black canvas. Because of the bright city lights, she'd never seen the stars in New York. Here, it was more than just the stars that felt like a proverbial hug. It was everything. The air was sweet and clean and smelled of all that was righteous. Birds sang, crickets chirped, and people laughed—filling the air with a melodic symphony. And even though they had never laid eyes on her before, residents' faces glowed warmly as they greeted her with *hello* or referred to her as *hon* or *sweetie.*

Bella wondered what her life would have been like had her parents settled in a town like Lawson Beach instead of traveling the world. Would her father have been drunk on the night he and her mother died? Would they still have been too busy for their only child? The string of nannies that drifted in and out of her life had been her only friends, and most of them had been less than cordial. They only saw her as a paycheck.

In the five thousand heartbeats since her arrival, Bella felt different here. In New York, she hadn't let people into her fortress until she had fully vetted them. Her past was too painful. Bella had become good at hiding in plain sight, protecting her secrets. Being raised by nannies and passed between foster homes did that to you.

After rechecking the address, Bella crossed the street and made her way up the crushed shell walkway. Suddenly, she stopped. This old two-story would most likely be her home for the next twelve months. "If I'm lucky," she whispered. "If I'm lucky," she repeated louder with a slight snort. *Lucky?*

A ribbon of yellow light streamed from the windows, across the porch, and into the yard. Hugging the house along the front was a whitewashed porch. Unlike the stoops in New York City, this one felt like home.

This was it, the house where she would slide into the abyss. After everything that had happened, Bella no longer believed in heaven. The utopian afterlife with a god who was all good had been a lie her mother had told her—like one of the many Russian fairy tales she'd heard as a child. God was as bogus as Santa Claus or the Easter Bunny. Yet, he was still her go-to punching bag when she needed someone to yell at.

Bella shivered. A wave of anger roiled inside. *Twenty-three years.* Twenty-three years was all she'd been given. Twenty-four, *maybe*. There were so many things she would never experience. So many things that would be left undone, unsaid, when her light was snuffed out and she was counting worms. Her jaw tightened, ensnaring the scream that threatened to escape. Tilting her head back, she looked up at the sky. *How could you?* she thought as she tightened her fists. *After everything I've been through, why couldn't you pick on someone else for a change? And if you're real, prove it.*

"I been waitin' for ya," a voice boomed.

Bella jumped. It was as if the god she didn't believe in had answered her. With her heart racing, she scanned the porch. An outside light burst on, and the woman who belonged to the voice stepped into view. With her arms crossed, she slowly moved toward the stairs, focusing on her feet as she wobbled unsteadily. Her ebony skin glowed like the moonlight on the ocean. Her shoulder-length gray hair had been brushed away from her face and tucked behind both ears. She wore a pair of small gold hoop earrings and a matching necklace. A white apron hung around her neck and was tied at her waist, concealing the front of her floral dress.

"Ya must be my new tenant, the one Maggie called 'bout."

Bella nodded.

"What? Cat got yer tongue?" The older woman tsked three times, but Bella remained silent. "Well, come on, now," the woman commanded. When Bella didn't answer, she swiped a hand through the air toward the house. "Suit yerself, but I ain't sittin' out here all night waitin' for ya to have the good sense to haul yerself inside."

The wooden steps groaned beneath Bella's ninety-two-pound frame.

"Did ya eat?" the woman asked.

"Yes," Bella said softly.

The old woman gave her new tenant a death stare. "You ain't from these parts, are ya? 'Cuz if'n ya were, you'da known to follow that *yes* with a *ma'am*." Her eyebrows knit together. "And ya woulda answered in a full sentence."

Bella fumed. "Yes, ma'am. I've already eaten."

"See there, girl. Words're free. They don't cost ya a cent. Try usin' 'em." She pulled the screen door open and clumsily stepped over the threshold.

Bella followed the elderly woman as she shuffled into the kitchen. "Now, let me git a good look at ya. I don't just let every Tom, Dick, and Harry stay here. It's my home, ya know." She swirled a finger through the air. "Turn 'round."

Grudgingly, Bella turned in a circle. Halfway around, she stifled a yawn with her fist.

"Ever been to prison or killed anybody?"

"No, ma'am."

"Do ya steal?"

"No, ma'am," Bella snarled through clenched teeth.

"Are ya good fer the rent? 'Cause I don't let freeloaders live here neither."

"Yes, ma'am." Bella rolled her eyes and yawned again.

The woman sighed. "Tell ya what," she said, dropping the contract back onto the table. "Ya can sign yer life away in the mornin'."

Bella could feel her anger brewing, on the verge of overflowing. The woman had no idea how true that statement was. "Yes, ma'am. I'll sign my life over to you in the morning."

The old woman nodded before painstakingly climbing the fourteen steps to the second floor. Bella followed her to a room at the front of the house. The woman snapped on a lamp. With her gnarled fingers, she unlatched the wooden shutters and slid the window open. Fresh ocean air flooded into the room. Once again, Bella drew a deep breath and held it.

"Maggie didn't give me time to git up here to dust, but it's yer room now. So…" She looked toward the bed. "The beddin' is clean. I 'spect ya know how to wash sheets."

A frail smile crossed Bella's face. "Thank you. *Ma'am.*" She added the last word quickly, lest she be taken to task again.

"Bathroom's in the hallway. Towels and washrags're in the cupboard. The water heater's on the fritz, so make yer showers short." She turned to walk away but stopped. "I also 'spect yer room to be tidy and yer bed made every morning."

"Yes, ma'am." Bella was suddenly too tired to argue with her new landlady. Stiffly, she extended her hand. "I'm Bella."

The old broad shrugged. "Don't make no difference to me who ya are—so long as y're quiet, do as I say, and pay yer rent on time. Y're all the same to me."

Tears filled Bella's eyes. "Yes, ma'am," she said softly. Bella had never been a crier. Being tough was how she'd made it through every day of her life. But here she was, kowtowing to some iron-willed, ornery old biddy.

"Breakfast's at seven sharp. Be in the kitchen a half-hour b'fore so ya can set the table and squeeze the oranges." The woman slowly lumbered out of the room.

Bella nodded. "Yes, ma'am." She exhaled sharply.

At the top of the stairs, the old woman grabbed the railing and slowly turned around. "Tilly," she said. "My name's Tilly."

"Goodnight, Tilly." Bella smiled. But it hurt her to watch her landlady painfully begin her descent.

***

Bella dragged an old rocking chair in front of the open window and pulled a knit throw up under her chin. The floorboards creaked as she rocked herself with one foot. If she listened hard, she was positive she could hear the waves lapping the shore behind the newer homes on the ocean side of the street. It didn't matter if it was in her imagination or if it was real. Nothing felt real anymore. The life she had worked so hard to forge was fading. Before long, Bella would slip into nothingness. No one would even remember her.

Alone in the last room she would ever sleep in, her courage slipped away. Her throat tightened, and she struggled to swallow. Tears streamed down her cheeks. Dislodging the small pillow from behind her back, she held it to her face and smothered her sobs. An hour later, exhausted and still fully dressed, she crawled beneath the homemade quilt.

She had one less day than she had yesterday. Only three hundred and sixty-four remained, *if she was lucky.*

More than anything, she wanted to be lucky.

CHAPTER 3

Let the head-butting begin

The dark sky was dappled with spots of gray early morning light. Bella hadn't seen 6:30 a.m. since one of her foster families equated the completion of morning chores with the right to eat breakfast. Early on, there had been many days she'd gone to school with an empty stomach.

Bella stumbled into the kitchen, still garbed in the same clothes from the previous day. Not knowing her way around the old house, she followed the light that streamed through the narrow hallway. Timeworn music crackled from an old metal box with yellowed knobs.

"What's this thing?" Bella asked, pointing to it.

Tilly wiped her hands on the front of her apron. "Well, good mornin', sunshine," she sarcastically quipped as she drew closer to Bella. "That there's called a radio," she said slowly, emphasizing each word. "I woulda thought you'da seen one b'fore."

Bella rolled her eyes. "I know it's a radio. But the sound is terrible. They still sell them in stores, you know." Her snarky personality had returned, swiping away the amiable act from the previous night. She wasn't about to let the old woman get the better of her.

Tilly returned to the counter, picked up the pottery bowl, and continued to stir. "That's what's wrong with ya kids today.

Ya wanna buy new when old'll do."

Bella's ears burned. "First of all, I'm not a kid. I'm twenty-three. And second, why wouldn't you want the best that money can buy?" She pointed to the radio again. "That thing sounds…tinny."

A sharp laugh cut across the kitchen. "Listen, I lived through the Great Depression, and I heard a lot worse. Back in my day…"

The young woman loudly sighed. "Oh, please spare me. Just tell me what you want me to do." Bella flicked the radio off. "I can't listen to that—music, or whatever you call it, this early in the morning."

Tilly pointed toward the clock hanging on the wall. "Six thirty isn't early. I've been up since four. Who do you think made these cinnamon rolls?" She picked up the bowl and a wooden-handled spoon and began drizzling glaze over the top of them.

Bella poked her nose in the air and sniffed. The kitchen smelled like a New York bakery. The oven door hung open, so she lifted it with her foot, slamming it shut.

"Leave it open," Tilly snapped. "We waste nothin'. There's heat still comin' outta that oven. I'd rather eat in a toasty kitchen."

Bella glared at Tilly. "What do you want me to do?"

"I done yer jobs already." The old woman stared at her new boarder. "You can set the table."

The first drawer Bella tried opened no more than a few inches before exhibiting its stubbornness. No matter how hard she pulled, it wouldn't budge. Seconds later, Bella was keenly aware of the old lady's scrutiny over her battle with the old wooden drawer.

Suddenly, Tilly opened a cupboard door and grabbed a well-used hammer from the lower shelf. She hoisted it to chest height and squared her shoulders as she narrowed in on her new tenant. Bella scurried backward, unsure of her landlady's intent. Tilly swung the hammer, slamming the metal head into the side panel of the drawer, dislodging it from its current state. Without a word, the old gal shoved the drawer in with a quick push of her hip and returned the hammer to its rightful place.

"The silverware's two drawers to the right," Tilly told her as she pulled a frying pan from a lower cupboard. "We're havin' scrambled eggs and ham. Ya better tell me now if y're one of them meat haters."

Unsure if she was more shocked at what had transpired with the hammer or Tilly's reference to *meat haters*, Bella could feel her heart thudding inside her chest. "It's called a vegetarian. And no, I eat meat."

"Good. Now don't just stand there. Set the table or the food'll get cold by the time ya figure out where everythin's at."

When Tilly stuck her head into the beat-up green refrigerator, Bella mocked the woman, narrowly shutting her mouth before her host turned around. *Let the head-butting begin.*

While the cantankerous woman cooked breakfast, Bella plopped two plates in the center of the kitchen table and dumped a handful of silverware on top. A pair of small jars with handles served as juice glasses and a chipped cup from a hook under an upper cupboard held Tilly's coffee. It was the blackest cup of joe Bella had ever seen. She was positive it was deadly.

On the way to the table, the coffee sloshed over the top and onto the floor. After abandoning the cups near the plates, Bella followed the trail of dark liquid, swabbing it up with her sock. Finally, she grabbed the cinnamon rolls and set the pan on the table before settling into a chair. She cut a piece from the center and took an enormous bite. Tilly cleared her throat.

"Manners weren't somethin' yer folks taught ya, were they?

Now separate the plates."

Tilly put a piece of ham and a pile of yellow, fluffy eggs on Bella's plate before filling her own. "Here we wait 'til everybody's seated b'fore we eat."

The old woman returned the pan to the stove before settling into her chair. She looked at the table, clicked her tongue, and shook her head. "Fer yer information, we set the table the right way whether there's two of us or twenty. Fork on the left; knife and spoon on the right. The napkin's folded and placed to the left of the fork. The drinks go 'bove the spoon." She glared at Bella. "And a pan ain't never set on the table. Pots and pans are fer cookin' and bakin'." Next, she held the cinnamon rolls toward Bella. "And I better never catch ya helpin' yerself to food from the middle of a pan again. Understood?"

Bella warily lowered the roll to her plate.

"*And* we always say grace b'fore we b'gin."

A sigh of frustration escaped from Bella as she tipped her head backward. "I don't believe in your god or any of that other crap churchgoers try to shove down our throats."

"Well, I do," Tilly said decidedly. She scowled at the young woman. "And you'll kindly be respectful while I pray."

Bella stared at the ceiling and clenched her jaw, once again, holding the god she didn't believe in, or even like, responsible for sending her to live with this woman.

"Dear Lord, thank ya fer this food, fer the hands that grew it, and fer those who prepared it. May ya bless everybody..." She opened one eye and looked at Bella. "...includin' those who eat it. In yer name, we pray. Amen."

Tilly lifted her napkin, folded it across her lap, and stared at the young woman. Bella's fork was halfway to her mouth when she stopped. Grabbing her napkin in one hand, she awkwardly laid it across her lap and shoved a heap of eggs into her mouth.

"And another thing: we don't wear hats at the table." Before she even finished the sentence, she had tugged Bella's stocking cap from her head.

Tilly's mouth dropped open. "What in the heck happened to yer hair? Overcolorin'? You young white girls are always tryin' to be somethin' y're not."

Bella's eyes narrowed and the short hairs of her eyebrows bunched together. With a clang, she dropped her fork onto the table. "Cancer," she hissed. "Cancer happened." Angrily, she stood and knocked the heavy wooden chair to the floor. She stormed out of the kitchen and retreated to her room, where she crawled beneath the covers and sobbed.

***

By the time Bella woke, the metal alarm clock with the two bells on top read *11:35*. She yanked the covers back over her head to block out the light. Her stomach complained loudly. Shoving an arm out from her sanctuary, she felt along the floor until she found her backpack. Pulling it into her hideaway, she opened it and helped herself to a handful of trail mix.

An abrupt noise startled her, and she threw back the covers. Tilly stood next to her bed with a tray of food. From one of her misshapen fingers hung Bella's stocking cap.

"Ya didn't eat much fer breakfast this mornin'. I thought ya could use a bite."

For the first time since Bella met Tilly, the woman seemed almost kind. Bella knew this was as close to an apology as she would get.

"Thank you," she mumbled. She sat up in bed and took the tray. It had to have taken a toll on Tilly to climb the stairs without using the railing for support. For that, Bella was appreciative.

The woman watched her take a bite of the turkey and cheese sandwich. "If y're up to it, we oughta finish up the roomin' paperwork this afternoon. Do ya wanna come downstairs, or do ya want me to haul my tuchus all the way back up here—again?"

"I'll be down in a while." Bella smiled softly.

"Y're right about that. This might be the last time ya ever see me up here."

"Then why'd you ask?"

Tilly shrugged. "Not a clue." She slowly withdrew from the room.

CHAPTER 4

Spare Parts

The smell of fresh bread and pine cleaner attacked Bella when she walked into the empty kitchen. She deposited her tray of dirty dishes and trash on the counter next to the sink. Then, carefully positioning her arms and feet, she rotated in a half pirouette and nearly collided with Tilly.

"Holy crap!" Bella's hand flew to her chest, and she sucked in a sharp breath. "For an old lady, you sure are stealthy."

"It's the orthopedic shoes." Tilly chuckled. "And just so ya know, I ain't just quiet; I'm good with a rifle too." She winked. "I can part the hair on a squirrel's tail from a hundred yards away."

Bella's eyes grew wide. "Why are you telling me this? Should I be worried?"

Tilly's mouth twisted as she nodded toward Bella's tray. "Not if ya clean up after yerself. Y're payin' fer a room; ya ain't gettin' maid service to boot."

After her landlady's alarming admission about the squirrel, Bella cleared the counter and scrubbed it down in just under a minute. The dishes were stowed in the dated dishwasher, and the garbage was dropped into the mint-green trash can held together with a yellowed strip of box tape and a piece of jute string.

The woman pulled out a kitchen chair, backed toward it, and

dropped onto the cushioned seat. "Now, let's git this paperwork signed b'fore you knock me on my can with one of those wild dance moves of yers."

With her foot pressed on the seat of the chair and her knee against the table, Bella studied her landlady. Tilly pulled a wadded tissue from beneath her bra strap and swiped it under her nose. Bella's upper lip rose, and her nose wrinkled as the old lady tucked the dirty tissue back into its holder.

"Did they not have pockets when you were born?" Bella asked, repulsed by the woman's action. "How old are you anyway?"

"Hmm," Tilly snorted. "Has nobody ever told ya it's not polite to ask a woman her age?"

Bella lifted her palms upward and shrugged. "What difference does it make?

Tilly gave the tabletop a forceful slap. "'Cause it just ain't done. I don't give a flyin' fig what y'all do up north, but down here, ya respect yer elders."

"Well then, *everybody* in the whole world must respect you." Bella smirked. "Hell, I bet you're even *God's* elder."

Tilly planted one hand on her hip and squeezed her wrinkled lips into a tight line. "Might be, but I'd rather be old and wise than a young, smart arse like yerself."

Bella dropped her fists onto the table and guffawed. "Arse? You southerners make up swear words, don't you?"

The old lady poked a finger across the table. "Don't go takin' the Lord's name in a fit'a anger, and ya can say whatever turns yer crank." Tilly twisted her lips. "But fer yer information, southern women know how to act like a lady. They ain't gotta go 'round cussin' everybody out. Even our anger sounds sweet." She shoved the contract across the table. "Now, let's review this thing b'fore I toss yer arse back out on the street. *Bless your heart.*"

Bella nodded slowly. A weary sigh slipped through her pursed lips. She picked up the skinny, yellowed pen, courtesy of the Lawson Beach State Bank, flipped to the back page and attempted to sign her name. The indentation of the letter B was noticeable, but the ink was undetectable. Raising the pen above her head, she violently shook it and tried again—still nothing. Bella scribbled deep circles on the top of the page, but they too were invisible. Finally, she pitched the pen toward the trash can.

"Now, what'd ya go and do that fer?" Tilly demanded. "That's a fine pen. All it needs is a refill." She pressed a hand against the table and rocked once before launching herself upward. "Go fetch it while I track down some ink."

Bella scowled. "You've got to be kidding. They make refills for pens?"

Ignoring the comment, Tilly left the room—shaking her head and mumbling. Minutes later, she hobbled back in, holding a skinny metal tube with a tip on one end. She replaced the innards and slid the pen toward her renter.

Bella clicked the top of the pen again and traced the capital B she had drawn before. "Well, what do you know? It works." She finished signing the contract and dropped the pen on the paper. "I can't believe they can replace parts on a pen…" Her eyes and shoulders drooped. "But they haven't figured out how to fix people."

Tilly folded her hands and rested them on the edge of the table. "People ain't s'posed to live ferever, girl. If we were, we'da been born with a bag'a spare parts." She looked toward Bella. "It ain't what God intended."

Bella laughed. "Oh, yeah. That's right. You *would* know. I'm pretty sure you were with God when he created the world, weren't you?"

Tilly acknowledged the comment with nothing more than a sneer. "Do ya wanna go over the contract?" she asked.

"Don't need to." She pushed the paper packet back across the table. "Not planning to be here that long."

The woman turned to the back page, looked at Bella, and back at the contract. "What kinda name is Bellarina? Who saddles a child with a name that appallin'?"

Bella snorted. "A ballet dancer and her agent husband." She frowned at Tilly. "I used to think it was the most beautiful name. For a year after my mother died, I continued to call myself Bellarina. I was so proud of it. It reminded me of her. But after being passed from stranger to stranger who, just like you, tormented me about my unusual name—I decided to go by Bella."

Tilly studied Bella's signature. "Levitsky?" Her eyes narrowed as she looked at her new tenant. "Y're Alina Levitsky's daughter? *Thee* Alina Levitsky?"

Bella nodded. "I was until I became an orphan. Then I was nobody's daughter."

The old gal nodded. "Now I git that spinnin' move ya did. I'm guessin' you learnt it from yer ma. But ya got my curiosity up. When the apple didn't fall far from the tree, did it conk ya in the head or somethin'?" She raised an eyebrow and stared at her housemate. "I'm kinda worried about ya."

***

Dusk painted Lawson Beach a deep gray. The new roommates shared a meal of fried chicken, turnip greens, sweet potato casserole, cornbread, and sweet tea. Bella attempted a bite of everything but quickly turned her nose up at the greens. They were as bad as they sounded.

With the dishes out of the way, Bella threw herself onto the tufted gold sofa. The threadbare spots made it look as worn out as Tilly. It creaked when she landed.

"Fer the daughter of a professional dancer, ya ain't exactly the most graceful creature, are ya?" Tilly raised an eyebrow.

24

Bella huffed. "Never took dance lessons. My parents were too busy when I was young, the nannies refused to waste their time with a *passing interest*, and none of my fosters were exactly willing to haul my ass to some dance class a couple times a week." She lifted her skinny legs and pointed her toes as her mother had done years before. "So, no. Not graceful." Every turn, move, or jump Bella made, she had learned from watching old videos of her mother.

The woman's shoulders rose. "It shows."

Tilly snapped on a white marble lamp next to her recliner. Slowly, she backed to the front of the chair and collapsed into it. From a large basket on the floor, she picked up a skein of pink yarn and a pair of knitting needles. "Tell me 'bout yerself," Tilly commanded. Her twisted fingers worked the metal skewers and fiber into a wide tube.

"Not much to tell. I'm twenty-three and I have cancer. Oh— and I suppose you should know I'm dying. I've got about a year to live." Bella dropped her legs and rolled onto her side. She bent her arm under a soft pillow and rested her head on it.

Tilly kept her eyes on her work. "We're all dyin', Bella. Ain't nothin' special 'bout you." She took a few more stitches. "Maybe start from the beginnin'—b'fore the cancer."

The grandfather clock ticked loudly as Bella swam through the memories of her life. Finally, she sat up and quietly cleared her throat.

"Well, my parents were from Belarus in Eastern Europe. At one time, it was part of Russia. During the revolution in 1991, my folks, Alina Bellin and Josef Levitsky, escaped. No one knew what was going to happen." Bella drew a deep breath. "My mother was fifteen and my father was eighteen. They were both dancers. But my mother was amazing. She was considered a national treasure. So that made leaving extremely dangerous."

"What 'bout their families?"

Bella watched Tilly nimbly loop the thin cord into a series of stitches. She wondered how someone whose digits barely resembled fingers could move so swiftly.

Bella shrugged. "I'm assuming they didn't make it. I don't recall my parents ever mentioning them. I don't even know their names." Again, she pointed her toes. "My mom and dad made it to the United States. But after being injured in their escape, my father couldn't dance anymore."

Tilly laid her work in her lap. She repeatedly opened and closed her hands, working out the kinks. "I vaguely recollect hearin' yer mother died, but I don't recall how."

Bella snorted. "I killed them."

"Ain't nothin' to joke 'bout."

She pushed herself up and sat cross-legged on the couch. "It's true. I didn't kill them in the way most people would think. But I may as well have." She bent forward, pressed her elbows to her knees, and rested her chin on the backs of her hands. "When my mom got pregnant with me, my father insisted she have an abortion. But she refused. She was four months along before anyone realized she was pregnant. At that point, the company forced her to stop dancing."

The woman nodded. "Well, she musta loved ya or she wouldn'ta refused to abort ya."

"Maybe. But sometimes, I wonder. I was barely three months old when she returned to dancing—and traveling. Ultimately, my parents ditched me in a New York City apartment in the care of a long line of nannies." She watched the old grandfather clock. "I lived in the lap of luxury with a crapload of strangers who were only there for the money."

"So, help me git this," Tilly stated. "How exactly are you responsible for their death?"

Several deep breaths audibly passed through Bella's lips before she answered. "My father *never* wanted me. And my mother did. When I was a toddler, she wanted to quit dancing and raise a family, but he wouldn't let her. He controlled her life with an iron fist, and each year, it got worse. By the end, she lived in constant fear of him."

Bella jumped when she saw her reflection in the picture window. She'd avoided the mirror and the young, unrecognizable bald woman who watched her from the other side of the glass plate for months. "Over time, he grew extremely jealous, and he began drinking—heavily. He started buying himself expensive gifts—diamond cufflinks, high-priced suits, and even sports cars." She bit her lip.

"He reinvented himself with my mother's money. Then suddenly, he got what he always wanted—to be noticed. There were lines of women throwing themselves at him—even in our home. I used to hide at the top of the stairs in our penthouse apartment when they threw fancy parties. I was the proverbial *fly on the wall* in my flannel nightgown and thick robe." She sighed heavily. "I saw the women touch him in places they shouldn't have. I doubt he turned any of them down."

Bella went to the window and tried to see beyond her reflection, into her past. "There were a lot of close calls in those fancy cars he bought. So many, in fact, my mother refused to ride with him anymore—until that last night."

She ran her hand over the top of her head. "I don't even know what really happened. They'd gone out for dinner to some small, out-of-the-way place in the country—somewhere my mother wouldn't be recognized, and my father could be the star for the evening. I'm sure of that. Sometime around midnight, I woke up to my newest nanny screaming at me, *Your folks are dead! They're dead! Killed in a car accident. Did you hear me?*"

Tilly dropped her hands on top of her knitting. "What kinda person does that? That musta been awful."

On her toes, Bella spun toward Tilly. "The worst part wasn't that my parents were dead. I barely knew them. No, the worst part was how the nanny reacted. She raced around the house yelling that she didn't want to be saddled with a twelve-year-old little brat. *I'm supposed to be going on vacation next week.* She grabbed the front of my nightgown. *Did you hear me? Vacation! And you've ruined it.*"

"Good Lord, what a terrible thing to say to a child."

The young woman shrugged. "I suppose. But I was numb. Once she let go of me, I crawled into my bed, pulled the covers over my head, and bawled."

Tilly gave a half-smile. "I've witnessed that move recently. It's kinda like watchin' the groundhog run back inside his hole."

Bella rolled her eyes. "I didn't care about my dad. His drinking and need to control everything had made life miserable for us. I missed my mom, though. At least she tried to make my life good."

"How'd ya end up in foster care?" Tilly returned to her knitting.

"Well, my parents had no real friends, not ones who'd raise their kid anyway. And they hadn't left a will. So there was no one." Shoulders back, chin up, and arms curled in front of her, Bella crossed the room on her toes, following a seam on the scarred floor. "It was just me, so I ended up in the system. By that point, I was too old for anyone to want to adopt and too quiet to be noticed."

"I'm sorry." Tilly lifted the footrest of the recliner.

"On the morning of my eighteenth birthday, a woman from social services came to see me at the home where I was staying—a house with two young foster kids the family planned to adopt. She opened a folder, studied it, and closed it again. Then, she offered me three choices: remain in foster care until I graduated from high school, or until I turned twenty-one and had most of my college completed, or set out on my own."

Bella spun in a one-eighty. "For the most part, I was the live-in babysitter for the other two fosters. I hated it, but I didn't know how I would survive without a job, and I really wanted to graduate from high school." Bella followed the same line on the floor back toward the picture window. "That's when the social worker told me about my inheritance. My parents had left me more money than I could comprehend. So I packed my stuff into a paper bag, showed my detestable foster parents my inheritance the social worker told me about, and moved out. Of course, they tried to stop me, but I walked out. I learned how to adult fast."

Tilly's forehead wrinkled. "Where'd ya go?"

"I rented a tiny apartment, bought furniture from a second-hand store, and snagged a few clothes from Goodwill. Then I finished high school and, with the help of my guidance counselor, applied to college."

"Were ya scared?"

Bella nodded. "Yeah. Mostly because I wasn't smart with money. I'd never really dealt with money. I had no idea how long it would last."

"What'd ya study in college?"

"Design and Visual Communications."

"Sounds like a foreign language to me. Where'd ya work?"

Bella shrugged. "I didn't. The day after I graduated, I found the lump on my breast."

Typical of Tilly, she clicked her tongue. "Well, they say everythin' happens fer a reason."

Bella angrily spun around. "Who says that? Is that one of your moronic god lines?" She planted her hands on her hips. "You explain why my parents died. And why I got cancer." Her eyes burned as tears streamed down her cheeks, dropping onto her dark blue t-shirt. "Whose brilliant idea was it to kill me off before I got a chance to live?" Her fingers white-knuckled into tight balls. "Explain to me why your god is punishing me."

The room was thick with emotion—unanswered questions. Bella struggled to breathe.

Tilly dropped the footrest of the recliner and scooted to the front of the chair before standing. "A year, ya say. Then we got ourselves a lot of livin' to do in the next three hundred and sixty-five days."

Bella looked at the clock. It was nearing 7:30 p.m. "Three hundred sixty-three," she told her as she collapsed back onto the couch. "Three hundred and sixty-three days is all I have left. *If I'm lucky.*"

CHAPTER 5

More complicated

Sleep would not come. No matter how much Bella tried to relax, it eluded her. As the clock left yesterday behind and ticked into the new day, she pulled the covers over her head and sobbed. Would she see her birthday again, or would she spend the first day of October buried under six feet of dirt? There was nothing inside her that believed she'd ever celebrate another birthday.

As unlikely as it seemed, the previous night's exchange with Tilly had helped. It had lifted her spirits slightly, releasing the pressure that made her feel like she was drowning in her secret. Her landlady's comment about everything happening for a reason had sent Bella over the edge, but sharing her story had been therapy. Tilly wouldn't have been her first choice as a confidant, but she wasn't the worst person either. If they were going to co-exist for the next year, they had to learn to get along. In those couple of hours, something in their relationship had shifted. The iciness had thawed ever so slightly. And best of all, the old gal no longer insisted Bella call her *ma'am*.

Bella moaned. The clock read *6:22*. Commander Tilly would be expecting her downstairs in eight minutes. *Who gets up at this hour?* she wondered. *And for what?* It wasn't like they had any place to be or anything to do—besides stepping a little closer toward death. Still, Bella climbed out of bed, raced to the bathroom, and slipped on her jeans and a clean shirt, dashing into the kitchen with two minutes to spare.

The kitchen smelled of—nothing. Not only was there no hustle and bustle over breakfast as there had been the previous day, but Tilly was quietly reading the newspaper.

"Ah, what's going on?" Bella asked. She looked at the empty countertop.

Tilly lowered the paper. "Ya drive?"

"Yes," Bella answered hesitantly. "Why?"

The elderly woman held a finger in the air, directing her to wait. As always, she rocked in the chair, lifting herself a little higher each time, until she was standing, but winded. "Good! We're goin' on a little adventure today." She smiled. "And y're gonna drive."

Again, Bella scanned the kitchen. "What about breakfast?"

"We'll eat at the bistro. I wanna officially introduce ya to Maggie and Lou. After that, we're gonna tour Lawson Beach. I ain't gonna let you waste a minute of the time ya got left."

"Three hundred and sixty-three days," Bella reminded her sullenly.

"Listen to me. There ain't gonna be no complainin' today. None. Got it? 'Cause I ain't gonna attend yer pity party."

"Mmmm. 'Kay."

Tilly pulled a patent leather purse from a cupboard in the kitchen. She held it up for Bella to see. "I had this purse since I was sixteen." She twisted it to show Bella the other side. "Only purse I ever spent money on. Used it every day'a my life."

"Well, okay then." Bella rolled her eyes and followed the old woman through the door and down the front steps. "Aren't you going to lock up?" she asked.

Tilly stopped so suddenly, Bella swerved off the sidewalk to avoid a collision. "If somebody comes into my house and helps 'emself to somethin' I got, then they must need it a heckuva lot more'n I do." Tilly arched her eyebrows. "B'sides, this is Lawson Beach. Ain't nothin' but good folk here."

The two continued toward the old garage. Tilly reached up and twisted the wooden latch. She looked toward Bella. "This ain't a movie, girl. Ya gonna help me or just stand there and pick yer seat?"

"I have no idea where you come up with the crap you say. It's like you memorized some southern dictionary."

"Jus' git over here."

Bella moved toward the garage and pulled one door open while Tilly tugged on the other. She nearly fell as she stepped back into a small hole.

An archaic car nearly filled the old garage. Surprisingly, it looked new. The red sides juxtaposed the white top and the silver trim. Statuesque fins curved outward toward the back of the vehicle. The white-walled tires nearly glowed in the early morning light. The silver spoked hubcaps were polished and spotless. Bella wasn't sure if she was excited or mortified to drive such a monstrosity.

"What is this thing?" Bella asked. She ran a finger over one of the fins.

Tilly lightly slapped her hand. "Don't be touchin' my car." She headed toward the passenger's side. "If ya gotta know, it's a 1957 Ford Fairlane."

Bella's eyes grew wide as she mouthed *1957*. "Whoa!"

"It was the only new car my folks ever bought. They scrimped and saved every penny of the three thousand dollars it cost 'em. When my ma died, she left it to me. It's the only one I ever owned. B'fore then, I walked, took the bus, or rode with her."

The two women climbed into the car. Tilly dangled the keys above Bella's lap before dropping them.

"I can't believe it still runs!" Bella exclaimed.

"Take good care of things, and they last ferever."

"Not true of people," Bella said.

Tilly narrowed her eyes. "Were ya not listenin' when I told ya 'bout the no complainin' rule today?" When Bella turned away, she poked her chin toward the house next door. "My neighbor comes over time and again to make sure it still purrs like a kitten. Course, he thinks I'm leavin' it to him when I die. So he prob'ly stops more often than he should. I'm pretty sure he drools when he's over here."

Bella lightly touched the instrument panel behind the ultra-thin steering wheel. But recalling Tilly's earlier comment about not touching the car, she pulled her hand back. "I don't even know what all these things are for. It's nothing like the car I had back home." She set her hand on the middle of the bench seat. "Where's the shifter?"

"Ah, fer Pete's sake. You young'uns gotta make everythin' more complicated than it's meant to be."

Tilly spent the better part of two minutes explaining the basics of the old car. "It's real simple. Got it?"

"Yes." She started the car and backed out of the garage. It felt like piloting the Titanic after driving her Volkswagen. Bella shifted into *park* and wiped her slick hands on the front of her jeans. She touched the odometer. "Holy crap! It's only got fifteen thousand miles on it."

"Nobody drove much back then. People walked most everywhere they went. Lawson Beach wasn't so big. It was a better time. People were healthier. Y'all've wrecked the world with yer fancy cars and yer need for everythin' to happen on the spot. What was wrong with the good ole days and how things were?"

After last night, mocking her landlady seemed wrong, but it didn't stop Bella from fluttering her eyes and mumbling fake words as Tilly explained.

"Are ya done?" Tilly waited.

Bella pursed her lips to keep from smiling. "Sorry."

The old gal opened her purse. "I got somethin' for ya." She removed a small package wrapped in brown paper and tied with a white piece of string. Reaching across the seat, she waited for Bella to take it.

"For me? What is it?" she asked.

Tilly scowled. "It's a turd wrapped in brown paper." She tsked. "It's a gift, Bella. Ya don't get to know what it is 'til ya open it for cryin' out loud."

Bella pulled the string and unfolded the paper to reveal a soft pink hat with an off-centered white flower. Her mouth dropped open. She turned toward her landlady. "Is this what you were making last night?"

Tilly reached over and snagged the blue hat from Bella's head. "I thought ya could use something a little…" She held the old hat in the air. "…cleaner." She frowned. "And maybe a little less *homeless* lookin'."

Centering the flower over her left eye, Bella turned the rearview mirror and studied herself. "It's beautiful, Tilly. Thank you," she whispered. An overwhelming feeling of gratitude rushed through her. She leaned over and embraced Tilly. "No one has ever done anything this nice for me."

The old woman patted her on the back. "Might need to ask yerself why," she grumbled.

"I'm not going to let you get to me today." Bella wiped away the few tears that had fallen and looked at herself again. "It's perfect!" She felt the skin at the corners of her mouth tighten as her grin grew wider than ever before.

"All right already. Stop all this gushin' and git this show on the road."

A few minutes later, the car was safely parked in a double-length space in the lot behind the Table for Two Bistro.

"Hey, ladies," Maggie called when they walked through the door. "Be with you in a sec."

Unlike Bella's first trip, the two sat at a table in the middle of the restaurant.

"That is a beautiful hat," Maggie told Bella as she approached the table. "I bet I can guess who made it." She winked at Tilly.

Bella touched her new hat. "And you'd be correct."

After studying the menu, Maggie convinced the northerner to try a plate of biscuits and gravy rather than a traditional breakfast. "If you're planning to live down here, you better get used to eating like the rest of us." Always frightened of the unknown, Bella was surprised by how much she loved it.

Lou exited the kitchen long enough to officially meet Lawson Beach's newest resident. He was the tallest man Bella had ever seen. He towered over Maggie. Like Tilly, his dark skin had a sheen to it. Bella wondered if it was lotion or the glisten of sweat from working in the kitchen.

"I loved breakfast," Bella effused.

Lou nodded. "Good to hear."

"Lou's Tilly's neighbor," Maggie said as she zipped between the tables with the coffee pot.

Tilly shook her head. "Not just Lou. Maggie lives there too. They've been married for pert near thirty years."

Maggie drifted past again, this time with a pot of decaf. "Hard to fathom, huh?"

"So, you're the one who keeps Tilly's car running," she said to Lou.

The man shook his head. "Not me. That'd be my son, Malik. He's the one who's good with cars."

"Not food, though," Maggie called before stopping at another table. "That boy can't cook to save his soul."

Lou excused himself as a large group entered the restaurant.

Maggie stopped at their table. "Glad you enjoyed your breakfast, ladies." She nodded toward the older woman. "That biscuit and gravy recipe is Tilly's. It has a couple secret ingredients you won't find anywhere else."

"Really?" Bella seemed surprised. "I'm impressed."

"Evidently, she hasn't told you she used to own this place."

A loud huff exploded from Tilly. "Well, it weren't no hoity-toity *bistro* back then. It was just a café. I don't know why y'all can't leave well enough alone."

"Now I understand why your food tastes so good," Bella raved. "You were a professional cook."

"Food's food," Tilly grumbled.

"Are we splitting the bill, ladies?" Maggie asked.

Tilly took a gander at Bella. "No, ma'am. My new boarder'll be pickin' up the tab. It's the least she can do after I made her that nice hat." She winked at Maggie. They both laughed.

Bella again touched her head. "Yes, of course."

After wiping her mouth with a napkin, Tilly set the checkered cloth on the table next to her plate. "Now, if y'all'll excuse me, I gotta powder my nose."

Maggie instantly tucked her notepad into her apron pocket, grabbed Tilly's arm, and helped her to her feet.

"I have a mirror in my bag," Bella told her. "You don't have to go all the way to the bathroom."

The women laughed again.

"Ya got so much to learn, girl." Tilly shuffled toward the restroom.

CHAPTER 6

Life Lessons at the Piggly Wiggly

After leaving the bistro, Bella drove up and down the main drag of Lawson Beach, stopping wherever Tilly commanded. Sometimes it was at a small shop; other times it was a tourist site. Shortly after noon, they sat in the car and shared a turkey sandwich purchased from the Sand Bar.

Driving the old car was like going down the highway with your panic button jammed. It stuck out like a sore thumb. At stoplights, Bella hung her head and hoped no one would notice. But that didn't happen. Everyone knew exactly who was sitting in the car. People beeped and hollered greetings to Tilly. It was apparent she was loved by everyone.

As the late afternoon sun drifted across the sky, Bella pulled into the Piggly Wiggly. She held Tilly's arm as they slowly made their way to the front of the store. Instead of pushing a cart, Tilly opted for a scooter with a small basket. She plucked an organized list from a pocket in her seventy-four-year-old purse. As Tilly called out items, Bella retrieved them.

"Barbeque sauce." Bella grabbed the largest bottle from the shelf. Tilly raised an eyebrow and frowned. "So, ya love that stuff real good, huh?"

Bella shrugged. "It's all right. I don't use it a lot."

"Then put 'er back and git the small one," Tilly barked.

Narrowed eyes and a half-cocked frown showcased Bella's

confusion. "Why? If you buy a big one, you don't run out as often."

Tilly shook her head. "Who's pluckin' this chicken, girl—you or me?"

"I don't even know what that means. So I'm just going to assume you are."

"Dang tootin', I am. And there's a whole lotta other stuff ya need to learn 'bout dyin'. So hush up and listen. If anybody knows this stuff, it's me. I been dyin' for prob'ly…" she shrugged, "well, since b'fore ya ever popped outta yer ma's woo-hoo. So I'll beg ya not to question me when I tell ya somethin'."

Tilly watched Bella put the small bottle in the basket at the front of the scooter. "I ain't got no clue when the grim reaper's gonna cut me down, so I'm always ready. Let me explain some things to ya."

In the middle of the grocery store, Tilly spelled out a lesson on dying worthy of a tenured college professor. Shoppers smiled as they caught bits of their conversation as the two of them passed through the aisles.

"If somethin' is gonna last ya longer than six months, it ain't worth buyin'. Like this here barbeque sauce." She picked up the small bottle. "Stockin' up's fer people goin' be 'round a while." Tilly shook her head. "That ain't us.

"And if ya ever need a prescription, don't be gettin' those dang three-month refills. Stick with a month at a time. Ya ain't gonna save nobody no money if somebody just tosses it all out once y're dead and buried."

She moved her electric cart down the aisle. "Here's somethin' else to chew on. Don't be throwin' 'way good money on raffle tickets when the drawin' is more'n a couple weeks away." Tilly poked a finger toward Bella. "And even then, ya gotta ask yerself if the prize is worth spendin' the cash." Tilly shrugged. "A free embalmin' or a cremation might be worth a couple bucks."

Bella grimaced. She wanted to laugh, but she couldn't. It was all hitting way too close to home.

Tilly plucked a small jar of grape jelly from a low shelf. "And I don't give a hill of beans which scrawny-arsed kid comes a knockin' at yer door raisin' money fer their school. Don't be buyin' no magazine subscriptions. That's a year commitment, minimum." She shook her head. "If ya don't make it, it ain't only a waste a money, but the poor slobs at the post office gotta deal with yer crap."

She pulled the lever and moved the cart forward, talking as she steered. "Don't waste yer money on yearlong parkin' stickers or passes. Ya ain't even sure ya can use 'em a month from now, let 'lone a year."

Bella walked next to the cart. "And under no circumstances buy a lifetime warranty on anythin'." She shook her finger at Bella. "They get ya on that one. It's a trick those little nutbags play."

Tilly pulled a box of crackers from a shelf. "And it might seem like a good idea, but don't never pay bills ahead'a the due date. Ya ain't gonna be around for a refund, and that just screws things up fer everybody."

The woman stopped at the meat case and eyeballed a piece of salmon. "Remember, never say yes to anythin' more'n a week away. And even then, see how y're feeling b'fore ya commit."

She pointed to the piece of fish she wanted. "Thanks, Don," she said as he wrapped it in white paper and handed it to Bella.

Tilly held up a fist and ticked off more rules. "Don't be buyin' new clothes or new shoes. Make do with what ya got. And as for underwear, don't be throwin' it out 'less it's got more'n three holes in it."

Bella stepped back. "Three holes. That's a lot."

The old woman tsked. "Bella, y're makin' me wonder if New York is missin' its village idiot." She shook her head. "Three holes, Bella. Two legs and the top."

"Ah." Bella nodded. "But, still, it's nice to have good underwear in case…"

Tilly held her hand up. "I don't wanna hear what ya do when I ain't lookin'. That's b'tween you and the man upstairs." She scrunched her face. "And I s'pose the man in yer bed."

"Tilly!"

"What? Buy underwear if ya want to. It ain't my dime yer spendin'."

As she dropped a bag of Snickers in the cart, she whispered. "My downfall. I'd make 'em if I could." Bella grinned.

The two headed down the last aisle. "And finally, when those boneheads call 'bout extendin' yer car's warranty, either hang up or pretend ya got dementia." Tilly smiled. "Eventually, they hang up after ya ask the same question a few times."

Bella chuckled. "You're really something, Tilly."

Suddenly, the old woman stopped. "Oh, I almost fergot the most important thing. Don't be leavin' the house without lookin' yer best every day. Make sure yer hair and face're fixed the way ya wanna look."

Bella looked confused. "Why?"

Tilly shook her head. "Because if ya die and ya don't look good when they haul ya to the morgue, the funeral home's gonna have some wannabe beautician fixin' yer hair'n face. When they're done, y're either gonna look like an old lady or a hooker. Either way, it ain't gonna be pretty. But if ya ain't gonna do that, at least carry a good picture of yerself—just in case."

A man snickered as he passed by. Bella could barely catch her breath. She hadn't laughed that hard in weeks. There hadn't been much to laugh about.

Just before the checkout lane, she picked up a box of alfalfa sprouts and set them in Tilly's basket.

"What ya gonna do with those?" The old woman nodded toward the plastic container.

"I like these on salads and sandwiches."

Tilly shrugged. "Suit yerself, but if ya eat 'nough of those things, yer gonna start crappin' in the street like a horse."

Bella snorted. "Oh, my god! You're one crazy woman, you know that?" She hugged Tilly.

"Well, course I know that. Some people say I'm as crazy as a soup sandwich, but I'd like to think I got just 'nough crazy in me to make life interestin'."

"That you do." Bella nodded slowly. "By the way, what's the plan for dinner?"

Tilly scowled at her. "Dinner schminner." She flapped her hand through the air. "Let's go get us some ice cream."

CHAPTER 7

What if Tilly was right?

Thunder rumbled in the distance. Bella latched the kitchen window and checked the others before rejoining Tilly in the living room.

"It's comin' up a cloud," Tilly said. "I'm 'fraid we gonna git us a real gully washer."

"A gully washer?"

The old gal laughed. "Clearly, yer folks picked nannies with negative IQs." She shook her head. "This here's toad-strangling kind of weather."

Bella continued to shake her head.

Tilly tsked. "It's gonna rain hard, Bella."

"Got it."

Her landlady had been correct. The low rumbles and dark clouds had exploded into a storm of rain, hail, and wind. By the time the tail end had finally passed through, it had left a path of destruction across the neighborhood. Small branches littered the lawn. A large limb had been ripped from the twisted Southern Live Oak tree in the front yard. If a tree that size had caved to the storm, Bella was afraid to see the damage it had done to Tilly's flower garden in the back of the house.

The minute the rain stopped, Bella had been out the door ready to clean up. The small pile of sticks at the end of the deck continued to grow. Suddenly, the door flew open, and the old gal bellowed loud enough for the whole neighborhood to hear.

"Bellarina Levitsky! Ya ain't got the brains of a dead possum. What in God's green earth do ya think y're doin'?" She pointed up. "Do ya hear that thunder? Didn't nobody teach ya if ya can hear thunder, ya can git hit by lightnin'? Now, git yerself up on this porch b'fore I strike ya myself."

Bella grinned. No one had ever shown *concern* for her the way Tilly did. Not even her globetrotting parents. Her landlady didn't always demonstrate it in the nicest ways, but Bella knew she cared. It had been almost three weeks since she'd landed on Tilly Wilson's front step. In that short time, she became the owner of three new hats and had eaten better food than she had in her entire life. There was no doubt in Bella's mind that Tilly cared about her.

Instead of following Tilly inside, Bella planted herself on the wooden swing at the end of the porch. The kids across the street splashed in a knee-deep puddle courtesy of the storm. They were mud-smeared from head to toe. She gritted her teeth as the oldest child dove headfirst into the murky water. A second kid swung his arms outward and yelled, "Safe!" as the first emerged to a rumble of thunder. Obviously, their mother didn't care about them the way Tilly worried about her. Or maybe, unlike her parents and nannies—and Tilly, their mother believed in letting kids be kids. Bella couldn't recall ever stepping a toe in a puddle. Had she done so, she would have been banished to her room for life.

The yellowed thermometer on the far end of the porch read sixty-eight degrees. A violent shiver jolted through her. Lately, Bella was always cold. She pulled her arms inside the roomy second-hand sweatshirt she'd borrowed from her upstairs closet and continued to watch the escapades across the street.

Thirty minutes later, she picked up her empty lemonade glass and wandered into the house. Still wary of the wrath of

Tilly, she loaded it into the dishwasher exactly as the commander expected.

"Tilly?" Bella poked her head into the living room, but it was empty. "Tilly?" she called again, checking the bathroom and the laundry room.

It was so unlike her not to respond. Finally, Bella knocked on the door she'd come to know as the old woman's room. She'd never so much as peeked into the room before. It felt off-limits.

Bella's knock went unanswered. Finally, she eased the door open just enough to peek inside. She gasped. Tilly was on her knees in front of a tapestry couch in what appeared to be a sitting room. The upper part of her body was pressed face down into the cushions.

"Tilly!" Bella shoved the door open so hard, it slammed into the wall. She tripped on the corner of a rug as she barreled across the room and nearly landed face-first next to her landlady.

Tilly suddenly straightened. "What in blue blazes is wrong with ya?" she demanded. "Ya scared me half to death with yer carryin' on."

"Scared you? I thought you were dead lying like that." Bella sank onto the couch.

Tilly glared at her. "Just so ya know, when I die, I'll give ya a heads-up b'fore I go." Tilly lifted her Bible. "Now, if ya don't mind, I'd like to git back to my conversation with the good Lord."

"Praying? That's what you were doing?" Bella rolled her eyes. "Doesn't praying count if you sit in a chair?" The last of her adrenaline rush released its grip through a deep exhale. "How does someone who's—whatever your age is—even get off the floor?"

Tilly pursed her lips and narrowed her eyes. "Listen here,

missy, God's seen to it to git me off my knees every day for eighty-nine plus years."

"So that's how old you are? Eighty-nine?" Bella gave Tilly a smug look. "I had you pegged for like—a hundred and two."

Tilly grabbed Bella's chin and squeezed it. "The day God don't help me up is the day I die—on my knees prayin'—the way he intended."

"Well, okay, then." Bella shrugged and pulled away. As she stood, Tilly caught her by the arm.

"Maybe you should get yer scrawny backside down here and join me."

Bella froze. On the one hand, she didn't believe in Tilly's god, but on the other, if she just did what her landlady asked, Tilly would get off her back. Rolling her eyes, she dropped to her knees. As the old gal expected, she rested her elbows on the couch and folded her hands. She closed her eyes and drew a deep breath.

"Go ahead, Bella. Say somethin' to God. The least ya could do is thank him."

"For what?"

Tilly huffed. "Fer me not killin ya."

Bella closed her eyes. "Dear God." She opened one eye and looked at Tilly before closing it again.

"Go on. Say somethin'." Tilly poked her in the ribs.

"Dear God," she repeated. "Thank you for not making…" She shifted away from the old lady and pressed one foot to the ground. "…Tilly my mother." Jumping up, she ran from the room.

"Girl, ya'd better make it right with God b'fore ya go. And I ain't meanin' *leave this room.*"

Minutes later, Bella peeked around the corner and eavesdropped on Tilly's chat with the Almighty.

What if Tilly was right?

***

Bella heard her name called at least three times, but still, she ignored it. Tilly's comment about her god had seeped into her subconscious and screamed for attention. By her calculation, she had three hundred forty-two days left on earth—*if luck was on her side*. She'd been keeping track since that day at the clinic. *Would she make it to zero? If she did, what would her life be like? Would she be too weak or too befogged to care?*

Beginning waves of depression swam around her like sharks. She'd been on antidepressants when she first learned of her cancer. But since she raced out of Dr. Sloan's office without a word, she doubted the doctor would refill her prescription. Even if she would, Bella had no desire to contact her. She wanted nothing to do with doctors ever again.

"Are ya deaf?" Tilly stood at the top of the steps, clutching the railing as she struggled to catch her breath.

In the three weeks since her arrival, Bella had seen Tilly physically decline.

"Not deaf," Bella said. "Just…depressed."

"Depressed?" Tilly collapsed onto Bella's bed. "Well, diddly-fart. I shouldn'ta set my hind end down so fast." She held her arm out. "Here, git me up."

Bella climbed out of her chair. She pulled on Tilly's arm as she rocked on the soft mattress. After several attempts, the woman was finally upright.

Tilly moved behind Bella and aimed her toward the full-length mirror on the closet door.

"Take a look in the mirror," she instructed. "What'd ya see?"

"Me," Bella grumbled. "The same person I've seen since the day the doctor told me I was standing on death's door—an orphan dying of cancer."

"Is that who ya wanna see?"

"No." Bella snorted softly.

Tilly nodded. "When all ya focus on is the past, it's like walkin' backward through a cow pasture. Ya see all the crap y've already stepped in, but ya got no idea of the huge piles y're 'bout to hit. Start payin' attention to where y're goin', Bella. Leave the past alone." She pushed Bella closer to the mirror. "Now, who'd ya like to see?"

Bella tipped her head. "Well, I'd like to see Reese Witherspoon, Emma Stone, Kaley Cuoco, or…"

Tilly chuckled. "We ain't from the same generation, is we? I woulda said Etta James, Rosa Parks, or Pearl Bailey."

"Who?"

"Exactly!" Tilly exclaimed. "Different generations. Obviously, I didn't ask the question the right way." She reached up and tilted Bella's chin up so she would look into the mirror. "Are ya the person ya want to be? I ain't talkin' 'bout yer bald head or yer flat chest. I wanna know who ya wanna be while ya still got some breath left in ya."

Bella stared into the mirror but said nothing.

Tilly tried again. "When ya was growin' up, what'd ya always wanna do?"

Frowning, Bella said, "Don't laugh. When I was young, I always wanted to be a model."

The old woman slapped one hand across the other. "All right. Now we're gittin' somewhere," Tilly said unequivocally. "So that's what you'll do."

"What? Model?" Bella pushed past Tilly and threw herself onto her bed. "I have no hair and no boobs. I'm not exactly model material."

She pulled up her shirt and revealed a pair of ugly scars where her breasts had once been. Bella watched Tilly's expressionless face. Finally, she dropped her shirt and crossed her arms.

"So, no. Modeling's not an option."

Tilly headed toward the door. "Never say never. Ya got no idea what the Lord can make happen."

"Huh!" Bella grunted. "Yes, I do! Look what he did to me. I know exactly what he can do."

CHAPTER 8

Tough crowd

Tilly dropped the black leather keychain on Bella's side of the table. The red, white, and blue triangles and the word *Ford* were camouflaged in the shadow of her plate.

"Ww www gg?" Even Bella knew her question sounded cryptic. It was as if she were speaking a foreign language. A large bite of toast shifted around in her mouth as she chewed.

Tilly's chin lowered as she gave Bella *the look* across the table.

An excruciatingly painful swallow forced Bella's eyes shut. She guzzled her glass of orange juice and set it on the table harder than she intended. "Sorry," she said, wiping her mouth on her sleeve. "Where we going?"

"I got an appointment at nine." Tilly nodded toward Bella's plate. "Eat yer breakfast. We'll talk later." Tilly tossed Bella a napkin. "And ya might wanna change that shirt b'fore we go."

Bella shoved the last of her toast into her mouth and stared at Tilly. *Appointment? Was she sick?*

At precisely 8:30 a.m., Tilly pulled her purse from the cupboard and headed toward the door.

"We're leavin'," she announced. "And I don't give two hoots and a holler if ya ain't ready. I am."

Bella grabbed her backpack and kept a close eye on Tilly as they made their way to the car. Nothing seemed out of the ordinary. She still wobbled when she walked, but she didn't appear to move any worse than a week ago.

Since their last outing, Lou's son, Malik, had raised the top on the convertible. He'd done it on one of the days Bella had been too exhausted to leave her room. The sunshine didn't warm the November days enough to leave the roof down any longer.

"Where're we going?" Bella asked again.

Tilly stared straight ahead. "You'll see. Ya gotta learn yerself some patience."

Bella shook her head. "You said we'd talk about it after breakfast. Well, it's after, so obviously, that was a lie."

She backed into the street and followed the step-by-step directions Tilly delivered.

After backtracking a missed turn, Bella announced, "You know, they have these things on phones that give you directions. It's called *navigation*. You put in the address, and it tells you exactly where to turn so this doesn't happen."

For the second time in an hour, Bella got *the look*. Tilly could make a person with the worst case of logorrhea shut up with that glare. Bella drew a deep breath, tightened her lip, turned an imaginary key, and tossed it over her shoulder. Until they arrived, she wouldn't say another word.

A massive stone sign welcomed them to Lawson Beach University. "The college? You have an appointment here? What for?"

She pulled the tank of a car into an open parking spot where Tilly directed. "Seriously? Are you going back to college? Are you getting a degree in how to use twenty-first-century technology? Can we start with the navigation app?"

"Hush up," Tilly warned as she gently closed the car door.

"Are you speaking to the Horticulture Club about growing marijuana? I bet it would grow really well in your garden."

Tilly glowered at her as Bella moved in front of her and walked backward.

"Wait! Are you being honored for being the oldest person in history?" She grinned. "I still can't believe you're only 89. I think you're lying."

Tilly continued to shuffle toward the building named *Magnuson Hall*.

Bella circled in front of her again. "I know. You're donating your body to science. Is that it? Are they doing a study on the difference between being *almost dead* and being *dead-dead?*"

"Button yer lip!" Tilly snapped her fingers. Then she pressed the large handicap activation button. The door slowly opened, and the two stepped inside.

"Are you…"

Tilly pressed a hand over Bella's mouth. "I told ya to zip it. If ya ain't able to do that, I'll do it fer ya."

Bella smirked. "Oooh. Tough crowd," she whispered.

The old gal stopped outside room 117A and leaned against a handwritten sign taped to the doorframe. She gave Bella the once over and pushed her into the room.

"Hello. Welcome. If you'd like to have a seat, we'll call you when we're ready," a woman near the door announced.

A handful of other women were seated in the room. A plump blonde paged through a fashion magazine while the others scrolled through their phones.

"Why are we here?" Bella whispered.

Tilly ignored the question.

A door opened, and a woman in a pantsuit stepped in. "Tilly Wilson and Bella Levitsky," she announced.

Bella's eyebrows shot upward. "How do they know *my* name?"

Tilly rocked only twice to get out of the chair. She hooked her arm through Bella's and leaned on her as they headed toward the woman.

"Right this way," she said. The woman ushered them through the doorway and into a small room. She snapped on the light. "You can get undressed in here."

"What?" Bella asked harshly, clearly confused. "What are you talking about?"

"Shush!" Tilly told her. "It ain't polite to interrupt." She nodded to the woman. "You were sayin'?"

The woman cast a curious look toward Bella before continuing. "Leave your clothes in this room. Slip on one of the robes hanging in the closet, lock the door with this key, and ring the buzzer when you're ready. Any questions?"

"We got it." Tilly pushed Bella into the room.

"What the hell's happening?" Bella could feel her heart pounding inside her chest. "Why do I need to take my clothes off?"

Tilly removed her thin sweater and began unbuttoning her blouse. "You don't. *We* do."

Bella locked her hands behind her head, over her new yellow hat. "Why are we here?" Her voice pinched. She started to pace the length of the small room.

Tilly pulled off her top, revealing a bra with a row of large hooks running up the front. The contrast of the white bra against her dark skin caught Bella off guard.

"Look," Tilly finally said, "if ya don't do somethin' every day that gits yer blood pumpin', you ain't livin'." She took Bella's hand. "Y're only existin'. No one'll remember ya five minutes after ya die."

Tilly pushed her elastic waistband skirt and slip down and let them fall to the ground. "This here'll git yer blood flowin', Bella." She winked at her. "I promise ya."

"This is crazy!" she said softly.

Slowly, Bella pulled her sweatshirt off and dropped it on the bench. "There's something wrong with you, old woman," she whispered as she continued to undress.

"There ain't nothin' wrong with me. I spent eighty-nine years livin'. I'm tryin' to help ya squeeze a load'a livin' into a few months."

Bella sighed. Tilly's comment hit home. If she was going to make the most of what little time she had left, she had to stop being so afraid of everything.

Minutes later, feeling only the silk against their nakedness, the two women sat side-by-side on a bench outside a windowless door. Tilly pushed the button and giggled.

"Well, looks like this is it," she said.

The door opened; the woman in the pantsuit returned and led them into an empty classroom.

"Okay, ladies, I'm going to have you climb onto the platform…" She looked at Tilly. "I'm sorry. Are you able to get up there?"

Bella laughed. "Never underestimate Tilly Wilson. This woman can do anything she sets her mind to."

The woman nodded. "Once you're up there, drop your robes and be seated. I'll return with a small group of student artists. It shouldn't be more than five minutes." She glanced between the two women. "Any questions?"

"No," Tilly said.

The woman's shoes clicked as she crossed the shiny cement floor and exited through a different door. But even after she was gone, Bella heard the sound.

Tilly dropped her robe and sat down.

Bella slapped a hand over her mouth to stifle a gasp. "Seriously? You're comfortable having your…" She moved her hand in a circle toward Tilly. "…knockers and all your other parts hanging out for the whole world to see?"

The old woman shrugged. "Ain't gonna make no difference.

God gave me this body. He'd want me to be proud of it."

Bella slumped into the chair next to Tilly. She tightened her robe and stared straight ahead.

"I can't believe I'm doing this. It's insane."

"Ya said ya wanted to be a model. I'm just makin' yer dream come true."

"This isn't exactly what I pictured." Bella sank farther into her chair.

After a minute or so, she side-glanced Tilly and started to giggle.

"Is that what happens after eighty-nine years?" She wiggled a finger toward Tilly.

"What?" her landlady asked.

"The saggy boobs? If you spread your legs, they'd probably hit the floor." Bella doubled over in hysterics.

"I got news fer ya," Tilly said, pointing to her chest. "This happens a long time b'fore ya turn eighty-nine," Tilly huffed.

Bella straightened. "Seriously?" She peeked inside her robe. "I guess I dodged a bullet then."

Slowly, she laid her pale hand on Tilly's breast. She recoiled when the old woman slapped it.

"Uh-uh. 'Less y're buyin' me dinner and takin' me dancin' afterward, keep yer grubby hands to yerself."

As the door opened and a dozen or so people filed in, Bella giggled. "I'll buy you dinner, but I'm not dancing with you."

"Hush up." Tilly pulled her shoulders back, but her nipples didn't move; they still rested near her belly button.

As each person took a seat, the woman in charge announced loudly, "Ms. Levitsky, can you drop your robe, please?"

With wide eyes, Bella turned toward Tilly. She took a deep breath and stood. Beads of sweat dampened her neck and forehead beneath her knit hat.

"Before I do, you need to know that I'm not your typical

model.”

“Ma’am, we’re artists. For us, there is no typical,” a middle-aged man in the front row stated. “We like the unusual, the unique. Beauty is everywhere.”

A ragged exhale slipped through Bella’s pursed lips.

“That’s good. Because I have cancer.” Bella watched their faces as she tugged off the yellow hat to expose her short bristles. “I’ve had a double mastectomy.” She made eye contact with each person; she wanted them to see her—really see her. Finally, she admitted what she’d told no one except Tilly. “And I’m dying.”

The air felt oppressive as all eyes watched her. She didn’t know if her announcement had repulsed them or if they were stunned into silence. Then, knowing it couldn’t get worse, she pulled the knot on her robe, let it slip from her shoulders, and drift to the ground.

A moment of silence flooded the room before a slow, hollow clapping echoed through the large space. The sound grew louder as the others joined in and rose to their feet.

It wasn’t a pity clap. As Bella looked at each person, she saw their admiration. They saw her as brave.

“Ms. Levitsky.” A man in a gray suit standing in the back of the room stepped forward. “Dean Anders,” he introduced himself. “I just want to say we are in awe of your courage.”

A young woman moved closer to the platform. “Thank you.” She pressed her hands to her lips and sent her appreciation toward Bella. “I want you to know that you may see yourself as broken, but every person here sees you as a beautiful inspiration.”

Tears streamed down Bella’s face as she listened to the young woman. She tried to speak, but her words were tangled somewhere inside. Instead, she touched her heart.

“Thank you for coming today. Thank you for helping us

understand what true beauty is."

"Hey," Tilly called sourly. "What about me? Ain't this beautiful?" She ran a hand down her nakedness.

Everyone laughed as Bella winked at Tilly.

"You've always been beautiful, old woman."

***

For forty-five minutes, Bella and Tilly sat side-by-side as each student artist drew their version of them.

"All right, ladies. Go ahead and put your robes back on. I think you should come and see how the students saw you."

Tilly looked at Bella, "Oh, good Lord. This seemed like sucha good idea b'fore—when I didn't hafta look at myself neked as a jaybird."

Bella grabbed her arm and helped her off the platform. Together, the two walked from one easel to the next. Each picture had captured something Bella had never noticed in herself—strength, resiliency, confidence, toughness, and *life*. No one had drawn her as sickly or dying. If anything, after looking at their renditions, Bella saw herself as more beautiful than she ever had.

It wasn't until they were in the changing room that Tilly finally spoke again.

"Ya know, Bella, they drew ya the way I see ya," she said.

Bella laid a hand on her chest. "Thank you, Tilly. You have no idea how much that means to me."

"But, but…they just drew me like an old black lady." A crooked grin pushed up one side of her face.

"Tilly," Bella laughed, "you *are* an old black lady." Then, she knelt in front of her. She positioned her slip and skirt around Tilly's legs before pulling them up for her. "But if they would have drawn your heart, it would have been stunning. That's what they should have focused on."

Tilly flapped her hand. "Ah, I bet ya say that to all yer

landladies," she teased.

Bella stood and kissed her on the cheek. "Only the ones I love."

CHAPTER 9

Outta my misery

Temperature-wise, November was still unusually warm. By the time Bella got to the beach, the stiff breeze had plunged the beautiful day into the toilet. Still, she braved the weather; she needed the time alone. Clad in a thick sweatsuit, she wrapped herself from head-to-toe in an old quilt and burrowed into the sand.

A war of words had been fought between the two women—lots of nasty ones. Tilly had been as adamantly opposed to Bella taking the homemade quilt to the beach as Bella was in favor of it. They'd stood nose to nose and fought it out like a couple of schoolyard bullies embroiled in a battle over lunch money. Tilly was positive it wouldn't return, but Bella wasn't an absent-minded six-year-old. If she took it, she'd bring it back. Trying to convince Tilly of that was another story. Finally, in a rare win, Bella wore her down. She was grateful she had. As the afternoon wore on, the wind gusts forced her to retreat under the quilt time and again.

Few people had had the courage to endure the wind. Those who did were buried beneath layers of blankets. The waves roared as they crashed into the beach, dragging shells and driftwood in and out of the water. It was a metaphor for her life—being pulled out to sea and tossed around, unable to control any part of her life.

Three hundred and twenty-eight days. According to her oncologist, it was the *most* she could expect. Her mind ping-ponged between what could have been and what was—between dreams and reality. Finally, Bella closed her eyes and relived Tilly's verbal slap upside the head from the previous night.

"Good Lord, Bella. Stop entertainin' that damn *poor me* attitude. If anybody's gotta right to feel sorry for themselves, it's a goldarn mayfly." Bella stared at her, wondering what a mayfly and dying of cancer had in common.

"They're born and die in twenty-four hours. But even after they croak, their skeletons cling to everythin' and irritate the H-E-double toothpicks out of pert near everybody. Just sayin', girl—but y're still here, ya still gotta chance to enjoy life. But yer constant complainin' is wearin' my nerves thin. I'm pritty sure if ya were a mayfly, I'd slap ya and put ya outta *my* misery."

Looking back now, Tilly was probably right. Every day, Bella wasted time wallowing when she should be living. She drew a deep breath and rolled onto her back. The billowy clouds that dotted the sky drifted past quickly, constantly reimaging themselves into new formations. Could Bella be like the clouds and let life play out around her, let destiny shape her life until she disappeared beyond the horizon?

Suddenly, panic squeezed her. Like the clouds, her days were passing way too fast. A minute earlier, Bella had succumbed to Tilly's belief that self-pity was for losers, but she was wrong. How could anyone be okay with dying? Tilly and her god were trying to make her believe there was more to this life than what was on earth. Bella wasn't falling for any of it. She was too angry.

Wrapped in the blanket, she tried meditating. She hoped it would drive away her anger—at least temporarily. It had been just over a month since Bella abandoned her ticket to Miami in favor of Lawson Beach. By choice, she'd met virtually no one. Soon, that would change. In Tilly's words, they were going to have a *practice Thanksgiving* with the neighbors. Anger poked at her again. *What did she have to be thankful for? What had she ever had to be grateful for?*

Bella had played the thankful game in the past, or rather, it had played her. Often, she'd sat through family and holiday dinners with complete strangers. Sometimes it had been at the kids' table of a foster family she didn't even know or like. Other times, it was with her nanny—just the two of them, eating lukewarm turkey mush from a plastic tray heated in the microwave. Only once could she ever remember having a Thanksgiving dinner with her parents. That meal had ended with the turkey carcass being hurled across the dining room and her father storming out drunk.

The only thing she was even remotely thankful for was Tilly—and even that was questionable. As the clouds swallowed the sun, she pulled the quilt over her head and waited for its return. Only for the old broad would she suffer through a group dinner.

Lou and Maggie would join them. Malik, their son, would also be there. How bad could it be? Bella had never met Malik, but she liked his folks. And if things went from bad to worse, perhaps she could always feign sick. That was the only positive thing about cancer; it got you out of a lot of crap you didn't want to do.

In a moment's reprieve from the wind, she shook the sand from the quilt and wrapped it around herself again. The worn fabric flapped in the cold breeze as she made her way home.

"Tilly! I'm back!" But there was no answer. *Not again. The woman spent more time on her knees than the pope.*

Bella wandered through the house, cringing at the severely outdated décor. From the living room window, she saw Tilly sitting in the same white wooden chair she always occupied when visiting her garden. Three matching chairs, each painted with the name and picture of a flower, rounded out the circle. Bella had been to the backyard only a handful of times since her arrival. Each time, she and Tilly had shared the swing on the other side of the utopia the old gal had built.

Tilly gestured with her hands, and her mouth moved in an animated conversation. Bella searched the yard, looking for the person the old gal was talking to, but she saw no one. The woman was much too old for imaginary friends. So, unless dementia had settled in, Bella viewed the conversation as a problem.

She bit her lip and studied the garden. It was rare for Tilly to be outside alone. Bella had become her crutch. With each passing day, Tilly physically leaned on her more and more, needing her help to get from point A to point B. Frankly, if she was out there talking to herself, Tilly would need her for mental support soon. But Bella knew it wouldn't be long before assisting Tilly would be too much for her. Day by day, her own body slowly deteriorated. She was keenly aware of every new twinge, pain, or weakness.

Continuing to observe Tilly, Bella realized she knew nothing about her landlady. The woman had yet to divulge anything about her life. It was all one big mystery. The house, her seeming lack of family, her past—Bella knew nothing. And Tilly was a master of diversion. Sound and light had nothing on her. She could change the subject faster than either could show their stuff.

The tall clock chimed once—2:30. The crockpot had been on low since early morning, filling the house with a sweet beefy smell. Tilly wouldn't begin the rest of dinner for a couple of hours. If Bella wanted to dig into her past, it was the perfect opportunity. It would take Tilly some time to get back to the house.

Dropping the quilt on the couch, Bella tiptoed toward Tilly's door. For all she knew, the woman had an internal *creak detector*. Cautiously, she pushed the door open. The sitting room looked no different than it had the day she had encountered her praying. A chill ran down Bella's spine, and she checked behind her before rounding the corner into Tilly's bedroom.

A sharp breath sounded, startling even Bella. An array of photos hung across one entire wall—floor to ceiling. There wasn't room for even one more picture. Like the game Booby Trap, touching any frame would have detonated the perfect arrangement.

Bella leaned in. She could identify photos of Tilly. In her younger days, she had been gorgeous. Truthfully, at 89, she was stunning. A man appeared in a few black and white pictures, but he quickly disappeared from the abstract timeline. Based on the story the wall told, Tilly had a daughter. Except for a dozen or more photos of friends and relatives, most of the wall was dedicated to one person.

She picked up a framed photo from the nightstand and tipped it toward the window. It appeared to be a graduation photo of Tilly's daughter. A small 1978 sticker was adhered to the bottom, right-hand corner. The crown of the girl's hair was flat, but her bangs and sides were a thick mass of black curls. Other than being born in different decades, she could have been Tilly's twin. They looked nearly identical.

"Put. That. Down." The command was vicious—low and disjointed.

Bella spun around to an enraged Tilly. The old woman was weaponed with a broom. She held it toward Bella, swiping at her several times. Instead of running, Bella froze.

"I told ya to put that down and git outta here," Tilly hissed.

Her eyes were ablaze. The droopy skin of her cheeks and neck trembled with anger.

"I, I…" Bella didn't know what to say. She had no defense. "I, I'm so…"

"Git out!" Tilly hollered. "Now!"

Bella dropped the photo on the bed and ran from the room, skirting the broom Tilly swung once more in her direction.

"If I ever catch ya in here again, y'll be gone long b'fore yer year is up. Don't be testin' me, Bella. Got it?"

She said nothing as she raced from the room, up the stairs, and into her bedroom. The slam of the door shook the framed art, jolting it askew. A cheap vase with a faded plastic rose dove off a small table near the door.

What had she done? And what was Tilly hiding?

***

At 5:30, Bella timidly headed downstairs to assist with dinner. Tilly was in the kitchen stirring the contents of the avocado green crockpot. Bella was sure it had been the first slow cooker off the assembly line.

"Tilly, I just…"

Tilly held a hand up. "After dinner, we got us an errand to run."

"Tonight? Can't we wait until to…"

"Listen here, girl. After what ya pulled today, ya owe me."

Bella nodded. "Got it," she said quietly. She stepped toward her landlady. "About that…"

"Don't wanna hear it." Tilly cut her off. "Just keep yer dang nose outta places it ain't got no business bein'."

A deep sigh from Tilly punctuated the end of their conversation. Bella went about her work silently. She set the table and prepared a bowl of salad greens. A small plate of cornbread and the butter dish sat in the center of the table. Finally, she folded the napkins and poured two glasses of sweet tea.

Bella carried the plates to the counter and set them near Tilly. She watched the old woman scoop barbequed beef over a pile of mashed potatoes. Tilly handed Bella both plates and nodded toward the table. Still sheepish, Bella waited for her landlady to sit before she joined her.

For the first time since their meaningful connection at the college, Bella felt more like a renter than a friend. Her heart ached. Tilly had been so angry. But she had every right.

Silence haunted the room as the pair ate. The same hush surrounded them as they cleaned up. Once the kitchen was spotless, Bella waited by the door.

"Where're we going?" she finally asked. She'd become familiar enough with the town not to need step-by-step directions any longer.

"Just drive," Tilly told her. "If I wanted ya to know, I'da taken out a billboard. Ya don't need to know everythin', Bella. Some things ain't meant fer ya to know."

Bella sighed. She did as she was told, turned when directed. Not a sound passed her lips. Making things right with Tilly was all she cared about.

Finally, after almost thirty minutes of driving up and down the main drag and side streets, Tilly yelled, "Pull over!" She pointed toward the curb in front of an abandoned storefront.

Three boys stood in the shadows beneath a burned-out streetlight. Their heads were pressed together in some secret conversation.

Tilly squinted at Bella. She stuck a foot out the door of the passenger's side and scowled. "Wait fer me. When I git back in, gun this thing. Don't stop fer nothin'."

Bella froze. "What's going on?" A tingling sensation grew on the top of her almost bald head.

"Shhh!" Tilly pressed a finger to her lips. "That's the

problem with ya, girl. Ya ain't gotta know everythin'. Just do as y're told, and nobody'll git hurt."

Bella's breathing quickened and her heart jackhammered in her chest. "What does that mean?" She grabbed Tilly's hand, but her landlady jerked it away. The old woman slowly climbed out of the car with her purse hanging over her forearm. She looked up and down the street before approaching the boys.

Bella watched the old woman speak to the teenagers. One of them angrily stepped toward her and raised a threatening fist but stepped back when another intervened. Several times, the boys glanced toward the car. Then, suddenly, they all looked in her direction for a few seconds. Finally, her landlady opened her purse and extracted her wallet. She handed the boys a thick wad of cash in exchange for a small plastic bag. Once again, Tilly checked the street before shoving it into her handbag.

A siren wailed in the distance but quickly grew louder. Bella squeezed the thin steering wheel, digging her fingernails into her palms. Sweat beaded on her forehead.

Was Tilly buying drugs? Were the cops coming for them or was the siren a coincidence? Bella rocked back and forth as panic surged through her. *She couldn't get busted. She couldn't spend the last year of her life in a prison cell.*

Red and blue shards of light flashed as the cop rounded the corner. She watched the boys take off down a side street in the opposite direction of the police car. Tilly moved too slowly. She would never make it to the car before the cop stopped.

"Come on, old lady!" she yelled. "Come on." She pounded the steering wheel with the palms of her hands.

Tears burned in Bella's eyes, blurring her vision. If Tilly was buying drugs, Bella was driving the getaway car. They would both get nailed. How could Tilly do this to her?

The squad car pulled up behind them as Tilly opened the door and fell in.

"Go!" she yelled. "Go! Drive!"

But Bella didn't move. It was too late. Her shoulders dropped and her forehead fell against the steering wheel. Tears streamed down her face.

The cop towered over the car. He bent down and knocked on her window, pressing his face close to the glass.

"Say nothing," Tilly hissed. "*Nothing*. Let me do the talkin'."

Bella searched for the button to lower the window, but she was too rattled. In her panic, she couldn't find a way to open the window in the ancient car. Finally, she gave up and shoved the door open.

"Ma'am," the cop held a hand toward her and wrapped the other around the handle of his gun. "Stay in the car. Do not leave the car," he barked. "Do you understand me?"

Bella nodded. Her shoulders bounced up and down as she shuddered.

"What business did you have with those boys?"

Tilly leaned over Bella and smiled. "Hello, officer." She squeezed Bella's arm—hard, steamrolling her into silent submission. "What young men ya referrin' to?"

The cop looked at both women. He pointed to the west. "The ones who took off running when I turned the corner." The cop scowled at Tilly. "From what I saw, there appeared to be an exchange going on." He tipped his head slightly. "Perhaps money for drugs. Was that it?"

Bella's eyes grew wide. She slowly turned toward Tilly.

"No, sir. That'd be illegal." Tilly waved a hand in his direction. "I think y're confused 'bout what ya saw."

Swishing swelled in Bella's ears, and her hearing faded in and out. She was positive the cop could hear her heart.

"Ladies, I need you both to step out of the car. Keep your hands where I can see them."

He yanked Bella's door wide open before going around to the other side.

"I want you both on the sidewalk." He looked directly at Bella. "Don't even think about running."

Bella's knees shook. If he thought she would run, he was gravely mistaken. She could barely make the dozen steps to the sidewalk without holding on to the car.

"So," he turned toward Bella, "tell me what happened?"

She opened her mouth, but no sound came out.

The cop turned toward Tilly. "How about you, ma'am? Why were you meeting with those boys? Was it drugs?"

Tilly glared at the officer. "Fine. I got myself some little red ones." She scowled. "Officer, ya don't know what it's like to get old. I can barely make it through the day without a little pick-me-up."

Bella's jaw dropped. Tilly had just sealed the deal. They were going to jail.

The cop held out his hand as Tilly dug through her purse. She pulled out a small black gun and waved it in the air. "How'd this get in here?"

Bella's knees buckled. She could barely breathe.

"Ma'am! Is that thing loaded?"

Tilly glowered at the officer. "Well, course it is. A gun ain't no good without bullets."

She laid the gun in the cop's hand. "Can ya hold it fer me?"

The cop took the gun and opened the chamber. He appeared to dump something into his hand.

Tilly pulled out the clear bag of red pills and shook them. "Here they are, officer." She smiled provocatively. "Want some?" She winked at him. "I'd be willin' to *share*."

Bella swiped at a drop of sweat that rolled between her eyes. Tilly'd just propositioned a cop. The word *bribery* swam through her head. They were *both* going to die in prison.

"I sure would." The cop nodded.

He reached in and scooped out a handful of the pills and shoved them into his mouth.

"Would you like some?" He held the bag toward Bella.

What was happening? She frantically shook her head and tried to hold back a single sob.

Tilly grabbed the bag from the cop and laid a hand on Bella's arm. "It's mini M&Ms, Bella. Just candy." She shook the bag toward her.

Bella stiffened in confusion.

Tilly grinned. "This here's Malik Jackson, Lou and Maggie's son. I thought ya might wanna meet him b'fore he comes to dinner tomorrow."

Bella glanced from Tilly to Malik. "Y-you're Malik?" she stuttered.

He nodded.

"And this was all just a big joke?"

Tilly grinned. "Is yer heart pumpin'?"

"I could have died. I could have killed us both in some high-speed chase."

Malik and Tilly howled. Their laughter echoed through the empty street.

"We don't have many high-speed chases in Lawson Beach." Malik smirked.

"And you thought I would see this as funny?" Her mouth went tight, and she glared at Tilly. Her landlady continued to laugh.

Still shaking, Bella walked around the car, climbed in, and drove away, abandoning the old woman on the sidewalk. Her sights were set on New York. Anger raged inside of her, and her cheeks burned. But the farther she drove, the funnier the night's events became. Only Tilly could have pulled off something so spectacular and yet so terrifying.

When she finally pulled into the driveway of 354 Sweetwater Lane, the lights in the house were alight. Her landlady had been right. The only way to truly feel alive was to do something that got your blood pumping.

Tilly was waiting in the entry when Bella walked through the door. "Revenge…"

"Zip it, old woman. I don't want to hear it," Bella grumbled.

Then, she draped an arm over Tilly's shoulder and aimed them toward the kitchen, where they shared a pint of ice cream and a good laugh.

CHAPTER 10

Oh, why the Sam Hill not?

Bella pulled the hand-crocheted blanket over her shoulders and curled up on the couch. Several days had passed since her bogus run-in with the law. Her heart still raced when she thought about it. Since that day, Malik had checked in on her daily. Guilt made people do all kinds of things.

While the police hoax had shaken her, it was nothing compared to her *artistic* debut at the college. In her state, she would never have seriously entertained the idea of modeling—let alone *neked*, as Tilly called it. The old lady had pulled a fast one that day. Her influence meandered far outside the lines of her comfort zone. Yet, she couldn't control her laughter whenever the memory of her and Tilly sitting side by side—au naturel—passed through her mind.

As November pushed on, the lack of daylight weighed on Bella like never before. Even on sunny days, the early sundown added a gloominess that left her disheartened. Dinner was served after the sun had sidelined itself for the evening now. Once the dishes were done, Bella wanted nothing more than to follow suit—curl up in her pajamas and get lost in the pages of someone else's story. It seemed like the best way to forget the final pages of her story were growing close. But tonight, Tilly had begged her to stay downstairs.

"Fer gosh sakes, Bella. It'd be nice to spend a li'l time with ya every once in a while."

Reluctantly, Bella agreed.

A door banged shut somewhere in the house; Bella sat upright. Her shoulders stiffened and her eyes grew wide.

"Hello?" Maggie called.

The air Bella was holding released in a blast. Her chin dropped to her chest and her head fell forward. "Holy crap!" she whispered.

Tilly rolled her eyes. "In here," she called. "This ain't New York. If somebody walks through yer door without knockin', it's a friend."

Maggie and Malik rounded the corner, and Tilly smirked at Bella.

"What?" The word was stiff, suspicious. Bella had seen that menacing grin before; the old broad had something up her sleeve.

Malik plopped down on the couch beside her and threw his feet on the coffee table, narrowly missing a small antique bowl.

"Sorry," he grumbled. Malik shot a quick look in Tilly's direction before patting Bella's leg. "So, Bella, are you ready?" He rubbed his hands together, grinned, and wiggled his eyebrows.

Bella's shoulders arched backward, and she sneered at him. His unnerving grin didn't disappear. Finally, she cast a death stare toward Tilly.

"What did you do, old woman?"

Tilly's smile disappeared. She laid a hand to her chest and shook her head indignantly. "I didn't do nothin'." A wink careened through the air toward Maggie. "This one's all on her." She nodded across the room.

Bella's eyebrows furrowed together, and she frowned as she shot daggers toward Maggie. "What did *you* do?" When her question was met with nothing but a shrug, she tried Malik.

"What did your mother do?"

Malik slowly shook his head and pointed toward Tilly. "It's on the troublemaker over there. She's one-hundred percent responsible for everything that happens tonight."

Tilly wrinkled her nose and huffed in his direction. "Boy, y're a blabber mouth."

Maggie helped Tilly out of her chair and into the kitchen.

Malik squeezed past them on his way to the door. "It's cold outside. I'll go warm up my future car." He beamed. "I just love that old girl."

"Keep spoutin' my secrets, and I'll cut ya from my will," Tilly hollered behind him.

Malik laughed. "Nobody's gonna haul you to Grayson's office to change your will. And you're too old to get there yourself. I heard on the news that the Dead Sea wasn't even sick when you were born."

She patted him on the back and smiled. "Hooey! I reckon y're gonna hafta work pretty dang hard to top that insult."

"I'm willing to put in the effort." Malik pushed the door open and disappeared into the dark.

Bella fidgeted with her zipper. "Would someone please just tell me where we're going?"

"Honey, it's a surprise. You need to relax a little, okay?" Maggie leaned Tilly's cane against the wall and held her coat for her. The old gal poked her arms through the sleeves and shrugged into it. "Just remember, whatever happens, you'll be just fine."

Bella reluctantly followed the women toward the car, muttering under her breath.

"What's that, Bella?" Tilly tittered. "Did ya say somethin'?"

"Very funny."

Bella climbed into the backseat as Maggie helped Tilly into

the front.

Malik pulled onto the street and headed south. "So, Bella, I just heard about your *modeling* gig." He snorted. "Care to share any drawings?"

Tilly backhanded him across the head. "Hush yer mouth, boy." She glanced into the backseat. "Bella was fabulous. And so was I."

Malik gasped. "Wait! You did it too? Nude?" He looked at Tilly. "Did you at least iron that body of yours before you stripped naked?"

The old woman glowered at him. "In a word—yes. In two words—clam the hell up!" She locked her fingers and laid her hands over the top of her purse. "Fer yer information, they thought I was beautiful and brave."

Bella faked a cough. "What? You told me they just saw you as an old black woman."

"Listen. We all hear what we wanna. The students saw me as a black woman with...*experience*."

"Experience? Really?" Malik grinned at Bella in the rearview mirror.

Bella laughed. "Looooots of experience. Oodles of experience."

"Eons. Decades. A ginormous number of years of ex..." Malik ducked as Tilly swung her purse at him.

"All right, ya two. Ya had yer fun. Now, button yer lips b'fore I sew 'em up."

"I'll give her this, once her bra came off and she let those things drop, it pulled the wrinkles right out of her face." Bella bent forward in a fit of laughter. "C-course, s-she couldn't open h-her eyes," she roared.

Tilly clicked her tongue and waited for Malik to stop laughing. "Not one word," she warned him.

"Word," he said. He and Bella burst into laughter again.

"Malik, I think she means it." Maggie touched his shoulder and gave him the heavy-handed *mom look*. "Just stop—" she bit her lip, "before her bra lets loose and kills you."

Laughter thundered. Malik fought to keep the car on his side of the road as he wiped tears from his eyes. Maggie and Bella high-fived.

Tilly waved a hand in the air. "Go ahead. Have yer fun. But y'all need to know, I'll be back to haunt yer arses."

Bella shrugged. "Won't matter. I won't be here that long anyway."

The car grew eerily quiet. Bella stared out the window, knowing she'd thrown cold water on everyone's mood.

"I wish I knew where we were going," she said.

Maggie took her hand and patted it. "It'll be fine."

***

The *OPEN* sign flickered when Malik pulled the door open and held it for the women. The light buzzed and hissed as they entered, a sure indication of a short in the time-worn sign.

Bella stopped in the entry. "What're we doing at a bar? And why's Tilly here? I've never seen her drink anything stronger than grape juice."

Malik's eyes grew wide. "This isn't just *any* bar, Bella. It's the Pour House." He raised his hands slightly outward. "This is the place to be on a Saturday night."

"It's Thursday," Bella corrected him.

He shrugged. "And Thursdays." He grabbed her hand and linebackered his way toward the middle of the huge room. "Dad saved us a table."

Bella awkwardly followed him through the crowded room to a round table near a small platform. A burgundy curtain hung across the back of the staging area. Based on the dust that clung to the top and a long tear held together with duct tape, it had seen better days.

Lou pulled out Tilly's chair and slowly lowered her into it. "What are you ladies drinking?"

"I'll just have water." Bella tilted her head toward Tilly. "Someone has to make sure the old broad doesn't drink too much tonight." She chuckled.

"That's *my* job." Maggie draped an arm over Tilly's back. "Bella, you go ahead and order whatever you'd like."

Bella tightened her lips into a crooked grin. "Well, okay then. I'll have whatever's on tap."

"I'll come with you, Dad." Malik squeezed between Bella's chair and an empty one at the adjacent table.

"I'll have an old-fashioned," Tilly said decidedly. "I haven't had one in years."

Bella's eyebrows pressed together. "An old-fashioned what?"

Tilly ignored her. She snapped her purse open and snagged a five-dollar bill from her wallet. "I'll buy the first round."

Malik and Bella laughed. Maggie slid the bill back across the table.

"I've got it." Lou smiled.

The old woman stared at Bella. "What in blazes is so dadgum funny?"

Bella shook her head. "When was the last time you stepped foot in a bar?"

Tilly lifted her chin and raised one eyebrow. "It's been some time, I reckon."

"Well, that five-dollar bill isn't even going to pay for *your* drink."

Maggie laid her hand on top of Tilly's. "Don't you worry about it. Tonight's on us."

Tilly arched an eyebrow. "Well, by gum! It ain't cheap to be a lush these days, is it?"

"That's for sure." Maggie tilted her head sideways.

Bella smirked. "Not sure what a *lush* is, but if you mean *a drunk*—yeah, it's not."

Suddenly, a microphone buzzed, and a man appeared on the platform.

"Welcome to the Pour House Karaoke Night. My name's Ace, and I'll be your host for the night."

The hooting and hollering grew so loud, Tilly covered her ears. Her purse hung from one arm.

"As always, we have a full lineup tonight. Some of your old favorites are back." He momentarily glanced down at the table in front. "And we have some new talent as well. So sit back and enjoy. First up, Willow Grady and Parker Ward. Come on, Pour House, let's give it up for our openers."

Bella stuck two fingers in her mouth and whistled loudly as the first dozen notes of "You're the One That I Want" played. She leaned into Malik and whispered, "This is fun. I always loved to sing, but I've never been brave enough to climb those stairs."

A nod was his only response.

Three-quarters of an hour had passed. More than a handful of singers had hit the stage. Most of them could somewhat carry a tune, but the last woman should have taken the stage *before* she started drinking or *long after* everyone else had begun. She was so wasted and off key, it made Bella cringe. When she finished, a polite round of applause cut through the crowded bar. It wasn't until her boyfriend carried her off the stage that people got to their feet and cheered.

Even though the woman hadn't been able to carry a tune, Bella appreciated her spunk. Bella had always sung in the privacy of her own bathroom or hidden between two other altos in the school choir. A public venue was not a place she could ever see herself.

"Alright, so, that was...*interesting*." Ace peeked at the

paper in his hand. "Next up, we have newcomer Bella Levitsky singing 'Don't Stop Believing' by Journey."

Bella's mouth dropped open as she looked around the bar. Surely, he meant someone else with her name.

Finally, she looked at Malik. Her eyes grew wide. "Never!" she hissed. She tightened her arms across her chest.

Malik clapped his hands together and shouted, "Bell-a! Bell-a! Bell-a!" The rest of the bar joined in.

Her heart raced and she felt her cheeks burn. "I can't!"

Tilly leaned toward her and pressed her forehead close. "Ya can! If ya ain't livin' outside the lines, ya ain't living. Now git yer arse up there."

The chanting continued. "Come with me?" Bella begged her.

Tilly drew a deep breath. "Tell ya what. I'll stand b'hind the curtain while ya sing. All right?"

A ragged sigh rushed from Bella's lips as she stood and helped Tilly to her feet.

"Malik, help me up the stairs."

As commanded, Malik assisted Tilly up the stairs and behind the curtain while Bella made her way onto the stage.

Her hands trembled as Ace handed her the mic. The room had gone silent, but the hum inside her head was like a freight train rumbling toward her. The microphone nearly slipped from her slick hand as they cued the song. She stared at the screen on the back wall of the bar. Notes appeared as the music began.

When the words on the screen turned from white to green, her mouth opened, but not a sound emerged. She missed the entire first line before eking out a couple of words from the second. Finally, a few hushed words linked together and were picked up by the microphone.

"Louder!" someone bellowed from the back of the bar.

Even though she tried, the words tied themselves into knots

and stuck in her throat. No matter how hard she pushed, they wouldn't cooperate. Before long, the patrons returned to their conversations. They ignored her and her pathetic attempt. Bella wanted to run, but her feet were planted in place.

"Woo! Woo!" a person in the back suddenly shouted. Everyone's attention returned to the stage. The sudden cheering coaxed Bella's voice out of her. Others joined in, pumping their fists in the air. From somewhere deep inside, Bella found the courage to give them more. She belted out the chorus as the cheering continued. A huge grin lit her face as she sang the last verse and finished strong. People were on their feet, hooting and hollering and pointing at her.

"We want more! We want more!" they chanted.

Bella stood there and soaked it all in. Malik retrieved Tilly from behind the curtain, and Lou wrapped his arms around Bella and lifted her off the stage.

"Wow, girl! Once you got going, you had a set of pipes." He planted a huge kiss on her cheek.

"That was incredible!" the emcee exclaimed. "Let's give it up one more time for Bella Levitsky and Lawson Beach's very own Tilly Wilson."

Bella looked at Tilly. "Thank you for being there for me tonight. And for pushing me out of my comfort zone."

Tilly patted Bella's hand and smirked. "I support like a Playtex bra."

Bella laughed. "Well, thank you."

Another three people took the stage before a twenty-minute intermission. Yet Bella heard nothing after her song. She was lost inside an adrenaline rush and the buzz of a second beer. Her grin never left her face.

"I can't believe I actually got up there," Bella announced to her table. "I would have never been able to do that a few months ago."

Maggie took a swig of her Diet Coke. "Your performance was astounding. I didn't think such a big voice could come out of such a little person."

A group of people approached their table. "Oh, my gosh. You were so good—once you lost the butterflies."

"Thank you." Bella beamed.

The man touched Tilly's shoulder. "And you, wow! You are a character and a half. I haven't laughed that hard in a long time."

As the group walked away, Bella's face fell. "I feel like I missed something." She looked at Tilly. "What'd I miss?"

"Nothin'," Tilly said. "You didn't miss a gosh darn thing."

Bella stared at Malik. "Tell me."

"Malik," Maggie warned.

"She's going to find out anyway."

Reaching across the table, he grabbed his mom's phone and pulled up a video of Bella on stage. Behind her, Tilly danced provocatively, swinging her yellow scarf above her head like a lasso.

Bella watched to the end. Everyone watched *her*.

"So." She turned toward Tilly. Tears threatened a flood. "You didn't believe in me enough to let me get on stage alone?"

Tilly pointed to the stage. "Wasn't my idea to go up there."

Bella dropped Maggie's phone on the table. "I didn't ask you to perform. I just wanted moral support."

"Listen, if I didn't think ya could do it, I wouldn'ta signed ya up. But ya said singin' was another of yer ambitions. I knew ya could sing 'cause ya always got somethin' comin' outta yer mouth. Malik picked the song 'cause he heard ya hummin' it yesterday." She took a draw from the same glass that had been in front of her all night. "And once ya quit mumblin', I went back b'hind the curtain. By then, they was cheerin' for you. I just got the ball rollin'."

"Bella, honey, you really do have a beautiful voice," Maggie said. "I don't think you give yourself enough credit. You're every bit as talented as your folks were."

"I agree." Malik smiled. "You were amazing! I didn't know you could sing like that."

Tilly shook her finger at him. "And, fer a cop, ya sure as shootin' can't keep yer trap shut."

"Oh, he's always had a big mouth," Lou said sternly. "I knew it when he was two. I put one little dent in Maggie's car. Ice cream didn't even buy his silence. You don't trust this boy with secrets."

Tilly shook her head. "Now you tell me." She laughed.

A woman at the table behind Bella touched her shoulder. "You were unbelievable. I hope you come back next week. I'd love to hear you again."

Lou and Malik were on their third beer. Bella and Maggie had switched to water by the time Ace showed up at their table.

"Excuse me," he said to Bella. "We just had someone drop out of the last slot of the night. There's a request for you to close. You game?"

The corners of Bella's mouth turned up slightly as she eyed Tilly. "Only if the old woman goes with me."

"Well?" he asked Tilly.

After a few seconds, Tilly swiped a hand through the air. "Oh, why the Sam Hill not?"

Ace looked at Bella. "What song do you want to sing?"

She didn't even need to think about it. "How about 'Stand by Me' by Ben E. King?" She winked at Tilly. "And this time, instead of dancing, all you have to do is hold my hand." Bella raised her eyebrows. "Because if you dance, I'll push you right off the stage."

"Wow! A li'l success and sud'ly ya think y're Rosemary Clooney."

"Who?" Bella asked.

"Never mind." Tilly took the last draw of her drink and held the empty glass toward Lou. "Git me 'nother one'a these, would ya?"

CHAPTER 11

Cut the backtalk

November had disappeared without fanfare. At the click of the hands of the old clock, the month dropped from the calendar. Bella knew she would never see another November day again. She could feel it. When the month faded away, she'd pulled the covers over her head and cried herself to sleep. The number was etched in her brain. After crawling into bed each night, she'd blow across her open palm, sending the imaginary number adrift. Each morning, she'd angrily face the new, smaller number. The three hundreds were sailing away like a scrap in the wind.

The December temperatures dipped into the fifties, yet Tilly continued to visit the garden daily. In the past week, she'd traded her cane for a walker. On her good days, she would make the trip independently. But, when the difficult ones battered her with pain, she wanted Bella to walk behind her—just in case.

Since Bella had known her, Tilly hadn't *asked* for anything. *Told* and *demanded* were her style. The old gal was snarky and quick-witted. She was always so busy telling Bella how to live her life that she never shared anything about her past. Bella was confident the concept of sharing wasn't even in her wheelhouse.

Undeniably, Tilly was a creature of habit. She insisted Bella always turn right out of the driveway and drive around the block so they could turn left at the light. Meals were served at seven, one, and six, and under no circumstances did that deviate. Bedtime was at 10:00 p.m.—not one minute after. When she was in the garden, she always sat in the same chair, and she always spoke toward the empty chair on her right.

Hiding behind the edge of the thick aqua and gold drapes, Bella watched the old woman. Finally, unable to control her curiosity one second longer, she grabbed two quilts and a cup of hot coffee and joined Tilly on the round flagstone path. Bella set the cup in her landlady's hands and tucked a quilt around her legs. Finally, she dropped into the chair where Tilly's fictional friend always seemed to sit.

"No!" Tilly bellowed. "Not there."

Bella sprang up almost as quickly as she sat down.

"Sit yer cheeks over there." Tilly pointed to the chair on her left.

"What? Is *Jasmine* broken?" Bella teased as she headed past Tilly.

Tilly shot daggers in her direction. "Ya ask way too many questions fer yer own good. Jus' do what y're told and cut the backtalk."

After shaking out her quilt, Bella wrapped it around herself and settled into the *daisy* chair on Tilly's left.

"Jasmine, huh?" Bella stared at the pristine chair with the small white flowers painted against a greenwashed background. "It's pretty. It kind of looks like a star."

Tilly ignored her.

She tried again. "Is there only one kind of jasmine?"

The old gal rolled her eyes. "Comes in lotsa colors—white, yellow, pink," she muttered.

"I bet they're all pretty."

Bella didn't care about the flowers. If she could just get Tilly talking, perhaps she would share something about her past.

Tilly nodded to the center of the round walkway. A wooden trellis had been erected in the middle, leaving an opening for her to see the other three chairs. "Jasmine's planted in this here garden. It should bloom in the next couple months. Up to the weather." She shrugged. "My gard'ner cuts it back every year. B'fore long, it'll start climbin' the slats."

"You have a gardener? Like a gardener-gardener? Like a company that comes out and does work back here? I've never seen anyone else back here."

Tilly sipped her quickly cooling coffee. "Y're fulla questions today, ain't ya?" She looked toward the gardens behind Bella. "I use'ta do this by myself. Now, I need help. So, yeah, I gotta gard'ner."

"Does your gardener have a name?"

"Of course, he does. Everybody's got a name." Tilly grumbled. "Not that it's any of yer business, but his is Leon."

Bella rolled her eyes and mimicked Tilly. Suddenly, aware she was being watched, Bella smiled awkwardly.

"So, how'd you meet? Was it *glove* at first sight?" She chuckled. "Get it?"

But her landlady appeared to be too distracted to notice.

Tilly set her mug on a side table and pulled the quilt over her arms. "I knew his pa years back. When Leon r'turned to Lawson Beach, his folks had already passed, and he had no place to stay. So, 'til he could get his feet on the ground, he stayed with me. I gave 'im a place to sleep at night, and he took care of my gardens. Still does. Usually shows up b'fore you get outta bed."

Bella leaned forward and scanned the garden. "Is that who you're always talking to out here?" she asked.

"What?" Tilly's voice exuded anger. "You been spyin' on me?"

"Not spying so much as…" Bella shrugged. "Yeah, spying,"

she admitted.

For several minutes, Tilly said nothing. Emotions morphed across the old woman's face as thoughts ran through her. Bella watched her like a hawk, waiting for her to speak.

A mass of clouds gave cover to the sun. Tilly shivered. Her eyes narrowed as she looked at Bella. "Well, if ya must know, I talk to my daughter, Jasmine."

"Is she dead?" Bella looked toward the chair opposite her. "Do you see her when you talk to her? Is that why you yelled at me not to sit there?" She was marginally teasing but also a bit concerned.

"Hush up. I swear yer mouth drives itself sometimes." Tilly shook her head. "No. She ain't dead." The old woman stared at the empty chair. "But she might as well be. She wants nothin' to do with me. I ain't seen her in thirty-four years, five months, and twenty-two days."

"You've kept track?"

Tilly tilted her head and scowled. "Just like you *think* ya know how much time ya have left, I keep track of how long it's been since my daughter walked away." She plucked her coffee from the table, but the cup never touched her lips. "Jasmine's got a set of twin girls." Tilly stared at the empty trellis. "My granddaughters are most likely married with crumbsnatchers of their own by now. But I wouldn't know. I ain't never seen 'em or been told one iota about 'em."

Bella's mouth dropped open.

"Ya see, Bella, whether ya know it or not, what y're countin' ain't the days 'til ya die; it's the days until ya meet yer folks again. Me? I ain't got no specific timeframe 'til I meet my maker. I could drag on another ten years, or I could die tomorrow. My life's got no definite endin'. I just keep countin' the days, hopin' Jasmine returns b'fore the good Lord comes fer me. That'd give me the chance to explain things to her."

Bella tucked the patchwork quilt under her legs. "Like what?"

The breeze had picked up. Tilly adjusted her white stocking cap. A red ribbon had been fed through a series of holes and was tied in a bow on one side.

"Everythin'." She drew a sharp breath and looked toward her daughter's chair. "Jasmine and me never got along. She was headstrong like her pa. If things weren't fer her or 'bout her, she wanted nothin' to do with 'em." Tilly looked at Bella. "But there's a lot she don't know." Tilly's shoulders rose. "So, I sit out here and explain things—hopin' the wind'll whisper it to her wherever she's at."

A knot grew in Bella's throat, and her eyes welled with tears. If she spoke, her voice would crack, so she remained quiet.

"I married young, too young. I met my husband James at a box social. I spent the entire mornin' fryin' up chicken and makin' deviled eggs and dinner rolls. An extra piece of my famous blueberry pie went into that wicker basket. I tied a wide red bow 'round the handle. It was a fine lunch for the perfect man."

The red bow on Tilly's hat wasn't lost on Bella. She wondered if it was the one that had been tied on the basket handle.

"Only that perfect man wasn't James." She looked into the sky, shielding her eyes against the sun that had been set free again. "I told Charles exactly what my basket looked like and to bid on the one with the ribbon that matched the bow in my hair. But when the biddin' started, James outbid Charles by five dollars."

"Who's Charles?" Bella asked quietly.

Tilly's eyes went soft. "Charles Isaiah Washington. He was the boy I fancied since the third grade when he put a toad in the teacher's desk drawer." She smiled into the distance. "Oh, sure, he teased me, but that meant he was sweet on me too. If a boy don't like ya, they don't pay no never mind to ya. A girl ain't worth the time of day to 'em." She winked at Bella.

"When Charles and me got older, we'd sneak down to the beach after dark and talk 'bout our future." She slowly shook her head. "Ma and Pa never knew—at least I didn't think they did—'til the picnic. Turns out, Pa paid James to bid on my basket."

"Why would he do that?"

Tilly absently fingered the red bow on her hat. "Charles was from the wrong side of town. Pa used to say, *People on the south side of town don't have a pot to pee in or a window to throw it out of.* And he weren't wrong. The Washington family was poorer than church mice. But it made no difference to me."

Tilly stared into the distance and smiled. Bella knew Tilly was watching ghosts from her past.

"James' father worked in the only bank in town. Pa figured James'd follow in his footsteps. And he did. Like his pa, he was a bookkeeper—'til he started his love affair with the bottle."

"So, because of the picnic, you fell in love with James and left Charles?"

Tilly nodded. "James was older. And like I said, he had himself some money. He courted me, swept me off my feet with flowers and candy. A week after I turned seventeen, we got married. I quit school and made a home fer us while he headed off to work every day." Tilly twisted her lips. "James wanted a whole slew of kids, and he was hell-bent on startin' right away. Fer years, we tried, but God didn't see it to be the right time. So I got bored and went to work at the cafe."

She raised her eyebrows. "Oh, James was fit to be tied. He said it made him look weak, like he couldn't provide fer his wife." Tilly shrugged. "But I needed somethin' to do, anythin' to keep my mind off not bein' a ma when all my friends were poppin' out kids like pimples on teenagers."

She looked into the sky, watched a cloud press in on the sun again. "Durin' our trials, my husband developed a wanderin' eye. I tried to talk to my ma, but she told me to hold my peace. Said all men were like that. It was a wife's place to accept it. And if I didn't want to be tossed onto the street, I should be the best wife I could and, in time, maybe I'd be 'nough for James."

"Whoa. That's not right. You deserved so much better. You were enough *without* him."

"Ya say that, but it happened to yer own ma too. Had she thought she was 'nough without your pa, she might still be livin'. But life was different back then, Bella. Ma used to say, 'Que sera, sera. Whatever will be, will be.'"

Tilly returned to the past again. "Anyway, after pert near ten years, God planted the baby seed. But by then, it was too late. On the same night I told James our excitin' news, he told me his. He was leavin' me for another woman he'd met on one of his rendezvous in the next town over. I was twenty-seven, pregnant, and couldn't afford rent on the house we lived in. So I moved in with Ma and Pa." Tilly pointed toward the house. "This here was their place."

Bella looked at the picture window and tried to imagine someone else sitting in Tilly's old recliner. "Did you ever remarry?"

"No. And I never divorced James either. Pa died shortly after I came back here. Ma helped take care of Jasmine—'til James returned."

"What? You took him back after all that?"

"Turns out the other woman pitched his sorry arse to the curb when his eyes started wanderin' again."

"Why would you let him come back?" Bella was angry.

"'Cause I was still married to him. 'Cause our daughter was

three years old and needed a pa in her life. That's how things were."

The wind picked up, and the sun disappeared behind the graying clouds that had seized the sky.

"Looks to be comin' up a cloud. Help me inside, would ya?"

Bella hoisted Tilly up by the arm and aimed her walker in the direction of the house. She grabbed both quilts and the coffee cup. Once inside, she settled her into her recliner. Massive raindrops pelted the windows. Before settling in to wait out the storm, Bella tossed a blanket over Tilly's legs.

"Did you and James make it?" she asked.

Tilly huffed. "We stayed married. I honored my vows. He didn't. We hid our gummed-up marriage from Jasmine. I wasn't gonna let her suffer just 'cause we couldn't make things work."

When Tilly grabbed her knitting, Bella was certain she had heard as much about Tilly's life as she was meant to. The old woman had moved on to something else. As the storm wailed outside, she sat quietly, hoping she was wrong. After several minutes, Tilly continued her story.

"Even though James had nothin' to do with his daughter fer the first three years of her life, she sud'ly b'came the apple of his eye. He spoilt her. If I disciplined her, he gave her candy. If I told her no, he overruled me. It was a constant battle—one I was never gonna win."

Tilly yawned. "Ma was slowly deterioratin'. I was takin' care of her and Jasmine and working a heap of jobs to make up for James' lack of ambition and his drinkin'. When Jasmine turned sixteen, Ma died. After the funeral, I took on another job and was gone pert near day and night. By the time Jasmine graduated, she wanted nothin' to do with me. Told me I abandoned her."

"Didn't James try to talk to her?"

"Huh!" Tilly snorted. "James? He had no scruples. That

man was as crooked as a dog's hindleg. Day after day, he fed our daughter a kettle of lies 'bout me—'bout how I was off shoppin', spendin' his hard-earned money, and runnin' 'round with every man in Lawson Beach. In her eyes, her pa could do no wrong. Jasmine loved him and despised me. He won."

"Wow. Just wow," Bella uttered softly.

"After she graduated high school, Jasmine moved to Charleston fer college. She ain't never been back. Oh, she'd see James when he went to the city. *Business trips* was what he told her. I always wondered what kind of business he was conductin' since he didn't have a job—but I think I knew. Whenever I asked to tag 'long, he told me I couldn't afford the time off work. When I called Jasmine, she was too busy to talk, and she never called me back. As mother and daughter, there was nothin' left *of* us or *for* us. James saw to that. A few months after she left town, I heard rumors she was pregnant. James didn't even have the decency to let me know she had a baby, let alone twins, or that she'd gotten herself a husband. I learnt that from somebody else." She took a few more stitches before setting it down. "I sent some baby gifts with him, but I never got so much as a thank you—from either of 'em."

"I'm so sorry," Bella said. "That must have hurt so much."

"It did." Tilly's head bobbed. "But then James got sick, and he finally came clean—to me. Jasmine was married and in her twenties when he met his maker. She had her own life, and she didn't leave the door open fer me. I tried to reach her, but I didn't know her last name or even where she lived."

Tilly continued to knit the ball of red yarn into a long tube.

"The funeral wasn't in the church. It was at the cemetery. James wasn't a church-goin' man. He made me promise no preachers and no Bible readings. Jasmine never came to the funeral. I reckon she didn't wanna face me."

Tilly released a long sigh. "A month after James died, I

finally got 'hold of her. I found her number when I was packin' up James' belongings. As far as she was concerned, I was a jus' some stranger. She carried on 'bout how I ruined everythin' I touched—her father's life, our marriage, and even the relationship b'tween us. What hurt most was that my daughter accused me of not havin' a church service in hopes of sendin' her pa straight to hell. When I tried to tell her it was what he wanted, she told me I could join him there."

"What? Oh, my god. How did she even know about his funeral or that he died?"

"She musta stayed'n touch with somebody in town." She tipped her head. "In no uncertain terms, Jasmine told me that without her father cleanin' up my messes and takin' care of me, I'd be ruined. Said I'd be out on the street in two shakes of a lamb's tail. Then, she said she wished it was me who'd died insteada her pa. I told her I wished the same thing."

"Tilly, I'm so sorry. I can't believe how awful she was to you."

"When she hung up, I knew it was the last time I'd talk with her." Tilly sighed sadly. "Like I said, that was thirty-four years, five months, and twenty-two days ago."

Bella knelt next to Tilly's chair. "So, what do you tell her when you talk to her out in the garden?"

"The truth. I ain't defendin' James no more. I ain't gonna let him take one more day from me."

"But if you just talk to her in the garden, how will she ever hear the truth?"

Tilly shook her head. "She ain't gonna. But she wouldn't listen to me no how."

"Then we have to find a way to make her listen. I have an idea. I just need a little time."

***

For the next few weeks, Bella snapped pictures of Tilly with the camera on her phone. Sometimes Tilly insisted on seeing the pictures; other times, she barely noticed Bella had taken them. When the old woman was busy, she snuck in and took photos of the wall in Tilly's bedroom.

The pieces were coming together. Tilly would no longer have to hold her peace as her mother had told her. Soon, Jasmine would understand what a wonderful mother she'd had. She would know the truth.

CHAPTER 12

Words with God

Almost overnight, Christmas exploded in lights, trees, and fake snow. It had happened like the flip of a switch. Holiday music played in every store, seeping into the street. The day after Thanksgiving, the season had changed.

Bella couldn't help but notice how different things were here than in New York City. New Yorkers embraced winter. They bundled up like snowmen—wrapped in heavy coats and bright scarves. Barely an inch of skin lay exposed to the elements. Boots were worn for warmth, not fashion. Steaming cups of coffee served a dual purpose: hand and belly warmer. And they rarely grumbled or complained when they trudged through the snow on the sidewalks.

But cold was a relative term. In South Carolina, on *cold* mornings, Lawson Beachers opted for sweatshirts with hoods. They traded their flip-flops for pairs of fur-lined Crocs. In extreme cold, they even wore socks. Residents shivered in the fifty-degree sun-drenched days. When temperatures dipped into the forties, or God forbid, the thirties, they donned quilted jackets and wandered the streets cussing out Mother Nature. In December and January, when a few flurries drifted to the ground, they would take refuge and hole up in a warm house. Hot chocolate laced with vanilla vodka warmed their core.

For Bella, Christmas in the south felt contrived. It was like living in front of a painted canvas or inside a snow globe where everything was plastic. Snowmen were made of fabric, and wreaths were nothing more than a long sprig of plastic garland. Santa arrived in a boat rather than a sleigh. And in the holiday parades, he and his elves swiped at the perspiration that grew under their hats.

Still, there was something magical about a southern Christmas, something she'd never experienced in NYC. Even without the seventy-five-foot tree of Rockefeller Center, the ice rinks, or the scarves wrapped so tightly you couldn't recognize your friends, Bella was intoxicated with excitement. Everything made her smile—the reflection of Christmas lights rippling across the moving water and Christmas shopping in warm sunshine. No matter where she went, people greeted her by name. It was a homespun holiday like the ones she'd dreamt about when she was old enough to understand *hope*.

For the first—and the last time—Bella saw Christmas as more than gifts from an imaginary man in a red suit. It was about people like Tilly, Maggie, Lou, and Malik. It was about the customers at the bistro and the merchants who smiled every time she stepped foot into their store. It was about the hugs from individuals she barely knew. Yes, Bella was home. She only wished she'd discovered Lawson Beach years before.

As she strolled down the street, she hummed the song that pealed from speakers on each corner. It didn't matter that she had so little time left. What counted was what she did with that time. And right now, that meant selecting the perfect gift for Tilly.

She crossed the street and entered the store on the corner of Sunrise and Main. A doorbell sound radiated through the General Store as she stepped over the threshold.

"Hey, Bella," Judson called, looking up from the counter. The register was open, and he held a handful of cash. "Lookin' for anything special?"

"I am." She glanced around the store. "Do you have any handheld voice recorders?"

He set the wad of bills in the till and shoved the drawer shut.

"I've got a few." He pointed in the general direction and led the way.

Bella followed him past the computers and cellphones. The General Store stocked everything from appliances to electronics—from movies to cameras. His selection was limited, but you could always find what you needed. And, if he didn't have it, you didn't need it. Just to make sure you knew that he'd posted it on the sign out front.

"Don't know a lot about them. I'm from the generation of cassette recorders." Judson frowned. He pointed to three different devices hanging from hooks above Bella's head.

"And I'm from the generation of *just record it on your phone*." She picked up the third recorder and read the back. "But Tilly's older than…"

"Me?" Judson laughed. "That old woman's older than everybody in town. I'm guessin' she doesn't even own a cell phone."

Bella nodded. "You'd be right about that."

She scrunched her lips and pressed her eyebrows inward. Her voice shook as she mimicked Tilly. "The only one you need to answer to twenty-four hours a day is God. He doesn't need a phone, so neither do I."

Judson chuckled. "That woman'd be madder than a wet hen if she heard you make fun of her like that."

She pressed a finger to her lips. "I've never seen a wet hen, but I'm guessing it's not pretty."

"Trust me. It's not." He walked behind Bella. "Anything else you need?"

Bella looked around. "A flash drive."

"Next aisle." Judson hooked a thumb toward the row. "Middle on this side." He looked up as the door opened. "I'll meet you upfront when you're ready."

"Sounds good."

After selecting a large capacity flash drive, Bella made her way toward the small appliances. She studied the slow cookers for several minutes before dropping one into an abandoned cart she found at the end of an aisle. She smiled when she tossed in a bag of Snickers. Since she wouldn't be here for the following Christmas, Bella was determined to make it one for the books.

Judson rang up her purchases. "Did you drive down here?"

Bella twisted her mouth. "No, but I'll walk back to Tilly's and get the car. Can you hold on to the crockpot until I return?"

"Are you done shopping?"

Bella nodded. "I just came down for the recorder and flash drive. I got sidetracked with the crockpot. You should see the one she has. It's so old, the words are worn off, the knob's missing, and you have to turn the metal thingamajig where the knob was with a pair of pliers. And on top of that, you can't take the pot out, so it's a bear to wash. I think it might be time for a new one."

Judson shook his head. "Tilly's never gonna go for a new crockpot. Until hers dies—and I mean *dead*—she isn't even gonna open that box."

"Well, then, I guess I'm just going to have to prove you wrong."

"Nick," he called across the store. "I'm gonna be gone for about ten minutes. Watch the store, will you?"

"Sure thing, Dad."

Judson slipped on his jacket and scrunched his face similar to how Bella had earlier. He raised his voice and pinched his lips together. "If God wanted me to have a new crockpot, he would have made them disposable."

Judson tucked the box under one arm and held the door for Bella. They took turns making Tilly comments all the way to his pickup.

***

Tilly was asleep in her recliner when Judson dropped Bella out front. Careful to miss the creaking steps, she tiptoed upstairs with her gifts. She shoved them under the bed with the personalized aprons she'd had printed for Maggie and Lou. Her real gift was the creation of a website for the bistro.

Maggie had been talking about hiring a web designer since Bella arrived, but she hadn't gotten around to it. So Bella took it upon herself to design one—complete with new menus and framed photos of Lou's meals. Under the guise of needing something to do, she had spent hours in his kitchen—*helping out*. While she dropped fries into the fryer or cut veggies, she snapped pictures. She was more than a little excited for the big reveal.

Deciding on the perfect gift for Malik had been like finding a needle in a haystack, though. Besides being a police officer and having a penchant for old cars, Bella didn't know much else. Finally, at a loss for ideas, she hid across the street from the police station one morning and waited for him to drive away. She spoke to nearly anyone who would give her the time of day. Her solution came in a pair of tickets to the car show in Charleston, a t-shirt with a gear stick that touted *Shift Happens*, and a framed photo of him sitting in Tilly's convertible—the car he would one day own—if Tilly didn't kill him first. She'd taken the picture one day when he'd come over to change the oil. It had been dumb luck that she'd gotten the perfect shot. Behind the car, a rainbow arched across the sky. The kaleidoscope of colors landed directly on his *pot of gold*—the Ford Fairlane. She couldn't wait to give it to him.

***

It was Christmas Eve when Tilly finally allowed Bella to drag out the decorations and put up the tree. The inner child in her had wanted to decorate the day after Thanksgiving. But Tilly had been adamant it would not happen until she said so. Finally, she could wait no longer.

"The twelve days of Christmas begin on Christmas Day and end on Epiphany."

Bella stared at her wide-eyed.

"Oh, for Pete's sake." Tilly frowned. "January 6th—when the Wisemen paid homage to Jesus, the new king. That was the day they arrived with their gifts of frankincense, gold, and myrrh."

Bella shrugged. "Weren't they a little late to the party? They should have had their gifts there on Christmas Day."

Tilly sighed and dropped into her recliner. "You can't change the Bible, girl."

Bella removed the oversized black bag from the artificial Christmas tree. She studied the tree. Could she even call it that? It looked like a branch from a sickly fir. It was barely five feet tall. Most of the needles had abandoned it over the years, choosing a dustpan and a garbage pail over commitment. At some point, tinsel had been strung over the branches. Bella was certain it was to make up for its lack of—*needles*.

Shims had been shoved against the trunk, into the wooden cross stand, to keep the tree from leaning. Nothing about the tree was even remotely beautiful. Yet Tilly's eyes lit up when she saw it.

"What?" Bella asked. "Why are you smiling?"

"I know it ain't the prettiest tree. But, to me, it's like the bedraggled surroundings where Jesus was born."

Bella rolled her eyes.

After much pushing, Tilly admitted the tree had been her mother's. She'd won it in a raffle at a hardware store that had long since closed its doors. The tree had first gone up in 1946, after the war. It had been the talk of the town—a fake tree that wouldn't lose its needles. *Clearly, that had been a lie.* Some people loved the idea; others saw it as blasphemy.

"My mother was prouder than a peacock," Tilly told her. "She strutted around all Christmas season that first year."

At some point, someone had sprung for modern lights in an array of colors. Bella tested the string before wrapping them around the tree. Tilly critiqued, or rather criticized, the entire operation.

You missed a spot. Wrap 'em tighter. Ya ain't never gonna have enough lights. And on and on she went.

Bella clenched her jaw. *You don't have to join every argument you're invited to.* Instead, a revised version of *The Night Before Christmas* danced in her head.

I spoke not a word but went straight to my work.
Wrapped the tree all in lights, ignoring the jerk.
I should be used to this by now; this is always how it goes.
So, up went my hand, and my middle finger quickly rose.

Bella slapped a hand across her mouth when a snort escaped with her laughter. It was her best silent poem yet. There had been many since she'd come to know Tilly.

When she opened the flaps on the box of ornaments, she frowned. "Did these come over on the Mayflower?"

"Just you never mind. Put 'em on the tree."

Tilly's decorations had been stored in a red and tan Campbell's Soup box. The cardboard was deteriorating, and Bella knew it was only a matter of time before the decorations would fall to their death. Maybe that wasn't such a bad thing.

Inside was an eclectic array of dime-store ornaments. These had obviously been the strongest of the bunch. They had endured almost eighty years of repeatedly being dropped, hung, and packed away in a dark closet, waiting for the light of another Christmas.

The few glass balls had broad stripes of glitter that escaped onto her hand when she touched them. A pair of icicles, painted in ugly non-Christmas colors, had also lived to see another hanging. Two unidentifiable plastic birds, a few gouged foam pears, and some plastic snowflakes lay in the bottom of the box. Much as with an older person's face, even a new coat of *paint* wouldn't have been able to hide the deep scratches or hairline cracks of Tilly's decorations. Age was age—person or object.

A small green and white checked box was all that remained inside the bigger box. Bella lifted the lid.

"What the hell is this?"

"Really, Bella?" Tilly chastised. "It's a pickle. Ya ain't smart enough to know that?"

"Ha-ha. I know it's a pickle. Why would you have a pickle ornament?"

For a moment, Tilly was lost in thought. "It was somethin' my ma always did. She hid it on the tree on Christmas Eve, and the first kid to find it on Christmas mornin' got a special treat."

"That's stupid."

"It was an old German tradition."

"Still stupid." Questioning lines slowly grew across Bella's forehead. "You're…*German*?"

"Just 'cause I ain't German don't mean we can't enjoy the tradition."

Bella grew even more bewildered. "And weren't you an only child?"

"Just hush up. Finish decoratin' the tree so ya can git rid of these boxes."

Bella pirouetted, stopping in front of the tree. She held the pickle in front of her, moving it from branch to branch.

"There's nowhere to *hide* it. Your tree's *dead*."

The old woman ignored her. Instead, she climbed out of her

chair and retrieved a small gift box from the closet. Tilly handed it to Bella to hold while she lifted the lid. Inside was a bedraggled angel that looked to be about her landlady's age.

Her white dress was yellowed and had a darker yellow stain in one corner. Silver cardboard wings with bent tips rose from her shoulders. A jagged line of glue marked one cheek of her ceramic face. The angel's dark hair stood on end, giving the impression she'd just woken up *from a long winter's nap.*

"She's, ah..." Bella tightened her lips. "Is she going on the top of the tree? Really?"

"She certainly is." Tilly pulled her from the box and settled her over the top of a single sprig.

Bella stared at the tree topper. "Has she been painted?"

Tilly nodded. "Dern tootin'. My mother painted her. She lopped off a chunk of my hair and glued it to the angel's head." Tilly touched the hair. "Back then, they didn't have black angels." She shrugged. "Ya do what ya gotta do."

Bella scrunched her nose. "Don't you think she looks kind of...rough?"

"Ya know, Bella, I'd be willin' to bet ya a dime to a donut yer guardian angel looks a lot worse'n she does."

Bella arched an eyebrow. "I doubt it. My guardian angel checked out long before my folks did." She walked around the tree, studying the angel. "This one looks...like she stuck her finger in a light socket."

"I'm guessin' yers does too. Her halo's prob'ly busted, and her clothes are torn. I'd wager a bet her wings are bent from runnin' into the walls you keep puttin' up."

Bella stared at the angel as she thought about Tilly's declaration. Three months ago, Bella wouldn't have uttered the word "angel." She would have laughed at the thought of a god. But today, she wondered if maybe her landlady knew something she didn't.

She picked up the boxes and returned them to the closet. If there were a god, she was positive he wouldn't like her very much. Before she'd given up on him, she'd done her fair share of letting him have it. But if Tilly was right, and this afterlife she believed in was real, then she and God were going to have words—soon.

CHAPTER 13

Won't matter a year from now

The clanging rhythm of the pots and pans blended with Lou's baritone voice. Bella knew it would be an early morning, but 4:30 was ludicrous. She rolled over and pulled her pillow over her head. For a good two minutes, the banging of a wooden spoon against Tilly's countertop reverberated up the stairs and into her head. Lou belted out the melody for "Jingle Bell Rock" while Maggie sang a questionable harmony.

A quick shower was all the unreliable water heater would allow, but it was Christmas morning—the day of hope and miracles. She hoped for enough hot water and wished for a miracle. Bella was an old soul. Because of her circumstances, she'd grown up quickly. She'd never been filled with the childlike wonder of Christmas. To her, it was just another day. But today felt different.

She raced through the shower, quickly dried off, and ran a comb through her hair. Before cancer, her locks had been coarse and wavy—much of the time, unmanageable. In the past few months, it had returned as the same butternut blonde, but it now felt downy soft and had a gentle wave. The strands were finally long enough to lie down with a little persuasion, but they did nothing for her appearance. So Bella opted for a red scarf. A long red and white sweater borrowed from her closet paired perfectly with her black leggings and the red and gray wool socks she'd found in the dresser.

"Talk about a lazy head." Maggie threw her arms around Bella and kissed her cheek. "Merry Christmas, honey."

"Same to you." Bella kissed Lou's elbow and quickly ducked as he pulled a large pan from the oven.

Tilly stuck a spoon in her crockpot— stirred, tasted, and stirred again. She looked around and turned her back toward the crew before dumping in some unknown spice.

"Morning, roomie! Merry Christmas!" Tilly mumbled something unintelligible as she quickly shoved the container into the cupboard. Bella hugged her—longer than her landlady could stand. She finally let go when Tilly began to squirm.

The old gal frowned. "It would be if this crockpot wasn't so doggone stubborn some days."

The corners of Bella's mouth turned upward slightly. She couldn't wait to tell Judson he had been wrong. The slow cooker would be the perfect gift after all.

"There's orange sweet rolls on the table for breakfast." Maggie glanced up at the clock. "Lou, grab Bella a piece of egg bake." She set a glass of grape juice on the table. "Eat as many of those rolls as you want. As usual, my son is late. If they're gone, it'll serve him right. He was supposed to be here by 5:00."

"I am here." Malik walked through the door with a stack of Christmas gifts so high that no one would have recognized him had he not spoken. "A little help here."

"Squat," Bella told him. She reached up and removed the top two foil-wrapped presents and led the way to the living room.

The gifts seemed to have amassed overnight. When she'd headed up to bed, there had been only one small gift under the tree—an unmarked box wrapped in paper so old, it could have drawn Social Security. The brightly wrapped piles of secrets made the holiday feel magical.

After adding Malik's gifts to the others, Bella circled her arms in front of her and spun, but she clumsily stopped halfway around. Five beautiful hand-knit stockings hung in front of the fireplace. Each had a name stitched on it. The last one read *Bella*. Tears filled her eyes, and she swiped at an errant tear with the sleeve of the borrowed sweater. Hesitantly, she moved toward the fireplace, afraid the stocking lived only in her imagination and would disappear if she so much as blinked. She held out her hand and traced the letters of her name. *When had Tilly made her a stocking? Why had she spent so much time on something that wouldn't matter a year from now?*

"Even though I give her a lot of crap, she's a pretty amazing person," Malik whispered in her ear. "She'll drive you crazy one minute, and the next, she'll surprise the hell out of you."

The lump in her throat had grown so large, Bella couldn't speak.

"Let's go eat." Malik nodded toward the kitchen. He rubbed his hands together. "Mom makes a mean Christmas breakfast." With a hand on each shoulder, he steered Bella toward the kitchen.

"It's a good thing I wore stretch pants today." Bella laughed as she sat down.

"Get used to it. This is how Christm…" Malik pressed a fist against his mouth and blinked slowly. "I'm such an idiot. Bella, please forgive..."

Bella laid a hand over his. "Don't. Don't blame yourself for one second. If Tilly's even remotely right about there being a heaven, I'm pretty sure Christmas is going to be even better up there." She poked her index finger upward before leaning close to Malik. "Somehow, I think the old woman and her crockpot will be in charge."

"Bella!" Tilly growled as she shook a wooden spoon in her direction. Then, finally, she shrugged and walked away. "Well, if God wants me to lead Christmas, who am I to say no?"

Maggie shot a mouthful of coffee toward Lou. "Oh Lord, Tilly! You are something else."

***

By the time dinner was over, Bella thought she would explode. It had been a mistake to fill up on breakfast and eat dinner too—but she had. The leftovers alone could feed the entire neighborhood. She moaned in either pain or deep satisfaction; she wasn't sure.

There was nothing she hadn't tried—roast turkey and whipped potatoes with cider gravy, creamed spinach, sweet potato souffle, cornbread and sausage dressing, and sweet pocketbook rolls. Between bites, Bella washed it down with sweet tea—something she realized was a mistake after the first glass.

Bella held her stomach and groaned louder. If she made even the slightest movement, she was sure everyone would see the *reverse rerun* of her gluttonous meal.

Maggie stood and began stacking plates. "Lou and I'll clean up. You three go sit down and enjoy yourselves." She nodded toward the living room. "Now, git."

"When Ma talks, you listen." Malik laughed as he hoisted Tilly out of her chair.

"Me next," Bella whined.

In the other room, Bella stretched out on one of the couches. She hadn't felt the snare of a food coma since her pizza binge study sessions in college. Bella had just begun to doze off when Maggie arrived with a tray of desserts. Like a couple piranhas, Lou and Malik attacked the plate in a feeding frenzy. Malik plopped down next to Bella's feet with a plate of rum balls, divinity, and pecan finger cookies. He held it toward her. Her answer came in a groan.

"Girl, you gotta learn to pace yourself." Malik laughed as

107

Bella buried her face in a pillow. "You and I almost went head-for-head on dinner. I just have a lot more room to put it." He patted his stomach.

After finishing dessert, Malik got up and retrieved the stockings from the mantel. He delivered each to its owner.

Bella studied the beautiful gift. "This is incredible, Tilly. I've never had a Christmas stocking before. Thank you so much!" She hugged it to her chest and smiled at her landlady.

Malik playfully patted her on the shoulder. "Don't get too excited. It's filled with the same thing every year."

Seconds later, an orange walloped him in the side of the head.

He squinted at Tilly. "Damn! For an old lady, you've got one hell of an arm."

Bella laughed. "I assume one of the things in the stocking is an orange?"

Malik rubbed his temple and looked intently at Tilly. "How'd you guess?"

The others waited while Bella emptied her stocking. Tilly provided commentary.

"The oranges represent balls of gold. Ya see, St. Nick once tossed three gold balls through the window of a poor family. As luck'd have it, one ball landed in each one of the daughters' stockings." She raised an eyebrow and stared at Malik. "The foil-wrapped chocolate coins are fer gold too. Started puttin' those in there when Malik bawled that all an orange did was take up space that could be filled with good stuff."

"I didn't cry, old woman."

"Bull!" Lou smirked. "You tossed your stocking, pitched yourself onto the floor, and screamed. It was a full-blown temper tantrum."

Bella poked him with her foot. "How old were you?"

"How old *were* you last Christmas, Malik?" Maggie smiled

and winked at Bella.

Malik frowned at his mother. "Looks like I'll be returning that new car I bought you this year."

"That'll be the day." Maggie sipped her coffee.

Bella pulled out a handful of nuts and held them toward her landlady. Her face was tight in question.

Tilly shook her head. "That one's too easy. Y're all a little…" She twirled a finger slowly around her ear.

Bella grinned. "Well, thanks for that!"

She removed a plastic-wrapped brown roll of something squishy and examined it. "What's this?"

"Oh, let me tell her," Lou begged. "It's a fudge log. That's Tilly's way of reminding us that we're not only nuts, but we're all full of crap too."

Bella grinned as she retrieved a lump of coal from the heel of the stocking. "Hmmm. I always heard about this. My friends were always threatened with coal if they didn't behave."

"Exactly!" Tilly said. She pointed at Bella. "That's why ya got coal."

"Pfft! I don't think I deserve coal." Bella rolled her eyes and pulled out the last item—a candy cane.

"Turn it upside down," the old woman told her.

She did as she was instructed.

"It's a J—for Jesus," Malik said softly.

Bella stared at it for a minute before snapping off the curved end. She unwrapped it and shoved it in her mouth.

Holding up what remained of the J, she said, "Look at that. Now it's an I—for *idea*. As in, your ideas are idiotic. No god would put anyone through all the crap I've had to deal with."

"Believe what ya want, missy. But when it's yer turn to fill the stockings, you can decide what goes in 'em."

"Perfect! I'd love to live long enough for that opportunity."

The room grew silent. Lou's stare fixed on the floor.

Maggie looked directly at Bella. "You okay, honey?"

Bella sighed. "You don't have to worry about me so much. I'm fine."

To prove her point, she grabbed a green and red striped box. "Thank you, Tilly. I really do appreciate all you did to make my last Christmas special. The stocking would have been plenty. I love it."

Tilly flapped a hand in her direction but said nothing.

Bella handed the box to Maggie and Lou.

"This is for both of you." Her stomach flip-flopped. "I *think* you'll like it. Oh, I hope you do."

She wiped her hands on the front of her sweater and watched them open the box.

A hand-written note lay in the box. Maggie read it aloud.

"Dear Maggie and Lou." She smiled at Bella. "Thank you for treating me like a daughter. For the first time ever, I feel like I have a family who truly loves me. And because of that, I wanted to do something special for you. Merry Christmas. I love you both! –Bella."

"We love you too, honey." Maggie made a small heart with her hands and held it in front of her chest. "I saw someone do this in the restaurant one day. I hope it means *I love you*, and it's not some kinky sign for sex or something."

"Ma!" Malik pressed his hand to his forehead.

Bella chuckled. "It's a heart," she assured her.

Lou reached into the box and removed a pair of gray aprons. He handed one to Maggie. An artsy rendering of two people sitting at a table was printed on the front. Above the picture was the name of the bistro—Table for Two.

"Did you design these?" he asked.

Bella nodded. "I did." She sighed. "I thought you could use a little…branding."

"I don't even know what that is. But I like it," Lou said.

"These are incredibly nice."

She nodded toward the box. "There's more."

Lou's expression shifted to confusion. "You bought us a used laptop?"

"No!" Bella said. "That's *my* computer. It's what's *on* the computer that's yours."

Bella wiggled into the small space between the couple. She opened the website she had designed and the menus she planned to print for them.

Maggie's eyes grew wide. "This is incredible! It's exactly what we've been talking about…"

"Since I met you." Bella snickered. "I figured it was about time."

She closed the laptop and tucked it behind her. "Come upstairs with me. I have something else for you."

"Don't mind me," Tilly whined as everyone headed toward the stairs. "I'll just sit down here and wait 'til y'all come back. I ain't goin' nowhere—'less I die."

Maggie frowned. "We'll be back in a few minutes."

"Y'all'll be sorry if that happens while you're up there celebrating Christmas without me."

Malik opened his mouth, but Lou elbowed him in the stomach. "Okay," he grunted. "We'll be back soon." He rubbed his belly. "Maybe next time, don't hit so hard, Dad."

"Maybe next time, think before you open your mouth." Lou glared at him.

Tilly laughed. "He can't do that. He's dumber'n dirt."

With an open mouth, Malik pointed toward Tilly but said nothing.

Lou, Maggie, and Malik followed Bella upstairs and into the extra bedroom. The photos she had taken and framed for the restaurant lined the room.

"Oh, my goodness, Bella! These are gorgeous. We couldn't

have paid someone to take better pictures." Maggie walked from one frame to the next.

Lou embraced Bella in a bear hug. Her feet dangled near his knees. "You're really something. Do you know that? This is the perfect gift!"

Bella felt like her heart would explode. "I have a picture for you too, Malik. But close your eyes first."

She opened the closet door and removed the twenty-by-thirty framed photo of him in Tilly's car. Lou grabbed the heavy picture and held it for his son to see. When he turned it, Maggie gasped.

Malik's eyes popped open, and his mouth followed suit. "Are you kidding me? Are you kidding me right now? Oh my God! That's amazing!"

For the second time in less than two minutes, Bella's feet didn't touch the ground.

"This is the best gift I've ever gotten." He stared at the picture. "And that includes the year Alicia gave me he…"

Maggie cleared her throat loudly.

"What? I was going to say *headlights* for that old Mustang I had."

Lou slapped him on the back and winked. "Sure, you were, son. Sure, you were."

Back downstairs, the rest of the gifts were exchanged. Bella folded her legs beneath her, sat back, and watched. For twenty-three years, she'd missed out on a real Christmas celebration with a family. Today made up for it.

Bella fingered the gold locket Maggie, Lou, and Malik had gifted her. Inside were pictures of her mom and dad. She'd never been close to her parents, especially her dad, but it wasn't the photos that touched her; it was the effort they'd put into finding them. Tonight, she felt more loved by four people who months earlier had been strangers than she had in her entire life.

"Malik, get my gift for Bella, will you?" Tilly told him.

As instructed, Malik retrieved a large box wrapped all in red. It had a big silver bow tied around it.

"Did you wrap this," Bella asked Tilly. "The paper doesn't look like… Well, it's not…" Finally, she stopped talking.

"Pffft! I woulda given it to ya in a plastic bag. Maggie's the overachiever."

"It's beautiful! Thank you, Maggie."

"You shouldn't oughta be thankin' her. I'm the one who paid fer it," Tilly grumbled.

Bella shook her head and smirked. "Well, let me see how good it is first."

Her mouth dropped open when she lifted the flaps of the box. "Whoa!" Bella looked at Tilly. "This is crazy. It's way too much."

She set the box on the floor and pulled out a leather bag. Inside was a top-of-the-line camera and several lenses.

Bella laid a hand on her chest. "Why would you do this?"

"'Cause y're always takin' pictures with that stupid phone of yers. Everybody knows phones are fer talkin' and cameras are fer takin' pictures. Thought maybe ya could git some good ones if ya set yer mind to it."

Bella stepped around the box. She nearly fell into Tilly's lap trying to hug her. "You are one of a kind!"

"I know." Tilly smiled. "And everybody else knows it too."

"Lord, woman. You are something else." Lou smirked. "But you wouldn't be Tilly if you weren't such a spitfire."

Bella picked up the last box and took it to her landlady. She whispered in her ear, "This is your *in front-of-everyone-else* gift. I have a special gift for you later."

Tilly nodded as she picked at the tape on the box.

"Christmas paper's meant to be torn. Tear the stuff already," Bella told her.

Unconvinced, the old woman continued scraping at the tape. Finally, Bella grabbed a corner and ripped it open.

"What the hell? A crockpot? What am I gonna do with another crockpot?"

Bella sighed. "I thought maybe you could use one that actually worked. Maybe then, we could throw out that one you were complaining about this morning."

"No way. Not gonna happen," Maggie said.

"Why not?" Bella asked. Her heart began to unravel. "It's old, and it barely works."

"Maybe so. And maybe Tilly'll even find it in her heart…" Maggie made a face at the old gal, "to *use* your gift…and enjoy it, but that old crockpot can never be thrown out."

"Why's that?" Bella asked.

Maggie sighed. "How many times a week does Tilly use that slow cooker?"

The corners of Bella's mouth turned down as she thought. "Practically every day, I guess."

"Exactly. Around here, Tilly's known as the *crockpot queen*. If you're hungry, she always has something cooking in that thing. Doesn't matter who you are." Maggie smiled at Tilly. "So Tilly decided that when she passes away, she'll be cremated and buried in that old thing."

"What?" The word rebounded in the room. "Are you kidding me? Buried in a crockpot?"

Tilly snapped the footrest down. "Listen here, missy. I've used that thing my entire life. I'm takin' it with me when I go." She shrugged. "Besides, you was the one who said God might put me in charge. So, I wanna be prepared."

Laughter erupted.

"Okay, but if you come back and haunt me, don't bring that thing with."

***

For the first time in hours, the house was still. It was well after dark when the neighbors headed home. Bella was energy bankrupt. She knew Tilly was also spent because, instead of knitting, she sat and stared at the Christmas tree.

Bella retrieved a small, wrapped box from the closet.

"This is your real gift, Tilly. I just didn't think I should give it to you in front of the others."

Tilly held it in her lap. "Ain't nothin' Maggie and Lou don't know 'bout me. I known 'em forever."

"I didn't know that." She nodded toward the box. "Well, go ahead and open it."

As before, Tilly picked at the tape, planning to reuse the paper. Bella was too exhausted to care.

"What is this?" Tilly held up the gift she'd unboxed.

"Well, you know how you sit in the garden and talk to your daughter?" Bella knelt next to Tilly's chair. "This is a recorder. You can record your conversations so, at some point, Jasmine can hear the truth about you and James."

Tilly stared at the machine.

"Once you're done, I'll take the recordings and put them on a flash drive so Jasmine can listen to them whenever she wants."

Tilly put the recorder back in the box and closed the flaps. "Don't ya think if I wanted to talk to her, I would?" She stared at Bella. "I don't think she should hear what I really want to say."

Instantly, Bella's cheeks burned. "I'm sorry. I guess I wasn't thinking. I thought after our conversation a couple weeks…" She sighed. "Never mind."

She stood and headed toward the stairs. "Merry Christmas, Tilly. Thank you for my camera. It was so kind of you. I can't wait to use it. And thank you for my stocking. It means more than you'll ever know."

Her fatigue was thick as she climbed the stairs. She held on to the railing for fear she would stumble.

"Ya gonna help me learn how to use this thing or ain'tcha?" Tilly called.

A wide grin spread across Bella's face. She turned toward the wall to hide it.

"On my way," she said as a second wind blew through her.

CHAPTER 14

A big word

Commitment rather than habit sent Tilly, armed with a recorder and a heavy quilt, to the garden every afternoon. No matter how hard Bella tried to convince her landlady she could record inside the house as easily as out back, Tilly wasn't having any of it. She'd spoken to her daughter in the garden for as long as she could remember; recording it wouldn't change that. So Bella gave in.

The trip out back had grown arduous for Tilly. Bella could see the toll it took on her every day. At least she'd agreed to let Bella serve as her pack mule, walking next to her with her arms loaded as Tilly wheeled her walker along the path. Bella insisted Tilly dress for the January temperatures of the forties and fifties. A thermos of hot coffee always sat on the side table.

Tilly did not want Bella in the garden while she shared her tightly protected secrets with the recorder. But Bella wasn't about to leave her alone. The old lady grew weaker by the day. She'd gone from a cane to a walker in a week. Now, she was leaning on it like a lifeline. If she let go, Bella was sure she would topple over. She couldn't take the chance, so she quietly remained out of Tilly's view—out of earshot.

Life and death commingled in the garden—from seedlings to the desiccated leaves of the previous season. And then there was Tilly—like Bella, she was alive for now, but soon she would be like the plants that clung to the tiniest bit of green. Everywhere she looked, the garden held the beginnings of life and death.

Was there a beginning of death? Was that what Bella was feeling each time she felt another twinge of pain? Was it death poking at her—reminding her it was coming for her?

A row of bushes gave Bella the perfect cover to make Tilly the subject of many of her pictures. From one certain angle, she looked much younger than her eighty-nine years. From another, her face held the shadow of darkness, of death. Bella finally saw it—the beginning to the final curtain. It didn't start on the day you were born, as most people asserted. It happened later—slowly. One minute, you were healthy, and the next, you noticed one small thing that didn't feel right. Each day, something else felt off—pain, tightness, shortness of breath, weakness, a dull ache. It all pointed to the beginning of the end. Tilly's days were numbered. Bella saw death grow as she watched her. She wondered if Tilly saw the same in her.

***

The strong wind wrestled with the gray Spanish moss hanging in the trees that outlined the garden. March was the month that was supposed to enter or exit like a lion or a lamb, but the last day of January roared in. Bella insisted it was too cold and windy for Tilly to sit outside. After a heated disagreement, she set her up in the living room with a new skein of yarn and a book of hat patterns.

Tilly insisted it was Bella's turn to cook dinner. She gave her two options: calico beans or stew. Bella opted for beans and cornbread—following the old woman's recipe, of course. But it wasn't the one Tilly had handwritten on the recipe card. Those cards were simply the skeleton of any dish—something a non-cook would happily throw together. The secret ingredients that made it stand out lived inside Tilly's head. There would be no deviating from the instructions Tilly called from the living room.

Bella pulled the new crockpot from a cupboard. Shortly after Christmas, she had unboxed, washed, and stowed it for Tilly to use. Thus far, she had refused to give up that tired-out slow cooker she'd had since the dinosaurs were expunged from the earth. But if Bella was cooking, the new crockpot was coming out. She would prove the new one worked just as well, if not better.

Bella poked her head into the living room. "The beans are cooking. I need to run to Maggie's for a bit. Are you going to be okay if I leave?"

Tilly snorted as she dropped her hands into her lap. "What in tarnation do ya think I did b'fore ya got here? I took care of myself fer almost ninety years. Fer Pete's sake, ya can leave me alone fer a few minutes."

Bella bowed before her. "I'm sorry, your highness. I won't ask again."

The old gal cleared her throat. "B'fore ya go, fetch me that heavy blanket off the couch. I'm a little chilled."

"Are you okay?" Bella asked as she walked toward her chair. She reached toward Tilly's forehead. "Do you have a fever?"

Tilly shoved her hand away. "I'm just dandy. Just git me the dadgum blanket and git outta here fer I slap ya into the middle of next week."

Bella spread the blanket over Tilly. "You've got to be fine. You're as ornery as ever."

Without another word, Bella headed next door.

***

"Did you know Tilly's turning ninety on March 3rd?" Maggie poured Bella a glass of sweet tea and shoved a plate of cookies toward her. "Lou and I would like to throw her a

119

birthday party at the Legion, but we don't want to interfere with any plans you have for her big day."

Bella frowned. "Well, since I didn't know it was her birthday, I have no plans."

"By the way, when's your birthday?" Maggie asked.

A deep sigh escaped. "Remember the day I arrived in town?" Bella grabbed a cookie and broke off a piece of the benne wafer.

Maggie nodded. "Beginning of October, right?"

"Uh-huh. It was October second. The day before was my birthday. That was the day I found out I was terminal." She tightened her lips. "Happy birthday to me, right?"

Maggie squeezed Bella's hand. "Oh, honey, I'm so sorry."

She finished the cookie. "It doesn't matter. Birthdays were never important to anyone in my family. My folks were usually gone, or the nannies and foster homes didn't care enough to celebrate."

"That's not right. Birthdays are meant to be celebrated."

Bella shook her head. "Let's talk about Tilly. I love the idea of a party. What do you have in mind?"

Maggie got up and grabbed a notebook from the counter. "I've written down some ideas, but I also want to hear yours."

Thoughtfully, Bella skimmed the list. She made suggestions and helped flush out other ideas. Nearly an hour had passed by the time they finished talking.

"Oh, my gosh! I didn't realize it was so late. Tilly's going to have my ass in a sling if I don't get back over there and stir the beans. If dinner isn't ready on time, she'll melt down."

One corner of Maggie's mouth lifted into a crooked smile. "You could set your clock by her eating schedule. That woman's as stubborn as a mule." She shook a finger toward Bella. "But if you ever tell her I said that, I'll deny it."

Bella smirked. "Oh, don't worry. I'm sure she knows we

talk about her behind her back."

She slipped on her jacket and hugged Maggie.

"I'll get my part done in plenty of time. If there are other things you need me to do, just let me know."

"I will." Maggie walked Bella to the door. "I'll share your ideas with Lou and Malik too." She glanced at her watch. "Lou's working late tonight, but my son should have already been home. He's in charge of dinner tonight."

"Hmmm. We should have coordinated. He could come get some beans." She laughed. "Thanks for the treats." Bella waved as she headed down the front stairs and across the adjoining yards.

She tossed her jacket over a hook in the entry. "I'm back, Tilly. Sorry I was gone so long. But you know how Maggie is. She loves to talk."

Bella stopped in the kitchen and stirred the beans. "I'm going to get everything ready for the cornbread. I have the recipe card here, but I'm sure you're going to tell me how to make it anyway?" She washed her hands and grabbed the towel from a plastic hook that hung on the side of an upper cabinet. "Tilly?"

There was only silence.

"Are you taking a nap, or are you ticked at me for being gone so long?"

Bella wandered into the living room.

"Tilly!" she screamed. "Oh, my god, Tilly!"

Tilly was lying in a heap on the floor. Bella kicked the overturned walker to the side and dropped to her knees.

She gently touched her. "Are you hurt?" But Tilly remained still. "Wake up, Tilly." Bella continued to shake her. "Please wake up?"

After rolling her onto her back, she touched her cheek. Tilly was burning up.

Terrified, Bella dialed Maggie instead of 911. Malik and Maggie were on the floor next to Tilly in seconds.

"Tilly?" Maggie cooed. "Come on, honey. It's time to get up." She gently tapped her cheek.

She rotated to Tilly's other side. "Bella, get a cold washrag."

But Bella didn't move. She knew Maggie wanted something, but she couldn't comprehend anything at all. The screaming in her head and the swishing inside her ears compounded the problem. Bella pressed herself against a wall and pulled her arms to her chest as she stared at her landlady.

Malik tapped his mother's arm and pointed to Bella.

Maggie looked from Bella to her son. "Go get the washrag, and call…"

"I already did," he said. "They're on their way. I can hear the sirens."

Still flattened against the wall, Bella watched the EMTs work on Tilly before lifting her onto the gurney. Malik tucked one arm around her as his mother spoke to the paramedics. When the stretcher left the room, Bella's knees gave out, and she collapsed. Malik caught her and carried her to the couch.

"Ma, get her some water."

Bella shook her head. "I-I knew she was sick. I knew it. But she wouldn't tell me the truth when I asked her." She turned toward Maggie. "This is my fault. I should have been here instead of at your house."

"Honey, this is no one's fault. People get sick all the time."

"B-but she fell. If I had been here…"

"Oh, Bella, *if* is a big word. We could *if* ourselves to death. Always questioning what we could have done won't change anything." Maggie held her. "If you hadn't come to my house… If Tilly hadn't gotten out of her chair… If she had told you she wasn't feeling well… Don't do that to yourself."

Maggie looked at Malik and then back at Bella. "Do you want to go to the hospital and check on Tilly, or do you want to stay here with Malik?"

Instantly, Bella was on her feet. "No, I want to go. I need to be with her."

"Okay. Then let's go check on our girl."

***

The words *We don't know anything yet* could have been put on a recording and played repeatedly every few minutes. It was the only news the hospital shared for the first few hours. Bella paced while Maggie and Malik whispered behind hands pressed to their mouths. She could only speculate what they were talking about. Tilly dying? The house and what would happen to it?

Her stomach sank. *What would happen to her if Tilly died? Where would she live? Tilly's place was her home.* She rushed to the bathroom, barely making it into a stall before Maggie's tea and cookies erupted in a volcanic spray.

"Bella?" Maggie pushed the door open and squeezed into the stall with her. "Oh, honey."

She unrolled a long strip of toilet paper and handed it to Bella before helping her to her feet.

Bella never needed a mother more than she needed one right now. Maggie was the closest she had. Her legs wobbled, refusing to support her. Her hands felt clammy as sweat dampened her back and the short hair on her head. Maggie pulled the door open, and the two moved out of the stall as one.

"I-I usually don't sweat this much—except at night," Bella confessed. She swiped the thin toilet paper across her forehead. "Usually, I'm freezing." She splashed water on her face. The mirror reflected Maggie's concern.

"I'm okay. Don't worry about me." She dried her face with a brown paper towel. "I just wish they'd tell us something about

Tilly. It's the waiting that's killing me."

Maggie shook her head. "Have you been throwing up a lot lately?"

Her shoulders dropped. "Not a lot. Just once in a while."

"Do you think you should see…"

"A doctor?" Bella asked bitterly. "So she could tell me what? That I'm dying? That there's some stupid trial in Oregon that could extend my life for an extra two months? That there's some questionable treatment in South America that has a five percent chance of curing me—if it doesn't kill me first?" She shook her head. "No, I'm not going to see another doctor."

Maggie took Bella's hand. "You know you can always change your mind."

"I won't." Bella smiled uneasily at a woman who cautiously entered the bathroom. "We should probably get back and see if there's any word on Tilly."

When they entered the waiting room, Malik was speaking with a doctor. He waved them over.

"This is Tilly's…granddaughter." Malik stumbled over the word. "She's family. You can share the information with her."

Bella glanced at Malik but didn't protest his lie.

The doctor offered his hand to Bella. "I'm Doctor Hastings. We've just moved your grandmother to the ICU."

"What's wrong with her?" Bella asked. She nervously played with the zipper of her jacket.

"She has pneumonia. We've started her on antibiotics and fluids and put her on oxygen."

Bella squeezed Maggie's hand. "Is—my grandmother going to make it?"

"I'm not going to lie to you. It's touch and go. Whether your grandmother makes it or not is up to her. Her body's either going to fight this or let it win. We can only pray it isn't the latter." He looked at his chart. "Do you have any other questions for me?"

"Is she awake?" Malik asked.

"I'm afraid not." He shrugged. "Sometimes sleep's what's needed to heal the body."

"Can we see her?" Maggie asked.

Doctor Hastings held a finger in the air. "Just a minute." He backed up and intercepted a nurse from the desk. Seconds later, they both joined the small huddle.

"This is Hillary. She's one of the ICU nurses. She'll take care of you from here." He looked at Bella. "I want to warn you. Your grandmother looks rough. I don't just mean from the pneumonia. When she fell, she must have hit her face on something. She looks like she's been in a brawl."

Maggie grabbed Bella's arm. "This isn't the time for *ifs*, Bella," she whispered.

"Keep your visits short. And only one person at a time. Okay?" Dr. Hastings was already moving toward his next mission.

"Come with me," Hillary said. "I'll get you set up to visit Matilda."

Bella mouthed "*Matilda?*" as they passed through the long hallway.

Maggie grinned. "Tilly hated that name. She said it made her sound like a hundred-year-old woman."

Malik snorted. "Well, she's close."

Maggie gently shoved him with her shoulder. "*Now* it fits. But it didn't when she was nine. Some boy she liked back in grade school gave her the name *Tilly* and it stuck."

"Charles Isaiah Washington," Bella said, emphasizing each part. "She told me she'd been in love with him since they were in third grade. But her father disapproved."

"Tilly had a boyfriend way back then?" Malik laughed. "I assumed she'd deck any boy that looked at her."

"Me too." As they walked, Bella stared at the red line that led toward the ICU.

Maggie pulled Bella out of the way of an oncoming gurney. "I had no clue Tilly had a schoolgirl crush on anyone but James."

"I think it was more than that. She still thinks about him—a lot."

"Wow! The things you learn from Tilly's *granddaughter*," Maggie teased.

CHAPTER 15

The moment didn't last long.

By 10:00 p.m., the ICU waiting room had dwindled to a few distressed people waiting for a crumb of news about a loved one. The Jacksons and Bella belonged to the consort of worriers. None needed or wanted anything except information.

Earlier in the evening, Lou had appeared with an assortment of sandwiches, salads, and desserts he'd packed up after closing the bistro. He swept in with three grocery bags full of provisions. There was enough food to last for days. Once he set the bags down, Bella planted herself under his arm and hugged him. Food was how Lou showed love. Maggie often referred to him as the *food devil*.

Making their way around the waiting room, Maggie and Lou personally invited each person to share in the meal. While Maggie hugged strangers, Lou talked them through their options.

Malik disappeared, returning with a box of sodas and bottled water. Bella did nothing but watch. Her heart ached with sadness for Tilly and with love for the unconventional family she'd been lucky enough to fall into. While everyone helped themselves to food, for a few brief moments, the voices and quiet laughter almost made life seem normal. Had it not been for the sterile surroundings, it could have been a party. If Bella blurred her vision enough, she could imagine being in the bistro with Tilly, laughing about the most mundane events. But the moment didn't last long.

After finishing their meals, people withdrew back into themselves, battling with their own *what ifs*. Even though Maggie had forbidden her to think about them, Bella couldn't do anything but.

The four of them had settled on perpendicular couches. From the wide eyes, furrowed brows, and the tight jaws, Bella knew they were as worried about Tilly as much as she was— maybe more. The Jacksons had known Tilly longer. The thought of losing her had to be gut-wrenching. If her heart was breaking, she couldn't even imagine how they felt.

"How you doin', honey?" Maggie softly asked. She draped an arm over Bella's shoulder. "You should probably go home and get a good night's sleep. Malik can take you." She shoved his foot with her toes.

Malik opened his eyes and sat upward. "Of course. I can take you home. If you want, I can stay with you."

Bella shook her head. "I can't go. I wouldn't sleep anyway." Bella felt the weight of the unknown pull her under. Her voice cracked. "I need to be here in case…" She stared at the floor. "I just need to be here."

"Then I think you should get some sleep," Lou told her. "You'll land yourself in a bed next to Tilly if you don't take care of yourself."

Once again, Malik vanished. As Maggie settled Bella onto the too-short couch, he returned with a thin hospital pillow and blanket.

"Here," he said, holding them toward her. "These should help."

A faint smile crossed her face. "Thank you."

Bella squished the pillow into a lopsided ball and pulled the blanket over her head. The thin material quieted the harshness of the lights but did nothing for her spinning thoughts. She silently counted, sang songs in her head, and pictured her mom dancing, all attempting to squelch the blistering hum of the lights. Nothing dampened them enough to let her sleep.

Suddenly, a voice spoke to her. The voice wasn't a familiar one. Was it Tilly's god? She couldn't remember the last time she'd listened hard enough to hear him. Her belief in a divine being was buried deep beneath her parents' death, the revolving door of foster homes, and her cancer diagnosis. His decision to condemn her to a death sentence before she'd even started to live had been the final straw.

On October 1st, when she'd walked into her oncologist's office, Bella had been positive things had turned around. After all, it was her birthday. What kind of god would destroy her on the anniversary of the day he had given her breath? But her hopes and wishes and dreams of the future were all for naught. She'd raced out of the office, knowing he had taken everything.

So, under the covers on the small sofa, with Tilly balancing on the edge of two worlds, would he forsake her again? He'd better not. He owed her. After everything she'd been through, he had to leave her with something good—even if it was only for a few months. He couldn't keep taking from her. Other than Tilly and the Jacksons, she had nothing left to give.

Over the years, God's nagging voice periodically found its way into her head. But after all that had happened, she wasn't about to give him the time of day. *Still.* If there were any chance of saving Tilly, she wasn't above begging—this one last time.

I don't know if you're real or not, and I don't know if you can even see me or hear me, but on the off chance you're listening, please don't let Tilly die. You've taken enough from me. I beg you not to take the one good thing I have left. Please, don't do this to me again.

Suddenly, the weight she felt began to lift. Bella drew a

deep breath and held it until her lungs screamed. When she released it, she heard Tilly's voice as clearly as if she were standing next to her in the antiquated kitchen on Sweetwater Lane. *Bella, Bella, Bella. Oh, ye of little faith. I told you I'd let you know when it was my time. This ain't it. Now, quit your bellyachin'.*

A tiny smile lifted the corners of her mouth and she drifted off to sleep.

***

The sound blended into her dreams. She could hear someone whimpering. It was barely audible, like the mewl of a newborn kitten. It was paled by the high-pitched hum above her. Bella tried to pull herself from the depths of the darkness she had fallen into, but it was like swimming through mud. Finally, she threw the covers back and bolted upright. Her shoulders rose and fell with each deep breath.

Maggie moved to the floor next to her. "Honey, are you okay? You were crying."

The waiting room had exploded with strangers while she slept. Her fellow worriers from the previous night had vanished, and new faces had taken their place. Bella was keenly aware of the newbies' prying eyes. She threw her legs off the couch and ran her hands through her hair as she leaned forward and clutched her stomach.

"Tilly?" Her mouth was dry, and she was keenly aware of the huskiness of her morning voice.

Maggie shook her head. "We don't know any more than we did last night. The doctor stopped in shortly after you fell asleep. He said we just have to be patient. The antibiotics need time to work."

"Where are Malik and Lou?"

"Malik had to go to the station. And Lou, well, he can't stay in one place longer than a hummingbird, so I sent him back to work. It's probably for the best." She sat next to Bella. "How're you feeling?"

Bella turned sideways, rubbed her aching shoulder, and tucked a leg beneath her. "I can't explain it, but I honestly believe Tilly will be okay."

One of the lights above them flickered before it flashed and died. Bella's resolve faded, and she wondered if the dying light was an omen.

Maggie squeezed Bella's hand. "We can only pray, honey."

Bella stretched her neck and looked up. Most people would think she was checking out the burned-out bulb, but Bella was looking far beyond the dark light.

***

By evening, Maggie and Bella had relocated to Tilly's room. They were gawkers, intently watching for Tilly to wake. Bella paced while Maggie sat. Words between them were sparse, but they both spoke to Tilly, reminding her she was a fighter.

Three days later, Bella remained a fixture in ICU-5. Maggie had returned to work, leaving her alone to wait for Tilly to come back to them. The doctor darted in and out of the room from time to time. Based on his loud sighs, Bella knew he was growing concerned. Her belief that Tilly's god would work a miracle had begun to wane, and she angrily yelled at him multiple times each day.

Bella had spent the last two nights hunkered down in the aqua recliner. Multiple times each night, she would wake and fret over Tilly. The blanket Malik had brought her the night Tilly was admitted had become her only comfort. She rubbed her hand against the rough material day and night. Her exhaustion and worry battled with her need to be awake—no matter the outcome.

Each morning, someone dropped off clean clothes and an

insulated bag filled with breakfast and lunch. She'd changed her clothes daily and washed her hair in the bathroom sink, but the food almost always went untouched. No matter how hard they tried to convince her, Bella refused to leave Tilly's room. If the old gal died, she didn't want her to be alone. If she woke, Bella wanted to be the first face she saw.

The morning of the fourth day dawned without fanfare. Tilly remained asleep. Along with the bag, Malik delivered a cup of piping hot coffee. He set her camera bag on the floor.

"I thought you might want this. Don't know what you'll take pictures of, but I don't think I've ever seen you go this long without that thing hanging around your neck."

"Thanks. Maybe just looking at some old photos will help."

"I know you don't want to hear this, but you look like hell."

Bella rolled her eyes. "Well, thanks," she mumbled.

"You can't keep this up, Bella."

She frowned at him. "I'm fine, Malik." She dropped onto the edge of the recliner. Gently, she lifted the old woman's hand. "Until Tilly comes back, I'll be right here."

Malik shrugged. "Okay, then. I'll let Mom know there's no change—with you or Tilly."

Slowly, he backed out of the room. Bella knew he hoped she would follow, but she remained fixed to the chair.

Bella stared at the case. Finally, she unzipped it, removed her camera, and set it on the edge of the bed. After searching the room, she grabbed Tilly's Bible from the bedside table and opened it to the ribbon-marked passage Maggie had read to her the night before. Bella read it aloud.

She stared at Tilly, willing her to open her eyes. "That should make you happy, old woman. I read from the Bible, and I didn't burst into flames."

Carefully, she closed the book and tucked it into Tilly's hands. Next, she turned off the overhead light and altered the settings on her camera. Bella snapped several pictures of Tilly's hands and the tattered Bible, each time adjusting this knob or that one before taking another shot from a different angle.

When she finished, she stood next to the hospital bed and clicked through the photos. She gasped. Something was amiss, or maybe it was as it was supposed to be. Perhaps it was the morning sun shining through the large window or some anomaly with the flash of her camera, but every picture had a circle of light around the old woman's ashen and wrinkled hands. It wasn't bright or particularly noticeable; you really had to study the image to see it, but once you did, you couldn't unsee it.

"You've got an in with the man upstairs, don't you?" She snorted.

Exhaustion suddenly won out. Bella's legs grew weak. Making it to the folding chair had been almost more than she could do. She leaned forward, rested her head on the bed, and watched Tilly.

"I can't believe you're still not awake. What are you waiting for?" Bella didn't expect an answer as much as she hoped for one. "Is this because I used the new crockpot? If it is, I promise to use that crappy old slow cooker from now on." The machines continued their rhythmic orchestra. "Or is it because you're mad at me for putting that small dent—that I can't even see—in the fender of your precious car?"

Bella felt her lids grow heavy as her eyes filled with tears. She squeezed them shut and let them fall onto Tilly's blanket. "Don't die on me, old woman," she whispered as she felt herself giving way to sleep.

"Who ya callin' old?"

The voice was so soft that Bella was certain she'd only imagined it. She smiled. It felt good to hear Tilly's voice, even if it was just a dream. She didn't want to open her eyes, fearing

Tilly would disappear.

Suddenly, she felt a hand on her head. Her eyes popped open.

Tears rolled down Bella's face as she sobbed. Snot bubbled from one nostril. "T-T-T-Tilly? I-I w-w-was s-so w-worried y-you were g-g-gonna d-d-die."

The old woman's voice was weak but as snarky as always. "Fer cryin' out loud. Get yerself a hanky and wipe that disgustin' nose. And quit bawlin'."

Tilly was back. Bella sucked in a deep breath and smiled. She grabbed a tissue and wiped her face and blew her nose.

"Now, what's all that blubberin' about?" she whispered.

Bella rocked back and forth as she held Tilly's hand. "I thought you were going to die."

Slowly, Tilly raised her eyebrows. "Didn't I tell ya I'd let ya know when that was gonna happen?"

"You did." Bella nodded.

"Then quit yer snivelin' and tell me what I'm doin' here."

Bella kissed her landlady's hand. "Yes, ma'am." She beamed at the old woman.

CHAPTER 16

Death can't be stopped

Mid-February unexpectedly ushered in a string of seventy-degree days. Each one drenched the earth with warm sunshine and hopes of an early spring. With someone keeping watch over Tilly, Bella had wandered to the beach a few times, but the coolness of the sand on her bare feet was a shocking contrast to the warm air. Mother Nature was sending mixed signals.

With the warm afternoons, Tilly insisted on retreating to her garden. After her unforeseen brush with death, the matter of demystifying her life for her daughter seemed more crucial than ever. She talked a good game, claiming it hadn't been her time, but Bella was confident she'd been more frightened than she let on. There were brief moments when she caught Tilly staring at the spot where she'd collapsed. And on outings, the old gal would often direct their trip so they would pass the hospital or the cemetery. Both places gave Bella the heebie-jeebies. Not because of the grim reaper's pseudo appearance at Tilly's door, but because she knew she would land in one or both before year's end.

214. Bella continued to count the days each night before bed. Crossing off the date was symbolic of erasing another day of her life. When she had first started college, her philosophy professor asked—*Would you rather know when you would die or not?* Back then, she was young and invincible. Time felt infinite.

The question had been a fictitious scenario used to teach the questioning of self and others. Stupidly, Bella had chosen to know when she would die. Defending her choice had been easy. She justified her answer with a load of crap about experiencing everything you ever wanted to before you were pushing up daisies. And, of course, she'd added the typical eighteen-year-old response, "Plus, it lets you know how much time you have left to party." She'd ended her soapbox speech with a *woo-hoo*. And the rest of the class had joined in. Never had she expected God, or whoever was puppeteering her life, to put her choice to the test. She wanted to go back and change her answer.

Knowing you had approximately two hundred and fourteen days made life feel brittle. It was like standing on the glass walkway over the Grand Canyon and looking down. One minute, everything seems fine, and the next, the glass begins to crack. Unsure what to do, you stand perfectly still, hoping your inaction halts the fracturing. But it doesn't. Death can't be stopped. How and when you die is based on a series of choices, the twisting of events, and, if there is a god, his manipulation of your life.

Yes—two hundred and fourteen days. Most nights, Bella sobbed until she fell into an exhausted stupor. Each day slipped away, like water through her fingers. She grieved each one. Since the day Bella received her death sentence, she could focus on little else. No matter what she was doing, it was never far from her mind.

After her parents died, she knew how fragile life was, how quickly the days could lapse into nothingness. Her mother always told her that each day could be wasted or enjoyed. The choice was hers alone. But no matter which she chose, it wouldn't slow their passing.

Tilly's hospital stay and near stumble into the grave made

Bella painfully aware of her own final exit. Unlike the time-killing video games she'd played in college, she would never level up, and she could never win. From this point on, she would always be on *Level One*. Bella's entire life had been spent there. The October appointment with her oncologist had made that clear. Oh, she'd made a few decisions that had moved her forward, but the ones that held her back had been made for her. In real life, she hadn't broken enough bricks or collected enough coins or power pellets. And, it was obvious, the ghosts who chased her were closing in—quickly.

Pong! That was the game her life emulated. It was like a slow game of table tennis, popularized in the 1970s. Bella hit the pixelated ball and waited for the computer to return it. The waiting was her life. After her parents died, the game had been put on *pause*. Then, after graduating from college, when she was finally ready to smash the ball, cancer tripped her. For two more years, her life went into *pause mode*. Then, the computer got bored with her. In seven months, she would lose.

Nearly every night, the same nightmare collared her. It always started with Bella standing in a long hallway with a thick wooden door on the far end. Who or what was on the other side of that door remained a mystery. As each day passed, she moved closer to finding out.

Calendar numbers, displayed on sticky notes, lined the brick walls in her dreams. As she stepped closer to the door, they drifted downward, giving up. The floor was littered with numbers written on squares of colored paper. Frantically, she collected them and attempted to reattach them. She hoped to buy herself another day, another week. But the numbers wouldn't cling to the unforgiving brick any longer. Panic rose inside of her, drawing her deeper into the nightmare.

A pattern of colors finally began to emerge in her dream. Days Bella had lived joyfully were brightly colored. Wasted days, the ones she lived in self-pity, were represented by dark, ominous colors. She'd expected the days she'd spent at Tilly's bedside to be black; instead, they were neon yellow and orange, the colors of the sun. Bella tried to connect the dots, but it didn't make sense.

From the hallway, only two hundred and fourteen days remained. Two hundred and fourteen white squares that would change color depending on the choices she made for each day. Two hundred and fourteen breakfasts, lunches, and dinners. That many sunrises and sunsets. An equal number of *sleeps,* as she referred to them when her parents traveled. One spring and one summer. If she was incredibly lucky, she might see the leaves begin to change one more time.

For those not dying, two hundred and fourteen days was an eternity. But to Bella, it was but the tick of a clock.

***

Bella snapped the macro lens onto her camera and twisted it. She had dropped some breadcrumbs near an anthill, hoping to capture the strength of the tiny creatures. After a few minutes, she switched the lens again and turned her focus to Tilly.

Hoping not to be noticed, she worked her way to the far side of the garden and planted herself on the ground behind a climbing vine and watched. At some point, Tilly had traded the recorder for her Bible. Unlike in the hospital when Bella planted the book in her hands, Tilly was a willing participant this time. She searched for a verse or a page or some other Godly reference Bella didn't understand. After a few moments, the old woman cradled the book against her chest and held it in place with folded hands. When she looked up, Bella captured a photo of what she'd never experienced—faith.

Knowing the *jasmine* chair was off-limits, Bella walked in front of Tilly and dropped into the one on her left.

"How's the recording going?"

Tilly frowned. "I'd say 'bout as good as tryin' to cook an entire alligator in that old crockpot of mine."

Bella fake coughed. "Did you just admit my crockpot is better than yours?"

"I did no such thing. I'm just sayin' there's a place fer both slow cookers." Tilly raised her eyebrows. "The place fer yers is in the cupboard."

"I knew you'd never admit the one I bought you was better than that obsolescent piece of junk you own."

The old woman shrugged. A crooked smirk tugged at her lip. "Don't matter if it is or it ain't. When I was on my deathbed, I heard ya promise ya'd never use that poor excuse of an appliance again."

Bella stared at Tilly and tipped her head. "You heard that? You heard what I said when you were supposed to be unconscious? How long had you been awake?"

"Long 'nuf to know ya love me more'n yer confounded slow cooker." Tilly laughed. "Now, how 'bout ya help me inside so I can start dinner."

Bella stood and stretched. "I have a better idea. How about we eat at the bistro tonight. I need to pick up some prints from the drugstore later."

"Fine, but y're buyin'."

Bella smiled. "I figured as much."

CHAPTER 17

Heads would roll

Malik walked into Tilly's house just as she lifted the lid off the old, slow cooker. The beefy aroma wafted through the dated kitchen with the patched red and white wallpaper.

"Hoo-wee! Is that Mississippi pot roast?"

He snatched a utensil from the cutlery drawer and aimed it toward the pot. The tarnished silver fork never made contact. Tilly slapped his hand with lightning speed and slammed the cover back down, narrowly missing his fingertips.

"Try that again, and ya better be dang sure ya gave yer heart to Jesus, 'cause yer backside'll be mine." She swung the dirty wooden spoon at him.

Malik ducked the spoon and plowed a hip into the corner of the stubborn drawer that hadn't closed. "Ohhh," he moaned as he kneaded the spot on his side. "Well, are you planning to share?"

Tilly pushed him away from the counter and pulled out the big hammer she used to convince the drawer to shut. "If ya don't irritate the bejeebers outta me, boy." She shook the hammer in his direction before smacking the side of the drawer and closing it.

Malik grabbed a can of off-brand root beer from the fridge. "Seriously? Steve's root beer? This stuff tastes like toilet water." Still, he popped the top and drank it down.

Tilly watched him with narrowed eyes. "What're ya doin' here anyhow?"

Malik slapped a hand to his chest. "Oh, Tilly, that hurt! Can't a guy just hang out with his favorite gal?"

She arched an eyebrow. The corners of her lips curled downward. "A guy can come over and visit when he don't try'n eat an old lady outta house and home."

Holding the can of root beer in the air, Malik smiled. "Thanks for the soda. I'll be helping myself to some of that pot roast before I go."

Bella had been hiding in the living room, watching the exchange. Malik was right on time. Maggie had asked for her help with last-minute plans for Tilly's party. And since the four of them had agreed not to leave Tilly alone anymore, it was Malik's turn to *old lady sit*. They would never tell Tilly of their plan. Heads would roll.

She rounded the corner into the kitchen. Her camera bag was slung over her shoulder.

"Oh, Malik." The naturalness of her faux greeting surprised even her. She winked at him while Tilly slowly pushed her walker toward the living room. "Why are you here?"

"Dang! The old woman just asked me the same thing. Can't a guy just stop in for a visit?"

"Shut your pie hole, boy," Tilly growled before disappearing into the living room.

Bella turned toward the living room and spoke loudly. "I was just heading over to show your mom some pictures. Want to come?"

He made a face and wagged his tongue at her. "Nah, I think I'll spend some time with old Grandma Moses."

"If ya keep callin' me old, you'll be eatin' yer share of pot roast outta the trash can. I'd just as soon feed *it* as you."

"Sorry," he groveled. "Sorry, Miss Tilly." He waved Bella

out the door and hurried into the living room to do some butt-kissing.

Bella stepped onto the front porch and drew a deep breath. A cool breeze brushed her cheek and ruffled her short hair. She loved Tilly, but there was something to be said about freedom—and not being solely responsible for the woman. It wasn't that she wasn't grateful for everything Tilly had done; it was just so exhausting.

As she crossed the lawn, the tiny yellow and white fertilizer balls sprang up and pinged against her shoes. It was Malik's day off. Not only had he fertilized both yards, but he'd also washed Tilly's car.

"Hey, Maggie," Bella called when she came through the door. She hung her jacket on a hook and wandered into the kitchen.

"In the den, Bella."

Maggie had one leg tucked beneath her. The wooden chair was pulled tightly against a massive oak desk that nearly filled the room. A handwritten list lay on the top of the dark, scarred desk.

"Just going over the checklist for Tilly's surprise party." She looked up. "How's everything coming along on your end?"

Bella ignored the question. Instead, she knocked on the top of the desktop. "This thing looks like it was built with wood from the *Mayflower*."

A raised eyebrow settled on Maggie's face. "Where do you think it came from? *Waste not. Want not.* You know her saying. I wanted a *new* desk. But you don't say no to that woman."

"That's an understatement and a half."

From her bag, Bella removed an envelope with a stack of pictures and spread them out in front of Maggie. "I was hoping you'd help me decide which photos to enlarge for the walls."

Maggie lightly clapped her hands together and held them in

front of her. "My gosh, Bella. These are all wonderful. You have such a photographic eye."

She lifted the photo of Tilly's hands holding her Bible. "What's this?" She plucked her glasses from the top of her head and slipped them on. "There's a faint circle. How in the world did you do that?"

Bella lifted her shoulders upward. "I didn't. That's how it came out."

Maggie continued to stare at the picture. "That's incredible. I've never seen anything like it."

"Me either," Bella admitted. "If I didn't know better…" Her words drifted off.

"What?"

"Well, I swear the woman has an in with…" She pointed a finger upward. "Whoever lives upstairs."

Maggie laughed. "That's called *faith*, Bella. Tilly wholeheartedly believes in God." Her eyebrows raised. "I do too."

Bella sighed. "Someday, you're going to have to try to convince me of his existence. Just not today. If I don't get back soon, Tilly'll have Malik handcuffed to the sofa."

Maggie laughed. "Malik can hold his own. If he gets in Tilly's craw, that's on him. Those two fight like cats and dogs."

The sun streamed through a stained-glass iris flower hanging in the window. An array of pinks and burgundies melted across the top of the desktop, changing shape as the afternoon sun shifted.

Ninety minutes later, photos had been selected, and the list that was supposed to have decreased grew instead.

"I need to run down to the drugstore and order the prints tomorrow. I know you're working in the morning, but can you sit with Tilly after lunch for a little while?"

"How about I bring lunch from the bistro. You can go after

we eat."

A wide smile crossed Bella's face. "Oh, thank god. If I have to eat one more hodgepodge of random foods from Tilly's crockpot, I swear I'll scream."

"Well, then, what would you like for lunch tomorrow?"

"Mac and cheese—plain and simple."

Maggie closed one eye and tilted her head. "Hmmm. Pasta, cheese, milk, onion, and whatever else Lou throws in. I'd call that a hodgepodge."

"Well, at least it doesn't have mushy green leaves in it."

"True. Very true. Tilly is a fan of those green leaves. That may be why she's lived to almost ninety."

***

Bella blew into the house and raced up the staircase. She was concealing things she didn't want Tilly to see.

But when she stepped into her room, she froze. In the short time she was gone, the room had been reverted to its original layout. She'd been erased from 354 Sweetwater Lane.

Bella didn't own much, but she'd hung some pictures on the walls and picked up some second-hand items at the thrift store to make it feel homey. All those things had vanished. The closet door was ajar. Slowly, she pulled it open and found nothing but a couple of dated prom dresses and a few pairs of high-heeled shoes.

She raced down the stairs. "What in the hell happened to my room?" she demanded. Anger seethed inside her as she looked from the old woman to Malik. Bella poked her finger into his chest. "What did you do? She couldn't have done this by herself."

The footrest of the recliner snapped. Like always, Tilly rocked several times before standing. She pushed her walker toward Bella.

"Come 'ere." She led the way down the hall toward a room

Bella had never entered before.

Tilly pushed the door open. The suite mirrored her landlady's.

"What is this?" Bella walked around the front room.

"This here's yer new room. Malik moved everythin' down here so ya ain't gotta climb the stairs no more."

"I don't understand."

Tilly sighed. "Last night, I stood at the bottom of the stairs and listened to ya retch. Just when I got to thinkin' ya was done, ya started all over again." She touched Bella's arm. "I wanted to come up and check on ya, but I didn't have the energy. Believe me, I tried."

Bella walked around the stub wall into the attached bedroom. The walls had been covered in pink floral wallpaper. She pressed a hand to the wall.

Tilly stood near her. "That there's the original paper."

"No kidding." Bella snorted softly. She touched a tiny bud before tracing the stem to the next flower.

Her pictures had been rehung in nearly the same location as upstairs. She pulled a dresser drawer open and touched her clothes. The things she'd borrowed from the upstairs closet had also found their way downstairs.

"There's a private bath over there." Tilly pointed to a closed door. "This was my ma's room." She looked up. "In all the years I took in boarders, I never let anybody stay in here." She wheeled toward Bella, so close Bella could feel Tilly's warm breath on her face. "No one deserved this room—'til now."

A sob cut through Bella. "Thank you. But why did you do this?"

Tilly shook her head. "Bella, y're only gonna get sicker and weaker. I'm just tryin' to make things easier for ya."

A ragged sigh fell from Bella. "I love you, old woman," she whispered into Tilly's ear.

"Don't go gettin' all soupy on me." She shuffled past Malik and out of the bedroom. "And don't call me *old*."

"She loves you, you know," Malik said.

"I know. But just once, I'd like to hear her say it."

"She did. Look around. She just didn't use the words you wanted to hear. But someday, when you least expect it, she'll say them."

Bella stopped in front of Malik. "Thanks for doing all of this. It was incredibly nice of you." She walked toward the other room but suddenly spun around. "Oh, man. I hope like hell you didn't help yourself to a pair of my underwear as a little thank you gift." She grinned.

"Don't flatter yourself." He came toward her and wrapped his arms around her. "I saw your undies. There wasn't enough there to blow my nose on."

She wiggled her way out of his arms. "You're disgusting."

"Not as disgusting as those things you call underwear."

"Y're both disgustin'," Tilly hollered from the sitting room. "Now, git out here and help me off this dang couch."

CHAPTER 18

Cheese and crackers got all muddy

The morning after the big move, Bella smiled when she opened her eyes. Malik was right. Tilly loved her, or she wouldn't have given her this room.

At breakfast, Bella beamed at her landlady.

"What?" Tilly asked suspiciously.

Bella shrugged. "Nothing."

"Well, quit lookin' at me then. Y're starin' like a hungry old dog." She shoved a forkful of grits into her mouth.

Bella pushed her bangs to the side and laughed.

"And that's another thing. What're ya gonna do with that mop of hair sproutin' from your head? Ya look like one of those teenage white boys from the seventies. Ya know, the ones who didn't know combs existed."

"Well, since I wasn't born in the seventies, and barely in the last century, I have no idea what you're talking about. But I think I'm going to keep my hair short."

"Good!" Tilly said decidedly. "Then after breakfast, I'll cut it fer ya."

"You? What do you know about cutting white people's hair—or cutting hair at all, for that matter?"

Tilly scowled. "I grew up durin' the Great Depression. Couldn't pay fer a stick of butter, let 'lone a haircut. My ma cut my hair with her sewin' scissors. And when they weren't sharp 'nough, my pa cut it with a butcher knife."

"Now I know you're lying."

After several attempts, Tilly stood. "Sounds like a challenge. I'll go sharpen a knife and show ya."

"No, you won't! You're not getting within a hundred feet of my head with a knife."

"Well, then, scissors it is." Tilly picked up her plate. "Now, let's git these dishes done so we can git to that shaggy mess ya call *hair*."

"Can't I just make an appointment at a salon?" Bella repeatedly moved between the table and the refrigerator.

"Ain't ya learned nothin'? In this house, we ain't wastin' money on frivolous crap."

Bella's eyes narrowed. "A haircut's frivolous?"

"It is when ya got somebody who'll do it fer free. My ma cut hair fer everybody in the neighborhood. There weren't a day I didn't come home from school to a head in the sink and a body waitin' at the kitchen table."

"Was the, ah…" Bella put her hands around her neck. "Well, was the head in the sink attached to a body?"

"Well, course, it was. Bella, sometimes I swear most rocks gotta higher IQ'n you." Tilly pointed to her temple. "Think, girl! Think."

"It was a joke. But sometimes, I don't know if what you're telling me is the truth or some bogus southern tale to keep me off balance."

Tilly started running water in the sink. "If I say it, ya better by God b'lieve it's true."

An hour later, Bella stood in front of her bathroom mirror. Tilly had done an incredible job of overhauling the hair that had sprouted in the past five months. After a quick wash and dry, and a butterfly clip she swiped from a drawer upstairs, she felt like *precancer Bella*. Once again, she had a hairstyle, a real hairstyle. There was no way she would have ever believed the old woman could have pulled it off.

***

Plans for Tilly's party were coming to a head. Maggie, Lou, and Malik had been in and out of Tilly's house on and off for days. Each time, Bella would sneak out on some errand or another.

The evening before the surprise party, Bella and Maggie walked in as Lou walked out.

"Hold yer horses, Lou!" Tilly yelled. "Git back in here."

Like a small child, Lou sheepishly returned to the kitchen.

"Do y'all think I only got one oar in the water or what?" Tilly shook her finger at each of them.

Bella sighed. They'd been caught; all their secretive planning had been for naught. "Tilly, you know your b..."

Maggie slapped a hand over Bella's mouth. "Of course, we don't think you're stupid, Tilly. But maybe you should tell us why you think we do."

Tilly shuffled to a kitchen chair and dropped into it. "Y'all're up to somethin', and don't think I don't know what it is."

"Tell us, old woman," Malik said as he stepped through the front door. "What's everyone up to?"

"Call me old one more time and my dentures will permanently take up residency on yer backside."

Malik tipped his head slightly and arched an eyebrow. "You'd have to catch me first."

Tilly scrunched her face and gave each of them her evil eye. "Don't think fer one second I don't know 'bout yer ridiculous plan."

Lou sent Maggie a questioning look. She pressed a finger to her lips but faked a yawn when Tilly turned toward her.

"I'm gonna say this once, and once only." She looked at

149

Malik. "So, fer those of you who are slow, pay attention."

"Whoa!"

"If the shoe fits, sonny, wear it."

Tilly returned her attention to the whole group. "I know all y'all got some idiotic plan…"

Bella's shoulders fell. Somehow, she must have said or done something for Tilly to know about the party.

"…to make sure somebody's here with me pert near all the time. Let me be perfectly clear. I don't want no dang babysitter. *Cheese and crackers got all muddy!* Stop treatin' me like a baby."

"Cheese and crackers?" Bella whispered to Maggie.

Malik leaned in and whispered in Bella's ear. "It's Tilly's ultimate swear without really saying it."

Bella nodded.

"I ain't six." She turned toward the kitchen window. "I swear, y'all could make the pope cuss."

A snort of laughter escaped from Bella. She slapped a hand across her mouth and clenched her jaw before looking at Malik.

"Stop it." Tilly swiped at her. "What happened b'fore I went to the hospital ain't gonna happen again. So I want y'all to stop hoverin' and leave me the hell alone."

The four conspirators did not move. They cautiously glanced at one another until Tilly pointed toward the entry. "Now git!"

"Oh, you mean, now?" Maggie pointed to the door.

"Yes. Git the heck outta here b'fore I force-feed y'all a bowl of chitlin and roadkill stew."

Bella gagged as she stumbled toward the front door.

Tilly slammed the front door behind them and turned the deadbolt before they ever made it down the steps.

Lou laughed. "Oh, my God. I don't think I've ever seen her that mad."

"I seriously thought you were going to lose your cookies in there." Malik nudged Bella with his elbow.

"So did I." Bella rolled her eyes. "Just last week I asked Tilly what a chitlin was. Just…" Bella gagged. "…thinking…" A second, louder gurgle escaped, and she snapped her mouth closed to keep it from bailing.

"Stop!" Maggie said. "If you throw up, Malik will too. He's a sympathy puker." She jabbed him in the ribs.

He snorted. "Yeah, that didn't go over well in police training or at college parties."

Bella nodded and grinned. "Now I understand why you're still single."

Lou let out a howl so loud, it could have stopped traffic. He bent forward and held his arms across his stomach. The deep laughter echoed through the neighborhood.

"Shut up, Dad!"

But Lou couldn't. Neither could anyone else. Finally, Malik joined them.

CHAPTER 19

Wishin' is for fools

Tilly's birthday dawned bright and sunny. The warmer spring had doused Lawson Beach with an abundance of rain, leaving Bella wondering how the day would play out. The weatherman had called for a sixty-percent chance of morning rain, but they'd beaten the odds. Bella hadn't prayed for a beautiful day, but she'd spewed a promise into the night sky. If the weather for the party were perfect, she would go to church the following day with Tilly rather than drop her at the curb. Based on the sunshine and clear sky, it looked like she was going to have to put up or shut up. Her landlady was going to have a field day walking into church with Bella by her side.

Unable to relax, Bella had risen before the rooster down the street. Truth be told, she hadn't seen the inside of her eyelids for more than a dozen or so blinks each hour. The fluorescent hands of the old alarm clock had taunted her all night long with its inability to speed time. Since the day she arrived at Tilly's, there had only been a handful of nights she hadn't cried herself to sleep. Last night was one of them. Instead of feeling sorry for herself, she focused on giving Tilly the best birthday ever. All their planning would come together in a crescendo in the next six hours or so. Bella could hardly wait.

"Morning, Tilly." She pulled out her landlady's chair and set a hot cup of coffee on the table. Tilly's favorite white chocolate and raspberry bakery scones sat in a basket on the table. Two small jars of orange juice had been placed next to red and yellow poppy plates, a wedding gift from Tilly's mother. The once stylish plates were worn, chipped, and cracked. *If they serve their purpose, they're as good as when they entered the house.* Bella could hear the words as if the old woman were standing in the kitchen chastising her for entertaining the thought they should be tossed out.

"A little birdie told me it was your birthday today."

She whipped three large eggs the way she'd seen Tilly do many times. A pinch of salt and pepper were blended into the frothy mixture before Bella poured them into the sizzling, buttery pan. Bella had never been a cook. Her knowledge of food amounted to deciphering a menu and knowing how long takeout food was edible before it killed you. Before moving in with Tilly, boiling water had been a challenge. But little by little, she was learning. She'd almost mastered the crockpot.

"Well, that little birdie don't know his head from his b'hind," Tilly hissed.

Bella glanced over her shoulder. "Normally, I would agree with you, but I confirmed it with Maggie. And we both know she wouldn't lie."

Tilly dropped into her chair. "That girl oughta learn to keep her dang mouth shut." She took a sip of her coffee and cringed.

"This is your day, Tilly. Prepare to be pampered."

"Pampered, my patootie. Far as I'm concerned, it's just another day. A bigger number'n yesterday. Age don't mean diddly squat. It's not like I did anythin' to be born."

A piece of toast shot out of the toaster and landed safely on the counter with Bella's intervention. She rolled her eyes. How the relic still worked was beyond her. The cloth coating on the cord was frayed, and at least one wire was exposed. Bella didn't know the first thing about wiring, but she knew the cord was an accident waiting to happen.

She screwed a nearly spent pink candle into the middle of Tilly's buttered toast and lit it. She curved a hand in front of the candle and slowly carried the old girl's birthday breakfast to the table.

"Happy birthday to you! Happy birthday to you! Happy birthday, dear Tilly! Happy birthday to you!" Bella smiled at her landlady. "Go ahead. Make a wish and blow out the candle."

"I ain't makin' no cockamamie wish. Wishin's fer fools. When ya b'lieve in the Lord, ya got everythin' ya need."

Bella retrieved her plate from the counter and plopped down opposite Tilly. She sighed loudly. "I just thought…"

"Fine! I'll make a stupid wish." Tilly closed her eyes and went silent for a few seconds. She opened one eye. "Told ya wishes didn't work. Y're still here."

Tilly took a sip of her coffee and closed her eyes again. "Wait! I got 'nother wish. I wish Bella'd learn to make a decent cup of coffee." Tilly opened her eyes and arched her eyebrows. "'Nother wish that didn't work. Ya happy?"

Bella scowled. "Sometimes, you're just mean. You know that?" She picked up her glass and lifted it into the air. "Well, I can be mean too." She cleared her throat and held her juice glass in the air. "On the day you were born, the sun filled the morning sky." She smirked at Tilly. "For the very first time—ever! Happy birthday, old woman!" She tapped Tilly's coffee cup with her juice glass and took a sip.

Tilly glowered at her.

"You asked for it, Tilly. All morning long, I've tried to be nice, but you weren't having any of it." She got up and opened the cupboard where Tilly kept her purse and extracted a small, brightly wrapped package. "I bought you a gift. But, if you'd rather, I can return it."

Tilly studied the box. "Well, it'd be rude if I didn't least open it."

Bella guffawed. "Like that's ever stopped you before."

As she had done with her Christmas gifts, Tilly picked at the tape until the paper opened. Carefully, she peeled the pieces of tape from the shiny paper, smoothed it, and neatly folded it in four.

"Make sure this gits into the wrappin' paper box. I don't wanna find it in the garbage can later," she told Bella.

Bella squeezed the arms of her chair until her knuckles grew white. "Of course, I will. Because, after all, reusing this eight-inch piece of paper will save…what? Like thirteen cents?"

"Obviously, we're very different people, Bella. Y're wasteful, and I'm frugal." Tilly wagged a finger between the two of them. "Which one of us do ya think'd survive another depression? Just 'cause ya won't be around to reuse that paper don't mean I won't."

Bella's face fell. She fought back tears as she stared at Tilly. "That was mean, old woman."

She shoved her chair backward, slamming it into the wall, and stormed from the room.

Tilly huffed. "Don't ya dare pitch a hissy fit, missy. If y're gonna dish it out, ya dang well better be able to take it when it's thrown back at ya."

The ancient door rattled when Bella slammed it. She felt no satisfaction, so she jerked it open and slammed it again. Pressing her ear against the thick wood, she listened for anything that would let her know Tilly was on her way to ask for forgiveness. Bella knew that even in the unlikely event of an apology, it wouldn't be heartfelt. That would anger Bella enough to slam the door a third time—and probably a fourth time.

The few bites she'd eaten sloshed around, causing a storm of revenge in her stomach. Bella's breakfast reappeared almost before she got the toilet lid open. The scrambled eggs looked nearly the same as they had on her plate. She fought through a second wave of dry heaves.

When she was positive her stomach had nothing left to give, she flopped on top of the old quilt in the bedroom. Her visits to the porcelain god happened a couple of times a week now. It wasn't a good sign. She already knew she would lose the battle. Adding the increased puking sessions was just rubbing it in. But it wasn't her cancer that upset her stomach this morning; instead, it had everything to do with the cantankerous old woman on the other side of the door. Bella had tried to give Tilly a perfect day, but the old broad fought her every step of the way. Tilly was snarky and rude, but in the five months since her arrival, she'd never been cruel—until this morning.

Bella rolled onto her side and curled into a ball. She fished her phone from her back pocket and texted Maggie. *Problem. Tilly's in a mood. I'm ticked. Send backup. Can't get her to lunch.*

Instead of hearing from Maggie, a text from Malik appeared within minutes. *Bringing my handcuffs and gun. Be there in a few.*

She got up, stowed a second freshly charged battery in her camera bag, and closed the flap. Bella set it next to the door before heading to the bathroom to brush her teeth. After a quick check of her hair, she pulled on a clean blouse that wasn't peppered with tears. Quietly, she pressed her ear against the door and listened for Malik's arrival. It wasn't more than a couple of minutes before the front door banged shut, and the bickering began. Tilly was in a mood, but Malik stood his ground.

She threw a nylon bag over one shoulder and her camera bag over the other. Lately, she went nowhere without an extra set of clothes and toiletries. The tote was her lifeline. She'd needed it no more than a couple of times, but it had saved her from total embarrassment.

Bella quietly opened the door and stepped into the hallway. A shudder cut through her. Malik and Tilly were waging an all-out war in the living room, neither stopping to take a breath. Malik returned fire as fast as Tilly launched her grenades. With her face aimed toward the floor, Bella crept past the battle and out of the house.

The American Legion was a three-minute walk. Taking the car was counterproductive. It would take less time on foot than to find a spot big enough to park Tilly's tank. Besides, the solitude and the sunshine would burn off her anger. Later, when Tilly decided she'd had enough of the party, someone else could drive the tyrannizer home. After their morning row, she wasn't about to get into the car with that woman—not today, maybe never again.

When Bella stepped into the party room, her jaw nearly hit the floor. Maggie's vision for Tilly's birthday celebration rivaled even the most stylish weddings. Because Bella's days had been spent taking care of the old woman, she hadn't seen the pieces come together. With the bistro closed for the day, Maggie hired their staff to work the party. From decorations to food, everything screamed perfection. A silver, pink, and white balloon archway ushered guests into the hall. White lights sparkled inside the tulle that swagged from the ceiling and around the room. Round tables were topped with crisscrossed silver runners. Pink roses, white jasmine, feathery greenery, and tiny fairy lights sprouted from clear vases on each table, and small mesh bags held chocolate treats for the guests. The crowning glory was the twenty large canvas prints Bella had taken of Tilly. They hung along all four walls.

Bella slowly turned in a circle to take it all in. She wanted to believe Tilly would love and appreciate everything that had been done. But based on their morning blowout, Bella couldn't trust her instincts. Tilly was Tilly; how she would respond was anyone's guess. Hope and reality hung on opposite ends of the spectrum.

Slowly, she wandered the perimeter of the room, stopping to admire each picture. Bella had looked at the photos at least two dozen times but seeing them enlarged made her teary. For the first time, she really saw Tilly. The old broad was beautiful; she almost had an angelic glow around her. But how could someone with such a sharp tongue be so beautiful on the outside?

"She looks so pretty, doesn't she?" Maggie wrapped her arms around Bella from behind. "You did an incredible job with these pictures. She's going to love them."

Bella snorted. "Really? Are we talking about the same Tilly Wilson? This morning, she was beyond horrible to me. All she wanted to do was argue." She stared at a picture of Tilly in the garden. "I swear she could start an argument in an empty house."

"Oh, my God, Bella. Where'd you hear that?" Maggie laughed loudly. "I haven't heard that since…" Maggie dropped her arms and smoothed the front of her dress. "Anyway, that was an old Tilly line."

"Exactly, just not so old. She says it all the time."

Maggie nodded knowingly. "Remember what I told you the first day we met? Tilly's an acquired taste."

"Well, it's been five months. I'm not so sure I like the taste at all. There are a lot of days I'd just as soon chew her up and spit her out. I don't think I will ever get used to her barbaric side."

Maggie looked up at the picture. "You don't have to understand people, Bella. You just have to love them."

Bella nodded. "I get it." She looked around the room. "So,

what do you need me to do?"

"I think we're good. Most of the guests are here. We're just waiting for Malik and Tilly."

The click of the microphone brought a hush to the room. Lou lifted it to his chest. "Thank you for being here. Tilly and my son just pulled into the parking lot. When she walks in, please do *not* yell happy birthday. No one wants to be responsible for her biting the big one on her birthday." Laughter quietly cascaded through the group.

He lowered one palm toward the floor. "Maybe let's just whisper it."

Maggie grabbed Bella's hand and pulled her toward the door. But while Maggie was focused on Tilly's arrival, Bella let go of her hand and slowly slipped deeper into the crowd.

Lou peeked through the doorway. He quickly returned and thrust his hand above his head. Silently, he counted on his fingers. *One. Two. Three.* A loud whisper flooded the room when Tilly stepped through the door. "Happy birthday, Tilly!"

The old woman looked startled. Finally, a smile grew. "Well, butter my butt and call me a biscuit! I can't believe y'all're here to celebrate my ninetieth birthday."

Bella scowled. This was not the Tilly who sat across from her at breakfast—the one who reminded her in no uncertain terms that she wouldn't be around much longer. Who was this woman with the smile and the grateful heart? How had she completely transformed in just a few hours? From her corner of the room, she watched the old gal greet her guests. Finally, she and her landlady stood face-to-face.

"Happy birthday, Tilly," Bella whispered. Every muscle inside her tightened as she leaned in to hug her. The old gal put her hands out and held her at bay.

Tilly released a long breath. "Seems I got up on the wrong side of the bed this mornin'. I don't even know why, but I had a burr in my bum, and I took it out on you. I'm 'shamed of myself." She took Bella's hands. "I hope ya can fergive me. My old lady orneriness was not nice, and fer that, I'm sorry."

A crooked grin lifted one of Bella's cheeks. "Did you just call yourself an *old lady*?"

"Hush-up!" Tilly took Bella's hand. "Ya know, girl, our relationship's like comparin' a fart an'a turd."

Bella tipped her head in confusion. "How's that?"

"One of us is just full'a hot air, but the other's the real deal. Today was the *only* time I was ever the fart."

A grin slid across Bella's face. "I wouldn't say *only*."

Tilly pressed a finger to Bella's lips. "Didn't I tell ya to hush up?"

Bella nodded. "You sure did." She touched the small ruby brooch she'd bought for Tilly from the second-hand store. "I see you wore my gift."

Tilly glanced down at it. "Malik made me."

Bella's eyes narrowed. "Did he tell you about your party?" She studied Tilly's face. Suddenly, her eyes grew wide, and she drew in a sharp breath. "He told you, didn't he?"

Tilly frowned. "Well, course, he did. That boy's mouth is bigger'n his brain. He's such an idiot. I'm pretty dang sure he could throw himself on the ground and miss."

Bella pressed her fist to her mouth to silence a giggle.

Tilly shook her head. "How he got into the police force is beyond me." Her brow furrowed, and she glared at Bella. "If ya tell anybody I knew 'bout this here party, I'll kick yer behind from here to Charleston."

Bella hugged her. "Happy birthday, Tilly. Your secret's safe with me," she whispered. "And I hope that every surprise today makes you smile."

"Well, it dang well better. It's my birthday, and somebody promised me a day of pamperin'."

"It'll happen." Bella hooked her arm through Tilly's and led her to the place of honor.

CHAPTER 20

In my dreams

Bella placed an enormous cupcake in front of Tilly. For most, it could have been dessert for a week. The chocolate cream-filled cake was decorated with white and pink roses. A silver number *90* protruded from the top.

Tilly's eyes grew wide. "Ya think I can eat that whole thing? 'Cause if ya do, you're dumber'n I tell people."

"That's why I brought two forks." Bella pulled them from behind her back and held both toward her landlady.

Tilly plucked one from Bella's hand and pulled the plate toward her. "Then again, if ya think I'm gonna share, ya got another think comin'."

Bella grinned. "And that's why I ate part of Malik's before coming over here." She set her clean fork on the table.

The old gal nodded as she shoved a forkful of cake into her mouth. "Smart."

Suddenly, Tilly fell silent. Her eyes grew wide, and she froze. Bella followed her gaze toward the door. "Who is that man?" she murmured, but she already knew.

Bella quietly sidestepped beyond the table. She wasn't about to miss Tilly's reaction when she came face to face with her first love. Unbeknownst to even Maggie, Bella had tracked down the man's only son.

Tilly's face glowed. The years had slipped away. Her spine

straightened, and she pulled her shoulders back and lifted her chin. Tilly flapped a hand in front of her face. Bella grinned. Goosebumps grew on Bella's arms. After more than seventy years, she could tell Tilly was still very much in love.

A woman in a pale blue dress with a white lace collar pointed toward Tilly. The man's eyes widened. He leaned heavily onto his walker and steered it in her direction.

"Well, well, well. If it isn't Matilda Violet Robinson." The gray-haired man's grin widened as he wheeled closer.

"It's Wilson now. Been Wilson fer quite some time," Tilly mumbled. She never took her eyes from his face.

"It'll always be Robinson to me, pretty lady."

"Charles Isaac Washington, you ain't changed one bit. Y're still the old sweet-talker ya always were." Her eyes sparkled. "Who invited ya to my party? Or did ya decide to crash it?"

The man shrugged. "Don't matter. I'm here 'cause you gotta birthday that needs celebratin'."

Music from Tilly's teen years played in the background. The room quieted as one song ended and another began. The first few notes made Tilly's eyes go soft.

Charles drew a deep breath and held one hand toward her. "May I have this dance?" he asked.

Without the rocking and groaning that always accompanied her launch out of the chair, Tilly stood. She glided toward Charles without the aid of her walker. The once stooped-over man was suddenly a good head taller than he'd been when he entered the room. He gently rested his hand on Tilly's back and took her small hand in his. For nearly three minutes, the couple stared into one another's eyes, never talking, just swaying to the song *Confess* by Doris Day and Buddy Clark. The room went still as all eyes watched them. Bella was positive neither of them even noticed.

"Look at her. It's like she's lost fifty years." Maggie leaned into Bella. "Did you invite him?"

Bella nodded. "Yes. I think I need to confess. There's something you don't know about me." Maggie looked concerned. "I'm an internet stalker." She winked. "Actually, it was something Malik said that made it easy to track down his son. He agreed to bring him today." She pointed toward the front corner of the hall. "That's him in the corner next to Lou."

Maggie hung an arm over Bella's shoulder. "You sure know how to spice up a party, don't you?"

As the song wound down, it was like watching the inflatable air tube people. One minute, Tilly and Charles were standing tall, and the next, they were hunched over, grabbing for their walkers.

After helping the couple into chairs opposite one another, Maggie and Bella joined them at the table.

"Charles, I'm Maggie. I'm…"

Charles nodded. "I know who ya are. Ya don't live in a town this long and not know people." One eye narrowed as he looked at Bella. "But I don't know you."

"I'm Bella, Tilly's boarder." She stood and offered her hand to Charles. Completely unexpected, he planted a kiss on it.

"Nice to meet ya, young lady."

For nearly an hour, Charles and Tilly talked as if the time that passed had been mere minutes instead of decades. Jointly, they relived stories. When Charles lost his train of thought or repeated something, Tilly was there to save the day. Seeing the joy on Tilly's face drove out the darkness of the morning's breakfast fiasco.

Lou appeared with Charles' son in tow. "Happy birthday, Miss Tilly. I'm Charlie." He pointed toward his dad. "I was named after the old man."

"Ya look just like him." She pointed across the table at Maggie.

"This is Maggie, my neighbor. And this young thing is Bella."

Charlie nodded. "I've already met Bella—on the phone. She found me in Charleston."

"Oh, really?" Tilly squeezed Bella's hand under the table as she gave her a quizzical glance.

He laid his hand on his father's back and leaned close. "You doin' okay, Dad?"

"Uh-huh."

Bella wondered how honest Charles was being with his son. His smile had started to fade.

Charlie squeezed his dad's shoulder. "Okay, I'll be back to check on you in a bit. Ladies." He nodded toward them before turning and heading toward the dessert table, where Malik appeared to be testing out every flavor of cupcake.

"So, where ya living?" Tilly asked Charles. "Still in yer folks' house?"

Charles didn't respond. His eyes no longer appeared to be focusing on anyone. He stared at the back wall.

"Are ya still married?" Still nothing. Tilly's brow furrowed, and she glanced toward Maggie.

Maggie cleared her throat. "Is Charlie your only child?" She laid her hand on his arm when he didn't answer.

Finally, Charles shifted his gaze to Maggie. "Nurse," he said slowly, "can ya help me find my room?"

Bella drew a sharp breath.

Maggie took both of Charles' hands in hers. "Of course, I can." Then she jerked her head backward, indicating for Lou to get his son.

"Would you like to tell Tilly goodbye before you go?" Maggie asked.

Charles looked back at Tilly. A toothy childlike smile spread across his face. His words were metered and slow. "I know you."

Bella held her breath as she watched Tilly. Her landlady's eyes were still as bright as when Charles first walked through the door.

"And I know ya too, Charles. I can't never could ferget ya even if I tried."

Charlie, Lou, and Malik rejoined the group. Bella's face slowly began to crumble, and tears threatened to fall. Malik gently shook his head toward her.

"Okay, Dad. Let's get you back home."

Lou took one arm and Charlie took the other. Together, they pulled the old man to his feet. Malik positioned his walker in front of him.

Suddenly, he turned and smiled at Tilly. "Sometimes, I see ya in my dreams," he said slowly.

Tilly smiled. "I dream 'bout ya too, Charles."

Then the men were gone.

"Oh, Tilly." A few tears broke free and trickled down Bella's cheeks. "I'm so sorry. I didn't realize…"

The old woman pressed her forehead against Bella's. "Don't ya be sorry fer one minute. This was the best birthday gift I ever got. Ya gave me somethin' I never thought I'd ever have again." She closed her eyes in an extra-long blink. "We only had a short time today, but it was more'n I ever expected. Thank you."

"Thank you," Maggie mouthed to Bella when she pulled away from Tilly. She tapped her finger over her heart. "Thank you," she whispered.

"Tilly," Maggie said, "I have another surprise. Your daughter sent a gift. Would you like to open it?"

For the second time in just over an hour, Tilly's face lit up. "Well, does a bear crap in the woods?"

Bella frowned with confusion.

Maggie left and returned with a shallow white cardboard box. Maggie's name and address had been written on the outside, but a note on the bottom indicated the gift was for Tilly. No return address had been included, just the word *Jasmine*. The package was postmarked Virginia Beach, Virginia.

Bella hoped beyond hope there was something in the box that would heal Tilly's heart. Jasmine was supposed to be here, but the mailed gift told them she wasn't coming. Her heart ached for Tilly.

Maggie lifted the end of the tape enough for Tilly to peel it off. Then, she set the box on Tilly's lap. The flaps popped open once Tilly removed the wide tape. She reached in and plucked a wad of crumpled tissue paper from the top of the box and set it on the table. Inside appeared the back of a picture frame. Tilly gingerly lifted it from the package and held it in her hands for several seconds. Bella knew she was imagining who might appear in the frame: her daughter, the two granddaughters she'd yet to meet, or a son-in-law she'd only imagined into existence. Slowly, Tilly flipped the frame over.

Bella's heart sank. For the second time that day, her stomach churned, threatening to expel everything she'd downed in the past few hours.

The frame was devoid of pictures of Tilly's family. Instead, the bogus couple who graced every similar frame across the entire country mocked her.

"Oh, Tilly, I'm so sorry," Bella said quietly.

"Why?" The old woman blinked several times. "Ain't nothin' wrong with it. It's a perfectly good frame."

Maggie snatched the box from Tilly's lap and looked inside. "There's a card."

She handed the envelope to her and made eye contact with Bella.

Tilly pried the flap of the envelope up and opened the card.

Almost instantly, she closed it and laid it on top of the frame. Bella picked it up and tipped it toward Maggie. All it said was *J.* It contained no birthday message, no personal greeting. It was just a single letter.

The old woman drew a deep breath. Her shakiness wasn't lost on Bella.

"Well," Tilly finally said, "this cake ain't gonna eat itself."

As Bella handed Tilly her fork, she noticed the old woman swipe at a lone tear.

***

An hour later, Malik drove Bella and Tilly home. Maggie and Lou had stayed to clean the hall.

"Anybody hungry?" he asked as he got Tilly settled into her chair. "I can go grab some dinner or I could whip something up in the..."

"None fer me," Tilly said firmly. "And keep yer grubby hands outta my kitchen."

Bella gently shook her head in his direction.

"Well, how about we watch some TV, then?" Malik grabbed the old remote and pressed the *power* button.

"I'd rather have me some quiet."

Just as quickly, he pushed the button again, darkening the screen of the bulky old TV.

Malik dropped onto the couch next to Bella. Side-by-side, they watched Tilly.

"Are ya gonna sit there and stare at me all night? It's annoyin'. But if ya are, I'd just as soon go to bed." She snapped the footrest down.

Malik held his palm outward toward Tilly. "Fine. We won't look at you." He shifted on the couch to face Bella.

"You can go," Bella whispered.

"You sure?"

"Yeah. It might be better."

"There ain't no *might* about it," Tilly grunted.

"Well, okay, then, I'm going to head out." Malik stood and stretched. "I'm going now." He watched Tilly. "Here I go. I'm really leaving." He pointed toward the doorway.

"Go!" the women said in unison.

Malik pressed his hand to his heart. "Wow! A guy sure can tell when he's not wanted."

"'Bout time ya learned to read a room," Tilly yelled as Malik walked into the kitchen.

After the front door shut, Bella dropped onto her knees next to Tilly's chair. "I'm so sorry, Tilly. Nothing about today went as it was supposed to. Breakfast was a disaster. Thanks to Malik, the party wasn't a surprise. I had no idea about Charles' memory loss." She sighed. "And your daughter was supposed to be at the party—not send some cheap drugstore frame. I feel sick about the whole day."

Tilly sighed loudly. "Bella, ya gotta learn ya can't control everythin' life hands ya. You, of all people, should know that sometimes things happen that ya can't understand. It ain't our place to figure it out." She laid her hand against Bella's cheek. "We can't expect people to be anythin' more'n they are." Suddenly, Tilly picked up her knitting and held it toward Bella. "Sometimes people are like this. We poke 'em and twist 'em into what we want 'em to be, but from time-to-time, things happen—a needle breaks, ya got yerself a bad thread, or ya drop a stitch—and everythin' b'gins to unravel. It ain't part of *our* plan, but…" She shrugged. "Anyway, nothin's perfect. There's a bigger plan out there, and we can't change it. We just gotta accept it."

The old woman knit a couple of stitches before returning her work to her lap. "And fer the record, I had a very nice day. When y're ninety, ya wonder if anybody ya used to know is even still breathin', let alone remembers who ya are." Her eyes grew soft. "And as for Charles, like I told ya b'fore, I had a moment I never thought I'd have again. Fer that, I'm grateful."

The woman continued to knit. "And Jasmine? Well, I learnt a long time ago ya can't change anyone but yerself." She smiled at Bella. "One day, my daughter'll realize she's missed out on a lifetime with me." Tilly shrugged. "I might be gone by the time that happens. But either way, I still love her."

CHAPTER 21

Bonus days

Ribbons of color from the stained-glass windows of the small white church bled onto the sidewalk. Bella stopped on the walkway, frozen. A sign to the right of the building read *African Baptist Church of Lawson Beach*. She wasn't fixated on the sign; it was the arched double door that bothered her. Once she stepped a foot inside, she was admitting she'd been wrong about there being a god.

People veered off the sidewalk and around the two women. Finally, Tilly pushed her walker onto the grass and pulled Bella out of the traffic.

"What's got yer undies in a bunch? Does it bother ya it's an African church? There are other churches in town if that's..."

"No." Her eyes narrowed, and she gently shook her head. "That's not what bothers me. It's the *church* part—the God part."

Tilly's shoulders dropped in frustration. "I didn't ask ya to come." She shuffled toward the door. "You were the one who insisted ya needed to be here today."

Bella caught up to her and hooked her arm through Tilly's, making it difficult for her landlady to use her walker. But Bella didn't care.

"You ain't gotta come in." The old woman pointed to the sky. "God's out here the same as inside."

Bella shook her head. "I have to. I promised."

"Promised who? God?" Tilly walked through the door with Bella firmly attached. "The good Lord ain't gonna love ya no less if ya don't keep yer word. He don't like it none, but he ain't gonna fight ya on it."

Tilly led the way toward the front of the church. She left her walker in the aisle, pulled tightly against the wooden panel on the end of the bench. Clutching the top edges of the third pew, she maneuvered her way through the narrow passageway just far enough to leave Bella a spot to sit. The old seat creaked as she dropped onto it. Bella quickly sat next to her. Her body folded inward as if she were trying to hide.

Several people greeted Tilly. Belated birthday wishes from those who hadn't been able to attend her party were abundant. While Tilly visited, Bella stared at the cross. She hadn't been in a church since she'd lived with her last foster family. There had been nothing left to believe in back then. Her parents were gone, and no one had wanted her for more than a few months. No god was going to change those circumstances. People didn't just come back from the dead.

Yet somehow, being here today was different. Bella hadn't come because she was forced to; she was there to fulfill her promise for the perfect weather on Tilly's birthday. But more than that, if she was honest with herself, it was really to beg Tilly's god for a favor.

Suddenly, live gospel music began to play, and several people robed in burgundy and white danced up the center aisle and into three short rows in the front of the church. The choir sang with a commitment Bella had never seen. It wasn't the church music of her foster days. This music was powerful, like a concert. Within minutes, members of the congregation began leaping up. They joined in the singing and clapping. The elderly, like Tilly, remained seated but were no less part of the celebration. There were only two other white women in the entire church. Even they were on their feet. Bella was the lone holdout.

When the song slowed, a minister appeared at the podium. He was a big man who quieted the room with only his presence. Evoking the rockstar in him, he jerked the mic from the stand and moved with purpose toward his flock.

"Praise the Lord!" His voice boomed, but he wasn't hollering. Power and excitement radiated from him and spread through the church. The more excited he became, the more engaged his congregation was. People called out *Amen* and *mmm-hm* when something touched them. Their hands waved in the air as if they were trying to touch Tilly's god.

Finally, Bella began to relax. The unknown had been what she'd feared the most. From what she'd read about southern churches, she'd expected fire and brimstone, punishment over love. Smiling inwardly, she drew a deep breath and focused on her needs.

If the old woman's god was here, he should hear her when she spoke to him. She closed her eyes. How did one talk to someone they couldn't see? Was she supposed to introduce herself? Or did he already know her name? Maybe it was like therapy where you laid out your problems, and the therapist listened and asked questions. Perhaps this god already knew her issues. Finally, she drew a deep breath and let her vision go still, dark. After curling her thumb and index finger on each hand into a perfect circle, she rested them on her thighs and continued to breathe deeply and slowly, waiting for the ideal moment to address the being Tilly referred to as God—*thee* God.

The pastor grew louder. Bella heard the increase in volume, but she had moved so far inward that she didn't recognize his words. Her internal conversation had begun. She laid her requests before the being she didn't actually believe in. Even in her deep state, she knew she wasn't praying. She was begging.

"Amen!" The woman directly behind her stood up and bellowed it again. "Amen!"

Startled, Bella jumped out of her seat and responded with the exact word she shouldn't have said in a church. "Jesus!" she screamed. Her hands shot into the air, and her heart thudded inside her chest. Eyes wide, she dropped onto the bench and shrank down behind a woman with an oversized hat.

"Yes!" The pastor pointed at her. "Feel the love of Jesus! Let him speak to your heart."

Tilly slapped a hand over her mouth to silence the laughter that threatened to explode. Her shoulders bounced up and down. Bella crossed her arms and glared at her.

"Just shut up, old woman," she hissed quietly. "That wasn't funny."

"Oh, yes it was." Tilly folded herself forward and laughed silently.

Finally, when her convulsions eased, she slid away from Bella, leaving a space for an extra-wide person between them.

"What are you doing?" Bella whispered. She was keenly aware of several pairs of eyes peering at her. It wasn't because she was the palest person they'd ever seen in their church; it was because she had doused herself in stupidity.

With an eyebrow arched and her chin tucked down, Tilly glanced at the space between them. "I'm makin' sure I keep my distance in case God's fixin' to strike ya down where ya sit."

The old woman started laughing again. She swiped at the tears that streamed down her cheeks. Finally, she straightened, drew a deep breath, and moved back toward Bella.

Bella could no longer pay attention to the god Tilly professed loved her no matter what. If he did, why had he allowed her to make a fool of herself? No, she had to stay vigilant; she couldn't embarrass herself again. So, when the music started again, and the congregation were on their feet, she escaped.

Once the double doors swung shut behind her, she drew a deep breath and slowly released it.

"That bad, huh?" Malik was lying on the grass, propped on one elbow. He had a dopey grin on his face. Bella had come to know that look well over the past several months.

"Why are you here?" she grumbled.

"Mom told me you were going to church with Tilly this morning. We made a bet about whether you'd make it through the whole service. I figured I'd come down and see if I won." He winked at her. "Looks like I did." He stood and brushed off his backside. "How bad was it in there?"

Bella's mouth slid sideways as she contemplated her faux pas. "Well, you know when you're thirteen, and you do something so incredibly stupid, like so stupid that not only does everyone laugh at you all day long, but you're the butt of the joke for the next several months?"

"Yeah." The grin widened on Malik's face

"It was a million times worse than that."

"I think you're exaggerating." He started toward the bus bench at the corner of the church lot.

Bella followed. "I'm not. It really was that bad."

Traffic moved slowly along the street. Malik locked his fingers behind his head and stretched his legs out in front of him.

"So why *did* you go to church anyway?"

Bella shrugged. "Because I promised Tilly's god I would."

Malik turned sideways, rested an elbow on the back of the bench, and cradled his head in his hand. "Bella, He's not *Tilly's* God. He's God. Period."

A loud huff exploded from Bella. "If he's God, *thee* God, then why doesn't he cure me? Why is he letting me die?"

Malik considered her questions for a few moments. "Bella, you can't look at life that way. When things happen, we learn from them. Maybe it's not fair to you, but someone else is growing because of what you're experiencing." He touched his chest. "I'm better because of you and what you're going through."

Bella got up and stood in front of Malik. She looked up. "Knowing you're going to die is like knowing the ending of a book before you even start reading it."

"True, but don't you think we all know the end of our story? I mean, come on. we're born; we die." He leaned forward and rested his elbows on his knees. "It's what we do with the in-between days that's called living."

Bella slowly circled the bench. She kicked at a clump of grass as she passed behind Malik. "According to the doctor, I have two hundred and eleven days left. And that's if I'm *lucky*." She nearly spit the last word. "*Lucky!* If I were lucky, my cancer would disappear. Or I would never have had it at all. Lucky isn't an extra day or two or even a week or a month more. It's living your whole life—the one you expected when you were twelve. *College. Jobs. Marriage. Kids. Grandkids.*" She bit her lip. "And then you die."

Malik pulled her onto the bench. "Let me try to explain something to you. Most prisoners with short-term sentences count the days until their release. It makes sense. At some point, they'll have served their time and can return to their life." He watched Bella. "But those who receive a life sentence with no possibility of parole know they aren't getting out, so they often wallow—being miserable day after day." He paused. "That's how you're looking at your time. You're seeing it as a miserable existence—life without parole."

The breeze was cool. Bella pulled her sweater tighter around her, folded her arms across her chest, and dropped onto the bench. "Why wouldn't I? That's exactly what it is. I don't see how it's any different."

"It's not, Bella. But what you're doing is putting yourself in a self-created prison cell, feeling sorry for yourself rather than realizing you're free to live out the rest of your days however you want. You have something those prisoners don't have—freedom." Malik frowned. "Okay, so you have two hundred and eleven days left, right?" He raised his eyebrows. "If you're lucky. Stop thinking of them as days marching through your life sentence and start thinking about them as…*bonus days.*"

Bella scowled at him. "Bonus days?"

Malik wrapped an arm over her shoulder. "Your doctor could very well have said you had six months or three months or a week to live. No, he…"

"She," Bella corrected.

"*She* gave you a year. That's more than some and less than others. But every minute of that time is *yours*. Stop wasting it."

Bella leaned her head on Malik's shoulder and stared at the closed flower shop across the street. They sat in silence for a long time.

"When I was with one of my foster families, the dad brought home a huge bouquet. There was no special occasion. He just wanted his wife to know he loved her and that she was important to him. The flowers didn't last long, maybe a week. Every time the mom walked by them, she'd smile." Bella sat up. "Finally, the flowers died, and my foster mom threw them out. But for weeks afterward, whenever she walked by the counter where the flowers had been, she'd still smile." Bella stared at Malik. "I always wondered why. Then, one day, I got the courage to ask her. Do you know what she told me?"

Malik rested an ankle on his opposite knee and shook his head.

"She said it wasn't the flowers that made her happy; it was

the memory of the day her husband brought them home—that he had done something so special for her. She knew he wouldn't remember surprising her with those flowers a year from then. But what she said next has always stayed with me. *We don't do things for ourselves. We do them so others will always have the memory, know how much we cared.*" Bella's eyes lit up. "Seeing Tilly with Charles yesterday was incredible. It was a gift Tilly will always carry with her." She poked a finger into her chest. "I did that."

Malik twisted his face in thought. "And how exactly does this relate?"

Bella rolled her eyes. "Keep up. Life isn't about the memories we keep; it's about ones we leave for others."

He made a face and shrugged. "Still lost."

"You called them *bonus days*. So, I have two hundred and eleven bonus days to give memories to others—memories they can carry around their entire life."

Malik shook a finger at her. "Yeah. That's what I was trying to tell you all along."

Bella swiped at him. "No, you weren't. You aren't that deep."

"Ohhhh. Hit a guy while he's down, why don't ya?"

"Okay, you helped me connect the dots. I'll give you that."

Suddenly, there was a loud commotion behind them. People were still singing and clapping as the church doors flew open.

"Thank you, Malik. I've been looking at the time I have left all wrong."

He stood and pulled her up with him. "Well, you know me—always willing to help."

Bella grinned. "Let's go find Tilly."

Holding hands, the two moved into the churchyard. Tilly finally appeared at the door, but she stopped to talk to a middle-aged man.

"Do you know who that is?" Bella asked.

"Yeah. It's Martin Tindall." He turned his head toward Bella. "And it looks like you're going to meet him since he and Tilly are both headed this way."

"Malik." The man extended his hand. "Haven't seen you since…yesterday." He chuckled.

He offered his hand to Bella. "Marty Tindall."

"Hi." Bella could feel her cheeks grow red. She was sure this was about her *episode* in church.

The man laid a hand on Tilly's back. "Tilly tells me you're the one responsible for those incredible pictures at her party yesterday."

"I am. Yes." Her brows furrowed together in question.

"Oh, don't look so suspicious." Tilly tapped the back of her fingers against Bella's arm. "Martin, here, just wants to ask ya a question."

"I have a gallery downtown. Every month I host a series of new South Carolina artists—painters, photographers, sculptors, and the likes. Your work is spectacular. I really want to include you, but I don't have an opening until July. Would you be interested?"

Bella looked from Tilly to Malik. She had no idea if Martin knew she was dying.

Malik held a finger in the air. "Hold on one second, Marty. I need to speak to Bella about something."

"Sure." He winked at Bella. "Tilly and I have lots to talk about. Maybe she can shed some light on what happened in church today."

Bella's shoulders dropped, and she shot Tilly a warning look. "If she knows what's good for her, she'd better not."

Malik grabbed Bella's arm and pulled her a good fifteen feet away. "Make memories, Bella. Yes, there's a possibility you may not be around in July, but others will. Make memories for *them.*"

Bella stared at him for a brief second. "You're right." She nodded. "You're right."

"Mr. Tindall," she called, "you've got yourself a photographer for your July showcase."

He clapped his hands together. "That's wonderful! But call me Marty, please. Tilly's the only one who calls me Martin, and my pa's the only one who gets called Mr. Tindall." He smirked. "Come down to the gallery tomorrow afternoon and we can talk specifics." Marty smiled at Tilly. "You got yourself one heck of a talented roomie, Miss Tilly."

Tilly's eyes were soft when she looked at Bella. "She's more like a granddaughter," she said.

Bella tipped her head to the side. "Ah, thanks, *Grandma*," she teased.

Her landlady touched Marty's arm. "But clearly, she ain't learned how to b'have in church yet."

Bella rolled her eyes while Marty roared with laughter explaining to Malik about her *Jesus* moment.

CHAPTER 22

The garden

An early morning storm rumbled overhead. Bella had hated night storms for as long as she could remember. When she was young, comfort and understanding were what she craved during a squall; ignored was what she got. When thunder shook the penthouse, she'd sought solace in her nannies. Their solution: a makeshift bed on the floor of their room. Her foster families showed even less compassion. For several nights, after her parents died, intense storms goaded her—inside and out. It was then that she realized how alone she was.

Bonus days. Bella had spent the night thinking about her conversation with Malik. For the second night in a row, she hadn't fallen asleep in a puddle of tears. Instead, she had lain awake long into the night, considering ways to make memories for other people.

Her *One year, if I'm lucky* countdown had been folded and tucked inside a t-shirt that once belonged to her mother. She turned on her bedside lamp and removed the page. The first number read 365; the last was 1. A black X cut through each number that had passed. The likelihood she'd see the number 1 was anyone's guess, but based on how her body failed her daily, she wouldn't bet on it.

Slowly, she ran an index finger over all three hundred and sixty-five numbers. The last one was the day before her birthday. She sucked in a deep breath and slowly released it before drawing a large black X across the entire page.

Bella jumped as a sharp flash of lightning and an immediate blast of thunder shook the house. Her window rattled long afterward. She closed her eyes for a few seconds before flipping the paper over. On the top, she wrote *Bonus Days*. Then, she added a single tally mark below the title. This was the first of an unspecified number. It was impossible to tell how many days she had left.

She ran her palms across the folded paper, flattening the creases. This was her reminder to make memories for others—ones that would last a lifetime—someone else's lifetime.

*** *** ***

For the next several weeks, Bella spent her afternoons visually eavesdropping on Tilly in the garden. The small recorder had been an enormous success. Only a single word here or there floated within range of Bella, but the expression on Tilly's face was worth every bit of crap the old woman had given her when she opened the gift.

A few afternoons each week, Maggie or Malik would stop by and sit with Tilly while Bella searched for extraordinary photos for her debut—*and swansong*—at the art gallery. Tilly had finally given in to the idea of never being left alone.

On Sunday mornings, with Tilly at church, Bella had ninety minutes of freedom. She drove up and down the streets of Lawson Beach, seeking opportunities to make a difference for someone. Within a couple of weeks, she'd settled on a plan.

It was a sunny day in early April when she asked for Tilly's blessing. The azure sky stretched to the edges of the earth, reflecting across the ocean. Everything was a month ahead of schedule this year. It was the March showers that brought April flowers. The warm days allowed Tilly to spend more time in her garden, clearing up the twisted illusion James had fabricated for their daughter.

After watching Tilly from the living room window for nearly an hour, Bella mustered the courage to present her proposal to her landlady. She walked in front of Tilly and curled up in the *daisy* chair.

"What?" Tilly set the recorder on the stone table next to her chair.

Bella bit her lip as she glanced around the garden. "Well, I was thinking."

Tilly leaned forward slightly, waiting for her to finish her thought. Then, finally, she sat up. "Well, clearly, ya ain't got the brain power it takes to think."

"Sorry." Bella chuckled. She slowly swung a hand across the huge garden. "What do you do with all these flowers?"

Tilly's forehead wrinkled, and she steepled her fingers. "B'sides sit here and enjoy 'em?"

"Well, yeah. But you and I are the only ones who ever sit out here, though. Sometimes Maggie comes over, but usually, it's just us. So, I was thinking, what if…" She stood and picked a hot pink, star-shaped flower from a plant and held it toward Tilly. "What if we shared them with other people? What if we cut bouquets and sold them on the street?"

Tilly snorted. She crinkled her nose and frowned at Bella. "Why on God's green earth would we do that? I don't need no money, and you certainly don't seem to."

Bella's head bobbed slightly in all directions. "True. But what if we donated the money to someone who did?" She studied Tilly's face, trying to read her expression. "I mean, there's a man who stands on the corner down the street almost every night around suppertime. He seems to need money. Sometimes he has his young son with him, but most of the time, he's alone."

"Nate Percy." Tilly picked up her lukewarm coffee and took

a sip. "His ma worked fer me at the café. She never worked a day in her life 'til then. Her husband up and ran off. Poor woman didn't have no choice." She took another sip and emptied the rest of the cold coffee on the ground. "That boy sat in the corner of the restaurant while his ma worked. Reminded me of me and Jasmine way back." She stared at the chair to her right before looking back at Bella. "Didn't matter how old he was, he was quiet as a grave." Tilly yawned. "He got married right outta high school. His son was born a few months later." She raised her eyebrows. "Guess ya don't need to speak much to make a kid."

"Tilly!"

"I'm just sayin'. Ya don't need a lotta words to get neked." Bella shook her head.

"Anyway, his ma died not long after his kid was born." She set her cup back on the table. "He tried to keep the mortgage paid up on her house, but the bank took it back right quick. Last I heard, they'd moved into a rundown trailer out behind the Pig."

"The Pig?"

"The Piggly Wiggly. The grocery store."

"Yeah. I got it."

"The boy ain't had an easy life."

"So, he'd be a great person to help, then. The flowers would make people happy, and the money would help…"

"Nate," Tilly finished.

Tilly took inventory of her garden. Many flowers were in full bloom. Others were just beginning to show their colors.

The old gal sighed loudly. "Well, fer one thing, I'm too dang old to do that kinda work. In case ya ain't noticed, I got 'bout as much energy as a UFO."

Lines folded across Bella's forehead. "UFO? Like the ones in the sky?"

"No. *Unidentified flattened object.* Ya know, all those dead animals on the side of the road that ya got no idea what they was? UFOs."

Bella's head bobbled. "Well, I'm probably too sick to take this on too, but I'm not going to waste my bonus days. I want to use them to help someone else."

"What in tarnation did ya just say?" Tilly questioned. "Yer *bonus days*?"

She folded her hands. "The days I have left."

Tilly uncrossed her arms. She slowly scanned the garden again. Finally, she nodded. "Okay. But don't expect me to help none."

Bella sat upright. "Awesome! I just need you to tell me which flowers will last if I cut them. I don't know a flower from a weed."

Tilly arched an eyebrow. "I ain't got no weeds growin' in this here garden."

Bella winked. "I got it, old woman. No weeds in your garden."

"It really gits my tail up when ya call me an old woman. I got half a mind to paddle yer backside with a switch."

The corners of Bella's mouth turned upward. "First of all, you'd have to actually get out of that chair without help."

Tilly's eyes narrowed, and her jaw tightened. "When I set my mind to somethin', ya got no idea what I'm capable of, girl. I can tell ya this, though. You're moving full speed toward my *don't press your luck* button."

That sucked the smile right off Bella's face.

* * *

The following morning, Tilly returned to her garden chair without her recorder. Bella followed her landlady's directions—cutting, arranging, and tying flowers with curly paper ribbon she snagged from the living room closet. Tilly had

185

told her where to find a box of glass vases in the basement. After filling a half-dozen with just enough water to keep the flowers hydrated, she hauled an old folding table from the garage and set it up on the sidewalk in front of the house. An old lace tablecloth lay across the table. The previous evening, after they had talked about prices, Bella printed a sign on a yellowed piece of tagboard. Today, she attached it to the front of the table.

To capitalize on traffic, Bella opted to sell in the late afternoon, hoping to catch the after-work crowd. By 4:00 p.m., she was open for business. Several cars passed before one finally stopped. A few minutes later, a man noticed the woman getting into her car with a bouquet and pulled in as she drove out. Within an hour, she'd sold every bouquet.

For the first time since she started the sale, Bella glanced back at Tilly. The old woman had said she wouldn't help. Clearly, she meant physically. She'd spent the afternoon in the shade of the big tree, barking directions every few minutes.

Bella handed the cash-filled envelope to Tilly before lugging the vases into the house and the table back to the garage.

"Not a bad haul for a day's work." Tilly closed the envelope. "Ya made $125." She nodded toward the young man holding the cardboard sign on the next block. "Nate'll appreciate it."

Even as busy as Bella had been selling flowers, she was acutely aware of his presence. From a block away, she could tell he was not happy she'd invaded his territory.

"I'll sit here and wait while ya take the money down to him."

Peering over the top of her sunglasses, she drew a deep breath. "Not yet. I'm going to wait until the end of the week."

Tilly tipped her head. "What makes ya so sure he ain't gonna need the money today?"

Bella sighed. "I'm not. But just because I want to do it differently than you do, doesn't make it wrong." Bella shoved Tilly's walker in front of her. "Do you need help getting up?"

"No." Tilly rocked until she gained enough momentum to stand. She wheeled toward the house. "Sometimes ya ain't playin' with all yer marbles." She shook her head. "I don't git ya."

"You know, Maggie once told me you just have to love people. You don't have to understand them."

"Well, Maggie should keep her dang, fool mouth shut."

***

As the week progressed, Bella cut, packaged, and sold more flowers each day. New varieties opened, and with Tilly's blessing, Bella turned them into beautiful arrangements.

Between sales, she watched the man on the corner, holding his small cardboard sign, waving it in the air as cars drove past, stopping to buy flowers instead. When that happened, Nate often kicked at the sidewalk or punched his hand through the air.

On Friday, Bella sold out in thirty minutes. Tilly had given up her supervision of Bella's sale. Instead, she kept company with a pair of knitting needles.

Once Bella cleaned up, she returned to the house with the last envelope of the week. She opened the cupboard where Tilly kept her purse and removed a thick stack of bills. Carefully, she counted and arranged them into like denominations. With today's take, Bella had over nine hundred dollars.

Finally, she sat down at the table and wrote a note on a sheet from Tilly's yellowed notepad.

"Tilly, I'm heading down to talk to Nate," she called. She folded the letter, tucked it into the envelope with the cash, and shoved it into her backpack. "Please stay in your chair until I return. I shouldn't be long."

"Yes, mother," she grumbled.

Bella rolled her eyes as she headed out the door. She turned right at the edge of the yard and headed toward the corner. A car stopped, and a woman flapped a bill out her window. Nate nodded to her and tucked it into his front pocket.

She had no idea why, but her heart began to race, and her cheeks burned as she crossed the street. Nate turned toward her. From his expression, it was clear he recognized her.

"Well, if it isn't my competition," he said. "You seemed to do well this week."

Ignoring his comment, she held out her hand. "Hi. I'm Bella."

Nate stared at her and tucked his hands under his arms. He raised an eyebrow and jerked his head slightly sideways. "It seems people are far more interested in buying flowers than helping someone down on his luck feed his family."

She pulled the envelope from her bag and held it toward him. "Well, I'm not one of those people."

Nate shifted his eyes from Bella to the white envelope and back to her.

"Here." She straightened her elbow, moving the money closer to him. "This is for you." Nate just stared. "It's all the cash I earned this week—nine hundred and twenty-five dollars."

Nate swallowed hard. "Why are you doing this? Is this a guilt thing? Did old Miss Tilly shame you into giving it to me?"

Bella looked up and sighed loudly. "First of all, don't let her hear you call her *old* or, in her words, *she'll tan your hide and kick your backside from here to kingdom come.* Second, this wasn't her idea. It was mine."

His face remained somber.

"I asked Tilly if it'd be okay to sell flowers out of her garden to help you and your family." Bella stepped closer to him. The envelope touched his chest. "So, take it."

"Why would you do that?" He took half a step backward.

Bella shrugged. "From time to time, we all need a hand. Maybe one day, you'll help someone else."

Nate's hand shook as he reached for the envelope. He opened the flap and stared at the thick wad of bills.

"Th-thank you." Nate looked down. "This is so much more than I could have collected in an entire month of standing on this corner."

A weak grin tugged at the corners of Bella's mouth. "Tell you what. Next week, you go home and spend time with your family. On Friday, I'll bring you the money I earn."

Nate's eyes grew wide, and his mouth dropped open. "Are you kidding me? You're going to do this again?"

Bella shook her head. "Tilly told me you've been down on your luck for a while now. I just want to help."

"Why? I know I keep asking that, but…"

"I told you. Everybody needs a little help sometimes. Today, it's you. Tomorrow, it might be someone else."

Nate slowly shook his head. "I can't believe this. I've been working two jobs for over a year now. In between, I stand out here for a couple of hours. Best corner in town." His eyes grew glassy. "The thing is, even with two jobs, I can't stay caught up. My wife lost her job when she got sick. And my son, Jacob, is growing so fast, we can't keep him in clothes or food." He looked at Bella. "You have no idea how much this means to my family."

"Then it's about time you get a break. I'll drop off the money next Friday. Tilly told me where you live."

Nate looked as if the air had been knocked from him.

Bella touched his arm. "Go home, Nate." She turned to walk away but spun back around. "See you Friday."

On the way back to Tilly's, she smiled. *Okay, God—that I*

still don't know if I believe in—that was how I used a week of bonus days. I hope you're happy.

Brightly colored chalk drawings on the sidewalk drew her attention. She hadn't noticed them on the way because she'd been so focused on Nate. A small pink heart nearly jumped off the sidewalk. The word *yes* was written inside. A shiver ran down Bella's spine.

CHAPTER 23

Wrong or different?

The night before, Tilly had been perfectly clear. They were to walk out of the house at precisely 6:00 a.m. The old woman wasn't about to miss the sunrise Easter service. It didn't matter that the sun wouldn't wake up for three-quarters of an hour after they were to leave. What Tilly said was gospel. Just ask her.

Bella hit the snooze button one too many times. When she finally climbed out of bed, she had barely enough time to tug on a pair of worn leggings and a sweatshirt and make it to the door before her landlady.

Tilly ran her eyes up and down Bella. She tsked several times, obviously judging everything from her uncombed hair to the blue flip-flops.

"Ya look like somethin' the cat dragged in. Please tell me ya ain't plannin' to attend church on this holiest of days lookin' like a stray."

"After last time, I'm never going to your church again."

Tilly harrumphed. "We'll see."

The old gal shoved the screen door open with her walker. She propelled it along the new ramp Lou and Malik had installed shortly after her birthday. One ramp ran along the front of the house and into the yard, and a second one curved around the back, into the garden. It had been their birthday gift, albeit loudly unwanted. Tilly let them know in no uncertain terms that *she didn't need no old person ramp.*

The weeklong event had sent Tilly into a tailspin like nothing Bella had seen. She sat in a rocker on the porch and raucously insulted Lou and Malik. While the men worked on the ramp, she hurled one brickbat after another. *Stop wreckin' my house b'fore I squeeze ya so hard, yer eyeballs'll pop out! Ya ain't got but three brain cells 'tween the two of ya. I ain't too old to kick yer arses! Did y'all wear yer belts so tight, it cut off the circulation to yer brain? Cheese and crackers! Get the barnacles outta my yard! If they gave points fer stupid, you two'd be the grand prize winners!* And Bella's personal favorite—*In a crap factory, you'd be the head turds: Captain One and Two.* Bella had to give it to her. Tilly could string together the most entertaining insults. If Bella was going to be around into old age, she would have borrowed from Tilly's library.

Except for an occasional snicker, the men ignored every word. When the ramp was completed, the complaints finally stopped. The first time the old gal wheeled down it, she almost smiled—almost. She'd never admitted the ramp was the perfect gift, and she'd never uttered a thank you. But then again, no one expected as much.

Bella took the stairs and waited for Tilly to meet her. The sky smoldered purple and blue with a line of orangish-gold just above the horizon. A few high clouds peppered the sky off to the east, far out over the ocean.

The church was a half mile away—too far for Tilly to comfortably walk. One time, Bella had suggested taking the wheelchair, but Tilly was an obstinate and vain woman. If looks could kill, Bella would have been dead on the spot. Even the walker made the old gal uncomfortable. So, after the wheelchair dispute, Bella never mentioned it again. Instead, she said nothing as she loaded Tilly into the old Ford Fairlane and headed through the dark streets.

When Bella pulled up in front of the church, the same two elderly women who always assisted Tilly were waiting at the curb.

"Cutting it a little close today, Miss Tilly," the younger of the two scolded. "Church is already mighty full."

Bella unfolded the walker and set it in front of her landlady.

"Well, whose fault do ya think that is?" Tilly looked directly at Bella.

"This isn't on me. I was at the door when I was told to be." Bella helped pull Tilly out of the car.

Tilly clicked her tongue. "Well, if ya'd keep yer goldarn mouth shut and not talk to me in the mornin', we wouldn't be runnin' late."

Bella exchanged a smile with Gladys, the older of the two women. She wore a black and white floral dress with a red belt and a white hat. Her purse, almost a twin to Tilly's, hung from a gloved hand.

"We saved you and Bella a seat." As Tilly had done earlier, Ruth, the younger woman, gave Bella a once-over.

"Sorry. I can't stay. I'll be back to pick her up after church. Will the service be longer than usual?"

Ruth looked at her watch and again at how Bella was dressed. "How 'bout we bring Miss Tilly home after church? That way, ya don't have to bother yourself by showin' up here when the church empties."

Bella clenched her jaw and swallowed hard. "That would be very nice. Thank you."

Like a group of old Saint Bernards, the three women lumbered toward the church. Neither of Tilly's friends was significantly younger than her. Bella stood on the sidewalk until she heard the music burst out of the propped open doors.

She looked up. "I'm here," she said to the great beyond. "I

came. I'm not going in, though. You'll just have to deal with that."

***

After a quick shower, Bella headed to the garden with four cheap plastic eggs. Each had a name scrawled across it. Wandering the garden, she chose strategic places to hide them. Unfortunately, Tilly didn't have the wherewithal to be able to search for her egg, so Bella placed it inside a flowerpot she set on the *jasmine* chair.

Once satisfied with her choices, she went into the house and hid the four Easter baskets. Each plastic egg gave them a clue about where to discover their surprise.

No one loved tradition more than southerners. Judson had shared that. Easter eggs and baskets were a tradition they held on to. Since Bella wouldn't be around to stuff Christmas stockings, she opted for the baskets instead.

A wave of rich, savory smells washed over Bella as she walked into Maggie and Lou's kitchen after hiding the baskets. Her nose tilted upward, and she sniffed multiple times.

"Oh my gosh! It smells amazing in here. What are we having for dinner?"

Lou grabbed a glass dish from the oven and set it on the granite countertop. "Pineapple casserole."

"What?" Bella's nose crinkled.

"Oh, you'll love it." Malik tugged his t-shirt over his head as he walked into the kitchen.

"Okay, I'll, ah, have to trust you on that one." Bella stared into the pan. Suddenly, she shifted her attention to Malik. "Wait. I thought you had an overnight shift."

Malik yawned. "I did. Got home a while ago. I'm exhausted, so if I drop face-first into my plate, leave me there. I'll eat when I get hungry." He winked.

Maggie set a mixing bowl on the island. "If you want

breakfast, there are some rolls on the dining room table."

"Ma also made some deviled eggs." Malik coughed.

"Oh, I love those. One of my foster moms used to make them all the time. They were the best."

"They may not be…"

Malik cut his mom off. "Yeah, they may not be as cold as you're used to."

"It doesn't matter." Bella rubbed her hands together. "I could eat a dozen of these myself."

Bella plopped down in a chair and grabbed a small plate from a stack. She studied the tray before choosing the largest egg. Malik poured a glass of milk and inched it toward her.

She pointed to her plate. "No thanks! This is all I need." Bella held the egg in front of her face.

Half of it made it into her mouth before she bit down, dividing it in two. Within three chews, her mouth flew open, and the partially ground egg spewed onto her plate. She grabbed the glass of milk and sucked it down.

"More," she mouthed. Bella grabbed the glass before Malik finished pouring.

"What in the hell was that?" she asked.

Lou and Maggie leaned against opposite sides of the dining room doorframe. Lou laughed loudly.

"I tried to warn you," Maggie said, "but Malik had other ideas." She slapped her son across the top of his head.

Bella poured more milk. "What is this?'

"Those are southern deviled eggs. The tabasco gives them a bite." Lou disappeared into the kitchen.

He returned with a plate of six half eggs. He set them in front of Bella. "These are for you. Northern deviled eggs."

Bella looked at the plate. "And why should I trust you?"

Malik grabbed a spoon from the table and handed it to her. "Taste it."

Bella poked the spoon into the yellow mixture. After several stops and starts, she finally touched it with her tongue before shoving the spoon into her mouth.

"This is what a deviled egg is supposed to taste like."

She picked up the egg and bit it in half. Thoroughly enjoying it, she slowly chewed and swallowed. "Why would you ruin deviled eggs by adding tabasco?"

"They're not ruined, Bella. They're just different. We like ours with tabasco, sweet pickle relish, and Durkee sauce. Is it wrong? Or just different?" Maggie watched her.

Finally, she grabbed one of Bella's eggs and took a bite. "I appreciate the northern eggs just as much as the ones we make." She ate the other half. "You know, if *different* wasn't judged as wrong, we'd have a lot less hatred in the world."

Bella's cheeks started to burn. "Wow. Wow," she said again. "I just realized I'm a big part of the problem. I'm not racist because of how I feel about you—but I'm biased because I judge what's different rather than accept and embrace it—period." She sucked her upper lip into her mouth. "I feel terrible."

Maggie kissed the top of Bella's head. "No, honey, not racist. You love us unconditionally. But sometimes words and thoughts—and judgments—drive us apart rather than bring us together."

Bella sighed loudly. "I wish I'd been told that years ago."

Lou slowly nodded. "I'd be willing to bet you were. You just didn't *hear* it."

"You're right." Bella frowned.

Malik shoved one of the hot eggs into his mouth. Bella noted his eyes never watered—not even when he ate the second half.

"It's like the pineapple casserole you turned your nose up at. You didn't even try it before you decided it wasn't your thing. I mean, it's hard not to like. It's got buttery crackers and cheddar cheese in it." Malik rubbed his stomach. "I could pretty much eat anything."

"Ain't that the truth?" Maggie said.

Bella smiled as he shoved another southern deviled egg in his mouth.

Maggie shook her head. "Now, there is something wrong with this boy, plain and simple. And since I'm his mother, I have the God-given right to judge him."

Maggie slapped Malik on the back when he choked on an oversized bite. "See?" She laughed.

***

"I'm fuller than a tick on a big ol' dog," Tilly proclaimed. She pushed her dessert plate toward the center of the table. "Grandma's coconut cake never gets old."

"That was your grandma's recipe?" Bella asked.

Maggie grinned. "Bella, down here, everyone's called Grandma or auntie or uncle." Maggie shrugged. "But I suppose it was *someone's* grandma's recipe."

"Got it. I should know that by now." She pointed to herself. "Slow learner here."

"You're not slow, Bella. Everybody has their own traditions and foods. I noticed you had seconds on the pineapple casserole."

Bella's face turned pink. "It was a whole lot better than it sounded." Finally, she waved a finger in the air. "Speaking of traditions, can we go next door? I have a surprise."

"Ooooh," Malik moaned. "Do I have to get up?" He stared at Bella. "Can't you just go get it?"

Maggie tapped her son with the back of her fingers. "A walk would do you good, son."

"Will we be long?" Lou asked.

"Not really." Bella felt her heart skip a beat. "It should be

197

pretty quick."

Maggie glanced into the kitchen. "Let's just leave things sit for a bit, then. We can take care of them later."

Tilly raised an eyebrow.

"My house, my rules, Tilly. Stop judging, old woman."

Bella led the way across the lawn and into the garden. Lou and Maggie flanked Tilly, ensuring she didn't take a header.

The short trip and full stomach had exhausted her landlady. Once they reached the backyard, she fell into her chair.

"This garden is still so gorgeous—even with all the flowers you've sold the last couple of weeks. How's that going, by the way?" Maggie asked.

"Really well. I took Nate another seven hundred dollars last week. I delivered it with three bags of groceries and an Easter basket for his son, Jacob."

Lou squeezed Bella's shoulder. "You're a good person, Bella."

"Thanks." For the first time in a long time, Bella felt seen.

"Okay, so here's the deal. This is an Easter egg hunt. You each have one plastic egg hidden somewhere out here."

"Not much of a hunt," Malik whined.

"Pipe down, boy. Let her finish." Tilly nodded to Bella.

"So, inside your egg, there's a clue that'll lead you to a basket hidden somewhere in the house. Once you figure it out, go get your basket and meet back here for the big reveal."

Malik took off but reappeared almost instantly. "How will we know it's our egg?"

"Your name's on it. If you find someone else's, don't give it away."

Everyone disappeared into the garden except for Bella and Tilly.

"Ya might as well tell me where my egg is 'cause I ain't gettin' outta this chair."

Bella smirked. "I figured as much." She waved a hand across the garden. "Your egg is sort of hidden in plain sight of your chair. You should be able to see it—sort of."

Methodically, Tilly scanned the garden—left to right, up and down. Finally, she noticed the flowerpot on the *jasmine* chair. "What's that?" she asked Bella.

"What?"

"That pot." Tilly pointed to the chair. "It wasn't there b'fore. Bring it to me."

Bella reached inside and extracted Tilly's purple egg and handed it to her. The old gal opened it, unrolled the paper clue, and read it aloud.

Breakfast. Lunch. Dinner. You use this often. It's a winner.

"Oh, fer the love of Pete. That's too easy."

Bella twisted her mouth and turned her head. "Is it, though?"

"'Course, it is. It's my crockpot."

"Really? You really think so?"

The others had already gone inside. Malik and Lou were back with their baskets. Maggie wasn't more than a minute behind them.

"I ain't gonna go git it, so just tell me," Tilly grumbled.

"Okay, it's not your crockpot." Tilly poked a finger in the air and opened her mouth, but Bella cut her off. "And it's not *my* crockpot—which you *never* use."

"Read the clue again," Malik insisted.

Tilly read it aloud.

Lou offered the fridge, and Maggie suggested somewhere near the sink. Bella continued to shake her head. Malik grew uncharacteristically quiet. Finally, he grinned at her and disappeared into the house. A few minutes later, he returned with the basket and set it in Tilly's lap.

"Where in the world was it?" Tilly lifted it and peered

inside.

"What do you use every day? Every meal? Silverware, right? But the basket wouldn't fit in that drawer. And speaking of that drawer—that never shuts…"

Bella watched Tilly's wheels spin. "The hammer? It was in the cupboard with the hammer?"

Bella nodded. "Yeah. I figured I'd throw you off with your crockpot."

Malik had already dug into his chocolate and was trying to make trades from his mom's basket. But Maggie wasn't having any of it.

"So, in your Easter basket, I added something special for each of you. Malik, you go first."

"Gladly!" He tore open the footlong package and stared at the wooden sign before holding it up for others to see. It read *Bonus Days*. He smiled at Bella. "This is perfect. Every time I look at it, I'll think of you."

"I know," Bella teased. "That's the point."

"Maggie, you're next."

Maggie removed the paper from a small black velvet box. Inside was a silver cross. "Bella, it's exquisite."

"You and Malik have both told me that it's not just Tilly's god. He belongs to everyone."

"Oh, fer cryin' out loud. I been tellin' ya the same dadgum thing fer months," Tilly snorted.

Everyone laughed.

"Tilly, you can't let anything go, can you?" Lou smirked at her.

"Maybe I'm finally starting to hear it." Bella touched Tilly's shoulder.

"About dang time."

Bella grinned at Lou. "Your turn."

Lou pulled a wallet from a box. "Thanks. A guy can always

use a new wallet."

"It's not about the wallet, Lou. Open it."

He flipped the leather billfold open and found two photos inside—one of Maggie and a second of his son.

His jaw dropped open. "When did you guys pose for these? They're great pictures."

Maggie and Malik surrounded Lou. "We didn't." Maggie looked at Bella. "When did you take these?"

"At Tilly's party. You all looked so nice."

"Especially me." Malik laughed.

Bella ignored him. "I just happened to get the perfect shots."

"This is wonderful!" Lou smiled at Bella. "Thank you."

Bella pulled another photo from the pot Tilly's egg had been in and handed it to Maggie. "And here's one of Lou. I thought you might like one of him also."

"They look so professional. Can we get enlarged copies for the house?"

"Already done. They're in my bedroom. I figured you'd want them."

Maggie hugged her tightly.

Finally, Bella turned to Tilly. "Okay, your turn."

Tilly took a flat package from her basket before handing the wicker container to Bella. She laid it on her lap, picked at the tape, looked up at Bella, and ripped the paper in two.

"Finally!" Bella giggled. "You're learning."

Tilly held the five-by-seven photos in front of her. She appeared confused.

"Those are pictures of Jasmine and your granddaughters, Aliyah and Kiara."

Tilly's face went slack; her eyes grew misty. She mouthed her granddaughter's names.

"Where'd ya get these?"

Bella released a deep breath. "Well, I struggled to find them because I didn't know the girls' last names. So I hired a private investigator. When he found them, he snapped some photos, but they weren't very clear. Once I had names, I searched the web until I located their pictures. The girls own a small cosmetics company, so they weren't hard to find. Their names are on the back so you can tell them apart."

She pulled a folded sheet of paper from the same pot that had housed Tilly's egg. "I located Jasmine before your birthday. That's how she knew about your party." Bella looked down. "Anyway, she's a physician's assistant in Virginia Beach. She works at a clinic there. Once I knew that, it made it easy to find a photo of her. This is the PI's report. It has addresses and other information you might find interesting." Bella handed the paper to Tilly.

Maggie stepped behind Tilly and looked at the photos as the old woman paged through them repeatedly. "Bella, this is so incredible."

Tilly never took her eyes from the pictures. After a few minutes, she blindly reached toward Bella. She squeezed her hand.

"I-I don't know what to say. I ain't got no words to thank ya fer bringin' my family back to me."

Bella kissed her landlady's cheek. "You just did, Tilly."

CHAPTER 24

Fertility rituals—May Day

Bella woke with a stiff neck. Her tongue had a thick film that reminded her of dirty gym socks. She sat on the toilet seat, leaned forward, and massaged her neck. Sleeping on the bathroom floor hadn't been her plan. One slightly damp towel had served as her pillow, and the second as a blanket. Her first choice would have included a good night's sleep in a comfortable bed, but she'd been afraid she'd be too far from the toilet.

Bella hadn't told anyone she was getting sicker. Although she didn't know how they couldn't see it just by looking at her. The circles under her eyes were darker, and she'd lost more weight. If she confessed too much, she was confident Tilly would move into her room. Her landlady believed being ninety entitled her to have an opinion about everything. The last thing she wanted was to have her landlady critiquing her puking technique. It was bad enough that their rooms were now adjacent to one another. Tilly would find out sooner or later. She always did.

The windows were open, and a chorus of birds serenaded her from the big tree out front. The brilliant sunshine and the alarm clock told her she'd slept through breakfast. She closed one eye when she stepped into the bright kitchen.

"Rough night?" Tilly asked from behind the newspaper.

Bella rubbed her eyes with her fist. "You could say that."

She poured herself a glass of juice and sat down at the table.

Tilly shook the paper out and folded it along the creases. Once the sections were stacked neatly, she eyeballed Bella. Her brows rose so high, they nearly melted into her hairline. "Hoowee! Ya look like y've been through a month of Sundays and a goat ropin'."

"I don't even know what a goat roping is, but if I look like that, it must be bad." Bella laid her forehead on the table; her arms fell to her sides. "Let's just say it wasn't one of my better nights."

Tilly hoisted herself up and shuffled to the stove. She turned on the tea kettle and dug through a cupboard. Minutes later, she set a steaming cup in front of Bella.

"Peppermint tea. Helps with the nausea."

The sharp aroma of peppermint rose with the steam. "I've never been a tea person." Bella leaned over the cup and drew in the crisp mint scent.

"It don't matter if ya like it or ya don't. Drink it. Ya'll feel better." Tilly pushed the cup closer.

Bella slowly sipped the tea. Each time she swallowed, she pressed her tongue to the roof of her mouth and scrunched her nose. Tea wasn't her thing, but it had done precisely what Tilly had foretold. Twenty minutes later, Bella downed a hardboiled egg and a cold strip of bacon.

"Sounds like somebody's feelin' better," Tilly called.

Bella looked toward the empty doorway, expecting to see Tilly standing there. "How'd you know?" she called loud enough for the old woman to hear her.

"Oh, Bella, I got better hearin' than an elephant with an ear trumpet. I can hear a dog take a dump on a pillow two miles away. Ya ain't figured that out by now?"

Bella uncomfortably chuckled. If that was true, had Tilly

heard her last night?

"Remind me not to talk about you behind your back."

"Oh, don't think I ain't heard everythin' you and Malik have ever whispered about me."

Bella rolled her eyes as she bit into a second egg. After last night, she hadn't thought she'd ever eat again, but Tilly's tea had changed her mind.

Ten minutes later, the old gal appeared in the doorway with her walker. A heavy canvas bag hung over her shoulder. As she wheeled toward the table, the bag slid down her arm and nearly threw her sideways.

"Do you know what tomorrow is?" Tilly asked. The bag made a thud when she dropped it on the table.

Bella pursed her lips. "Ahhh, May first. As I recall, May always follows April. Unless they changed it this year."

"Don't get fresh with me or I'll be shovin' this bag where the sun don't shine." She sneered at Bella. "Fer yer information, it's May Day."

"May Day," Bella repeated. "What's May Day?" She chewed the last bite of egg.

Tilly clicked her tongue. "What do ya mean? What's May Day?"

Bella frowned. She'd come to recognize that click as Tilly's disappointment in her. It was always followed by some snide remark or life lesson.

"Didn't nobody teach ya nothin' when ya was growin' up?"

Bella picked up her phone and held it in the air. "We have these things called phones. I can look up anything I want to know."

"Pffft! Cellphones-smellphones. I can tell ya everythin' ya *need* to know." Tilly gently tapped Bella's hand. "Put that thing away. I'll give ya the Tilly version of the day."

"That's what I'm afraid of."

"Pooey! I went to school when ya actually had to keep things in your noggin." She pointed to her head. "Pure and simple, May Day's a celebration of the changin' of the seasons. Stupid people tried to make it 'bout everythin' else—includin' some foolish fertility rituals with the May pole and a wreath." She raised one eyebrow and stared at Bella. "It's beyond me why anybody'd wanna take a fun day and make it disgustin' like that."

Bella's eyebrows knit together, and her eyes narrowed. Suddenly, she grinned. "Ohhhh. *Male. Female. Pole. Wreath.* I get it."

"Now, get that disgustin' thought out of yer head." Tilly waited. "Down here, we celebrate the true meanin' of May Day. We make May baskets and hang them on people's doorknobs."

Bella snorted. "No matter how you say it, all I hear is that male/female thing."

Tilly's jaw tightened and her lip quivered in anger. "Get yer mind outta the gutter." The old woman looked at Bella. "Back when I was just a wee bit of a thing…"

"Did they even have doorknobs back then?" Bella interrupted.

"Listen here, girl. There's miles of nerves in the human body and right now, y're hangin' on every one of mine. So hush yerself up, or I'll do it fer ya."

Tilly's stare was uncomfortable. "Go ahead." Bella nodded. Her face had gone expressionless.

"As I was sayin', when I was young, ya hung a May basket on the door of somebody ya were sweet on. Then, they'd come out'n chase ya. If they caught ya, ya had to kiss 'em."

A howl exploded from Bella. She slapped the table. "No-no matter how you look at it, it's a day about *doing it*, isn't it?"

Tilly slapped the table too. "Ya, hush up! Y're as full of wind as a corn-eatin' horse. And no, it ain't about *doin' it*. Git your mind outta the gutter."

After a few seconds, Bella clenched her teeth to stop laughing. Finally, she drew a deep breath and exhaled slowly. "Okay, so what is it you want us to do?"

Tilly extracted a stack of foil and white doilies from the bag and set them on the table. Then she upended the bag to expose a handful of fuzzy bendable sticks, an ancient tape dispenser and stapler, some half circles of yellowed tagboard, some faded strips of construction paper, and several feet of ribbon and lace in a variety of colors.

"And?" Bella leaned back and folded her arms across her chest.

"And you and me's gonna make May baskets. Tomorrow, we'll be leavin' 'em on folks' doorknobs."

A slight squeal escaped through Bella's clenched teeth. "Still sounds…"

Tilly angrily cleared her throat.

"…like fun." Bella punched a bent arm through the air in front of her. "But how in the world are you ever going to keep yourself from getting caught if someone chases you?" Bella howled. "I can just picture you fighting some hundred-year-old guy off with your walker."

Tilly frowned at her. "*I'm* not." She pointed to Bella. "You are."

Bella shook her head. "No! No way. I'm not doing that."

"Oh, fer the love of Pete. Don't be such a wet blanket."

Bella planted her hands on the sides of the table and stared at the foil paper. "Fine, but I want something in return. If I hang them on the…" She grinned at Tilly. "…*doorknobs*, you're going to drive."

Tilly's face was deadpan. Finally, she pulled out her chair and dropped into it. "Fine with me." She shrugged nonchalantly. "Ya got yerself a deal."

Ninety minutes later, a dozen small, cone-shaped baskets, and a large nontraditional one, lined the kitchen counter. After lunch, Bella drove Tilly to Sweet Cheeks Candy Store.

Bella hooked a bright red plastic shopping basket over her arm and trailed behind Tilly. The old woman searched for candy for the small baskets, while Bella selected larger items for Nate's son, Jacob. Modern candy, chocolate, and miniature toys were her choices. On the contrary, Tilly narrowed in on sweets from her youth—old-fashioned candy sticks, necklaces, and buttons seemed a must. She also added taffy, Chuckles gummies, bubble gum cigars, and anything that evoked memories.

"How much candy do you think those little cones hold anyway?" Bella shifted the basket higher on her arm.

"This ain't my first rodeo. I done it b'fore. Just carry the basket and keep yer lip buttoned."

Without a word, she placed Tilly's purchases on one side of the plastic container and hers on the other. When they got to the register, she removed her items, explaining to the clerk there would be two separate sales.

Tilly poked her in the ribs. "Put 'em all up there. Ain't no reason to make the poor woman do double the work."

Bella shrugged. "O—kay." She placed all the items on the counter and returned the basket to the stack by the door.

"Thirty-seven dollars and twenty-nine cents," the woman announced.

Bella waited for Tilly to open her wallet; the old gal kept her hands folded across her stomach and her purse tucked into the crook of her arm. The clerk looked from Bella to Tilly and back. Finally, Bella pulled two twenties from her back pocket and handed them to the woman behind the counter. She shoved the change in her front pocket, picked up the two plastic bags, and headed toward the car ahead of Tilly.

"You think you're pretty funny, don't you?" Bella said as she drove out of the lot.

"Give it up, Bella. God don't like ugly."

***

At ten the following morning, Bella backed the car out of the garage and turned it around, front end to the street. While Tilly grabbed her sweater and scarf, Bella loaded the May baskets into the back and covered them with a blanket to keep things from blowing around. Then she climbed into the passenger's seat and waited. The addresses of the recipients lay in the center of the bench seat.

At the bottom of the ramp, Tilly stopped and stared at Bella. She knew her landlady didn't think she'd hold her to the deal, but Bella had no problem playing chicken with the old woman. Bella pointed her thumb toward the driver's door. Finally, Tilly tucked her head down and wheeled that way. She folded her walker, awkwardly hoisted it into the backseat, and climbed behind the wheel.

Without looking at her landlady, Bella dangled the keys toward her. Tilly sighed loudly and snapped the keys out of Bella's hand. The old gal turned the key and started the engine. After a few moments, she adjusted the rearview mirror. She untied and retied her scarf and checked her lipstick in the mirror. Between each step, she glanced toward Bella. Finally, she shifted the old convertible into gear and waited. Once again, Tilly looked at Bella.

"Don't play dumb with me." Bella pointed at the gear stick. "Put it in *drive*."

Tilly twisted her mouth and shifted into *drive*. She straightened her back and stretched her neck to see over the steering wheel. Bella wondered how she'd ever driven such a big car when the dashboard seemed to block her view.

Tilly studied her feet. She kept her left foot on the brake.

Cautiously, she pressed her right foot down on the gas pedal, lifting her left foot only partway. The engine raced as the car lurched forward and came to an abrupt stop at the end of the driveway.

Bella swallowed hard but showed no expression. "Well," she said, pointing to the street, "go ahead."

Tilly stared straight ahead. Her hands clutched the thin steering wheel, holding tightly at ten and two.

"Fine," she hissed. "Ya win. I can't drive no more. Does that make ya happy? Ya made me look like a fool."

The air rushed out of Bella, and her body collapsed inward. She closed her eyes before turning toward her landlady. "Oh, Tilly. I'm so sorry."

She threw her door open and helped her landlady from behind the wheel and into the passenger's seat. Then, she rearranged the baskets, sliding them behind the driver's side. When she crawled into the car, she just sat there. Finally, she reached over and laid her hand on Tilly's.

"I never meant to make you feel bad because you can't drive." She shook her head, admonishing herself for playing such a childish game. "I was just getting back at you for yesterday at the candy store."

Tilly said nothing. Instead, she turned and stared out her passenger's window.

Bella's eyes stung as she pulled onto the street and turned right, heading toward the far end of town.

"Tilly, please forgive me." The old gal still didn't respond.

The car purred as Bella drove through town. Tears rolled down Bella's cheeks, and her stomach twisted in knots. She sniffed and brushed away the droplets before they reached her sweatshirt. Tilly's shoulders bobbed up and down as she gasped for air, sobbing uncontrollably.

Bella's heart broke for Tilly. She hadn't meant to hurt her.

All she'd wanted was to beat her at her own game. She eased the car to the side of the road and shifted into park. She slid across the seat and rested a hand on her landlady's back, again trying to apologize. Finally, Tilly turned toward her. She howled with laughter.

"What the hell?" Bella said, giving Tilly's shoulder a shove. "What in actual hell?"

"Oh, my goodness, Bella!" Tilly swiped at her face, wiping away the tears. "Ya should see yerself. Y're sweatin' like a hooker in church." Her entire body shook with laughter.

Bella moved across the seat and squeezed the steering wheel. "Why would you do that?"

"Ahhhhh." Tilly took a deep breath. "Again, the winner. Ya don't mess with somebody as old as me. I been 'round the block more'n a few times."

Bella stared at her. "I have so many things I'd like to say to you right now, but…"

"But ya ain't gonna. So let's quit piddlin' 'round. These baskets ain't gonna deliver themselves."

After shifting into drive, Bella pulled onto the street. She tightened her mouth and peeked at Tilly several times before her scowl morphed into a grin.

"You suck, old woman. You know that?"

Tilly glowered at Bella. "Call me an old woman again and I'm gonna cream yer corn."

Bella laughed. "That I'd like to see."

***

Bella parked the old convertible next to the rundown trailer. She grabbed Jacob's May basket and a thick white envelope from the backseat.

"I'll just be a minute."

She knocked on the door. A young boy in a torn shirt excitedly threw the door open and stepped onto the small porch.

211

He wrapped his arms around Bella's waist, nearly knocking her down the stairs. Bella bent forward and handed him his basket.

"Happy May Day, Jacob."

The young boy jumped up and down. The candy and small toy cars hopped around in the basket.

"Ma, look! Bella brought me a May Day basket."

Destiny pressed her hands on his shoulders. "I see that, buddy."

She poked her head out the door and waved toward the car. "Good to see you, Miss Tilly."

Tilly nodded.

"Who's that?" Jacob asked as he waved to the old woman.

"That's Tilly. She's sort of like my…*great grandma*." Bella smiled at him.

Jacob studied Tilly for a few seconds. "What makes her so *great*?"

Bella and Jacob's mom laughed. "Well…" Bella looked at Tilly. "I'll get back to you on that."

Jacob shrugged and sat on the tiny deck. He dug through his basket, ignoring the adults.

Bella handed the envelope to Destiny. "I just wanted to drop off this week's money."

"Thank you," Destiny said. She pressed the envelope to her chest. "You have no idea how much this has changed our lives."

Bella nodded. "I'm glad. You deserve a break."

She bent over and hugged Jacob. He planted a wet kiss on her cheek. "I love you, Bella," he said.

Her stomach flip-flopped, not because she was nauseous, but because she'd just gotten something she never thought she would—the pure love of a child.

"What was in that envelope?" Tilly asked as Bella backed onto the dirt drive.

"Cash." She checked traffic and turned left toward home.

"But ya didn't sell no flowers this week. We decided the garden needed a rest."

"I know. But that doesn't mean they didn't need the money."

Tilly sat in silence as Bella drove. Finally, she snapped her purse open and pulled two twenty-dollar bills from her wallet, holding them tightly, lest they be sucked away by the wind.

"I think I owe ya," Tilly said, handing the money to Bella.

Bella grinned as she grabbed the bills from Tilly's hand and shoved them into her back pocket as she drove.

"Winner!" she whispered.

Tilly sighed. "Just get me home soon. I gotta pee so bad, my eyeballs're floatin'."

CHAPTER 25

Not once had she been truthful

The sun had dropped below the houses behind Tilly's. Daylight would soon turn to dusk, and the remnants of light would fall to darkness. After leaving the bistro, Bella had begged Tilly to sit outside with her for a while. They were each draped in a thin blanket. As always, Bella's camera hung around her neck, ready to capture the perfect shot of the full moon. The weatherman had promised a cloudless night. He wasn't wrong.

A tiny spark of white flashed in front of Bella, then a second and a third. She lifted her camera, hoping to catch another in the darkening sky.

"What are these things?" She moved her camera through the air, trying to predict the next flicker.

"Fireflies?" Tilly chuckled. "Ya ain't never seen a firefly?"

"Well, yes, but what exactly are they?"

"Bugs." Tilly shrugged. "I don't know the fancy-schmancy reason fer why they glow. I just know they're flyin' bugs that light up. Some folks call 'em lightnin' bugs." Tilly tucked her hands beneath her blanket and watched Bella snap several pictures against the jasmine garden.

"Didn't ya have 'em in New York?"

"Out in the country, yes. Not in the city. Too many lights. I mean, I've heard of them, but I've never actually seen one."

Bella got up and followed the flashes around the garden.

"Help me inside." Tilly threw her blanket off and rocked back and forth until her bottom reached the front edge of the chair.

"Why?" Bella whined. "I thought we were going to sit out here and watch the moon."

Tilly huffed. "I ain't got time to sit 'round and watch ya chase bugs."

Bella helped the old woman up. "Really? What else could you possibly have to do?"

"Stuff," Tilly replied. "I got important stuff to do."

After settling Tilly into her recliner in the living room, Bella returned to the garden. The light of dusk had vanished, leaving a deep bluish-black backdrop. A white glow bled onto the dark canvas sky around the moon. A few fireflies continued their dance, but it was the moon that grabbed Bella's attention.

Bella changed her lens and snapped several pictures. Without clouds to add interest to her photos, the moon was nothing more than a glowing ball. She dropped into Tilly's chair and looked up. Her heart skipped a beat. Kneeling on the walkway, she shot several pictures. It wasn't the moon that made her photos interesting; it was the angle and shadowy objects she captured against it. Within thirty minutes, she'd snapped a hundred or more photos, each with a shadowy twist.

Laughter cascaded from the living room when she walked through the front door.

"Tilly, you must be going deaf. I've never heard the TV that loud before," Bella called from the kitchen.

When she rounded the corner, she was surprised to see the neighbors.

Bella glanced around the room. "So, having a party without me was one of the important things you had to do?" She set her camera on top of the old box TV.

The old woman shrugged.

"Tilly tells us you've never seen fireflies before," Maggie said.

"I've only seen them in books and online." She frowned at her landlady. "Is nothing sacred?" Tilly ignored her dig.

Bella looked at Maggie. "They're kind of amazing! I got a few pictures. Here, let me show you." She picked up her camera and clicked through pictures to find the shots of the glowing bugs.

Malik grabbed her camera. "How many fireflies did you see?"

"Hmmm. A half dozen or so." She grabbed for her camera, but he held it out of reach.

"Suppose you could see thousands of fireflies—all flashing simultaneously?"

"Where?" Bella was doubtful. "Is there some little firefly convention going on somewhere?" She smirked.

Lou cleared his throat. "He's not kidding, Bella. Every year between the middle of May and mid-June, they gather in Congaree National Park. They go there looking for a mate. That's why fireflies flash. In small numbers, they flicker randomly, but a large group will all flash simultaneously. They're called synchronous fireflies. We've all seen it. We thought you might like to see it." He shrugged. "It's so popular that you have to enter a lottery to get in. Maggie enters every year. We won again this year." He winked at his wife. "I told her she was gonna get *lucky* last week."

Maggie swiped at Lou.

"Y'all got the dirtiest minds I ever did see. Try actin' a little more mature rather'n like yer pickled outta your mind."

Bella heard nothing Tilly said. Her eyes twinkled with excitement. "That sounds incredible." She looked at Tilly. "Can you imagine the pictures I could get for my gallery show?"

Malik shrugged at his dad. "Well, that's why Tilly suggested it." He looked down. "But—I want to make sure you're up for the trip. There's a two-and-a-half-mile trek out to the best viewing spot. And to get the best pictures, that's where you'll want to be. They don't allow wheelchairs or strollers, so you have to be able to walk it."

Bella's shoulders fell and her smile faded. "Tilly could never walk that far."

"Pish-posh." Tilly waved her hand at Bella. "I've seen 'em b'fore. You and Malik can go."

Bella's chest inflated with excitement but deflated nearly as fast. She shook her head. "I can't leave you."

Maggie pursed her lips and nodded. "I figured you'd say that. So—I'll stay here, and Malik'll take you. You can spend Saturday night and drive back on Sunday."

Bella looked at Lou. "But what about the bistro? I know Maggie only works the morning shift, but if she's here with Tilly…"

"Bella, you worry too much. You let me deal with the schedule. I have people." Lou put his hands in the air. "And my people have people." He laughed.

"And when did this plotting start?" Bella scanned the room, stopping at her landlady.

"As soon as ya got me in this here chair. Well, in the garden, actually." Tilly smirked.

Bella turned toward Malik. "I want to go. But are you okay taking me?"

Malik frowned. He dropped his head back and looked toward the ceiling. "I don't know," he whined. "I'd probably have to hold your hand in the dark and help you up when you trip over your own feet. And I'm sure I'd have to buy you dinner." He tilted his head and looked at her. "It's an awful lot of work." Slowly, he gave her a lopsided grin. "Of course, I'll take you. I love seeing the fireflies. I'll especially enjoy seeing them through your eyes. Sometimes you're kind of like a little kid. You get so excited about everything."

Bella punched him in the shoulder. "Isn't that how you're supposed to live life, old man? At least that's what Tilly tells me."

"Hey! Watch it. I'm only five years older than you."

Tilly snorted. "And now ya know how it feels to be called *old*."

"Don't even." He gave her a hard stare. "There's a huge difference between twenty-eight and someone born in the Stone Age."

A magazine flew across the room and landed near his feet. "If I wasn't so dadgum comfortable in my chair, somebody'd be gettin' a butt whoopin' with that magazine."

Malik gave her a half-smile and stood. "How about I come to you?"

Tilly raised an eyebrow and bared her teeth. "Sit yer fanny back down on that couch and shut yer trap."

He pressed his lips together, pretended to zip them. Then he tossed an imaginary key over his shoulder.

"Oh, if it was only that simple," Tilly grumbled.

***

At 7:00 a.m. Saturday morning, Malik walked into Tilly's kitchen. "What's for breakfast?"

"For cryin' out loud, boy. The least ya coulda done was give me a heads up you was comin' for breakfast."

Malik pointed a thumb over his shoulder toward Bella. "Well, the least you could have done is feed me for taking this one off your hands for a couple of days."

Bella jumped up and grabbed the carton of eggs from the fridge. "Tilly taught me how to make a mean omelet. Do you…"

He held a palm toward her. "I'm kidding, Bella. Ma fed me enough to last until…well, lunch."

Malik poured a cup of coffee and sat down at the table. The steam rose as he blew into the cup. "So, Tilly, what are you going to do without Bella?"

"Enjoy some peace'n quiet. Nap in my chair without somebody wakin' me up to ask me if I'd sleep better in bed."

"Oh, I can do all those things. It'll be like Bella never left." Maggie stepped into the entry. She set a small overnight bag on the bench. "By the way, son, thanks for carrying this over here for me," Maggie said sarcastically.

He shrugged. "Well, you know what they say. Muscle building's good for old people."

Maggie huffed. "I think you and Bella'd better get out of here before I smack you with that bag."

Malik made a face. "Crap! I ticked off the old lady."

"Watch yer mouth." Tilly glowered at him.

Malik pushed his lips outward and tried to see them. "It's kind of hard to do without a mirror. But I was thinking…"

Tilly shook her head. "Boy, if ya ever had a thought, it'd die of loneliness. Now git b'fore I regret my decision to give ya my car when I die."

Malik jumped up. "Yes, ma'am. Yes, Miss Tilly. I'm going right now." He raced out the door.

Bella picked up her overnight bag and held it up. "Don't feel bad, Maggie. He didn't help me with mine either."

Maggie rolled her eyes.

"Bella, there's a bag of peppermint tea and some mint candies on the counter fer ya."

She kissed the old woman's cheek. "Thank you. I don't know what I'd do without you."

Tilly shook her head. "Me neither."

***

The conversation between Bella and Malik barely left room to breathe. The only time there was silence was when one of them visited the bathroom at a random gas station. They stopped several times for photo ops along the way. At one vista, Bella drifted off. Malik caught her camera before it hit the ground. It was nearly noon when they reached the small town near the park.

After lunch, they headed to their hotel for an early check-in.

"I got us a suite. Separate bedrooms, separate bathrooms, but a shared living space. Is that okay?" He slid his keycard into the slot but waited for her response before opening the door.

"That works. But the first thing I need to do is take a nap, or I won't be much good tonight."

Malik's lips tightened as he watched her. "You okay?"

"Just tired."

"You're sure you're up for this, 'cause we don't…"

Bella nodded. "I'm fine. Don't worry."

She pointed toward a doorway to the left of the shared room. "I'll take this room."

Around 5:00 p.m., she emerged with her hair combed, teeth brushed, and a smile. "Let's go eat dinner. I'm famished."

The restaurant appeared to have been unchanged since the day it opened. The curved orange booths, the pitted tabletops, and the yellowed and torn wallpaper with outlines of brown coffee mugs had to have been original. Even the ceramic plates with the brown ring around them looked dated.

Malik ordered a double serving of black-eyed peas, rice, pork, and sauerkraut. Bella asked for a chef salad with no dressing and a dinner roll. Fifteen minutes later, the server set a large platter in front of Malik. Strings of sauerkraut hung off the side of the plate.

"*Bon appetit*," Malik said as he swiped a long-pronged fork across his plate, capturing some of everything and shoving it into his mouth.

Bella made a face as she waited for her salad to arrive. "How can you eat that stuff?" Her face contorted. "Especially the sauerkraut?"

The server set a salad in front of her. "Is there anything else I can get you?"

She pointed to Malik's plate. "How about a barf bag?"

The man nodded. "That's a lot of food." He grinned at Bella. "But I have a feeling your guy can make it disappear."

Malik quickly shook his head. "Oh, no, no. We're not together. We're just friends."

The server set the bill on the table. "Let me know if you need anything else."

Bella cut her salad into small pieces before shoving a small bite into her mouth. She watched Malik mow through the now blended goo on his plate.

"Do you want some?" he asked, finally looking up.

"Not on your life." After a few bites, Bella abandoned the salad and picked at her roll.

Twenty minutes later, they were heading toward the park. In a long line of unruly children with oblivious parents, young couples holding hands, and a few elderly folks, Malik and Bella waited for the gates to open. Bella wondered how others saw the two of them. Did they think they were a couple? Did they suspect she had cancer? Did they wrongly assume they would live a long, happy life with a Malik and Bella Jr. in the mix?

Over one shoulder, Malik carried a backpack with two umbrellas, a couple of bottles of water, two extra sweatshirts, and a small folding stool in case Bella needed to rest. Bella's camera bag hung over his other shoulder. The only thing she held was her camera.

For the first half of the walk, Bella held up her end of the conversation. But the last mile was torturous. It was everything she could do to put one foot in front of the other. She knew she would make it, but at what toll? Malik had taken her hand shortly after she stopped talking. She didn't know if he was pulling her or keeping her upright. Either way, it would have been so much worse without his support. When they finally reached their destination, Malik opened the stool and forced Bella to rest.

By the time the fireflies started their mating dance, thousands of lights blinking on and off simultaneously, Bella got her second wind. She was so busy snapping pictures, the exhaustion faded away.

Visitors left and arrived at varying times. Around 8:30, Malik and Bella joined a line of people headed back to the entrance. They started near the front, but it didn't take long before others overtook them. Malik questioned her ability to make the return trek several times. Each time, Bella responded in the affirmative, but not once was she truthful.

From the gate, their car was still half a mile away. Bella stumbled on the dirt road; Malik caught her before she fell. Without missing a step, he scooped her up and kept walking. She didn't fight him; she didn't have the strength.

Relief raced through Bella when Malik pushed the hotel door open. She quietly thanked him and retreated to her side of the suite. After a quick shower, she slipped on a pair of knit shorts and a tank top before crawling into bed—literally. Her eyes closed before her head hit the pillow. But by midnight, her face was plunged into the toilet bowl. Pieces of lettuce floated on the surface of the water, making her gag again.

"Hey, you okay?" Malik stood in the doorway.

Tears rolled down her face as she retched again. Her stomach pulled so far inward, she thought it may have touched her spine.

"What can I get you?"

"There's peppermint tea in the outside pocket of my bag. Can you make me some?"

Malik didn't even wait for her to finish her request. Within minutes, he reappeared with a steaming cup and two hard mints. Bella opened one and dropped it into the tea.

He sat on the cold tile floor, saying nothing, while she slowly sipped the hot liquid.

"Feeling any better?" Malik asked.

She nodded. "I'm so sorry. I thought I'd handle this trip a lot better."

"Don't worry about it. I'm a cop. I've seen lots of people puke before." His forehead creased. "Of course, it's usually some perp puking in the back of my squad car."

She closed her eyes and took another sip. "That's disgusting."

"Yeah, but it happens."

"By the way, tonight was amazing! Nothing I imagined even came close to how cool it was." Bella upended the cup and poured the last of the tea into her mouth. She set it down and stretched out on the floor, resting her head in Malik's lap. "I'm anxious to see the pictures when I feel better."

"I want to see them too." He ran a hand through her hair, tucking the short stands behind her ear.

Bella's eyes closed, and her breathing grew shallow. She could feel herself drifting off.

"How about we get you to bed?"

Malik pushed her into a sitting position and held her steady while he stood up. When Bella tried to rise, she fell into him. He picked her up and carried her to her bed. He pulled the covers up and clicked off the light. She could feel him watching her.

"Will you stay with me?" she asked.

"Sure. Yeah." He looked around the room. "I'll bring in the recliner from the living room."

"No." Bella held out her hand. "Will you lie with me? Hold me, at least until I fall asleep?"

Malik froze. "Are you sure that's what you want?"

She closed her eyes and tucked her arm back under the covers. "Yes. Please?"

Malik crawled in on the other side and slid across the bed. He wrapped his arms around her. Bella could feel him adjust the blanket.

She was nearly asleep when she woke herself. There was something she had to tell him—something he needed to know before it was too late.

"Malik?"

"Hmmm?" he answered softly.

"Can I tell you something?"

"Anything."

Bella paused for a few seconds. "If I weren't dying, I'd want you to be my forever."

Malik drew a sharp breath and held her tighter. Slowly, she rolled over and touched his face. His eyes were damp.

"I'd want you as my forever too," he finally said. He buried his face in Bella's shoulder and held her tightly. "But since we don't know when the end will come, I'd like to be your *for as long as we have*."

"I'm sorry. I'm so sorry you have to go through this with me," Bella whispered.

"Bella, I'd go through this a million times over if it meant we could have even a few minutes together."

Bella gently brushed her lips across his. But something was wrong. She felt it. Slowly, her mouth fell open; she couldn't speak. A long gurgle filled the air. She tried to fight it, but Bella knew the end was near.

CHAPTER 26

Soon was a relative word

Grief squeezed Malik's chest so tightly that he fought to breathe. Every breath was jagged and sharp and felt like a stab to the heart. Each sliced through the dimly lit room, leaving no doubt he was heartbroken. He sat at the front edge of the chair with his elbows pressed heavily into his thighs and his chin in his hands. Tears rolled down his face, pooling into tiny puddles on the white floor.

Maggie caressed his back with the palm of her hand. After a few minutes, she pressed her cheek to his.

"I should have known the trip was too much for her," Malik whispered.

His mother's voice cracked when she spoke. "Honey, I'm so sorry. You can't blame yourself."

Malik's shoulders heavily rose and fell in a storm of silent sobs.

"I knew you were close to Bella. I even thought you might be falling in love with her." She knelt in front of him and pressed her forehead against his. "I've been so worried about what this would do to you."

"Hey." Bella's hand trembled as she held it toward Malik. She had watched the mother-son interaction long enough to know being in the hospital bed, wired to a handful of machines, was not a good sign.

Malik swiped at his face and rubbed his palms down the front of his jeans. Maggie moved to the side.

"Hey, yourself. How you doin'?" He smiled weakly.

Malik rested his elbows on the edge of the bed and stroked the back of her pale hand. Maggie moved to the far side of the bed.

Bella licked her dry lips. "Ohhhhh, on a scale of dead to ten, I'm probably a two-point-three," she said softly.

She attempted to rub her face, but the IV cord tugged at the needle in her hand, and she winced. Bella shoved the oxygen cannula back into her nose.

"What happened last night?" she asked.

Maggie brushed Bella's hair back from her forehead. "What do you remember, honey?"

Bella studied the ceiling as if the answers would miraculously appear. Her memory felt whitewashed—not clear enough to remember anything but a few fragmented pieces of the previous night. It blended into a jumbled mess of impending doom, highlighted by a brief moment of passion.

"Wait." Her stomach tumbled as she turned toward Maggie. "If you're here, who's with Tilly?"

"Don't you worry about Tilly, honey. There's a lot of people in Lawson Beach who'd jump at the chance to spend a day or two with her."

Maggie tugged the covers up to Bella's chest and smoothed the thin blanket. Bella followed her eyes, but it was clear she was avoiding eye contact.

She grabbed Maggie's arm. "Don't lie to me. Tell me the truth."

Maggie glanced at Malik before finally looking at Bella. "Lou's staying with her."

"But what about the bistro?"

Maggie shook her head. "Bella, you don't get to start

worrying about everyone else right now. Just worry about getting strong enough to get out of here."

Bella stared at Malik. "The bistro?"

He touched the oximeter clip on her finger. "Dad's got it covered. Don't worry." Malik gently set her hand on the bed. "Do you remember anything about the fireflies?"

Bella stared at the wall behind him. Pieces of the night slowly began to emerge, and she smiled. "They were amazing." Bella nibbled on her bottom lip. "But I also remember puking—a lot. But everything from that…" She grew quiet. Suddenly, she turned toward Maggie. "Can you get me some water, Maggie?"

"Of course, honey." She quickly disappeared from the room.

Bella laid her hand against Malik's cheek. "I remember telling you I love you." She shrugged. "Maybe not in those exact words."

"Did you mean it?"

"Yes." She stared into his dark eyes. "Did you?"

"More than you could ever know." He drew a deep breath. "That's why this is so hard."

Bella felt her body tighten. "What's so hard? What are you talking about? Is this the end? Am I going to die here in this hospital? Today?" Bile and panic rose together.

Malik slid his chair closer to the bed just as Maggie stepped into the room with a water pitcher and a glass.

"Ma." Malik jerked his head toward the door.

Maggie smiled. "Got it."

She poured a glass of water and waited for Malik to raise the head of the bed. Again, he thrust his head backward, with more urgency this time.

"I'm going." Maggie kissed Bella's forehead as she handed her the glass. "I love you, honey. We all do." Then she was gone.

Bella took several sips before handing the glass to Malik. "What's going on?"

He released a long breath. His shoulders sagged. Malik's eyes welled with tears; a lone escapee rolled down his cheek. "The doctor doesn't think you have a lot of time left."

Bella turned away and stared out the window, contemplating his message. Her body had told her as much in the last couple of months. There was something new every day—dizziness, her negative response to food, exhaustion, and throwing up daily; they all foretold the end. No, the news wasn't a surprise. What was a few more days, a few weeks, or a few months? The end game had always been the same—she was going to die—soon. But *soon* was a relative word. Did it mean today or next week? Was it a month from now?

Turning back, she ran her hand over Malik's short hair and gave him a watery smile. "A wise man once told me that every day is a bonus day." Bella rested her hand on his cheek. "You wouldn't happen to know him, would you?"

The corners of Malik's mouth curved upwards into a sad smile.

"The only thing that changes, Malik, is that I have to live more each day. *We* have to take advantage of the time we have—together." She pressed the button on the bed railing to raise herself fully upright. "So, why exactly am I here?"

"When they brought you in last night, you were severely dehydrated. The doctor said it was all the walking we did and all the puking *you* did."

"The cancer's growing—fast now. But I knew that. I can feel it." She adjusted the covers before pulling her knees to her chest. "Anything else?"

Malik slowly shook his head. "He wants to put you on an antinausea medication that'll help keep fluids and foods in you.

Hopefully, you'll have a little more stamina then."

Bella laid her cheek on her knees and faced Malik. "How much time are we talking?"

"S.." The words stuck like peanut butter in Malik's throat. His voice was husky when he finally spoke. "S-six weeks—give or take."

With her head still turned sideways, Bella's eyes darted around the room behind Malik. There was nothing on the tan wall but a pain scale with a line of colorful faces. At that moment, the only pain she felt was over losing the two things she'd finally found—a family and the love of her life. Suddenly, a crooked smile spread across her face.

Bella's shoulders rose, and she glanced around the room. Finally, she set her gaze on a cupboard door. "Can you do me a favor?"

"Anything." Malik sat upright.

"Get me out of here."

Malik stood. "Yeah. Of course. I'll go find the doc…"

"No!" Bella cut him off. She held a finger toward him. "I don't mean in an hour or after the doctor fills out all the paperwork. I want to go *now*." She kicked her covers off and held her hand with the IV toward Malik. "And get this thing out of me."

Malik smiled widely. "You're such a troublemaker, Levitsky."

"Do you even know how to do this? 'Cause in the movies, they just jer…"

"Shh!" Malik moved to the other side of the bed and shut off the machine. He took her hand. "You're lucky I worked as an EMT before becoming a cop."

Once Bella was free of the monitors and the IV, Malik retrieved her shorts and tank top from the cupboard. She slipped them on and ditched the hospital gown, tucking it beneath the covers. Malik removed his sweatshirt and pulled it over her head. It hung to her knees.

"Listen to me," he said, "there's a door just to the left of your room. Once we get into the stairwell, I'll carry you. Otherwise, I'm not doing this. Got it?"

Bella knew he was serious. She nodded. "Okay."

"Stay in front of me, and whatever you do, don't look up."

Malik peeked into the hallway and relayed what he saw to Bella.

"Ma's on her phone. I'm guessing she's texting with Dad." He looked the other way. "Except for one person, the nurses' station's empty."

Bella shakily moved toward the door.

"Ready?" he whispered.

She nodded. "As ready as I'll ever be."

Stepping closely behind a barefoot Bella, Malik wrapped one arm across her chest. She felt him turn and peek into the hallway before pushing her forward and immediately into the stairwell. Malik quietly closed the door with one hand and held on to her with the other. When the door closed, he picked her up and carried her down the two flights. At the bottom, he pressed the automatic swing door button with his elbow. The door slowly opened into the parking ramp. Swiftly, he carried her toward the parking space he'd left his car the previous night.

When they exited the ramp, Bella breathed a sigh of relief. Malik checked the rearview mirror several times until they got onto the highway. His shoulders finally fell back against the seat, and he took a deep breath. Bella touched his arm and smiled. His furrowed brow and tight lips morphed into wide eyes and a huge grin. A deep clap of laughter erupted from him.

"That was like a TV show escape. What was that show? *The Dukes of Hazards*? Had you plowed through the stop arm and jumped a curb or two..." Bella laughed as she clapped her hands together. "I haven't had that much fun since… Well, I don't think I've ever had that much fun."

Malik set his hand on her bare leg as he drove. "You know, Bella, I'm a cop. I'm *not* supposed to help people escape. My job is to catch them."

Bella was silent. "Then don't think of it as escaping. Think of it as winning." She pumped both fists into the air.

A ringtone cut through the car. Malik looked at the screen. "Crap!" He nervously laughed as he hit the speaker button.

"Ma!"

"Where are you two?"

Malik looked at Bella and shrugged. She leaned toward the phone. "We're celebrating. Want to join us?"

"Where. Are. You?" Her words were sharp.

"Fine." Malik gave in. "We're in the car, driving away from the hospital. If I were you, I'd do the same. Get out of there before that doctor stops back in."

"Too late." The male voice was unfamiliar. "Bella, this is Doctor Landus." Bella looked at Malik with wide eyes. "Listen to me. If I were in your position, I'd be doing the same thing you are right now. But it's really important you take the antinausea meds so you don't get dehydrated again. I'll give the prescription to your mother-in-law."

Bella looked at Malik and held her palms up in question. "Mother-in-law?" she mouthed.

"That sounds good. Thanks, Dr. Landus," Malik said. "Thanks, Ma."

"Oh, don't think this is over. You two owe me—big time!"

Maggie and the doctor started laughing just as Malik hung up.

"Mother-in-law?" Bella asked again.

"Well, I may have made myself your husband on your admission papers. You know they'll only talk to family."

Bella nodded. "So, then how about you make an honest woman out of me?"

Malik spun his head sideways. "What?"

His shocked look made Bella howl with laughter. She tucked her knees under the oversized sweatshirt. "You should see your face."

"You know I'd do it. I'd marry you today, tomorrow, and every day until you're..." He frowned. "*Gone*."

Bella touched his temple. "And I love you enough not to let you."

CHAPTER 27

Deja vu or a premonition?

The streetlights had come on long before Malik drove into town. A warm yellow glow stretched downward in a fuzzy circle around each tall pole. Malik drove past a group of children dashing in and out of the beam. Bella rolled down her window and rested her chin on her forearm. Spurts of laughter and playful screams drifted through the night air. Sadly, she smiled. Malik would have been an amazing father. And she would have been the best mom. Their kids would have been raised in Lawson Beach, out of the limelight and away from the nannies. There wouldn't have been foster care, lonely nights, or uncelebrated birthdays. It would have been perfect. *They* would have been perfect.

"Stop!" she yelled.

Malik slammed on the brakes. Bella's seat belt locked, catapulting her backward after a short snap forward. She caught her camera before it landed at her feet.

"Quick! Turn around and drive back down this street. I want to get some pictures of the kids."

Loudly, he heaved. "I thought…" He shook his head. "Never mind."

After checking his side mirrors, he made a U-turn. He repeated the same move a block down the street. Keeping an eye out for inattentive children, he parked in front of the yard.

Through her open window, Bella took several pictures while Malik checked his phone. When she clicked through the photos, something odd came to light, something she hadn't noticed before. A small child stood away from the group, nearly concealed in the darkness. Bella couldn't determine if it was a boy or girl. Whoever it was appeared almost ghost-like. The streetlight revealed only the white glow of a t-shirt. The child's face was hidden in the shadows, and the dark pants and shoes faded into the night. Bella watched through the lens before taking *one* photo.

"Okay," she whispered.

Blindly, she reached toward Malik and laid a hand on his muscular forearm but kept her eyes glued to the youngster disappearing deeper into the night. *Was it deja vu or a premonition of something yet to come?*

Four minutes later, Malik parked in front of the boarding house. Maggie pulled in behind him.

Maggie hurried across the yard and yanked the passenger's side door open. "Are you okay, honey? That was a long trip."

Bella glanced toward the house. "I am." She sighed. "Telling Tilly is making my heart race, though."

Maggie pressed her knees against the running board and took Bella's hands in hers. "Sweetie, she already knows. Lou told her." She bobbled her head slightly. "I hope we didn't overstep. We just thought it might make it easier on you if you didn't have to do it."

Bella's body slumped, and her eyes closed. She squeezed Maggie's hand. "Thank you. I'm not sure I could have done it."

As Maggie stepped backward, Malik lifted Bella out of the seat.

"Put me down," she insisted. "I can walk." She squirmed like a toddler trying to free herself from her father's grip. "I walked almost six miles last night. I'm pretty sure I can walk into the house by myself."

Malik nodded. "Yes, you did. And because of that, tonight, you're not setting one foot on the ground. Do you hear me?"

He waited for Bella to stop wiggling. When she did, he shoved the door closed with his hip and headed up the walk. Maggie held the door and ushered them inside.

Lou's and Tilly's voices boomed from the living room. As usual, the two of them were in a head-to-head squabble over something or another. Whatever it was, it didn't matter. There was no way Lou was going to win. Tilly was eristic. Something inside her made her debate everything. Even if she *agreed* with the other person's line of thinking, she had to argue. If you said black, she said white. She was stubborn and opinionated.

The room went still when Malik stepped in with Bella in his arms. He stopped for a second before heading toward the couch.

"Well, fer cryin' out loud, Lou, git the girl some pillows." Tilly leaned forward over the top of her knitting and barked orders. "And make sure ya plump 'em up."

"Yes, ma'am," he snapped back.

Lou collected a handful of pillows from the second couch. One at a time, he handed them to Malik to stuff behind Bella's back and under her knees.

"Stop! Stop treating me like I'm broken." Bella pulled one of the pillows from behind her and chucked it to the floor. "I'm not dying *today*." Stubbornly, she crossed her arms in front of her. "And I sure as hell am not dying in the next few weeks. I have a gallery show to get ready for." Angrily, she tipped her chin downward and made eye contact with each person in the room. "Have I made myself clear?"

One corner of Lou's mouth pitched up. "Crystal." The smirk morphed into a full-blown smile. He pinched his face and mimicked Tilly. "As clear as pee after drinkin' a gallon of water." His laugh was cut short by Tilly's glare. "Well, she sounded an awful lot like you, Tilly."

"Good." Bella nodded at the old lady.

Tilly shook her head. "Bella, ya look like ya was rode hard and put up wet."

Bella's eyes narrowed. "That's disgusting."

Lou laughed. "It doesn't mean what you think it does. It has to do with horses needing to be walked before you put them in their stall."

"You got such a dirty mind, girl. All I meant is ya ain't lookin' so good."

"Like I need you pointing that out," Bella growled.

Silence loomed heavily as Malik picked up Bella's feet and laid them across his lap. One of her pale feet disappeared into Malik's large hands as he rubbed them.

"Hmm." Tilly wagged a finger back and forth between the two of them. "So, speakin' of rode hard, are ya two…" Her finger moved faster, and she scrunched her face. "…a, ah, sex thing now?"

Malik choked. "Oh, my god, old woman. What the hell?"

Tilly squinted one eye and stared at Lou. "Well, that's what Lou told me. Did I git bad information?"

"Yes. Ah, no. But…" Malik's mouth snapped shut. He silently implored Bella for help.

"Well, which is it boy? Yes or no?"

Bella bit her bottom lip to hide her grin. "What Malik was trying to say is—No, Lou didn't give you bad intel. And yes, we like each other." She snorted. "But as for the *sex thing*—as you so eloquently put it—*no*. We are not a *sex thing*."

Tilly opened her mouth, but Bella cut her off. "Annnnd, if it ever comes to be, it'll be none of your business. Understand?"

Again, Tilly's mouth opened, but she clamped it shut just as fast. Finally, she leaned back. "Yes."

"Yes, what?" Bella glared at her. "Yes, *what,* Tilly?"

Maggie turned her head toward Lou and covered the side of her face with her hand. She squeezed her lips together to silence her laughter. Bella winked at them before she gave Tilly the evil eye.

Like an angry dog, Tilly bared her teeth. "Yes. It's none of my business."

Bella tilted her head sideways. "Glad we're on the same page, old woman."

Maggie's shoulders bobbed up and down until Tilly hit her with a firm pillow.

Tilly gave both Bella and Malik the once over. "All I have to say is that it's 'bout time. For a while there, I thought I was gonna have to tie a pork chop around yer neck just to get him to notice ya." Tilly narrowed her eyes. "To be honest, I don't git what ya see in that boy. Most of the time, his brain rattles around like a BB in a boxcar."

Malik's eyes narrowed. "Not bad, old gal. Your insults are improving too." Suddenly, he arched one eyebrow. "But you know, Tilly, you *can* be a mean old cuss when you want to be. I can't believe I ever liked you."

Tilly shrugged. "Keep up, Junior. Everybody likes me."

Lines grew across his forehead. "I wouldn't say *everybody*. I wouldn't even say everybody in this room."

"Malik," Maggie warned. She stood, scooped Tilly's pillow from the floor, and returned it to her. "I think we should head home. It's been a long two days. Bella, do you need help getting ready for bed?"

Bella frowned at Malik. "No. And contrary to popular belief, I can walk, talk, pee, and dress myself just fine."

Maggie nodded once. "Then, Malik, how about you come with us?" It was a command, not a question.

"But…" Bella gave him a death stare the minute he opened his mouth. "All right. I'm going." He kissed the top of her head and followed his parents into the kitchen.

Once the front door closed, Tilly snapped her footrest down. "Six weeks, Bella. That's forty-two days—more or less. It's not…"

Bella raised her eyebrows. "What? A death sentence?" She watched the old woman squirm. "I think it is." Her legs wobbled as she stood. She clung to the back of the couch, waiting for her balance to kick in. "But you know what, Tilly?" She stood upright. "It doesn't matter. If your god is as great as you claim, then he's got a place waiting for me—with an incredible bed, the best chocolate, and the most comfortable shoes I've ever worn." She poked a finger toward the ceiling. "And I'll have perfect hair and a cancer-free body." Her chin lifted, and the corners of her mouth dropped. "Isn't that what you keep telling me?"

Solemnly, Tilly nodded.

Bella cautiously took a step. "But do you know what I won't have? *Malik*. And I won't have Maggie and Lou." She looked hard at Tilly. "And I won't have you there with me." She headed toward her bedroom, running a hand along the wall for support. "I hope you're right about this god, Tilly. Then I can experience all the things I never got to here—all the things that were taken away from me long before they should have been."

She slammed the door and stumbled into the bathroom.

Twenty minutes later, lying in the dark, beneath a sliver of moon, Bella cried herself to sleep for the first time in a very long time.

***

Bella could smell bacon before she opened her eyes. It was her downfall, the one food that beckoned her out of bed even on her worst days. Her legs no longer felt like they would collapse under her eighty-five pounds. For that, she was grateful. There was too much to do for her gallery show—and even more before *the end.*

In the bathroom, she shoved her arms and head through Malik's sweatshirt and dropped onto the toilet before pulling it down. Moments later, leaning against one wall, she tugged on a pair of thick socks. Lately, she was always cold. It didn't matter if it was eighty degrees outside; she was chilled to the bone.

When Bella rounded the corner into the kitchen, she had expected to see Tilly standing at the stove frying bacon. Instead, it was Maggie with the frying pan in her hand.

Bella gave her a once-over. "What are you doing here?" Bella pulled out the chair opposite Tilly and sat down.

Maggie set a steaming plate of bacon and eggs in front of her. "Hi, I'm Maggie," she teased. "I'm the new chief cook and bottle washer at the boarding house."

"What are you talking about?"

"I'm the new help. I'll shop, cook, wash clothes, and do anything else you two ladies need."

Bella scrunched her nose. "No." She shook her head. "No, I can still…"

"Girl, if ya think ya can keep takin' care of me in yer condition, then ya couldn't pour piss outta a boot even if the directions was written on the heel." She picked up a section of newspaper and held it in front of her face. "Maggie's gonna take care of us fer a while. And we're gonna let her." Slowly, she lowered the paper. "And I don't wanna hear another word 'bout it."

"Eat," Maggie said, waving the spatula at Bella. "Eat before it gets cold."

"Are you sure?" Bella studied Maggie's face.

Maggie nodded. "Bella, I want to do this. No one's asking me." She returned from the counter with a tall glass of water. She set a pill and the water in front of Bella. "Doctor's orders," she said as she quickly turned toward the sink.

Bella didn't miss the tears that tumbled down Maggie's cheeks.

CHAPTER 28

They sure don't make 'em like they used to.

Maggie had moved everything but her clothes into the boarding house. Small appliances, pans, utensils, and cleaning supplies had slowly made their way into Tilly's kitchen. Bella knew it went against every fiber of Tilly's being, and the old woman made sure everyone knew. But Maggie ignored her. From sun-up until sundown, she cooked and cleaned, making sure Bella and Tilly had everything they needed. In the rare moments when she found downtime, Maggie read or closed her eyes and rested. It hurt Bella to see her working so hard on her account. She hadn't come here to have someone take care of her. Her plan had been to simply fade away without anyone noticing or caring—but she'd become part of a family, had made friends—and that changed everything.

The new crockpot got its workout, but not without complaints from Tilly. She grumbled about the taste, texture, and temperature all the time. There wasn't a meal she didn't follow that up with—*They sure don't make 'em like they used to.* or *That ain't the way I woulda done it.* The old woman spent a great deal of time sitting in the kitchen, pretending to hide behind the newspaper—criticizing.

Malik had taken a partial leave, working only two days a week. If he wasn't at the station, he was at Bella's side. She loved spending the time she had left with him, but meals had become excruciating. Bella wanted to join the family for meals, but smells and tastes were like nails on a chalkboard. Her stomach rebelled, but she fought it down and stayed for the conversation. Malik had recently become self-conscious about eating in front of her, knowing Bella struggled with every bite. But no matter what she said or how much she pushed, he wouldn't listen. She wondered if it would be better to stop coming to meals altogether.

Lou often stopped for leftovers and to relieve Maggie from her duty—something she desperately needed but wouldn't admit. She hid her tears, busying herself when someone came near. It gutted Bella to see her suffer, but she didn't know how to make it better, so she stepped into the shadows and held her tongue.

Bella was no longer allowed behind the wheel of Tilly's car. The hammer had dropped, and the vote was unanimous. It infuriated her, but when push came to shove, even she knew it was no longer safe. Because she often lay awake at night, without warning, she would fall asleep during the day. She no longer had the strength or the focus to drive. So Malik did all the driving.

On Friday nights, the two of dropped off cash with Nate and Destiny. They had no idea she was dying or that she wasn't selling flowers any longer. Bella didn't want them to know. She wanted to live *and die* on her terms.

On days when Malik was gone, Bella crossed the yard and set up shop in Maggie's office. The house was quiet. After listening to Tilly complain about everything in life, the silence was music to her ears. The Jacksons also had internet, something Tilly had refused. "We don't need no stinkin' *inter-thingamajig* or whatever the hell it's called. It ain't safe. All it does is let the world snoop on ya. If y're okay with everybody knowin' yer business, then by all means—do it somewhere else.

That newfangled crap ain't comin' into my house." So Bella mooched "that newfangled," decades-old "crap" from the neighbors.

Every hour or so, Maggie wandered over to check on her. If Tilly was asleep, Maggie would sit and chat for a few minutes. Other times, she waved through the window and headed back. Bella's heart broke for Maggie and the relationship they would lose when she died. Maggie was like the mother she'd never *really* had, and Maggie treated Bella like her daughter. It had to hurt to watch her die.

For nearly a week, Bella pored over her photos, attempting to choose the perfect ones for the gallery opening. Some were so similar, no one else would have noticed, but Bella would. Finally, after narrowing it to ten, Bella ordered the professional prints. Marty was her savior. Not only had he allowed her the opportunity to showcase her work, but after learning her secret, he offered to frame them for her. She was grateful for his kindness—and for not dropping her once he knew this would be her only show.

Like every artist, Bella had been allotted space for ten items. She needed an eleventh. No matter how much she pleaded, Marty held firm. He'd never allowed an artist more than ten pieces. But Bella was persuasive. After much back and forth, she finally convinced him of the importance of this one unforgettable photo—actually, a grouping of several images in one frame. With his hard-fought-for blessing, Bella went to work on her final piece.

She should have felt an incredible sense of relief when her pictures were selected and ordered, but instead, knots in her stomach grew. Now that she had time to focus on other things, her anxiety grew, especially over one call she still needed to make. The *what ifs* swarmed her daily, but she still pushed it off again and again. Finally, Bella could wait no longer. That call signaled the end was imminent. Unable to even share the job with Malik, she made the call alone. She bawled through most of the conversation, sometimes needing a few minutes to gather herself before continuing. Bella was grateful for the kind and patient man on the other end of the line.

A few days later, that same man parked down the street and snuck in through Maggie's backdoor. With their heads pressed together in a back bedroom, in case Maggie popped in, they hammered out every detail. When he left, Bella expected to break down, but instead of the blubbery mess she'd been on the phone, all she felt was relief.

Then, three days before her gallery showing, Bella woke in an intense state of panic. She had a feeling of dread she couldn't shake. Physically, she was doing better than she had expected. Emotionally, she was a wreck. Malik had brought home a wheelchair, so she no longer needed to depend on her failing body. If only they made something to curb her racing thoughts.

What lived in Bella and played drums inside her chest was fear. The gallery show was what she'd been waiting for. It was the first thing she thought about when she opened her eyes each morning. To see your work through the eyes of others was every artist's dream. Bella's included. But as excited as she was, as soon as the show was over, there was nothing left. Other than Malik, there was little to keep her going. Her body would begin to shut down. The final curtain was closing at warp speed, like the blur of scenery out a car's window racing along the Audubon.

Three weeks and one day remained of the time the last doctor had given her. Twenty-two days wasn't a precise number—it was arbitrary. It was one person's opinion after spending a couple of hours with her. She could live longer. But then again, she could die tomorrow. *Was she ready? Would she ever be?* Panic pawed at her as she thought about closing her eyes for the last time.

"What in daylight is wrong with ya?" Tilly asked when she shuffled into the living room. "Ya look as nervous as a peacock in water."

Maggie set her book down. "What is it, honey? Are you okay?"

Bella's eyes grew wide. A lie, some fabricated story, would hide what she feared the most.

"I—I just realized I don't have anything to wear to the gallery opening." She twisted her hands and refused to look at either woman. "Maggie, can you take me downtown to shop for a dress and shoes?"

Tilly slapped the arm of her chair with the palm of one hand. "Cheese and crackers, Bella, buyin' somethin' new makes 'bout as much sense as tits on a bull." She dropped her knitting into the basket next to her chair. "Ain't we talked 'bout this already?"

Maggie glared at Tilly. "Of course, I will, Bella. It'll be my treat."

The snap of the recliner footstool made Bella jump. Tilly worked herself to the front edge of the chair and stood. She grabbed her walker and wheeled out of the room without a word.

"Is she mad?" Bella bit her lip.

Maggie's shoulders raised slightly. "Hard to tell with her." She glanced in the direction Tilly had gone. "Just the same, if I were you, I'd steer clear for a little while," she whispered.

The sound of the approaching walker sent a chill down Bella's spine. She took a small step toward Maggie as Tilly rounded the corner with a yellow chiffon dress draped over the front bar.

She stopped in front of Bella and held the dress up for her. "Here," she said, thrusting it toward her. "I wore this here dress in 1975. It was mine and James' twenty-fifth wedding anniversary. I kept it 'cause I knew somebody'd wear it again. It's a good dress. Well made. And I should know. Made it myself."

Bella studied it in horror. The hem of the old dress touched the floor. The round neckline was covered with a cape that buttoned in the back. At the end of the sheer sleeves were long satin cuffs closed with five pearl buttons pushed through fabric loops.

Maggie rolled her eyes. "Tilly! Don't be ridiculous. Bella can't wear that dress. First of all, she'd drown in it. But more importantly, it's almost fifty years old. No one wears dresses like that anymore." She set her book on the end table. "I'll buy her a dress. After dinner, Malik can stay here, and Bella and I will go shopping."

Tilly clicked her tongue and locked her eyes on Bella. "What makes ya think y're so goldarn special ya gotta have somethin' new even though ya ain't never gonna wear it 'gain?" She pointed at Maggie. "And you should be ashamed of yerself fer encouragin' her to throw 'way good money. Ya both got yer noses stuck so high in the air, ya could drown in a rainstorm." She jerked the dress from Bella's hand, turned her walker, and headed back down the hall. "I'll be in my room, and I don't wanna see or hear from either of ya. Do I make myself clear?"

"Do you want lunch?" Maggie asked hesitantly.

"No, I do not want lunch," Tilly replied mockingly. "If I want somethin', I'll git it myself. I don't need nothin' from the likes of you two."

Her bedroom door slammed shut. Bella had never seen Tilly so angry. She slowly backed up and dropped onto the couch.

"Honey, she just needs some time to cool off. It's probably best if we give it to her."

Maggie went into the kitchen to stir whatever was cooking

in the crockpot, but Bella didn't move. The last person she ever wanted to hurt was Tilly.

***

Around 6:00 p.m., Tilly reappeared for dinner. She ate her Carolina BBQ meatballs, coleslaw, and au gratin potatoes without looking up.

Malik cut a small chunk off a meatball and chewed. "Ma and Bella are going downtown for a while. Want to play cards or watch TV, Tilly?"

Tilly sneered at him before looking at Bella.

"So that's still yer plan, is it? Wastin' good money?"

Bella side-glanced at Maggie, silently pleading for her to answer.

"Bella wants to look nice for her show. You can't expect her to go in jeans and a sweatshirt. She has nothing to wear, Tilly." Maggie watched the old gal. "So, yes, I'm going to buy her a dress and a pair of sandals."

Tilly continued to stare. Finally, she hoisted herself up, left her plate on the table, and returned to her room, again slamming her bedroom door.

***

It was well past 8:00 a.m. by the time Bella woke. She rolled over and smiled. The dress Maggie bought was lying over the back of a cane rocker. To get the whole picture, she'd placed the nearly flat white sandals on the floor in front of the chair.

The night before, she'd tried on dresses until she had no strength left. Finally, she settled on the first one she'd picked up—white lace with a scalloped neckline and a circle skirt that hit the middle of her thighs. If Bella had the energy or the balance, she would have done a pirouette, just to feel the skirt twirl. But she didn't; she couldn't. The last time she'd tried, she landed on the floor in front of Tilly. Instead of showing the tiniest bit of compassion, the old woman let her have it. "I

247

wondered when ya'd stop doin' those stupid turns. Looks like that decision was made fer ya." Bella sighed. The playful skirt was lost on her now.

Maggie had bought her a padded bra and matching underwear too. Bella had lived flat-chested, with the scars of her mastectomy for so long, she wasn't sure how she'd look with breasts. She'd told Maggie she would be fine without the undergarments, but like a mother, Maggie bought them anyway. "You only get to do this once, Bella. You are so worth it—no matter what Tilly says." Bella wanted to cry. Maggie loved her beyond anything she'd ever known before. Malik had no idea how lucky he was to have such an incredible mother.

Bella slowly eased her way out of bed. As the pain increased, she felt her body betray her a little more each day. Last night's shopping trip had taken more out of her than she'd expected. She stood in front of the mirror, holding the dress; she wanted to put it on, but she didn't have the energy. What little strength she had, she needed to get herself through breakfast with Tilly. Her stomach fluttered just thinking about it.

The kitchen was unusually quiet. Maggie opened the fridge door when Bella sat down at the table.

"Where's Tilly?" Bella whispered.

"Not coming." Maggie set a glass of water and juice in front of Bella. "I thought you might have heard our war this morning." She held a palm toward Bella. "For the record, I did nothing."

"What happened?"

"I knocked, opened the door, and barely stepped into her sitting room before she told me to get out." Her eyes grew wide. "So I set a tray with coffee and toast on the small table inside her door, told her it was there, and barely escaped with my life before she flung a shoe at me."

Bella took several drinks of water. "Have you ever seen her

like this before?"

"Once." Maggie set two plates on the table: one where Tilly typically sat and the other in front of Bella. She sat down but didn't move. She stared at her Belgian waffle, covered in strawberries and whipped cream. "As I recall, it was a good month before she came around." She shook her cloth napkin and laid it across her lap. "We walked on eggshells the entire time."

Bella's mouth went dry. "Maggie, I don't know if I even have a month. I can't wait for Tilly to forgive me."
Maggie patted the top of Bella's hand. "Honey, this is Tilly we're talking about. I don't think you have a choice."

CHAPTER 29

Stop drooling. I'm taken.

Lightning flashed and thunder rumbled all morning on the day of the gallery opening. Ominous clouds surged eastward in varying shades of everchanging gray. The locals swore it was not commonplace to have so much unusual weather in one summer. But to Bella, the year had been nothing but storms. At least, according to the weatherman, the one brewing outside would be short-lived. Sunshine was to break through before noon, adding warmth to Bella's excitement. But for now, the gray sky matched her angst over Tilly's mood.

June hadn't exited the calendar on its own; July knocked it out like a linebacker. The days moved too quickly, dropping like autumn leaves in a windstorm. And while Bella was thrilled about the opening, she was also heartbroken.

She stared at the calendar hanging on the wall. If the doctor was right, July would be the month she drew her last breath. And if Tilly was correct, she'd be given another opportunity to live in heaven. Oh, how she wanted to believe, but so much had happened in her short life. Ninety percent of it was negative, sparking conflict between science and the drawing of the short straw.

Bella poked her legs into a pair of shorts, safety-pinned the waistband, and pulled a faded Huey Lewis and the News t-shirt down over the top of the fastening debacle. She would shower when she was ready to get dressed for the night's festivities. Right now, she had to find a way to entice Tilly to abandon her anger and attend the gallery opening.

Once again, Maggie was the sole inhabitant of the kitchen. Malik had gone in for an early shift.

"Still no Tilly?"

Maggie shook her head. "No. I was hoping she'd get over herself and join us for breakfast, but it…"

Suddenly, she tipped her head toward the hallway and pressed a finger against her lip. The oak floor creaked several times before Tilly appeared in the doorway.

Maggie closed her eyes and drew a deep breath. "Good morning. Would you like some breakfast?"

Tilly scowled at Maggie. "Woman, y're three gallons of crazy in a two-gallon bucket. Why else would I be in the kitchen at this hour?"

Bella wanted to laugh, but uncertainty and her thudding heart wouldn't let her. "Morning," she said softly. "I'm glad you're joining us for breakfast. Can I get you anything?"

Tilly arched an eyebrow. "Don't piss down my back and tell me it's rainin'. You know dang well ya ain't no more happy to see me than when I walked away with that dress the other night." She took a sip of the coffee Maggie set in front of her. "But ya will be. You'll see." She smirked.

Maggie hustled around the kitchen, preparing three meals instead of the two she'd planned for. She released a deep sigh when she finally sat down.

The women ate in silence. A mix of generations, backgrounds, locations, and races—and yet, they were family.

Suddenly, the stillness was louder than Bella could stand. She picked up a piece of crisp bacon but returned it to her plate with a sigh. Bacon no longer excited her as it once had. Even with the antinausea pills, a few small bites were all she could stomach.

With her heart still racing, a wave of courage swelled in Bella. "Tilly, are you planning to come to the gallery opening tonight?" she asked quietly.

Tilly tsked twice. "Well, course I am. Did ya think I'd miss yer big night?"

Maggie frowned at the old woman. "We didn't know what to expect. After the last two days, we thought you may never come out of your room again."

Tilly set her fork on her plate. "If ya honestly believed that, you haven't got the brains God gave a squirrel."

Maggie ignored the dig. Instead, she glanced at Bella's plate. "Sweetie, would you like something else?"

Bella's face grew pink. The tips of her ears burned. "Sorry, Maggie. I just can't eat today. Maybe I'm too excited. I'll help you do dishes, though."

"You'll do no such thing." Maggie gathered the plates and poured Tilly another cup of coffee. "This is your day." She laid a hand on Bella's shoulder. "You're our celebrity."

"Put yer dang butt in that chair, Maggie," Tilly growled. "I ain't done talkin' yet."

Maggie set the old metal coffee pot on the burner and lowered herself into her chair.

"Bella, go to my bedroom and get that yellow dress from my clos…"

"No!" Maggie slapped the table. "Tilly, we're not starting this again. Bella cannot wear your old dress. I bought her a beautiful…"

Tilly poked a finger in Maggie's direction. "Hush up." She turned back toward Bella. "Now, go git the dress."

Bella stared at Maggie, hoping for some help.

Maggie shrugged. "Go ahead."

Slowly, Bella stood and shoved in her chair with her hip.

Today was one of her better days, but she didn't want to overdo it. Anxiety took a lot out of her, and Tilly was generating a wave of stress big enough to drown in. She turned away, closed her eyes, and disappeared into the hallway.

Maggie touched the old gal's arm. "Tilly, this…"

Tilly pressed a finger to her lips and pointed toward the doorway.

"What the…" Bella carried the dress into the kitchen.

Maggie's forehead creased as she looked from the dress to Tilly and back again.

"Is that the same dress?" Maggie asked.

"It's the same material." She nodded. "I ripped my dress apart and made Bella a new one."

Unlike the one Maggie had bought, this dress had a straight neckline across the top of what would have been Bella's breasts. Narrow straps covered each shoulder. The dress was not fitted. The underlayer was satin and was covered in a layer of chiffon.

"Turn it around," Tilly told her.

Still in awe, Bella spun the metal hanger. Across the back, Tilly had sewn several overlapping pieces of chiffon in differing lengths. When Bella walked, the strips would flutter behind her, creating the illusion of flying—like angel wings.

Bella was speechless.

Maggie went to her. "Are you okay?" she whispered. "You don't have to wear it."

Bella shoved the dress toward Maggie and knelt on the floor next to Tilly.

"It's beautiful. Is this what you've been doing the last two days?"

Tilly shook her head in disbelief. "Well, of course. What'd ya think I was doin' in there? Sulkin'?"

"Well… Thank you! I love it." Bella hugged Tilly and smiled at Maggie. "Maggie, I hope you're okay if I don't…"

"This is your night, honey. You'll look beautiful no matter what you wear."

***

By 6:00 p.m., Bella was primped and ready to leave. She'd applied a little mascara and some lipstick that had been rolling around in her backpack since her arrival in Lawson Beach. With her face still too pale, she swiped a light layer of lipstick on her cheeks and smeared it slightly. Her bangs were held in place with the butterfly clip she'd worn nearly every day. The slight darkening beneath her eyes was the only indicator Bella was sick. But when she smiled, even she almost believed she wasn't dying.

Bella knew Malik was waiting for her in the kitchen. She heard his deep voice rumble through the walls. Stopping in front of the long mirror on the back of her door, she took one last look. Tilly's dress was more than perfect. The backward chiffon shawl dipped below the neckline, creating an illusion of breasts where there were none. It joined the flowing strips in the back. Whether Tilly had envisioned this when she'd started or not, she'd designed the perfect dress.

Days earlier, when Tilly had shown her the fifty-year-old dress, Bella almost cried. It wasn't just the size or the age; it was downright ugly. But clearly, Tilly saw more than a fifty-year-old dress. She saw possibilities—just as she had seen in Bella.

Like Tilly, Bella had recently begun shuffling her feet. The flat sandals provided her stability. Because the Lawson Beach residents had no knowledge of her impending death, she would need to focus on her demeanor and appearance, especially her walk.

To ward off exhaustion, she'd taken an afternoon nap. Before she'd fallen asleep, she tried talking to Tilly's god, but no matter what she said, it sounded like begging. Bella wasn't certain he responded to begging. But, if he was going to answer even one of her prayers, she needed him to get her through the night.

Finally, she looked up and smiled. She wiped away a speck of dried mascara and pulled the door open. She made a conscious effort to step, rather than shuffle, down the hallway and into the kitchen where her date waited.

The minute Malik saw her, his face went soft, and he inhaled sharply. Awkwardly, Bella turned in a circle and waited for him to say something, but he just stared. "Well?" she asked.

"Oh, my God! You look amazing," he gushed. His lashes fluttered. "I can't believe how beautiful you are." He shook his head. "That came out wrong. You've always been beautiful, but tonight, you're glowing."

Malik donned a light blue fitted suit. His chest muscles bulged beneath his white shirt, slightly stressing the buttons. The suit had been a gift from Maggie for the gallery opening, purchased on the same night they bought her dress. Bella had chosen a white dress to coordinate with his shirt. So, when she changed dresses at the last minute, she wondered if they would still match. But, somehow, Maggie had pulled off a miracle. The light blue tie with the tiny yellow flecks had somehow been purchased since breakfast.

"Thank you." Holding Malik's arm, Bella shakily rose onto her tiptoes. He bent down to meet her warm kiss. "You're not so bad yourself." She wrapped her arms around him and rested her cheek against his chest.

"Git a room, ya two." Tilly poked her head through the doorway. Maggie stepped into the kitchen around her.

"Wow!" She shook her head in disbelief. "Just wow!"

"Stop drooling, Ma. I'm taken."

"I was talking about Bella," she teased. She moved toward the couple and held them in a warm embrace. "I love you both," she whispered. Then she looked up at her son. "This will be a night to remember. Don't waste it, Malik." She took Bella's chin in her hand. "And as for you, your photos are incredible. You deserve every accolade you get tonight. Enjoy every second."

Malik kissed the top of his mom's head. "Thank you," he said softly. "Thank you for everything."

He glanced at his watch. "Okay, Bella and I have to go." He pointed to the wheelchair. "Your carriage awaits, madam."

Bella shook her head. "No. Not tonight. Tonight, I'm going to do this on my own. It might be the last night I can." She stepped toward the door. "Can we leave it in the car, just in case?"

"Of course." He folded the chair and winked at his mom. "We'll see the two of you in a while."

CHAPTER 30

Nothing lives in darkness.

Soft music wafted through the air inside the gallery. Marty winked in the direction of the artists before he opened the door to the line of people waiting outside. Malik was the first one through the door. Bella pulled her shoulders back and lifted her chin when she saw him. For three hours, this was the person Bella wanted everyone to see—confident and healthy. When residents thought back to this night, she didn't want them recalling the dying young woman.

A man in a slim-fit black suit held a tray of wine glasses toward Bella and Malik. She shook her head. Malik declined as well.

"Could you bring some water, though?" he asked.

"Of course." The man backed away and returned with two water bottles on the tray.

After a quarter-hour of listening to Marty talk about the artists and wishing she'd worn stronger deodorant, Bella finally moved toward her photos with Malik. The pictures of Tilly's hands with her Bible, the children playing, the nearly invisible child beneath the streetlight, and Tilly sitting in her chair praying were all on display. Bella had also chosen other photos, ones not even Malik had seen.

The booklet, the size of a half sheet of paper, appeared miniature in Malik's hands. Inside was additional information about each artist, their work, an artist statement, and the price for each piece. Items purchased tonight would stay in the gallery until the end of the month, when it would open with new artists.

"What's with this?" he asked, pointing to an empty hook near Bella's photos. "Did you already sell something?"

He opened the brochure, but Bella pulled it from his hands. As if on cue, Marty appeared with a picture and hung it on the empty hanger.

Malik stepped toward it. Bella hung back as he studied it. Butterflies swam in her stomach. "Wh-what is this?" He turned toward her.

Unlike all her other photos, this picture was black and white. It was a grouping of many images surrounding an abstract center of varying grays.

Bella pulled Malik backward and aimed him at the picture. "Who do you see when you look at the center?"

"You mean *what* do I see?" He shook his head and shrugged. "I don't see…" Then, suddenly, he leaned forward. "That's us. You and me. I don't think I would have seen that had you not pointed it out."

Bella nodded. "It is us." She swallowed hard. "And the photos around the center, the ones that show a person from birth through old age…" She waited for Malik to look at them. "That's our child."

"What?" Malik stepped back. "What are you talking about?"

"I used several different programs to create the first image of what our baby might look like. Then I used age progression software to show what he would look like throughout his life."

Malik moved toward the picture. "A child *you and I* would have?"

Bella could hear the torment in his voice. Her hands shook.

She'd been so sure he would love it that she hadn't given thought to the possibility it would send him over the edge. "Yes," she said softly. She laid a hand on his back. "Are you okay?"

"No."

Her heart jumped. "Talk to me. Tell me what you're feeling."

Malik's eyes shifted from Bella to the picture several times. "Why did you do this?"

"Because it felt right. It's the child I pictured since I fell in love with you." She looked down at her locked hands. "I wanted to know what could have been. I thought you might also."

He opened the booklet and turned to the section on *Bellarina Levitsky*. The photo was missing from her prints. Malik held the open pages toward her. "Where is it? Where's the picture?"

"It's on the wall, Malik. I'm not selling it. I am giving it to you." Her shoulders shook as she drew a ragged breath. "I made it for you—if you want it." Tears threatened to spill over. She hadn't prepared herself for this reaction.

"Malik?" She stepped in front of him.

His head moved in the tiniest motion. "Of course, I *don't* want it."

"Talk to me." Bella's stomach churned. "Please?"

"This is too much." His hands shot up near his shoulders before he turned and walked away, leaving Bella to stand alone in a gallery full of people.

Bella watched him go before plastering a fake smile on her face and greeting her public. She returned hugs and smiles and pleasantries with everyone, all the while searching for Malik behind them. Her thoughts were on his reaction—his rejection. She needed to find Marty and ask him to remove the photo, but that was impossible. What should have felt like adoring fans now felt like a roadblock.

An hour later, still surrounded by throngs of people, Malik walked toward the print. He, along with his parents and Tilly, stood in front of the picture. They were talking and pointing to different aspects of the image. More than anything, Bella wished to be a fly on the wall, listening to their thoughts. Instead, she continued to hold meaningless conversations.

Tilly, Lou, and Maggie made their way toward her, but Malik walked away. None of them mentioned that particular picture. Tilly and Maggie hugged her and told her how proud they were. Lou wrapped an arm around her shoulder and kissed the top of her head.

Tilly stopped in front of her and squeezed her hand. "I love ya, Bella," she said. "I'm so gosh darn proud of ya."

Bella's heart skipped a beat. Those were the words she had waited nine months to hear, but they were overshadowed by Malik's reaction to the picture.

"I love you too, Tilly." The old woman's hand slipped out of hers, and she wheeled her walker toward the door.

Someone touched her back. She turned and came face-to-face with Malik. Goosebumps rose on her arms, and a chill ran up her spine.

"Sorry, folks. I need to borrow the star for a few minutes," he announced.

Floating rather than walking, Bella let Malik lead her down a hallway to a back office. He nodded for her to sit. From a decanter of water, he poured a glass and handed it to her. Finally, he planted himself on the edge of the desk.

"Why?" He shook his head. "Why did you do this?"

Bella didn't respond. Nothing she could say could defend her actions.

"If things were different, Bella, we would have gotten married and had children. I would choose you as my *always*."

He crossed his arms. "But they aren't. You're dying…" He swiped at a tear. "And I'm dying with you—knowing I'm losing you—a little bit more every day. This is already so incredibly painful for me." A second tear fell. "And then you do this—remind me of everything I'll miss out on. Why?"

Bella looked down. It hurt too much to see Malik suffer. "I thought I was doing it for *you*," she whispered. "But now I realize it was for me. *I* needed to see what I was…" She gulped. "…losing."

She stood and moved toward Malik. "You stand there and say how much this hurts you. Well, what about me? There are so many things I'll never experience. I mean…" She looked up at him and frowned. "I'm still a virgin." Malik's eyes narrowed, and his mouth straight-lined. "That's right. I saved myself for my husband." She turned away. "But life has a funny way of ruining your plans, doesn't it?"

Bella clung to the glass with both hands. Water sloshed as she took a sip. "My whole life, I've wanted nothing more than a husband and a family. I found part of my family when I arrived in Lawson Beach. You, Tilly, and your parents *are* my family. But I wanted so much more. I wanted to be a wife and a mother."

Tears fell faster. "Do you know that sometimes at night, before I fall asleep, I pretend I'm not dying? I imagine our wedding, having kids with you, growing old together. I can see it all. But it's all make-believe, just like that picture out there. It's all pretend, Malik. That's all my life is."

She stood in front of the window and stared into the night. "That…" She pointed a finger outside. "That's all I see when I think about dying. Darkness. Nothing lives in darkness, Malik. So I have to imagine wonderful things to keep myself from falling into the abyss of panic and self-pity." She turned toward him. "That's what the photo did for me. I'm sorry it hurt you.

That was never my intent."

Bella looked at the clock on the wall. "I have to go back out there." Tears escaped, and she wiped them away. "I'm sorry. After tonight, I'll destroy the picture." She pointed to her forehead. "I have it here." Then she laid a hand on her chest. "And in here…for as long as I'm on earth."

She watched him for a second before walking out the door.

The crowd had expanded by the time she returned. Those who had missed her on their first time through flooded back into her space. A few people asked about the picture, but no one doubted her when she said it was a friend's child. Either they couldn't see the faded images of her and Malik, or they dared not mention it.

By the time 9:00 p.m. rolled around, Bella was ready to collapse. All ten of her photos had been sold. They would stay until the end of the month. The eleventh would go home with her. She would burn it in Tilly's pristine fire ring in the garden.

Maggie appeared from around a corner. "Hey, sweetie. It looks like you had a fabulous night."

Bella gave her a knowing look.

"In terms of the public, I mean." Maggie looked around the gallery. "Malik asked me to bring you home." She enveloped Bella in a hug. "I'm sorry, honey. I know you meant well." She rubbed Bella's back. "For what it's worth, I think the picture's amazing." She nodded toward it. "That boy could have been my grandson. But I just think it hit Malik kind of hard. He loves you, and… Well, maybe it was just too much of a reminder."

"I know that now," Bella sobbed.

"Let's go home. Tomorrow's another day."

"We need to take that picture with us."

Marty pulled it from the wall. "Great show, Bella. There was a lot of buzz about your photographs." He sighed when he looked at the empty space on the wall. "The show'll be here all month. Stop in whenever you feel well enough." He handed Maggie the picture. "I'll send you a check after all the purchases clear."

Bella hugged him. "Can you do me a favor?"

"Sure."

"Can you write the check to Nate and Destiny Percy?"

The line between Marty's eyes deepened. "Are you sure that's what you want?"

She shook her head. "Yeah. You can mail it directly to them. Just tell them it's from me."

"Okay. No problem." He hugged her again. "Bella, you are extraordinarily talented. If you don't mind me asking, who nurtured you as a photographer?"

"Tilly."

Marty looked confused. "I didn't know Tilly was a photographer."

Bella lightly snorted. "She's not. But she saw things in me I didn't see in myself."

Maggie put an arm over Bella's shoulder. "Come on, honey. Let's go home." She guided Bella toward the door.

***

The house was unusually dark when they arrived. "Is Tilly already in bed?" Bella asked.

"Uh-huh. Lou brought her home a while ago. He stayed until she was asleep."

Bella nodded. "Goodnight, Maggie. Thank you for being there for me tonight. I hope you know how much I love you."

"We all feel the same about you. You're a very special person."

She shook her head. "I doubt very much Malik feels that way anymore."

Maggie grabbed Bella's hands. "People don't instantly fall out of love. Give him time. He'll come around."

"I don't have time." Bella walked toward her bedroom.

Her backpack was lying on the floor near her bed. She hadn't remembered leaving it there, but then again, she'd been somewhat scattered when she'd been getting ready for the night. She picked it up and rummaged through it before returning it to the chair. Everything seemed in place, but she had this unnerving feeling something was wrong.

Her body ached with exhaustion. She could barely put one foot in front of the other. She felt an internal shaking, a buzz that coursed through her veins. No matter how many times she tried to think of something else, the foreboding feeling wouldn't go away. It clung to her as she shuffled into the bathroom.

Her reflection in the mirror stopped her. Even through the tears and exhaustion, she still looked beautiful. In the past, she would have never thought of herself as even pretty. But when Malik had told her she was beautiful, she finally believed it. She saw it.

The shorts and tank top she usually slept in hung on a hook. Reaching for them, the mirror again grabbed her attention. She drew a sharp breath. It was over. Tilly's god was coming for her.

Bella hung her pajamas back on the hook. If this was her final night, she wanted to look beautiful when they found her in the morning. So she crawled into bed in the dress Tilly had made for her, and even though she'd lost Malik, she fell asleep, imagining their perfect life.

CHAPTER 31

All that is lost

The curtains fluttered in the early morning breeze. Bella felt the bottom of the thin sheers brush against her arm, stirring her from sleep. Every morning since she'd received the crushing news, she lay in bed with her eyes closed and slowly counted to ten. She hoped beyond hope it had all been a dream and her body was strong and healthy. But this morning, even with her eyes shut, she knew it was real. The truth wound around her and squeezed so tightly, she could barely draw a breath.

Surprisingly, she'd woken to another day, one of an unknown number. Disappointment haunted her. She'd been certain she wouldn't see the morning light. It was the not knowing that pawed at her. *Would it happen today? Tomorrow?* Uncertainty stomped through her. After the gallery fiasco with Malik, she was ready to float away—disappear into whatever lay beyond clouds. Facing him again was more than she could handle. *Why hadn't Tilly's god come to find her?*

She ran her hand down the front of the dress, feeling the silkiness of the overlay. The dress was the kindest gesture she'd ever received. In her world, *kindness* had been nothing more than a word in the dictionary. It was a gift others received, never Bella. Her nannies, foster families, and even her parents had always served their needs and wants before hers. Even when her folks were alive, she steered clear of their endless squabbling and flying objects. Between travel and practice, they had no time for kindness; they had no time for their only child. Then, when she was finally on her own, it was difficult to determine whether her college friends liked her for who she was or for her bank account. She hadn't flaunted her money, but not having to work her way through college inevitably set her apart from everyone else.

Alone. Bella realized now that was how she'd always felt. *Unseen. Invisible. Ignored. Lonely.* But here, in Lawson Beach, Bella had found the things she craved: family, love, *and* kindness. And they saw her; they really saw her. Tilly, Lou, Maggie, and Malik weren't her family in the traditional sense, but did that matter? Wasn't family the people you chose—those who chose you?

Bella slowly sat up and lifted her legs over the side of the bed. They hung there for several moments before she tested them. When she tried to stand, she fell back onto the worn mattress. If she wasn't going to die today, it had to be closing in. It had taken every ounce of strength she had saved to get through the gallery opening.

Again, she tried to stand. This time, it took. She slid her feet along the floor as she clung to the bed. When she reached the wall, it became her support. Sitting on the bench in the large walk-in closet, she slipped on the shorts with the safety-pinned waistband and a worn t-shirt before shuffling to the door. Miraculously, the wheelchair had been left in the hallway outside her room. Bella dropped into it and clumsily maneuvered herself to the kitchen.

As always, Maggie was whipping up some fabulous breakfast Bella wouldn't eat. "I thought you might want the chair this morning. You looked pretty wiped out last night." She removed Bella's usual chair from the table and positioned her wheelchair in its place.

"Thank you." Bella gave her a thin smile. "No Tilly?"

"Not yet. I checked on her a few minutes ago. She's still asleep."

"I imagine it was a long night for her."

Maggie set a small scoop of scrambled eggs and a strawberry and whipped cream-filled crepe in front of Bella. "It was an amazing night. You should be incredibly proud."

Bella frowned. "Proud—and *not* proud."

"We're not going to dwell on that." Maggie swiped the back of her hand across her forehead. "Are you warm? I am. It's hot in here, right?" She flapped the neck of her t-shirt back and forth. "This menopause thing is for the birds. It's bad enough women have to suffer through childbirth, but then, add in their monthly visitor, and top it off with hot flashes and mood swings so bad you want to kill anyone who stands between you and a breeze."

Bella sighed. She would have loved the chance to suffer through all of it. "Well, I'm not cold—and that's unusual for me. So it probably is." Bella poked a fork into her crepe and tore a small piece off.

"Oh, honey. I'm so sorry. I didn't even think…"

"No, don't. I don't want you to have to watch everything you say around me."

Maggie uneasily pointed to the living room. "I'm going to open the windows in there and get a cross-breeze going."

Bella chewed the tiny piece of crepe, already wishing she hadn't. She picked up her napkin and wiped it out of her mouth. Her stomach flip-flopped, and she worried about what might follow.

Suddenly, Maggie shrieked. "Oh, my God! Tilly!"

She raced out the side door.

"What is it?" But Maggie was already gone. A sudden burst of adrenaline shot through Bella. On wobbly yet committed legs, she followed Maggie.

By the time she reached the garden, she saw what Maggie had seen from the window. Tilly was in her chair. Her head hung forward and tilted to one side. In one hand, she held the small recorder. She wore a long sleeve nightgown, and she was covered in a thin blanket. Depending on when she made her way outside, she couldn't have been warm enough.

"Tilly," Bella called as she shook the old woman's arm. "Tilly, wake up. Let's get you inside so you can warm up."

Maggie unsteadily stepped back as Bella moved closer. "Come on, Tilly. Wake up."

Suddenly, Bella's face crumpled into a sobbing mess. "M-Maggie, do something."

But Maggie didn't move. "Maggie, please? Help me wake her up."

Maggie reached down and tugged on Bella's arm. "I'm afraid she's gone, honey."

"No she's not. She's just sleeping." Bella shook Tilly again. "Right, Tilly? You're just sleeping, right?"

Tilly fell to the side.

"Noooo!" Bella wailed. She dropped to her knees. "Noooo!" She laid her forehead in Tilly's lap and sobbed.

Maggie rubbed Bella's back. "Honey, I'm so sorry. I'm so very sorry."

"Oh, Tilly. Please. You didn't even say goodbye."

"Bella, she did. Words aren't the only way to say goodbye. That dress was Tilly's goodbye."

"But *I-I* didn't get to say g-goodbye." Bella took Tilly's hand.

Maggie sat on the ground next to her. "Oh, honey, you can still tell her. Tilly knew how much you loved her." Maggie ran her hand down the back of Bella's hair several times. "You want to know what I think? I think Tilly willed herself to die before you. She'd do anything to head the welcoming committee when you get to heaven."

Except for the musical chirping of the painted bunting and the slurred tweet of the perfectly timed Wilson's plover, the air was still. Tilly had taught Bella to recognize the birds that frequented the garden by sight and sound. She had joked that the Wilson's plover had been named after her. Every time she said it, Bella rolled her eyes and played along.

"My heart's breaking, Maggie," Bella said softly.

"Mine too, honey," Maggie admitted. "Mine too."

***

Maggie had not left Bella's side since they found Tilly in the garden. Bella knew she carried a tremendous amount of guilt over thinking Tilly had been asleep in bed when she checked on her. The old woman had clearly wanted everyone to think that. The way she had cleverly arranged her pillows and fluffed the comforter gave the appearance of her body. Perhaps Maggie had been right. Tilly had wanted to die on her own terms—just like Bella.

Bella knew Maggie struggled with knowing Tilly died alone. She hadn't confessed it in those *exact* words, but when Maggie started sleeping on the couch in Bella's sitting room, she knew.

Since Tilly's passing, Bella again cried herself to sleep rather than conjuring up her make-believe life with Malik. Her heart ached for all she'd lost in recent days and all she would lose soon.

***

Three days later, on the morning Tilly was to be laid to rest, Bella couldn't get out of bed. Physically, she was able, but emotionally, she couldn't face the final goodbye. Since that dreaded morning, Bella had made a slight rebound. She'd done it for Tilly and for Maggie—who seemed to need Bella more than ever.

"Get up, Bella," Maggie insisted. "Tilly wouldn't want us sitting around mourning her. She'd want us to have a party. So that's what we're going to do. It'll be the best send-off party Lawson Beach has ever seen."

Maggie laid the white dress on the bed next to Bella. "Here, wear this."

"It's a funeral, Maggie."

Channeling Tilly, Maggie tsked. "It's a party. In the south, we don't even call it a funeral. It's a *Homegoing.*"

Bella bit her bottom lip. "Maggie, do you really believe that? Do you honestly think Tilly is going *home*?"

Maggie sat next to Bella. "With all my heart." She laid a hand on her chest. "I know we'll all be together again. You and Tilly are just lucky enough to get to go first."

So, instead of wearing black, Bella wore the white dress. Maggie donned a pink one that matched Lou's tie. Malik wore the same suit he'd worn to the gallery opening. They would stick out like *dog's balls*—as Tilly used to say, but Bella wasn't about to refuse Maggie anything.

At the same church Bella had sworn she would never visit again, Lou helped her out of the car. Bella had insisted on walking into the church. Today wasn't about her; it was about Tilly. A wheelchair-bound Bella would bring nothing but questions. When she looked at the church, she smiled. All this time, Tilly knew Bella would be back. When she'd said she would never return, Tilly's response had been, "We'll see." She knew Bella would return—for her *Homegoing.*

As they walked toward the church, they passed through rows of chairs that had been set up on the lawn—seats for latecomers who would not fit inside. It appeared the entire town had come for Tilly's send-off. Everyone loved her. Black or white. Young or old. Rich or poor. But, by some twist of fate,

Bella had been gifted the opportunity to be thought of as her granddaughter.

Heads pivoted when the four entered the church. Lou had Bella on one arm and Maggie on the other. Whispers washed through the open space, spreading from the back to the front. People poked one another and pointed as they passed by each pew. Lou, Maggie, Malik, and Bella were sunshine in a sea of black. *Disgraceful. Unacceptable. Disrespectful. It simply was not done.* And yet, here they were—doing exactly that.

Before entering the front pew, Maggie addressed the congregation. "No, we do not belong to your church."

"Or any church." A man on the other side disguised the barb beneath a fake cough.

Lou and Maggie both glared at him. "Maybe not, but that doesn't mean we don't believe. We all grieve in our own way. But today, we are *all* here for Tilly." Maggie smiled. "And you know Tilly. She'd tan our hides if we wasted an opportunity to throw a good party. So we dressed for that party." She pointed to their clothing. "Today, instead of crying for what we lost, we're here to celebrate the life of Matilda Violet Robinson Wilson—a woman clearly loved by everyone."

She slid in next to Bella. Lou winked at her, and Bella looped her arm through Maggie's. Malik smiled at his mother but avoided eye contact with Bella.

Since the night of the gallery opening, he had not said one word to her. For reasons Bella understood but hated, he'd kept his distance. He hadn't even ridden with them to the funeral. Instead, he arrived separately, seconds behind them. Bella felt the pit in her stomach grow when he made his way around the front of the pew to sit next to his father. *Today is about Tilly,* she told herself. She would deal with Malik tomorrow.

The old crockpot sat in the middle of a small table in the front of the church. It felt oddly out of place outside the walls of Tilly's kitchen, yet the missing knob and words had a familiarity that calmed Bella. On the day Tilly died, Maggie had taken an old toothbrush to the slow cooker, scrubbing off a lifetime of cooked-on grease. Bella saw it as busy work—something to keep Maggie from focusing on Tilly's death. She hadn't realized Maggie had been serious about laying the old woman's ashes to rest in the ancient pot. But there they were—Tilly in her crockpot. Tears rolled down her face and seeped between her lips as Bella smiled.

A large cross of white chrysanthemums and red roses stood to one side of the table. A wide ribbon with the words *Heaven called; Tilly answered!* hung across the spray. Tilly's picture rested on the easel on the other side. Maggie had borrowed it from the gallery for the service. A long line of people approached the front of the church. Each carried a vase or a handful of flowers picked from their own gardens. They placed them on long tables or added them to empty vases before stopping to pay their final respects by laying a hand on the old slow cooker.

During the service, congregants called out *Amen!* and *Praise the Lord!* This time, Bella was prepared. The solemnity she had expected for the funeral was cast out by the upbeat music Maggie had selected. The preacher's message was the same as Tilly's had been. *Get right with God before it's too late.* Was it already too late for Bella?

Malik, Maggie, and Lou told stories about Tilly. Some were hysterical; others curled her toes in irreverence, and some made Bella cry. Malik's stories came complete with an impersonation of Tilly's voice. The congregation smiled and laughed. Bella did not leave her seat; she couldn't. Since her landlady's death, her words had gotten stuck somewhere inside. She'd barely spoken about Tilly—even to Maggie.

At the end of the service, with the choir chomping at the bit to end on a high note, the pastor spoke one last time.

Staring at the slow cooker, he laid a hand on the glass lid. "It's a bit unusual for someone to be buried in a crockpot." He tipped his head slightly. "But then again, Tilly was a unique woman." A grin spread across his face as he retrieved a pair of wire cutters from a side table. "So, before we end the service, I have the honor of cutting Tilly's earthly cord and letting her go into the hands of the Lord."

The pastor opened the snips and cut the cord from the crockpot. He looked up and smiled. "Godspeed, Tilly." A lopsided grin fell across his face when he glanced into the church before looking up again. "And maybe hold off on telling God what to do—at least for a while."

Suddenly a bouquet fell off a table and onto the floor.

"Okay, go ahead. You're gonna do what you want anyway."

The congregation's laughter bled into the choir's version of Stevie Wonder's *You Are the Sunshine of My Life*.

At the cemetery, Bella tapped Maggie's arm. "Why's Tilly buried on one side of her parents and James on the other."

Maggie raised an eyebrow. "Well, her father died first, then James. When they buried her father in the second grave, everyone assumed her mother would be interred in the first, but Tilly insisted on being next to her mom when she died," Maggie whispered. "So..."

"So James had to be buried on the other side of her father. Do you think that was her plan all along?"

Maggie nodded. "Tilly planned everything."

"Do you think she'll forgive him when she gets to heaven?"

Maggie took Bella's hand. "Honey, in heaven, there's no hatred or anger. Forgiveness is for those of us down here." She smirked. "But Tilly's cut from a different cloth. She'll most likely figure out a way to make James suffer a bit before she forgives him."

Bella smiled. *Yes, she would.*

Maggie was joking. But if she was right, forgiveness wasn't needed in heaven. It was for those of us left on earth. That meant she had to find a way to forgive everyone who'd ever hurt her in the short time she had left. And that included Malik.

***

After the graveside service, everyone returned to the church. Tables had been set up outdoors to accommodate the enormous crowd. The church ladies had organized the repast, ensuring there was enough ham, funeral grits, biscuits, and tea cakes to feed the masses.

The preacher blessed the food before people helped themselves to the buffet. When he was done, an older woman threw her hands up and hollered, "Bless Tilly's soul! Now pass the ham." A wave of giggles fluttered across the churchyard as the choir serenaded the crowd.

Maggie set a plate of food in front of Bella and frowned. "Try to eat something, honey," she said. Malik sat at a table with several uniformed police officers. Bella wished he would have joined the family, at least for this final meal.

When they returned from the cemetery, Lou had insisted Bella use her wheelchair. Mourners stopped by on their way out of the churchyard. Rumors circulated about Bella's cancer. The handful of people who knew the truth shared it. The chatter was mainly about her joining Tilly soon. When they spoke to her, they hugged her too long or squeezed her hand too hard. It was uncomfortable—yet comforting.

When the yard had finally cleared, the church ladies began folding tables and chairs and stacking them on carts.

The preacher hoisted a table onto the cart before he approached them. "Are you ready?" he asked.

Maggie looked at Lou and nodded. "Yes, sir." She smiled at Malik before turning toward Bella. "Honey, we need to take care of some things inside. Do you want to wait out here?”

“Sure.” Bella wheeled herself into the shade of a massive tree at the corner of the church. She closed her eyes and folded her hands—and prayed. There was no begging, just praying. It wasn’t Tilly’s god she was talking to. It was God.

When she finally opened her eyes, Malik stood in front of her. She looked into the sky. *God worked faster than she knew.*

“Bella, I need to ask you to forgive me. I’m so sorry for the way I reacted at the gallery. That picture took me by surprise— to say the least.” He shook his head. “It’s not that I didn’t love it; it just reminded me of your…”

Bella opened her mouth, but Malik stopped her. “After I thought about it, I realized what an amazing gift it was.” He took a deep breath. “I don’t think you realize how much I love you. I’ve never met anyone like you. Even as sick as you are, you shine brighter than the sun and the moon and the stars. I don’t want you to fight this battle alone. I want to be next to you, holding your hand through it all.”

Bella launched herself forward and wrapped her arms around Malik. “I love you,” she whispered.

“I have somewhere I want to take you,” he said.

Malik pushed the wheelchair toward the church and through the double doors. Maggie and Lou stood up front on opposite sides of the pastor.

Bella held her palms upward, clearly confused. “What’s going on?”

Malik got down on one knee and reached into his jacket pocket. “Bella, I want you to be my wife.” Her heart raced as the news hit full force. “For the rest of our lives. Whether it’s three days, three months, or three decades—it doesn’t matter. I want our lives to be woven together for eternity. In heaven, I still want to be your *forever*.”

Bella stared at the gold band with the small diamond chips.

Tears tumbled down her cheeks. "Yes," she said. "Yes. Oh, yes."

Malik picked up a bouquet from the last pew. "Can I push you down the aisle, soon-to-be Mrs. Jackson?"

"Wait! We're doing this now?" Her eyes grew wide. "We don't even have a marriage license."

He removed a folded piece of paper from his front jacket pocket. "We do." A lopsided grin emerged. "Forgive me for digging through your bag the other night, but I needed a few things."

"Like my signature?" Bella questioned with a smirk.

"Technicalities." Malik turned toward the front of the church and laughed out loud. "Preacher, plug your ears." He pointed to his chest. "Cop with friends in high places." He pointed at Maggie. "And a ma who can forge dang near anything."

"Malik!" Maggie warned.

"So, what do you think? Do you want to marry me today?"

Bella pressed a foot to the ground. "Yes. I do. But I'm walking down this aisle."

Malik helped her to her feet before he moved toward the front of the church.

Lou came toward her. "May I walk you down the aisle?" He offered his arm.

"I'd like that." Bella hooked her arm through his and leaned her head against his shoulder.

Lou supported her as they slowly moved toward her husband-to-be. When they reached the front pew, Malik took her arm from his father. In a white dress, holding a beautiful bouquet of roses, Bella married the love of her life. After he kissed his bride, Malik scooped her up and carried her to her chair.

"Wait!" Bella said before he wheeled her out of the church.

Holding a hand into the air, she silenced everyone. A warm sensation washed over her, and she felt a hand on the back of her head. *Was it Tilly? Or was it God?* It didn't matter. She had just been blessed in ways she couldn't even describe.

"What is it?" Maggie asked.

Bella released a long sigh. "Nothing. I just wanted to savor the moment." She took Malik's hand and squeezed it. "Are you ready for our honeymoon, Mr. Jackson?"

CHAPTER 32

What if...?

While Bella waited in the passenger's seat, Malik retrieved her wheelchair and brought it to the side of his car. He had parked in Tilly's driveway, between the two houses.

"So…" Bella raised an eyebrow and stared at her new husband. "Are we going to live in my bedroom in Tilly's house?" She wagged a finger toward Malik's parents' house. "Or in your childhood bedroom with the blue sailboat wallpaper?"

Malik looked from one house to the other. Finally, his smile turned into a snort of laughter. "We are pretty pathetic, aren't we?"

"Maybe a little."

Bella clung to the door as she pulled herself up. Maneuvering the wheelchair closer to her, Malik alternately studied their options.

"Tilly's," he said unquestionably. "Your stuff's there. Besides…" Malik winked at her. "…my room's right next to my folks'." He pulled the wheelchair backward, shut the car door, and spun her toward him. "In the throes of passion, are you a screamer?"

"Oh, my God!" Bella laughed. Suddenly, her eyes darkened.

"What is it? What's going through your head?"

"Are we even allowed to stay here? Or does the house belong to Jasmine now?" She bit her bottom lip.

"For a loquacious old woman, she never talked about the critical stuff, did she?" He wheeled Bella toward the house. "Once you came to live with her, she changed her will. You can stay here as long as you…*need*."

Bella shook her head. "I didn't know that. She never said a word about her will."

The chair bumped over the shell-covered walkway. "By the way, Malik, please don't feel like you have to sugarcoat things for me. Don't stop yourself from saying I'm dying." He stopped at the bottom of the ramp and sat on the porch step facing her.

"What are you talking about?"

"You said, 'stay here for as long as you *need*.' You do that often. Just say *until you die* or *until you're gone*. If Tilly taught me anything, it's to say it like it is."

"In my head, I know that." He laid a hand against his chest. "But my heart doesn't always want to admit the truth."

Bella touched his cheek. "I'm pretty sure I figured that out after the picture fiasco at the gallery."

"Touché!" He laughed.

Carefully, he wheeled Bella up the ramp. He held the door open with his foot, lifted her from her chair, and carried her over the threshold.

"Welcome home, Mrs. Jackson."

Bella's heart swelled. Even with the end pressing in, she was happier than she'd ever been.

"What would you like to do first?" Malik set her on the couch before grabbing a couple of extra pillows.

She frowned. "This isn't going to be popular, but I really need a nap."

"Then a nap it is."

Malik pulled a blanket over the top of Bella and gently

kissed her. "Will you be okay if I run next door and grab some of my stuff?"

Bella closed her eyes. "I'm not going anywhere. Take your time."

***

A noise in the kitchen startled Bella, rousing her from the happiest dream she'd had in a long time. She wasn't even sure how long she'd been asleep. Had it been minutes or hours?

"Malik, is that you?" She stretched and yawned and threw the covers over the back of the couch.

A woman with shoulder-length dark hair stepped into the living room. "Who the hell are you?" she grunted.

Bella scooted backward on the couch and sat up. "Y-you're Jasmine. Tilly's daughter," she said. "You look just like her."

The woman scowled. "I didn't ask who I was. I asked who *you* are." She glanced around the room. "This place hasn't changed since I left forty-two years ago. It still has the same crappy furniture." Jasmine tapped the bottom corner of a picture to straighten it. "Even the decorations are the same." Suddenly, she turned her attention back to Bella. "So, who are you?"

"I'm Bella. I've been…"

"No. Don't tell me. You're another one of those strays my mother always brought home." Jasmine shook her head. "Cat, dog, human—didn't matter. She didn't have time for me, but she had time for everything and everybody else."

Bella kept her eyes glued to Jasmine, unsure how to respond. She was a stray. Tilly *had* taken her in, saved her like a homeless pet.

"Why are you even here? I thought my mother died." The woman was like a Category 5 hurricane—loud and destructive—not caring who she plowed over.

Bella flinched when she looked at the clock. Tilly's *Homegoing* had ended not more than four hours before. Where had Jasmine been then? Was she so hateful she would have purposely refused to attend?

Jasmine aimed the back of her hand in Bella's direction and flicked it outward twice, dismissing her. "Shouldn't you be on your way?" She ran her hand along the wide wooden trim. "I've got enough to do to get this place ready to sell without having some freeloader underfoot. I don't need my mother's leeches hanging around."

Uncharacteristically quiet, Malik appeared in the doorway. Bella felt the tenseness in her shoulders melt.

"And who are you?" he asked.

Jasmine spun around. "I'm the old woman's daughter."

Bella cringed at the phrase *old woman*. She and Malik had used it to tease Tilly from time to time, but hearing her daughter say it felt wrong. It wasn't teasing when Jasmine's words erupted from her mouth.

Malik nodded pointedly. "Ah. So you're Jasmine. Too bad you missed your ma's funeral today. It was standing room only—even in the churchyard. People sure loved her."

Jasmine rolled her eyes. "Well, clearly, they only came for the food. The deadbeats in this town'll go anywhere for free eats." She folded her arms across her chest. "And who are you?"

"Malik Jackson. I live—*lived* next door—until a little while ago. Now I live here." He pointed toward the floor.

"What the hell are you talking about? This is *my* house now. I'm Tilly's nearest living relative."

Malik's shoulders nearly touched the bottom of his ears when he shrugged. "That may be. Congratulations on staking that claim, by the way." He walked into the room and sat next to Bella. "But…and this is coming from my law enforcement background, being the closest living relative doesn't automatically make you the sole benefactor. Tilly had a will."

Jasmine's eyes narrowed. "Well, whoop de do! The woman

was nuttier than a squirrel turd."

Bella stifled a laugh. Malik grinned at her.

"And we thought Tilly had some interesting lines," he said.

"I could have her will contested. There's evidence dating back to the day she was born that shows she wasn't worth the paper her birth certificate's written on."

Again, Malik shrugged. "You don't know what you're talking about. Tilly was one of the most loved and respected citizens in Lawson Beach." A loud sigh filled the room. "There isn't a person in this town who would tell you any different." Malik squeezed Bella's hand. "And if the will was written and notarized in good faith, it stands as is."

He poked a finger in the air. "But, if you still want to fight this out, Grayson Bennett's her attorney—*thee Grayson Bennett.*"

Jasmine's mouth fell open. "Grayson Bennett?"

Malik nodded. "I take it you've heard of him. Anyway, you can contact him to find out what the will says. Or you can wait for him to get a hold of you. Ball's in your court. But like I said, if you choose to fight, you'll have to find yourself some big city lawyer, 'cause no one around here would ever take your case."

Jasmine's jaw tightened as she stared at Malik. "And where is Bennett's office?"

"Downtown."

Bella started to shake. She tightened her arms across her chest. "Malik?" she whispered.

"His office is on Coast Avenue, between Second and Third Street."

"Malik." Her voice sounded more urgent. She touched his arm. "Something's wrong."

His head snapped sideways. Bella was ghost white. Her entire body tremored. He dropped to his knees next to the couch. "Call 911!" he bellowed in Jasmine's direction.

Jasmine moved closer. "What's wrong with her?"

"Other than dying, you mean? She has cancer. For God's sake, call 911."

"Let me take a look. I'm a physician's assistant." She pushed him to the side with her knee. "Get my medical bag out of the backseat of my car," she snapped.

She sat next to Bella on the edge of the wide couch. Her voice was calm as she pulled the pillows from behind Bella's back and lowered her into a prone position. "*Bella*, you said. Is that right?" Jasmine didn't wait for her to answer. "How much time do you have left?"

Tears rolled down her pale cheeks. "A couple of weeks maybe," Bella said through chattering teeth.

"What kind of cancer do you have?" While Jasmine talked to her, she checked her pulse, pupils, and skin.

Sweat rolled down Bella's forehead. "Breast."

"When did you last see your oncologist?"

"Almost a year." Bella was shaking.

"I know you're sweating, but are you shivering because you're cold?"

Bella shook her head. "I'm hot. So hot, but I can't stop shaking."

"Your oncologist gave you a year?"

Bella nodded.

Malik rushed in and set the bag on the floor next to Jasmine.

"You haven't had chemo since then?" Jasmine unzipped her bag and removed a stethoscope. "Have you seen a doctor recently?"

Malik knelt next to Bella. "She was in for dehydration a few weeks ago. He gave her some antinausea pills. He thought they'd help…"

Jasmine looked directly at Malik. "Get me the bottle."

Bella continued to shiver. Black spots grew in her line of

vision. She tried to blink them away, but it was no use.

Malik handed Jasmine the amber bottle.

"Have you been taking these regularly, Bella?"

"No," she whispered.

Jasmine dropped the small container on the floor and rifled through her bag. She removed a glucometer and several other items. Then she tore open a packet that held an alcohol swab; she wiped it over her hands and dropped it to the floor. She opened a second and cleaned the tip of Bella's finger.

Jasmine turned toward Malik. "Hold her arm in the air, and don't let her hand touch anything." With precision, she slipped a small strip of paper into the meter. Taking Bella's hand from Malik, she pressed the machine against Bella's finger. "Small poke here." A drop of blood seeped out, and she set the edge of the paper into the globule. Within seconds, the meter beeped.

"Her blood sugar is extremely low. I mean, *really low.* When was the last time she ate?"

He shook his head. "She doesn't eat much anymore."

"Listen to me. I need a glass of soda—full sugar—or orange juice. If you don't have either of those, I need you to dissolve three teaspoons of sugar in a half glass of water." She looked at Bella. "Go, now."

Malik ran to the kitchen. Tilly still had several cans of her dollar store generic root beer. He grabbed a glass and raced back to the living room.

Jasmine opened it and emptied half the can into the glass. "I need her sitting. Get behind her and support her shoulders." Malik moved behind Bella.

"Bella, you have to drink this. Stay with me. Okay? We need to get some sugar in you."

Bella's hands shook as she tried to hold the glass. Malik wrapped his hands over the top of hers and raised it to her mouth. She took a small sip.

"Come on, Bella. You have to drink it all. Can you do that?" Jasmine put a finger against the bottom of the glass and tipped it up.

Bella took another small drink.

Malik brought the glass back to her mouth. "Come on, honey. You can do this. A big drink this time."

Bella took a gulp rather than a sip.

"More," Jasmine told her. "The whole thing. Down it."

She took another gulp, and another, until it was gone.

"Good girl," Malik said. He set the glass on the floor.

Jasmine fell onto the floor next to her bag.

"What do we do now?" Malik asked.

"We keep an eye on her and wait. In twenty minutes or so, I'll recheck her blood sugar. With any luck, this will have done the trick."

Malik smiled at Bella. For the first time in the last five minutes, she attempted a smile. Her mind raced with *what ifs. What if she'd been alone? What if this was the end? What if Malik had found her dead when he returned?*

"What happened?" Malik asked.

Jasmine returned the stethoscope to her bag. "Well, if I had to guess, her tumors are growing. Do you know when her last scan was?"

Malik frowned. "I'm sure it was when she left New York— in early October."

Jasmine looked at Bella. "With cancer, tumors often begin growing in other parts of the body. Bella, has anything like this happened to you before?"

She nodded. "A couple of times, but not this bad."

"What did you do when you felt shaky?" Jasmine asked.

"I ate something."

Jasmine nodded. "If the cancer's moved to her pancreas, it can create too much insulin, and her blood sugars can drop. Of course, if she's not eating much, she'll have low blood sugar anyway." She sighed loudly. "The antinausea pills the doctor prescribed are a steroid. Steroids tend to increase blood sugar, but since she hasn't been taking them regularly… Well…"

Malik exhaled through pursed lips. "She'll take them regularly now. I'll make sure."

Bella listened to the two of them talk. But, other than questions directed at her, their conversation still seemed muddled.

Jasmine slid sideways and leaned against the brick fireplace, keeping Bella directly in her line of vision. "So why are you here anyway?"

For the next ten minutes, Malik explained about being neighbors with Tilly, how Bella had come to live with her, and about the Homegoing and wedding earlier in the day.

"So, how long have you known my mother?"

"As Tilly would say—*since I was knee-high to a grasshopper*. Of course, when I was young, I used to call them *ass-jumpers*." He shook his head. "I couldn't quite get the whole grasshopper thing."

Jasmine smiled slightly. "And what was your opinion of my mother?"

"I loved her. She treated me like a grandson, and I thought of her as my grandmother. She didn't have a bad word to say about anyone."

"Except Malik," Bella mumbled.

"Well, well. Look who's back with us." Jasmine moved to the couch. "How're you feeling?"

"A million times better than I did." She touched Jasmine's shoulder. "Thank you."

Jasmine turned her head and closed one eye. "Mmm, don't thank me yet. We have to test your blood sugars again. I need to poke another finger."

"Great. Just what I was hoping for." She held a hand toward Jasmine.

"Is she going to be all right?" Malik asked.

"This isn't uncommon."

Malik looked concerned.

Jasmine checked Bella's blood sugar and gave her the *all-clear* for the time being. "Tell me about the will?"

Bella laid her head in Malik's lap. He rubbed her bare arm while he talked.

"The will gives Bella the right to stay here until…" He looked down at her.

"It's okay," she whispered.

"Until she passes. At that time, the house is yours." Malik watched Jasmine. "Also, the bistro my folks bought from Tilly…"

"Wait! What are you talking about?"

"You didn't know Tilly used to own a café?"

Jasmine shook her head. "No." She leaned backward. "Huh."

"Well, according to the will, upon Tilly's passing, my folks own the bistro free and clear." He smiled down at Bella. "As for her money, there are many organizations who will each get a piece. Your ma was known as a philanthropist around here. But don't worry, she left you some."

"How do you know all of this?" Jasmine again leaned against the fireplace.

"Ma's the executor of her will. I've known the plan since I was…"

"Let me guess. Knee-high to an *ass-jumper*?"

Malik pointed at her and clicked his tongue. "You got it."

"So." She looked around the living room as if she was seeing it for the first time. "It looks like I'll be sticking around a while then. It'll give me time to get the house ready to sell."

She stood. "I don't like that you're here, but until I speak with…" she swallowed hard, "Tilly's lawyer, I can't do much about it."

She picked up her bag. "Is my old room still open?"

"Which one was yours?" Bella asked.

"The one with… Well, when I lived here, it had brown wallpaper with huge gold, red, orange…"

Bella cut her off. "…and brown overlaid circles? You'll be happy to know the ugly wallpaper's still there."

"Well, clearly, you didn't know what was cool in the 70s." She started toward the stairs.

"Yes, that room's open, and it's all yours." Bella smiled at Malik. "*We're* in the downstairs room toward the front of the house." She winked at Malik. "And it's our honeymoon night." She smirked.

CHAPTER 33

We only see what we want

Hard rock 70's music throbbed through the house. It had been playing for over an hour. Bella rolled to her back and waited for her stomach to stop stirring. She longed for the quiet mornings of Tilly. Malik's pillow was pressed over his head and an arm laid over the top. His eyes were closed, and he snored softly. How anyone could sleep through the jackhammering music was beyond Bella.

Seventeen hours earlier, she and Malik had promised to love one another for all of eternity. Days earlier, she still questioned whether eternity existed, but somehow, Tilly had gotten through to her. The possibility that Bella could see Tilly soon made dying not as frightening. As infuriating as her landlady often was, the woman held tightly to one belief—God.

The previous night had not been how she'd envisioned, and she was positive it hadn't been for Malik either. In the eyes of the law, albeit a forged signature, they were husband and wife, but in every other sense of the word, they were not. Bella was too fragile, weak, and broken to consummate their marriage. No matter how much she wanted to give herself to her husband, she would die a virgin.

Malik asked for nothing from her. There was no guilt, frustration, or anger from him. Repeatedly, he tried to convince her having his arms around her was all he needed. But the horrible disease had robbed her of so much already. This was just one more thing. He cradled her all night long—until the rock concert began, courtesy of Jasmine.

Bella kissed Malik's cheek and waited for his eyes to open.

"Good morning, wife." He slid toward her and pressed his lips to hers. Seconds later, he pitched his pillow against the wall. Angrily, he sat up and sighed. "It's not even 8:00. She's got the music turned up so damn loud she could wake the dead." Malik glanced at Bella. "Oh, if only the ghost of Tilly would appear. I'd love to hear her lay into Jasmine."

Bella grinned. "That would be a sight to see."

Malik crawled out of bed, picked up Bella, and carried her into the bathroom. In the past couple of weeks, she'd given up her need for privacy. She didn't have the time or the energy to care who saw what, including her new husband.

With her hair combed, teeth brushed, and a clean shirt on, he set her in her chair.

"I have an idea." Malik pushed her toward the door. "Let's go next door for breakfast. I'm sure Ma would love to feed us."

"I thought she was going back to work."

"No," he said. "She's waiting…"

Bella nodded knowingly. "For me." She sighed. It was what they were all waiting for. Everyone's life had been put on hold.

When Malik opened the door and wheeled Bella into the hallway, the pounding bass attacked them. He stopped in the living room and stared. A mound of ancient, waxed cardboard boxes had been thrown out of the storage closet and into the center of the room. Jasmine poked her head out the door and hurled another box.

The woman lifted her chin and shoved her shoulders back. Smugness was written all over her face. "Oh, did I wake you?"

Malik shook his head and yelled, "Oh, no. Of course not. We love sleeping in the middle of a jet engine." He reached over, hit the pause button on her phone, and turned off the portable speaker.

In the loud silence, Bella gazed around the room. Tilly's pictures leaned against one wall. Her recliner had been shoved into a corner, and the couches were piled with knickknacks and memorabilia. The grandfather clock had been stopped, and Tilly's yarn had been dumped in a wicker garbage can.

"So, what's the plan?" Bella asked.

"Dumpster," Jasmine said flippantly. She pitched the Christmas tree toward the pile. "I've never seen so much crap in my entire life."

Malik righted the tree and moved it to the far side of the pile, out of harm's way. "Tilly was frugal. She grew up during the Great Depression. She didn't waste anything."

Jasmine upended the box of previously used wrapping paper. She snatched a piece with red and green candles from the floor. "There's thrifty, and then there's being a hoarder." She crumpled the paper and sent it sailing toward Malik. "For crying out loud, I'm pretty sure that piece was used to wrap a doll I got for Christmas when I was six."

Bella grew angry. "Seriously. I'm asking. What's the plan? What are you going to do with Tilly's stuff—and her house?"

Jasmine scanned the room. "Well, the house needs repainting and a serious cleaning, or it won't even get a second glance from prospective buyers—unless they plan to tear it down."

Bella's bottom lip trembled. "I don't know. I think it's kind of…charming. Anyone who knew Tilly would love it."

"Ha! Anyone who knew my mother would *know* she was a crazy old bat with a stick up her butt." Jasmine peeked at her phone. "I have to go." She shoved it into her back pocket. "You'd have to really know Tilly well to know that she'd lost her marbles years ago. Evidently, you didn't know her that well."

Bella bit the inside of her cheeks to keep from saying something she shouldn't.

"Where are you going?" Malik gathered the used paper at Jasmine's feet and stuck it back in the box.

"I'm meeting my mother's lawyer at nine o'clock. I'm going to be there when his door opens." She sneered at Malik.

"Oh, so no appointment, then?"

"Grayson and I go way back. We were close in high school." Jasmine grinned smugly. "If anyone can nullify her will, he can. He'll do anything for me. Anything."

"That's funny. You didn't mention that you knew Grayson last night."

"Not everything's your business."

Jasmine disappeared into the kitchen. Bella waited for the front door to close before she spoke.

"Can she really…"

"Contest the will?" Malik's head bobbed up and down. "Sure. But Tilly knew Jasmine would try. It's not going to happen—*legally*, anyway."

"But she said she knows Tilly's lawyer. She made it sound like they dated at some point."

Malik shook his head. "Years ago, maybe. Grayson's as honest as the day is long. He'd never succumb to Jasmine's demands."

"I hope so." She grinned slightly. "I don't think I could live in your sailboat bedroom—even for a few days."

"Hello?" Maggie called.

"In here." Malik stacked the paper box near the others.

"I saw your housemate leave. I thought you might like some breakf..." She held an insulated casserole case when she rounded the corner. Her shoulders fell when she saw the mess in the middle of the room. "Oh, my gosh. What in Sam Hill does she think she's doing?"

"Cleaning. She's getting ready to sell Tilly's house." Bella angrily shook her head.

"I knew she was a piece of work, but I didn't think she'd start showing her true colors this soon." Maggie looked at the bare walls and sighed loudly. "Where'd she run off to anyway?"

"Grayson's. She plans to contest Tilly's will."

Maggie laughed. "It'll be a cold day in hell before he'll ever help her."

The line between Bella's eyes deepened. "Why do you say that?"

"Well, Grayson and Jasmine were a *thing* during their senior year. They'd both been accepted to the Medical University of Charleston. Both being Type A, they had their lives planned down to the color of their bedroom. They were set to become physicians. And after their residencies, they were going to set up their own practice farther up the coast."

"But Grayson's a lawyer."

Maggie nodded. "Now, yes. But that wasn't his plan. The night before graduation, there was a senior party on the beach. Jasmine got wasted, and Grayson found her with someone else."

"I never knew that." Malik pulled Tilly's chair away from the wall and settled in.

Maggie nodded again. "Tilly told me years ago. Jasmine begged him to take her back, but he refused. So, the day after graduation, she left without him. She didn't even show up for her own party." She switched the casserole to her other hand. "Until yesterday, she hadn't set foot back in Lawson Beach. But being gone doesn't stop the gossip. Eventually, word got out she was pregnant—with twins. Everyone assumed Grayson was the father. But no matter how many times he tried to defend himself against the rumors, they wouldn't die. The lies and accusations were enough to make him turn his career choice to law. He returned to Lawson Beach after his dad died. His mom was struggling with dementia. He stayed because it was his home."

She walked toward the kitchen, holding the casserole dish steady. "You can be certain that as long as he lives, he'll never forgive her," she called over her shoulder. "People down here don't just hold grudges—they nurture 'em."

Malik and Bella followed Maggie to the kitchen. After Bella's episode from the day before, Malik insisted she take three bites at each meal and drink a glass of juice.

Maggie gave her son a knowing look. "Malik, that gift arrived today. Perhaps you could go get it this morning."

He nodded. "Great distraction. How about I go take care of that now while you're here with Bella."

"Sounds good. I'll finish cleaning up."

Maggie washed the dishes while she and Bella visited. After she dried the last plate, she stowed it in the cupboard and slid the kitchen window open. She leaned against the counter and shared her idea about transplanting some items from Tilly' garden into her yard.

A car door slammed. Maggie peeked out the window.

"Bella, I need to go take care of some things. Malik should be back in a few minutes."

"Okay. Thanks for breakfast."

Maggie left the kitchen and disappeared through the side door near the bedrooms.

Jasmine stormed into the house and slammed the front door.

Bella grinned inwardly. "Sounds like somebody didn't get what they wanted."

"The people in this town are as insane as my mother was." She whipped open the fridge door and stood in front of it. "Where'd this egg bake come from?"

"Malik's mom brought it over. Help yourself."

Jasmine scowled in her direction. "My house. My fridge. *My* egg bake."

Bella's eyes narrowed. "Who peed on your candy?"

A raucous laugh jarred the room. "You've spent entirely too much time with my mother. She had all these ridiculous phrases that made her sound like a hillbilly." She slammed the refrigerator and set the glass pan on the counter. "She was the most unrefined, simple-minded, self-centered woman I ever knew. I couldn't wait to leave this dump and get away from this ass-backward town."

She jerked the silverware drawer open, grabbed a knife and fork, and gave it a hip-butt. "Son-of-a…"

She kneaded her hip with her knuckles and fought with the sticky drawer. Bella smiled behind her hand. Finally, she wheeled to the countertop, grabbed the hammer Malik had left lying there, banged the side of the drawer, and shoved it closed.

"Sometimes, it just needs a little finessing." Bella held the hammer in her hand and scowled at Jasmine. "Just like people."

"Are you threatening me with that thing?" Jasmine stepped back.

Bella pressed a hand to her chest and straightened her shoulders. "Me? No. Of course not. I was just closing the drawer."

Jasmine rolled her eyes as she shoved her plate into the ancient microwave and turned the knob. "This hellhole is falling apart. I have no idea how I'm ever going to get rid of it. I swore when I left, I'd never return." She threw her hands out to her sides. "Yet here I am."

Bella fumed. Tilly's daughter was nothing like her mother. Jasmine was a sixty-two-year-old entitled brat. Yes, she'd helped Bella the day before, but that was her job. She must have taken some medical oath somewhere along the line. Bella clenched her jaw so tightly, she thought she would snap a tooth.

"So, who is the father of your twins, if not Grayson?"

Jasmine slammed the microwave door and spun around. "How dare you?"

Bella shrugged. "Lawson Beach is a small town. Word gets around." She shifted in her chair, dropped her feet to the floor, and pushed herself backward. "I take it things didn't go well in his office this morning?"

"You and your boyfriend sure like to stick your nose where it doesn't belong, don't you?" Jasmine hissed. "Not that it's any of your damn business, but I never even got to speak to Grayson. His secretary kept telling me to wait. Finally, I got sick of her games and stormed into his office. That got me an appointment for tomorrow morning."

Bella nodded. "What are you hoping for? Best outcome?"

Jasmine stared at the countertop. Bella was confident it had been the one she'd grown up seeing every day.

"For one, I want you and your boyfriend out of here…"

"Husband," Bella corrected, not letting it go a second time.

"Husband," Jasmine mocked. "Then I can get this place ready to dump on some poor unsuspecting buyer. And I sure as hell don't want any of my father's money to go to places that funnel it into their CEO's already padded paycheck. Besides, it was all my father's money. He was the one who worked, not her. Pa paid Tilly's mom for the house—fair and square. He'd want me to have the money."

Bella rocked her wheelchair back and forth. "You know, Tilly always told me we remember things the way we want to, not how they really were."

"Ha! Of course, my mother would say that. She was never home. She doesn't want me to remember that. No, Tilly spent her days gallivanting with her friends—and her *boyfriend*." She tilted her chin down and glared at Bella. "Don't tell me she never told you about her affair with some man named Charles. My father begged her to end it, but she wouldn't. It went on right up until my father's death."

Jasmine used the damp kitchen towel to extract the hot plate from the microwave. The heat seeped through the thin cloth, and she nearly dropped it before she reached the table. Forcefully, she shook her hand before shoving two fingers into her mouth. "Everyone else was always more important than we were. After I moved away, my father visited me often." She tipped her head sideways. "My mother couldn't be bothered."

Bella arched an eyebrow. "I think there's more to the story."

"Like what?"

Bella held a finger in the air, then pointed it over her shoulder. "Give me a minute."

Awkwardly, she maneuvered her chair into her bedroom and retrieved the flash drive with Jasmine's name on it. By the time she returned, she was out of breath.

"Here." She set the flash drive on the table and shoved it toward Jasmine. "This is from your mother. She knew she'd never see you, so she left you a message. There are several hours of her talking to you on there. I never listened to it, but she wanted you to have it."

Jasmine stared at the small black stick. Then, finally, she flicked it with her finger, sending it flying across the room. "Like I want to listen to her grovel for my forgiveness. She had her chance."

Bella sighed loudly. She pushed her chair toward the data stick. With her foot, she slid the flash drive close enough to grab. "She's not asking for your forgiveness. She's trying to set the record straight. There are things you didn't know."

Jasmine laughed out loud. "Then it's all a pack of lies. My father told me everything. He was the person who kept this family going. My mother couldn't see past her own desires.

And obviously, neither my father nor I made that list."

Bella's knuckles grew white as anger churned inside. "Like I said before, we sometimes only see what we want to see. Every story has two sides. How do you know James wasn't lying to you? Maybe his side was fabricated."

Jasmine stood so quickly, her chair tipped and slammed to the floor. She aimed a finger in Bella's direction. "Don't! Don't ever speak my father's name again. Do you hear me?"

She picked up her plate and pitched it into the sink. Bella heard it shatter in the ceramic basin.

"Now stay the hell out of my way so I can get rid of this fleapit and get out of this town before it turns me into my mother."

CHAPTER 34

Stop piddlin' around.

Bella wheeled herself through the front door and onto the porch. She wavered at the edge of the ramp, contemplating her strength to control her chair on the slanted walkway. There was no way she could spend one more minute anywhere near Jasmine.

"Oh, no, you don't." Malik came around the corner of the house just as she decided to chance it. "Why would you even try that?"

Music suddenly blared inside the house. He nodded once. "Makes sense now."

Cautiously, he pushed her down the ramp and toward the garden. "Are you up for sitting outside for a while?"

"Anywhere's better than being in there with Bloody Mary."

Malik laughed as he turned the corner. "Oh, I've called her worse names in my head over the past two days."

"Wait!" Bella said. Malik quickly stopped and almost sent her flying. "The chair." She pointed toward the daisy chair that sat to the left of Tilly's. "What happened?"

Malik parked her in front of the chair and squatted next to her. "Before Tilly died, she commissioned a local artist to repaint it. She wanted you to have your own chair in the garden. They're *bluebells*—for Bella."

Tears streamed down Bella's face as she stared at the

exquisite blue flowers. "Sh-she did this for me?"

He nodded. "Yeah. Tilly thought she'd get to see you sit in it, but the artist was behind schedule. It was delivered this morning."

Malik picked her up and lowered her into the chair. She turned sideways and ran her hand over the flowers. "This is incredible. It's like she considered me family."

"She did, Bella." Malik laughed softly. "You *were* her family." He pointed toward Jasmine's chair. "You were more of a daughter than Jasmine ever was."

A blue backpack sat in Tilly's chair. Malik removed his computer and Bella's earbuds. "There's something else too."

He turned on the computer and pulled up a file. He handed Bella the earbuds and set the opened computer in her lap. "Jasmine wasn't the only one Tilly left a message for. On the night she died, she left you a message too."

Bella shivered; her mouth dropped open. "Are you kidding me?"

He pointed to the file. "It's right here. I'm going to let you listen to it alone. Call me when you're ready, and I'll come get you." Malik looked toward the house. "For now, I'm going in to have it out with our new landlady." He raised an eyebrow and smiled at Bella. "It's quite possible one of us isn't coming out of that house alive."

"Just remember, you're the one with the gun and handcuffs." Bella laughed.

After kissing her forehead, Malik planted his hands on the arms of the chair. "I have no idea what message Tilly wanted you to hear, Bella. But I do know she loved you very much. So, no matter what she said or how she said it, keep that in mind."

Bella grinned. "She was definitely a feisty old gal."

She pushed the earbuds into her ears and watched Malik retreat toward the house. Trying to shake away her nerves, she drew a deep breath through her nose and blew it out through pursed lips. So many times since Tilly passed, Bella had wanted to hear her voice—just one more time. Now that she had the chance, she felt incredibly anxious.

With her hands trembling, she pushed the play button. There was a slight pause before Tilly's voice seeped through the speakers. As soon as she heard her name, the waterfall started.

"Bellarina Levitsky, this here's Tilly, yer landlady."

A laughing sob cut across the garden. Tilly and technology were like oil and water.

"Well, I told ya I'd let ya know when it was time fer me to move on to the next world. By the time ya hear this, I've prob'ly already gone. I just didn't want ya tellin' folks that Tilly Wilson lies like a no-legged dog. So, here's yer message."

Bella swiped at her damp cheeks. She had missed Tilly's outlandish aphorisms, the phrases that often made no sense to her, but seemed to help Tilly explain the world to Bella.

"I don't know where the years went. Heavens to Murgatroyd, I'm 90 years old. Seems like I was just a young girl, smokin' my ma's cigarette butts and practicin' cuss words in case I needed 'em. And yes, I needed 'em—many times over the years, 'specially after you showed up. Anyway, I guess it's true what they say 'bout yer life passin' quickly—one day y're an ostrich and the next a feather duster."

A lopsided grin curled the corners of Bella's mouth. That was a new expression. She'd heard so many of Tilly's utterances in the past ten months, but she'd never heard that one. Bella swallowed hard. Truth be told, she was feather-duster close too.

"I guess I knew when I was workin' on yer dress that I was reachin' the end. God was callin' me home. I could feel it in my bones. I could hear his voice growin' louder by the minute. Only thing I was worried about was gettin' that dress done and gettin' to see yer pictures hangin' in that gallery. So I made a deal with the good Lord. If he let me hang around long 'nough to see yer show, I'd be ready after. Well, it's time."

A wide smile spread across Bella's face. Leave it to Tilly to make deals with God—and have him agree.

"I sure as heck hope this thing's recordin'. I don't understand all these newfangled things." There was a slight pause. "Anyway, after Lou dropped me off, I got ready for bed. But I didn't want to die inside the house. I wanted to be out here in the garden when the angels came fer me. I ain't gonna kid ya. It was hard gettin' myself outside and down that ramp without bustin' my backside. These old legs of mine are about as useless as a screen door in a submarine."

Bella nodded. She understood Tilly's plight. In just a couple days, she'd gone from walking to being confined to her chair.

"Anyway, like I said, I knew it was time. Ya don't go makin' a deal with God and then break yer end of the bargain. Some people think if they had their druthers, they'd rather be sittin' out here unable to care fer themselves rather than up in heaven with the good Lord. I don't see it that way. God's got a place for all of us—one where we're not old or broken no more. You'll see, girl. Yer time's a comin'. We all trip, Bella." Tilly paused. "Well, that ain't true. Worms can't trip. At least I don't think they can." The old woman laughed softly.

"Ya know, I sit out here and look at the garden and think how hard I worked on it all those years ago. Back then, I was busier'n a moth in a mitten tryin' to keep it lookin' good. Then I got old and sittin' was 'bout all I could do. I guess that's why they tell ya to enjoy life while y're young."

Bella heard Tilly wince.

"I didn't even think what I was sayin' there. If I could go back and erase it, I would. But the only button I know is *on and off.* Maybe ya shoulda done a better job of teachin' this old dog new tricks.”

The computer weighed heavily on Bella’s boney thighs. She lifted it and tucked one hand beneath it.

“Anyway, I just want ya to know how dang proud I am of ya. Bless yer heart, girl. Yer photos at the gallery were nothin’ short of remarkable. Even though ya were just a minnow in a fishing hole, ya held yer own against all those big fish who had loads of experience. Ya should be doggone proud of yerself. I sure as shootin’ am. Anybody can fly, Bella. It’s the landin’ that’ll kill ya. But ya landed it tonight. Good job.”

Sobs tore through Bella. She hit the pause button long enough to regroup.

“As for you and Malik, well, I know I give that boy a lot of grief, but he’s good people, Bella. You were lucky to find him. Ya coulda done worse.”

Bella grinned toward the house.

“I hope ya both stop piddlin’ ‘round and… What do ya kids say? Hook up? Well, whatever that means—do it. Stop wastin’ time ya ain’t got a lot of.”

Tilly yawned loud enough for Bella to hear.

“Ya know, when ya walked into my house, I wasn’t sure I even liked ya. My pa used to say that northerners was like hemorrhoids. When they come down and go back up, it’s a relief. Ya can live with ‘em. But if they stick around, they’re a pain in the tuchus. For a while there, I wondered if ya were gonna be a pain in my backside. Then I got to know ya, and I didn’t hate ya.”

“She didn’t hate me.” Bella said aloud with a grin.

“Facin’ yer demise couldn’ta been easy. Still, ya hauled yerself down here where we still think of that sushi crap y’all eat as bait. I wasn’t exactly sure ya’d fit in, but over time, ya fit in like that odd button in a button jar. You might be different from the others, but from time to time, ya could be useful.”

Bella closed one eye. Was that a compliment?

"Anyway, these old bones're growin' tired. I can feel the angels circlin'. But before I close my eyes, there's somethin' I want ya to know. Over time, ya grew on me like age spots. At first, y're kinda disgusted by their appearance, but then ya realize they mean ya enjoyed a long life. Bellarina, ya helped me fancy life this last year. For that, I appreciate ya."

A river of tears streamed down Bella's face. She hiccupped as she heard Tilly's deep sigh.

"Just so ya know, I'll be lookin' for ya in heaven. I'll be the one next to yer folks, waitin' just inside the pearly gates. I love ya, girl. I'll see ya soon."

Sobs shuddered through Bella. She mopped her face with the sleeve of the old t-shirt. Tilly hadn't forgotten to say goodbye. She'd done it perfectly—in her own way.

Bella replayed Tilly's message. Then she played it again. She played it over and over until it made her laugh, instead of cry.

CHAPTER 35

Making me wait

Bella looked at the old alarm clock and rolled over. She drew a deep breath and closed her eyes. The thought of having a *husband* made her smile. Her heart soared as she popped one eye open and watched him. Within minutes, she drifted off to sleep, comforted by Malik's soft snoring.

She had barely fallen into a dream before the beat of rock music thudded inside her chest. A picture behind Malik tilted slightly as the old walls shook.

"What the…?" Malik threw the covers back and pulled on a t-shirt. "She has no idea who she's messing with."

The sound of his heavy feet marked time to the music as he crossed through the sitting room and slammed the door. Within seconds, the music stopped and the yelling started. Just as Bella couldn't hear the lyrics of the song, she couldn't make out who was winning their screaming match. Bella slid herself to the end of the bed. She watched the closed door intently.

Suddenly, it flew open, and Malik stormed in. Jasmine was on his heels, but he slammed the heavy door in her face and twisted the lock.

Jasmine pounded on the thick wood. "Give me my phone! I'll call the cops if you don't return it right now."

"Go ahead!" Malik set Jasmine's phone on his nightstand and sat next to Bella. "And I'll show them the rental agreement

Bella signed that guarantees her the right to a peaceful and comfortable environment. And that includes unnecessary noise by other guests."

Jasmine smacked the door twice. "In case you've forgotten, I'm not a guest. I own this property. I can do whatever the hell I want. And Bella's agreement isn't with me; it's with my mother."

Malik stormed across the sitting room and jerked the door open. Jasmine fell into the room, landing hard on her hands and knees on the worn rug. Malik moved into the bedroom; Jasmine followed. He clenched his jaw as he spun around to face the woman. "Technically, you don't own the house until Bella moves out. Until then, it's held in a trust in Tilly's name with my mother at the helm."

"Well, we'll see what Grayson has to say about that when I meet with him this morning." She stepped toward Malik and held her hand out. "Now give me my phone."

He tipped his head sideways and shrugged one shoulder. "No noise, and it's all yours. Respect us." Malik turned toward Bella. "Respect Bella and what she's going through. My God. What kind of a person are you?"

Jasmine stared at Bella. "You're just like my mother." Leaning into Bella's personal space, she seethed with anger. "That old woman should have died years ago. If she had, my life wouldn't have been so miserable. Now you're doing the same thing to me."

The remark pierced Bella. She drew a sharp breath.

"Hey!" Malik yelled. "Leave Bella alone. She's done nothing to you."

Jasmine angrily pressed a hand toward him. "Besides make me wait, you mean?" A deep line grew between her eyes. "I'm so tired of waiting for everything that should have been mine long ago." She pointed toward Bella. "And now, she's making me wait longer than I should."

Tears welled in Bella's eyes. A tightness squeezed her chest. "You're a horrible woman, Jasmine. Tilly would be embarrassed by the way you're acting."

She grabbed her phone from the nightstand, spun around, and stared at Bella. "Not as embarrassed as I am of her." She slammed the door when she left the room.

Malik wrapped his arms around her while she sobbed.

***

When she was done crying, Malik lifted Bella into the wheelchair and pushed her next door.

"Hey, Ma. We needed a change of scenery."

Maggie wiped her hands on her apron. Seeing Bella's tear-streaked face and swollen eyes and lips, her face fell. "My goodness. What happened, honey?" She tightly hugged Bella and gently rocked from side to side.

Malik laid a heavy hand on the counter. "One guess. That woman's a nightmare. I don't know how she and Tilly can even be cut from the same cloth. Tilly got in her fair share of digs, but she didn't tell people they should hurry up and die."

"What?" Maggie's mouth dropped open. "She said that?"

"Not in so many words, but that's what she meant."

"I can't believe that." She pushed Bella toward the table. "You and Malik will stay here. You don't need to put yourself through that."

Bella shook her head. "No." She took Maggie's hand and held it to her heart. "When I found out..." She looked down. "...about my year to live, I had no one I could count on. By some weird twist of fate, I landed here." She smiled at Maggie. "You were the one who led me to Tilly. It was the first place I felt safe and wanted. Even though I was dying, I never felt like I was truly living until I moved into Tilly's. So..." She dropped Maggie's hand.

"You want to end your life where it finally began. I completely understand." She looked at Malik. "Where does the law stand on kicking Jasmine out?"

"Well, because of how Tilly's will's written, and because you're the executor of her estate, you can kick her butt to the curb until..." He settled into the chair next to his wife. "I don't think we need to do that, though. I had a little talk with Grayson yesterday after my third round of the day with that woman. She's in for a rude awakening when she walks into his office this morning." Malik grinned at Bella. "Besides being on the wrong side of the law on this issue, he doesn't like her as much as she thinks he does."

Bella set her mouth in a hard line. "Is he single?"

Maggie nodded. "He and his wife divorced a couple years back. They had no kids, so it was a clean break."

"So, what if she tries to seduce him? I mean, she could get him in the office and..."

Malik and Maggie both chuckled.

"He won't let her get within a hundred feet of him without someone else in the room. That's how much he hates her." Maggie poured waffle batter into the hot iron.

"And so, there'll be a cop escorting her in and out of the office. The same cop will sit through the meeting with the two of them."

Bella's eyes grew wide. "Seriously? Is he afraid of her?"

Malik shook his head. "No. Not at all. He just doesn't trust her." His mouth twitched into a grin. "And after the meeting, the officer will deliver legal paperwork to us stating your rights as Tilly's renter."

A long sigh filled the kitchen. Bella leaned back in her chair. "That makes me feel so much better."

***

As usual, Bella ate no more than a couple of bites. Her

stomach felt better empty than with food in it. But waffles ranked right up there with bacon. She'd once told Tilly that if there were a heaven, there had better be a breakfast buffet where she could have waffles and bacon every morning. The old woman assured her she'd get her fill. When Bella asked how she could possibly know that, her landlady smiled. "With God, all things're possible. And heaven's a perfect place. It's different fer each one'a us. What feels like heaven to you might not be fer somebody else. But God looks out fer all of us. He gives us what we need and what makes us happy."

Tilly had patted Bella's hand. "So don't ya worry none. You'll get yer bacon and waffles." Then, she'd lifted her newspaper and said, "And if ya don't, ya come to me. I'll have a little talk with the good Lord." Her landlady was the only person confident enough to think she could convince God to fulfill Bella's breakfast request.

Bella's heart stirred. *Oh, how she missed that old woman.*

"Sweetie, I'm actually glad you're here this morning. We probably should iron out a few things around your…passing." Maggie pushed her plate aside and grabbed a notepad and pen from her junk drawer.

Malik squeezed Bella's hand. "I know this is hard, but we want to hear your wishes."

Bella smiled. "Don't look so glum. I've come to terms with dying. Tilly's message to me made me see it's a win-win either way." She looked from Malik to Maggie. "While I'm here, I'm with people who love me. If I'm up there…" She cast a finger into the air. "…Tilly'll be there." Bella nodded. "Win-win."

"Oh, honey. You have such an amazing attitude."

She snorted. "Well, I don't really have any other choice, do I?"

Maggie clicked her pen. "How would you like your life to be celebrated?"

Bella twisted her mouth and bit the side of her lip. "I've thought about this a lot lately. The one thing I know for sure is that I don't want a funeral." Bella pressed her hands against the side of the table. "I'd like a quiet burial at the cemetery—just a few people sitting in lawn chairs, sharing memories of me." She laughed. "Then I want you to go home and pig out on all of my favorite foods."

One corner of Malik's mouth inched upward, and he winked at her. "As I recall, you have a lot of favorites. Good thing we're going to the cemetery first, otherwise, I'd be too full to stay awake."

Maggie nodded. "We should probably contact the cemetery and get a plot. I think there's…"

Bella shook her head. "I was thinking, since I want to be cremated, maybe I could be buried next to Tilly in her plot."

"Oh, honey. That's a wonderful idea. She would love that." Maggie wrote something on the paper. "We can find a beautiful urn."

"No!" Bella said sharply. "I don't want an urn. I'd rather be buried in the crockpot I bought Tilly for Christmas."

Maggie laughed so hard, she snorted. "Oh, Bella. I would have never thought you'd want that in a million years."

Malik kissed Bella's cheek. "I love it. Depending on the cemetery regulations, maybe we could all be buried there…in slow cookers." He chuckled.

"Well, your dad would prefer to be interred in a whiskey bottle, but I don't imagine they'd allow that." Maggie laughed. "So, crockpots it is."

Bella smiled. Her new family was perfect.

"What about your finances? Have you made those arrangements yet? Tilly said you had some money from your folks. I just want to make sure it goes where you want it to." Maggie poised her pen over the paper, ready to capture any details Bella shared.

"I have. Actually, Grayson's partner's my attorney. He knows what to do with my estate when I pass. I've already moved most of the money into trusts, so it'll be easier to distribute after I'm gone. There'll still be a little money left."

Maggie shook her head. "You're so young, Bella. You shouldn't have to think about any of this." She made a note. "But you're an old soul, honey."

"Maggie, can I ask you to do me a favor?"

"Anything."

Bella looked at Malik. "I don't know how much time I have left. But every morning, when I look in the mirror and see how my eyes are sinking deeper and deeper, I know it's not long. I would love to have a really good picture taken of Malik and me. I want something for him to remember *us*." She squeezed his hand. "But the thing is, I look pretty rough. So…" She shredded a paper napkin in her lap. "I was wondering if you knew someone who would make me look like I didn't already have one foot in the grave."

She turned toward Malik. "Are you okay with this?"

"Absolutely. I would love a picture with my beautiful wife."

"Thank you." Bella squeezed his hand.

"Well, for the record, I think it's a great idea. I'll call the salon today. Kayla does make-up and hair." She scribbled on the pad. "I'll also call Marty. He's pretty good with a camera himself. Maybe I can convince him to take the photos. When and where do you want to have the pictures taken?"

"Well, I was thinking day after tomorrow—in Tilly's garden. I'd really like to wear the dress she made, but I'm afraid I may have ruined it." She twisted her hands. "After the gallery opening, I was sure I was going to die that night, so I slept in it." Bella sighed. "It's so weird. I didn't die that night, but Tilly did."

Maggie patted her hand. "Malik can bring me the dress, and I'll take care of it. If I can't line up Kayla and Marty, I'll find someone else."

A sad smile drifted across Bella's face. "I couldn't have picked a better surrogate family. I love you all."

CHAPTER 36

Carry a soft hammer

With the squeal of tires, clearly ready for conflict, Jasmine disappeared at 8:45 a.m. on her way to meet with Grayson. If he stuck to his guns, it would likely be the most uncomfortable meeting of her life. While she was gone, Malik returned all the boxes to the storage closet and hauled the twin bed from upstairs down to the living room.

After remaking the bed, Malik lifted Bella from her chair and set her on the clean fitted sheet. He pulled the top sheet to her waist and placed her backpack at her side.

"Did I forget anything?"

"No. But you know Jasmine will have a cow when she sees me in here." Bella adjusted herself against the old wooden headboard. Had she not needed to sit from time to time, she would have had him leave it off.

Malik snorted softly. "Do you think I give a rat's ass what she thinks? I'm so tired of her."

The front door slammed. "Brace yourself," Bella whispered.

Jasmine froze when she saw Bella in bed in the center of the living room where the boxes had been. "What did you do?" she snarled at Malik.

"I did you a favor. I'm sure Grayson told you that you have no right to do anything until after Bella passes. So I put all the boxes away. The way I see it, you owe me a thank you."

Jasmine stomped across the room and dropped onto the couch. She faced Malik but wagged a finger in Bella's direction. "Why is she in here?"

"I'm not dead yet," Bella said. "You could ask me."

"Fine. Why are you in the middle of my living room?"

Bella released a loud breath. She was tired of playing nicely. "It's not really *your* living room, is it? I'm sure Grayson filled you in on that this morning."

Angrily, Jasmine folded her arms tightly across her chest and gave Malik a death stare. "And I assume you're responsible for the police escort."

"No." Malik also crossed his arms, mocking her. "That had nothing to do with me or Bella."

"But you knew about it. You weren't surprised when I just told you."

"No. Not surprised at all."

"So you're telling me Grayson wanted the cop there?"

Malik slowly nodded. "Yeah. I guess he did. Turns out he doesn't like you any better than the rest of us."

Jasmine gritted her teeth. "I hate this town—and every person in it. It's the same judgmental hick town it's always been. It hasn't changed one damn bit. People only care about one thing—themselves." She pressed an elbow into the once padded arm of the couch but quickly pulled back when it made contact with the wood inside. "If any of these yokels ever got out of this dump and went to an actual city, they'd realize life doesn't work that way."

Laughter thundered from Malik. He threw his hands in the air. "Wow! Bella, tell her."

Bella nodded methodically. "Just so you know, I was born and raised in New York City. There are ignorant, self-serving people no matter where you go. I actually have more friends down here than up there."

"Not my problem you weren't popular in New York."

Bella closed her eyes and drew a deep breath before opening them again. "For someone who made it her life's mission to help others, you sure are an awful person."

Jasmine's eyes grew wide, and her mouth straight-lined. "How dare you? You know nothing about me."

"And you know nothing about me—except that I've inconvenienced you because I won't die fast enough." She clenched her teeth until her jaw started to ache. "And based on your need to constantly throw how awful your mother was in my face, I would guess it bothers you that I knew her a lot better than you did."

"Don't! Don't you…" Jasmine moved to the front edge of the couch.

"Cork it, Jasmine. The truth hurts, doesn't it?" Malik sat at the end of Bella's bed. "Your ma used to say, *God don't like ugly*. You're about as ugly as they come."

A knock on the front door cut through the house. Malik looked at Bella before he left the room to answer the door.

"Jasmine, did you come back for your dad's funeral?" Bella asked softly.

She shook her head before answering. "I had no interest in seeing my mother."

"So, then, it's true. You haven't seen Tilly since you graduated from high school?"

Jasmine shook her head. "I had no need."

"Wow. That's a long time. You're telling me you've spent fifty-some years hating her." Bella pulled her bag toward her and unzipped the top.

"You would have hated her back then too. She was nasty and self-centered."

Bella held her hand up. "Yeah, you've said that before. So,

in the medical profession, have you ever encountered a medical issue where you were positive a patient had one thing, but when you talked to someone else, you realized you were wrong?"

Creases cut across Jasmine's forehead. "Well, of course, I have. That's what I do for a living."

"So, you talk to other people—doctors, nurses, other PAs. You listen to their opinion about a patient. Why? Why get a second opinion rather than diagnosing it yourself?"

She rolled her eyes. "Because you're dealing with people's lives. No one wants to do something that will hurt a patient."

Bella nodded slowly. "But it's okay to hurt people, screw with their lives if it doesn't have to do with medicine?"

"What are you getting at?"

"As a physician's assistant, you seek out information from others to better understand the situation. But as a human being, as Tilly's daughter, you chose to listen to only one side—your father's." Bella held the flash drive toward Jasmine. "It might be important to hear the other side too."

Jasmine stared at the data stick in Bella's hand. Finally, she leaned forward and snatched it from her. "I highly doubt it'll change anything. My father was very clear about my mother's issues."

Bella brought her knees to her chest and wrapped her arms around them. "Well, here's what I think. While you're cleaning—perhaps upstairs—instead of listening to music, try listening to your mom's side of the story."

Malik walked into the room just as Jasmine shoved the drive into her pocket.

"It's awfully quiet in here." He looked from one woman to the other. "What's going on?"

"We were just talking," Bella said.

Malik dropped a set of papers on the corner of Bella's bed so Jasmine could see them. "These were just delivered by the officer who was with you this morning. Grayson's put everything you need to know in simple terms. No loud music. No dumping or throwing anything out—yet. Not until you own the place."

Jasmine leaned forward and snatched the packet from the bed. "I've got it. You've all made that loud and clear."

Bella rested her chin on one knee. "Jasmine, where are your daughters, Aliyah and Kiara?"

"How do you know about my girls?"

"Research. Tilly wanted to know."

Jasmine got up and walked toward the stairs. "It's really none of your concern, but if you must know, I haven't seen them in years," she whispered. "They turned their backs on me a long time ago. That was their choice."

Malik looked at Bella. "Hmm. Like mother, like daughter," he said quietly. "Hurts, doesn't it?"

"Wait!" Bella called. Jasmine froze at the bottom of the stairs, but she didn't turn around. "It doesn't have to be that way. You can't go back and make things right with Tilly, but you have time to change it with your daughters."

With her head hanging down, Jasmine climbed the stairs to her bedroom.

"Wow!" Malik sat next to Bella. "How did you do that? You almost turned her into a real person."

Bella pressed her forehead into her knees. "Nobody deserves to miss out on an opportunity to be with family. I wouldn't wish that on my worst enemy."

"Not even Jasmine?" Malik looked up the stairs.

She shook her head. "You know, Tilly used to say two things that never made much sense to me until now. *What goes around comes around.* Jasmine's suffering the same fate Tilly did. I don't think she's as hateful as she wants us to believe. She's more like a wounded animal who's trying to protect herself. It's all a front to keep us from knowing how much she's hurting."

"I supposed that could be true—based on what she said about her lack of connection with her daughters."

Bella turned her face toward him.

"So, what was the other piece of advice Tilly imparted on you?"

"If you're gonna change the world, assume everyone has good intentions, but carry a soft hammer."

Malik wrinkled his nose, and he tilted his head backward. "What does that even mean?"

Bella smiled. "Well, in Tilly's terms, it means every once in a while you have to knock someone upside the head to get them back on track."

Malik nodded. "Ahh, the *soft hammer*." He kissed Bella. "Ma was right. You are an old soul."

"No. I just had an old soul give me a lot of good advice this past year."

CHAPTER 37

Not having this conversation

Two days later, Bella woke before the sun even stretched. Her physical bandwidth was nearly depleted, but her mind buzzed with a million thoughts. The end was near, just as sure as the full moon would light the earth that evening. It was no longer a gradual regression. Each morning when she woke, she had less strength than the day before. If yesterday was a six, today felt like a three.

"Hey," Malik said softly. He slid toward her and pressed his forehead against hers. "Why are you awake so early? We're being spared Jasmine's early morning rock concert."

She touched the whiskers that had grown on his chin overnight. "I was just thinking how much I love you."

"Well, how could you not?" Malik smirked.

Bella smiled. He was the love of her short life. Why couldn't she have met him years ago? Why couldn't they have had more time together? Tilly had told her it wasn't her place to ask why; it was her place to accept God's will—to know there was a bigger plan.

Bella's brows dipped inward. "Promise me something."

"What?" He kissed her cheek.

"After I'm gone, and you're ready, you'll look for love again. Have…"

Malik pulled away. "No," he said sternly. "I'm not having

this conversation. Not now. Not ever."

"Please. For me. Malik, you'd be an amazing dad. Just because we can't have kids doesn't mean you shouldn't."

He angrily crawled out of bed and tugged on his shirt. "I told you I'm not having this conversation." The bathroom door rattled as it slammed shut.

Bella sighed. She'd said what she needed to. He knew where she stood. If the opportunity to love again ever presented itself, Bella had given him her blessing.

The metal springs creaked, and the mattress gave way to Malik's weight when he dropped onto the edge next to Bella. He caught her as she rolled toward him.

"I know you mean well, but I can't think about this now."

She touched his hand and smiled.

When Malik stood, the old springs launched Bella upward. She laughed out loud. It felt good to find joy in such mundane things.

"It's picture day. According to Ma, there's still a lot to be done. She said to tell you Kayla'll be here around noon." Malik carried her into the bathroom. "Is there anything you want me to set up in the garden?"

She grinned and told him she wanted one picture with everyone—Jasmine included.

***

Bella stared into the mirror. She'd been sitting in the kitchen chair for the better part of an hour while Kayla worked her magic. The dark circles that had grown more pronounced every day had miraculously disappeared. Her eyes looked enormous and bright. Except for her almost skeletal frame, no one would have believed she was dying.

Sometime before dawn, Jasmine had disappeared. In thick black marker, she'd scribbled a note on yesterday's newspaper, stating she would return after dinner. Her departure had ruined

Bella's plan. But Jasmine was her own person. It would be fine without her. Honestly, Jasmine's entire life had been a mystery. Until she showed her face after Tilly's death, Bella had wondered if she was just some mythical creature the old woman had invented.

"You are a miracle worker!" she exclaimed, looking at herself in the mirror.

"Paints only work well on high-end canvases. You, my dear, are as gorgeous as they come." Kayla dropped a brush into her kit. She looked at her watch. "Maggie, we have time to do your make-up, if you want. Lou won't recognize the supermodel he's eating dinner with tonight."

Bella folded her hands. "Please, Maggie. I want you and Lou in the pictures. You're already so beautiful, but every woman can use a little tweak here and there."

"Fine," Maggie finally conceded. She shook her finger at Bella. "You know I can't say no to you."

A half-hour later, Maggie looked more beautiful than ever. She helped Bella into the yellow dress Tilly had made. Then she wheeled her out to the garden.

Malik whistled when he saw her. "I thought you were beautiful at our wedding, but, Bella, you are… Wow! You're a knockout!"

He set her in her newly painted chair. Maggie smoothed Bella's dress and crossed her ankles for her. Minutes later, Lou walked into the garden in a pair of tan slacks and a navy polo shirt. No more than a few steps behind trailed Marty, lugging his camera bag and other equipment.

"Who's this beauty?" Lou bent and planted a kiss on Bella's cheek.

Maggie playfully slapped his arm. "Don't mess up her make-up. That's an hour's worth of work."

"You women and your paint. You should go au naturel like

me." He ran a massive hand over his bald head. "It saves a whole lot of time."

"Ha! No woman wants to look like you, honey." Maggie rolled her eyes.

Lou did a double-take when he looked at his wife up close. "Well, I'll be." He pulled her toward him. "You're as pretty as a peach, Miss Maggie."

"When did you start talking like Tilly?" She laughed.

Lou winked. "When I saw you in something other than an apron and a hairnet."

Maggie laughed. "Well, you don't look so bad yourself when you're not covered in burger grease and barbeque sauce."

"Okay. I'm ready." Marty aimed his camera at Bella and snapped a picture of her smiling at Maggie and Lou. He checked it and nodded. "The light's perfect. Let's get this show on the road."

Forty minutes later, he called it a wrap. Bella was grateful. She wasn't sure she had one more smile left in her. Her cheeks ached. And exhaustion had stolen her ability to function.

Marty shoved his camera in his bag and stepped toward Bella. "I'll pick some of the best shots and email them to you tonight." Bella slumped slightly to the side. His eyebrows pressed inward. "How about I send them to Maggie as well?" he said after watching her.

When Bella didn't respond, Malik shook his hand and helped him carry his gear to his car.

"Bella, honey. Are you okay?" Maggie asked.

She nodded slightly.

"Lou, let's get her in the house and out of the sunshine."

Lou gently picked her up and set her in her wheelchair. Maggie pushed her up the ramp and into the house.

"Bella?" Maggie handed her a small glass of the off-brand root beer. "Honey, drink this." She laid her hands over Bella's and brought them to her mouth. "Come on, honey, keep drinking."

Root beer dribbled from the glass and dropped onto her dress. Bella awkwardly swiped at the spots as tears tumbled down her cheeks.

"It's okay. I can get those out. Don't worry."

Maggie pressed the glass to Bella's lips again.

"What's going on?" Malik walked into the living room.

"Dehydration? Low blood sugar?" Maggie looked at her son. "I'm trying to get something in her. Has she eaten anything today?"

"She refused to eat this morning." He knelt in front of Bella. "Bella? Honey, are you okay?"

Her nod was almost non-existent. Her morning had been a three but had quickly slipped to a one. She was tired, so tired. All she wanted to do was close her eyes and go to sleep.

Malik picked her up and laid her in the bed in the living room. "I wonder if she got overheated. Dad, grab that fan. Let's get some air moving in here."

As exhausted as Bella was, she couldn't fall asleep. Just like that morning, her mind hummed with thoughts.

If she closed her eyes and fell asleep, would she ever wake again? How would Malik go on without her? Would he ever find love? Would he have children? Please, let him have children. What would happen to Tilly's house? Would the new family be as giving as Tilly? Would they love the place as much as the old woman had?

Bella opened her mouth to tell Malik how much she loved him, but she couldn't form the words. There was a disconnect between her brain and her lips. She opened her eyes. Malik was on his knees; his elbows were pressed into the mattress.

"I love you too, Bella," he whispered. Tears streamed down his face.

She hadn't needed to say the words. He knew her heart.

Finally, she closed her eyes and drifted off.

***

The full moon shone through the living room window, leaving a wide streak of light across the floor. Bella opened her eyes and tried to focus on anything. Tilly's chair was awash in light, emphasizing the emptiness of the place her landlady had spent much of the past year. A soft sob cut through the still air, and Bella pressed her face into the sheet. Malik had pushed the couch close to her bed, leaving only enough room to stand. He stirred but didn't wake.

"Bella?" Jasmine leaned in. Her stethoscope hung around her neck. "How are you?" she whispered.

She didn't know if she could speak any longer, so she nodded.

"Hey." Malik's whisper was sleep-filled. He sat up and dropped his legs between the couch and the bed. He held her hand as Jasmine checked her pulse. "Do you have any idea how much I love you?"

Bella nodded. She lightly kissed his hand and gave him a weak smile. Her eyes fluttered before they closed. The old box fan whirred in the distance, gently touching Bella's skin. Malik and Jasmine's words were clear, but their meaning was lost in a haze.

"What do you think?" Malik kept his eyes on his wife.

"It won't be long. Her breathing's shallow and irregular. I checked her feet a while ago. They're cool to the touch, and her knees look pretty mottled. I'd say a few hours, maybe less."

Malik drew a deep breath. "Can I ask a favor?"

Jasmine nodded.

"I'd like my folks to be here at the end." He looked up at Jasmine. "Just the four of us."

Again, Jasmine nodded. "I'll be upstairs." She handed him

a small piece of paper with the coroner's number written on it. "Call this number after she passes. He'll come when you're ready. But take as much time as you need. I'll stay in my room until you want me."

"Thank you."

Jasmine disappeared up the stairs, and Malik called his parents. Within minutes, Lou and Maggie were settled on the couch with their son.

Bella opened her eyes. She gave them a watery smile.

"Tilly," she mouthed, raising a finger slightly before closing her eyes again.

Maggie looked up. She swallowed a sob. "Yes, Bella. Tilly's waiting for you. It's okay to go, honey." She squeezed Malik's hand as he sobbed silently. "You have family waiting for you at home."

"I love you so much, Bella," Malik choked out as he pressed his forehead against hers.

Bella opened her eyes, stared at her husband, and mouthed the word *love*. She didn't have the energy to say more. Finally, she closed her eyes and let go.

JASMINE

CHAPTER 38

Lies. Lies. And more lies

The early morning wind gusted through the open windows, fluttering the sheers Jasmine had shoved to the sides. According to the weather station, it would be a cloudy morning before the sun attacked the earth with its intense July rays. A heat index warning had already been issued, encouraging people to stay indoors or in the water. Jasmine knew the beaches would fill quickly.

She drew a deep breath and stripped the sheets from the twin bed in the middle of the living room. Bella had been gone for four days. No one had come to remove any of her things. The young woman's items still cluttered the downstairs bedroom.

Not long after Bella passed, Jasmine had rummaged through her closet. Items from decades earlier hung on metal hangers from the makeshift rod chained to large eyehooks in the ceiling. Deleting Bella from the house was going to be a challenge. When other boarders came, they took their crap with them when they moved out. With any luck, maybe Bella's husband would take it all. After all, wasn't that his job? It would give her one less room to empty. Right now, she'd take any help she could get.

Jasmine jerked the heavy blue and white striped mattress to the floor, stood it on edge, and aimed it toward the stairs. Somehow or another, she would get it back up there. If she was going to sell this house, she had to make it presentable. And now that Bella was gone, it was hers—free and clear.

In the corner, the antique grandfather clock ticked loudly. Someone had started it again. The repetition made Jasmine's skin crawl. It reminded her of the childhood she hated. The bell chimed eight times. Jasmine went over and stopped the pendulum, squeezing it angrily. The clock was just one more reminder of the *things* Tilly clung to. She hadn't tried to hold on to Jasmine. Hell, her mother had driven her out of this house and Lawson Beach to boot.

8:14 a.m. Bella's funeral would have already started. She'd gotten a call from the lady next door, inviting her to attend. Jasmine had refused. Malik's family didn't want her there any more than she wanted to go. Helping Bella had been her job. She had assisted her out of a sense of obligation, not compassion. There was no familial connection. Jasmine's family lived in Charleston; her mother had been her only tie to this cesspool of a town.

On the day Bella passed, she had tried to see her girls, but they had been in meetings, too busy to even meet for lunch. Still, they were her daughters. At some point, they would see that—understand everything she had done for them—all she had given up for their benefit. Jasmine's relationship with them was nothing like the one she shared with Tilly. She actually loved her daughters.

Malik had stopped by only once since Bella died—for a crockpot. Jasmine assumed it was for Bella's funeral and would be filled with soft food for old people—like every other funeral. When he pulled it from the kitchen cabinet, she did a double take. It was the newest appliance in the house. Maybe it didn't even belong to her mother. Perhaps it lived next door and had made its way over here while Maggie cared for Tilly or Bella.

Jasmine retrieved her father's toolbox from the garage and

removed the headboard from the bed. Piece by piece, she transferred the bed back where it belonged. Once she got the room in order, she sprawled across the mattress and stared at the yellowed ceiling.

She had a mountainous amount of work ahead of her. Where should she begin? Should she start in the kitchen or the bedrooms? It was an overwhelming job to empty a house of ninety-some years of junk. Everywhere she looked held memories of being abandoned by her mother.

The house was a time capsule. Nothing had changed in the forty-some years that Jasmine had been away. *Nothing?* She got off the bed and went into her bedroom. After shoving the dresser against the end wall, she knelt on the floor and removed a footlong piece of flooring. Inside were the same treasures that had been there the day she drove away in the new-to-her car her dad had given her the day before. Letters from Grayson, their life plan, a pair of earrings she'd stolen from her mother, and an old joint had been left undisturbed.

She leaned against the wall and stared at the ugly, dated wallpaper from the 70s. Somewhere, her mother had gotten stuck in the past. Even with all the boarders she'd had over the years, she hadn't changed a thing. She was a miserable old woman who didn't see life passing her by.

Jasmine replaced the flooring and headed downstairs. Sitting around reminiscing about how awful her life had been wasn't helping her accomplish anything.

Her oversized Coach purse lay on the kitchen table; she dug through it for her phone. Instead, she pulled out the flash drive Bella had given her. *Lies. Lies. And more lies.* There was no way her mother could justify her actions, no matter how many hours of groveling she'd recorded. Jasmine shoved it back into her bag but didn't let go. Slowly, she took it out again. *Every story has two sides,* Bella had told her. What could her mother possibly have to say? All she had ever done was leave her father and her to fend for themselves while she slept her way across Lawson Beach. There were weeks she saw her mother for no more than a few hours. It was her father who had always been there for her.

Suddenly, a shudder of epic proportions passed through her. The hairs on the back of her neck stood on end, and she was positive someone had touched her cheek. She could feel her heartbeat in her throat. Still clutching the flash drive, she turned and raced from the room. She dropped onto the couch and took several calming breaths. Was she going crazy? Was there something inside this house that turned you into a raving lunatic like her mother?

Her laptop was on the coffee table. The lid was open. Jasmine never walked away without closing it. Not only that, but she was positive she'd left it in the kitchen under her purse. Someone clearly wanted her to hear Tilly's message. Could it be Bella? Or was it her mother? Or maybe she was just losing her mind.

Because her hands were trembling, it took several attempts to get the memory stick into the small slot. When the flash drive appeared on her screen, she drew a deep breath and clicked on the file. The voice was undeniably her mother's. Even if she hadn't identified herself, she would have known it was her.

"Jasmine, this is Matilda Violet Robinson Wilson. You'd 'member me as yer ma." There was a slight pause. "But maybe you fergot that after all these years."

The seconds turned to minutes and the minutes to hours. Dusk was beginning to settle by the time her mother signed off. "I love you to the moon and back, Jasmine. I always have."

Wadded-up tissues littered the tabletop and the floor. Except for a cup of coffee and a quick run to the bathroom, Jasmine had not moved from the couch in nearly twelve hours.

The fan blasted her with what felt like lukewarm air against her burning cheeks.

Her mother's story was one she'd never heard—one she didn't know if she could believe. Was it a lie? Or was it real? Even if it held the slightest kernel of truth, Jasmine had spent her entire life believing lies.

She started the message again. Finally, her eyelids grew heavy, and she drifted to sleep in a haze of confusion.

***

One of the sheers touched Jasmine's arm as it fluttered in the early morning breeze. She screamed. It took her several seconds to remember where she was—on her mother's couch in Lawson Beach.

She sat up and restarted the message. "Jasmine, this is Matilda Violet Robinson Wilson. You'd 'member me as yer ma." Her stomach flopped hard. It hadn't been a dream. Her mother had shared her side of the story. It was a far different narrative than her father had given. Was it the truth? Or was it just a fantasy nurtured in her mother's mind?

It was 6:30 a.m. when Jasmine climbed into the shower. She took her time getting ready. Within an hour, she'd had three cups of coffee and had eaten a scone that tasted as if it had taken up residency in the freezer on the day the house was built.

It was much too early for a visit. By 7:33, Jasmine began pacing the floor. The boards squeaked as she passed over them time and again. Finally, after several dozen trips past the stack of pictures she had pulled from the walls, she stopped. One by one, she rehung them.

At one minute to eight, when she could wait no longer, she walked out the door toward the driveway. She passed her car and stepped onto the porch next door. Her heart banged against her ribcage as she teetered between her heels and toes. Eyeing her car, she wondered if she should run, drive away and never return. Could she forget everything she'd learned in the past twenty-four hours? It wasn't likely. No, she had to know the truth.

Finally, holding her breath, she knocked.

Jasmine's knees buckled when the door opened. She nearly dropped onto the wooden decking. Maggie stepped out and grabbed her arm, pulling her to her feet.

"I wondered when you'd come," Maggie said softly. Then, she led her inside.

CHAPTER 39

Miss Tilly

Maggie set a glass of ice water in front of Jasmine. "I know it's early, but maybe you'd prefer something stronger?" She stood next to a small fridge. "Wine? Beer? Whiskey? Vodka?"

Jasmine guzzled the entire glass. "This is fine—for now."

She studied the kitchen. It looked nothing like her mother's. The house at 354 Sweetwater was frozen in time. Maggie's home had moved on without Tilly's approval: quartz countertops, state-of-the-art appliances, and refrigerator doors that blended with the cabinets. It was like passing through a time warp—visiting homes decades apart.

The chair screeched when Maggie pulled it away from the table. Jasmine closed one eye and ground her teeth as the torturous sound ran through her.

"Sorry. Lou was supposed to fix these chairs weeks ago." She smiled. "I could nag, or I could do it myself." Maggie rolled her eyes. "No matter which I choose, a woman's work is never done." She chuckled nervously.

Her smile fell when Jasmine didn't respond. Maggie leaned forward and folded her arms along the edge of the breakfast table. "Like I said at the door, I wondered when you'd come." She brushed a speck from the dark tabletop and wiped her hand on her shorts before looking at Jasmine.

"It's uncanny. You look so much like him." Jasmine

couldn't stop staring.

"I suppose that happens. DNA does that." She shook her head slightly. "I've been trying to forget I'm his daughter since the day I moved in with Tilly."

"Same—with my mother, I mean." Jasmine frowned. "I hated that I could have been her twin. I did everything I could this side of plastic surgery to change that. That's one of the reasons I stayed away. I was afraid if I looked like her, I might start acting like her." Jasmine looked back at Maggie. "But you're the spitting image of…"

"Our father?" Maggie chewed her lip. "There was never any question who my father was. That was clear from the day I was born."

"So how did you end up living with him and my mother?"

Maggie tilted her head. "Well…" She drew a deep breath. "My mother was nothing more than a passing distraction for James, someone to kill time with—since he couldn't keep a job." Maggie twisted her mouth. "As I got older and started to look more and more like him, he insisted my mother leave Lawson Beach. So we packed up and moved to a small town outside of Boston."

She got up and refilled Jasmine's glass before pouring one for herself. "Other than taking care of me, my mother had just one major problem with me. I wasn't white enough. The string of men she brought home all wondered why she was raising a *black* kid. Her line? *Ain't mine. Belongs to a friend. Just keepin' her for a while.*" Maggie shrugged. "So, the day after school let out when I was old enough to travel alone, she bought me a bus ticket for Lawson Beach. She handed me a note with James' address printed on the outside, and told me to ask for directions when the bus got in. Then, she shoved a couple pair of underwear, ten dollars, and my birth certificate in a plastic bag, and sent me packing."

Jasmine's eyes grew wide. "You've got to be kidding."

"I wish I was." She took a long draw from the glass. "When I arrived on Tilly's doorstep, James was MIA. Like always, he'd disappeared for a few weeks again. Turns out, he left for a month or so right after you did." She smirked. "Your room hadn't even gone cold by the time I arrived. We missed each other by a couple days." Maggie stared at Jasmine. "Did your dad ever tell you about me?"

Jasmine shook her head.

Maggie sighed sadly. "I didn't think so. I was his child, but your mother treated me more like a daughter than either he or my mother ever did."

Lines spread across Jasmine's forehead. "Isn't it possible my mother just fed you a crock of lies about him? Maybe he wasn't really that bad? If he was, why wouldn't she have kicked him out?"

She shook her head. "Tilly didn't tell me anything—at least not until long after I got married. I was there for all of it." She ran her finger through a tiny puddle on the table, separating the droplet in two. "The drinking, the stealing, and his disappearing acts. I saw it all first-hand. The way he treated your mom was atrocious."

Maggie got up and stood by the sink. With her hands pressed to the counter, she stared out the window. "I watched Tilly kill herself working four jobs while he sat around the house all day drinking himself stupid. Nobody else had any clue what the real James Wilson was like."

"But how could the neighbors not know? Old lady Fryer knew everybody's business before it even happened. Didn't she question why he was home so much?"

Maggie crossed her arms and slowly turned toward Jasmine. "James was a master manipulator and narcissist. He was the king of perfect lies. Everything he said sounded so legit. It made him look like the ideal husband. To hear him tell it, he was a big-shot banker who traveled from state to state overseeing dozens of other banks. Everyone wanted to believe that a black man had been hired for such a prestigious job, that they bought his lies hook, line, and sinker."

"And yet his car never left the yard?"

"He didn't own a car. He didn't need one. According to his tales, he flew everywhere he went."

"And my mother put up with all of this?"

"Back then, Tilly was worried about what people would think about her. Her mother told her that marriage was for life. Tilly wouldn't dare go against anything her mom said. So she stayed."

Maggie swiped at the droplets of sweat that had begun forming on her forehead. She adjusted the air conditioner before returning to the table.

"Did your mother mention that she raised you alone for the first three years of your life—while James was shacked-up with another woman over in Harper's Ridge? Tilly was eight months pregnant when he walked out the door. She hauled you with her to work every day."

Jasmine's eyebrows knit together. "No. She said nothing. That wasn't on the flash drive."

Maggie nodded slowly. "Even from the grave, she's still protecting you from our father's lies. That's what Tilly did. That's who she was. She protected everyone she loved."

Other than the soft hum of the air that blew through the vents, the room was silent for a long while.

"I'm still confused about something. My father—*our father*—came to visit me often. He had a car then." She took a long drink. "And I don't ever recall seeing him drunk."

A small snort came from the other side of the table. "Eventually, James had to sell his car. You can't pay for alcohol when you don't work. He sold a lot of stuff—things Tilly's mother had given her, antiques, signed copies of books…" She stared at Jasmine. "…and her wedding ring."

"He sold her wedding ring?"

Maggie nodded slowly. "He did. I sat on the stairs and watched him beat her until she gave it up."

Jasmine's face fell. "That's unbelievable."

"As for the drinking, he was what most people would refer to as a functioning drunk, a closet alcoholic, at least in public. James could drink with the big boys and still speak to a police officer like he'd never had a drop. It was only at home that he let himself get sloppy."

"So he never worked? That's why he was home when I left in the mornings and returned after school?"

"According to Tilly, when they first got married, he did work—in a bank. That made it easy to convince everyone about his fake job. But no, for the most part, he didn't work. Every gift you ever received from him was purchased with money Tilly either gave him or he stole from her or me."

Jasmine's jaw dropped open. "The car for graduation?" Maggie nodded. "The baby gifts?" Maggie nodded again.

"Tilly bought all of that. James knew where you were, but he never told your mother until just before he died. By then, she knew he'd filled your head with so many lies that you wouldn't believe her. So she chose not to destroy all the good memories you had of him. Tilly had a heart of gold. Our father didn't want you to see that."

Maggie leaned back. "Do you know that every year, on your birthday, Tilly baked a cake and bought you a gift—just in case you walked through her door? She did the same for Christmas. She didn't want to be caught empty-handed. The week before she died, she baked you a marble cake with chocolate frosting. I helped her—like I did when I was young."

The air felt heavy. Tears stung Jasmine's eyes. She looked up to keep them from falling.

"Those gifts are all up in the attic."

A sob ripped through Jasmine. She bit the inside of her cheeks to silence it. Jasmine twirled the ice in her glass while she pulled herself together.

"So, you said my mother worked four jobs."

"While James was alive—yes. At midnight, she'd head to the café to bake desserts. When her mother couldn't watch you, she took you with. During the day, she sold Avon. Tilly sold mostly on the east side because that's where the money was. But she had doors slammed in her face because, after all, how could a black woman ever know what a white woman wanted or needed?" Maggie clenched her jaw. "And when she got home, she took care of the boarders before sitting down to stuff envelopes for a penny apiece."

Maggie's phone buzzed. She looked at it and flipped it upside down.

"I know you think Tilly frittered away her days while our father was out making an honest living, but that couldn't be farther from the truth. If Tilly's mom hadn't given her the house and the car, she would have been up sh…" She cast her hands out to her sides. "Well, a creek without a paddle. After James died, she continued to work hard, stashing away every penny she could. Once she bought the café, she dropped her side job but kept the boarders. And when she got too old to run the restaurant, she sold it to Lou and me." She leaned back in her chair.

"I'd worked there since I was twelve. I couldn't stand to see Tilly busting her butt while our father spent every cent on booze." She twisted her mouth and bit her lip. "The week I landed on her doorstep, I realized I needed to work for my keep. If I didn't, Tilly'd have to work a lot harder. So I did everything

I could to help."

Maggie swiped at a tear that escaped. "I'm sure I was just another reminder of James' infidelity. How could I not be? But I never felt that way. Like I said, Tilly treated me like her daughter. I knew how much she loved me."

Maggie grabbed a bottle of wine and two glasses. She held the bottle in the air. "I think *I* need this." She poured two glasses. "Anyway, no one ever saw James and me together because he never left the house unless he was off visiting you— or another woman. So I was easy to pass off as a foster child from Harper's Ridge." She took a big sip of wine. "He didn't like me much. As far as he was concerned, I was a reminder of the moment he *got caught* with his pants down. Around James, I lived in *your* shadow." She raised an eyebrow. "Honestly, I wouldn't be surprised if a few more of our siblings show up over time."

Maggie suddenly stood. "I want to show you a couple of things. Come with me." She led Jasmine into the den.

From a closet, she extracted an old cardboard cigar box. "Here." She handed it to Jasmine. "This is all that's left of of James' things. But before you open it, I need you to know one more thing. Our father's obituary is in there. It says he died from an accidental fall. That's true, but it's only part of the story. On the day he died, he was drunker than I've ever seen him. Tilly'd refused to give him five hundred dollars for another bender. So he picked up a metal lamp and swung it at her. She ducked and…well, he tumbled down the stairs. That was the fall the paper referred to." Maggie swallowed hard. "I was there. I saw it happen."

Jasmine stared at the box.

"I've only looked at the contents of that box once. It was enough to make me sick. Please make sure you absolutely want to know who our father was before you open it."

"Why would Tilly have kept horrible things about him?"

Maggie shook her head. "Jasmine, everything about our father was horrible. Tilly protected us both from him. We were so incredibly fortunate she loved us."

Maggie looked out the window. "I have one more thing I want you to see."

She led the way out of the house, across the backyard, and into Tilly's garden.

"I don't know how much time you've spent out here since you arrived."

Jasmine looked toward the house. "This is the first time I've been in the garden. Flowers aren't really my thing. I tried to distance myself from anything my mother liked."

"I understand." Maggie pointed to Tilly's chair. "This is where your mom sat and recorded her message to you. Every afternoon, Bella would help her into the garden. This was her chair." Maggie ran a hand along the top edge. "This is also where she died. The flowers painted on the back are called *Miss Tilly*. They're bright and beautiful, just like she was."

She walked to the right.

"What?" Jasmine looked at Maggie. "She painted a chair with my name and a jasmine flower on it?"

"She hired someone to do it, but yes. When Tilly loved you, you knew it." She smiled. "No one, and I mean no one, was allowed to sit in this chair but you."

Jasmine gingerly lowered herself into the chair. "I can't believe this."

Maggie tugged her up and led her across the way. "This was Bella's chair. The woman you referred to as *a stray, one of the many she took in over the years…*" She raised her eyebrows and stared at Jasmine. "I heard what you said. Anyway, Tilly grew to love her fiercely. Bella was her family—the same as you and me. She thought of her as a granddaughter." Maggie laughed.

"The crockpot Malik came to get? Bella was buried in it—just like your mom was buried in that ancient slow cooker she refused to give up."

Jasmine's mouth fell open. "Seriously?"

Maggie led her to the backside of the circle, to the chair opposite Tilly's.

"Magnolia," Jasmine said quietly. She turned toward Maggie. "That's your chair?"

Maggie nodded. "My given name was Angela Michelle. Tilly always called me Angie. James died when I was nineteen. To protect Tilly, I stayed at the house and worked at the café after I graduated. Then one day, shortly after his death, she asked if I wanted to be adopted. I thought I was too old. But it turns out that's not true. My adoption was Grayson Bennett's first act as a lawyer."

Tears streamed down Jasmine's cheeks.

"I wanted to erase my past—the white mother who gave up her black child, the drunken father who pined for his oldest daughter—so I chose a new name. *Magnolia Rose Wilson.* From that moment on, I was Tilly's daughter. Grayson was sworn to secrecy. And the town's people just thought I was in the midst of a teenage rebellion. But Tilly and I knew the truth. Lou knows, but I've never even told Malik." Maggie sat. "This is my chair." She ran her hands along the smooth wide arms. "She didn't want it next to her chair. It's across the way, so we could always see one another—no matter who or what got in our way."

Jasmine squeezed Maggie's hand. Her pulse quickened. "Thank you for taking care of my mother."

"Our mother," Maggie corrected her. "*Our* mother."

5 YEARS LATER

EPILOGUE

The rule

Temporarily abandoning her dinner duties, Maggie cradled the newborn in her arms. "Oh my gosh, Malik, she's absolutely gorgeous." She sighed. "But I suppose I have to give her back."

"If we're ever going to eat, you do." Malik reached down and scooped the baby from her arms. "What time is dinner anyway?" he called from the living room doorway.

"Seriously?" Jasmine pulled a hot pan from the stovetop and sidestepped Lou and Grayson in a perfect dance. "I swear you're a bottomless pit."

"Boy, it'll be time to eat when I say it is. Now take that baby out of here so we can get this meal on the table." Lou dumped an array of spices into a large pot on the stove.

Malik walked into the living room and set the baby in the woman's waiting arms. "You're not gonna believe this, but baby Tilly got more attention in there than I did."

She smirked. "Oh, I can believe it," she said sarcastically.

Nate stepped into the living room with a matching infant. "Bella's changed and ready for..." A loud rumble ripped through the air. He scowled at Malik.

"Last one to touch her, dude. That's the rule. Last one to touch her." Malik grinned.

"Fine," Nate grumbled. He spun on his heels and again passed the barren Christmas tree with the ancient ornaments.

"Listen, little girl. It's Christmas. Maybe you could hold off on the crappy diapers for a little while."

Malik sat down and took in the commotion. Fifteen overlapping stockings hung from the mantel. The last two were labeled Tilly and Bella–reused, not new. He smiled, remembering the last Christmas when it had just been the five of them.

The room was wall-to-wall people. They were family outside the lines of the traditional sense, but it didn't matter. Family was family. Tilly would have been so happy to see her house filled with so much love.

"False alarm." Nate reemerged with Bella and set her in Malik's arms. He dropped a burp rag over his shoulder. "Keep in mind your rule, buddy—just in case."

Nate sat on the end of the couch next to his wife.

"Five years ago, I would have never thought any of this would have been possible. Bella changed our lives. I stood on that corner begging for money just to feed Jacob. Then she showed up with that first nine hundred dollars from selling Tilly's flowers. Now I've got a college degree, a programming job, a new house, and the twins." He smiled at the baby his wife was holding. "Had it not been for Bella's inheritance, we'd still be living in that rundown trailer across town."

Malik nodded. "She definitely had a huge heart."

"She and Tilly were cut from the same cloth."

The TV suddenly blared video game music. "Down!" Aliyah commanded her son, nephew, and Nate's son. "If I hear it again, I'm sending Grandma Jasmine and Auntie Maggie in here to whoop your behinds."

"God, Ma! You're such an old crab," Devon complained.

"Excuse me? When I was your age, I got away with nothing."

Kiara stepped toward the TV. "You do know that any of

these presents can go back—today? And that includes the gaming system Malik bought you to use while you're here."

Malik laughed. "Don't put me in the middle of this." A low rumble cut through the air. "Ah, man." His eyes watered, and he gagged.

Malik lifted the baby toward Nate.

"Sorry, buddy. Your rule. Doesn't matter if she *is* my daughter," Nate said.

A woman with dark eyes and blonde hair stepped into the room. "Merry Christmas, everyone," she called over the clamor.

She bent low and kissed Malik. "Sorry, I'm late, honey. My folks weren't real excited about sharing me, even for a little while." She poked a finger into the baby's belly. "Which one?" she whispered.

"Bella." He winked at Nate. "Want to hold her, Heather?"

"Oh, yes. You know I do!" She blew on her hands and rubbed them together as Malik abandoned the chair. She held out her arms. "Come here, you little cutie."

She sat down in the rocker and grinned at the baby. Suddenly, her face fell. "Oh. Oh, my goodness. I think she needs a diaper change."

Malik shrugged. "Well, you know the rule. The last one to touch her has to change her." He pointed toward the hall. "Diapers are in the first bedroom."

Heather gave him a dirty look as she carried baby Bella from the room, holding her away from her silk shirt. "Somehow, I think we were set up, little girl."

Malik laughed as he looked at Nate. "Well, to quote Tilly on this fine Christmas Day—*That worked slicker'n snot on a glass doorknob!*"

ACKNOWLEDGMENTS

To my Beta-Readers: Laura Chevalier, Bridget Christianson, DeeAnn Eickhoff, Barb McMahon, Cheryl Meld, Ruth Novack, Linda O'Neil, and Lori Schneider: Your masterful and fine-tooth comb reading of the rough draft helped polish this very emotional story.

To Beth at BZ Hercules: I wouldn't want anyone else in my corner when it comes to the *next round* of editing and revising. I appreciate everything you do—including answering my panicked emails so quickly.

To my husband, Mitch: I couldn't do this without your support. You are my number one cheerleader, my first reader, top critic, and best friend. Without your support, I would have thrown in the towel long ago. Somehow you know when my chocolate supply is low, and my water glass is nearing empty. I am also grateful for the backrubs, meals, and wall to bounce ideas. Without your love and support, I couldn't be following my dream.

To my son Brandon and daughter Taylor: Thank you for believing in my dream and supporting it as if it was your own.

To all of them: From my first vision of a new book idea to the published novel, it takes a team. You are my team. I am incredibly blessed to have all of you on this journey with me.

And to my readers: Your messages and kind words keep me writing. Thank you for continuing to believe in me. I am beyond grateful.

MESSAGE FROM MARY

For as long as I can remember, I have written stories. There hasn't been a day that I haven't authored something—either on paper or in my head. (Some things are never meant to see the light of day.)

The idea for *Outside the Lines* has been circling inside me for a long time. I have had too many friends succumb to this dreadful disease. And yet, even knowing their days were numbered, they never lost faith. Through all their suffering, they raised incredible families, nurtured beautiful relationships, and loved fiercely to their last breath. The world is a better place because of each of them.

Tomorrow is not guaranteed. So open your heart and love deeply. As these women reminded us—have faith over fear, be the light for someone else, choose joy, and remember, if you want magical things to happen, first you have to believe in magic.

Above all else, choose love.